STACI HART

Cover design by Quirky Bird
Photography by Perrywinkle Photography
Editing by Love N Books and Rebecca Slemons

Hearts and Arrows

Deer in Headlights (Hearts and Arrows 1)
Snake in the Grass (Hearts and Arrows 2)
What the Heart Wants (Hearts and Arrows 2.5 Novella)
Doe Eyes (Hearts and Arrows 3)
Fool's Gold (Hearts and Arrows 3.5 Novella)

Hearts and Arrows Box Set

Hardcore (Erotic Suspense Serials)

Volume 1
Volume 2
Volume 3
Box Set

Romantic Comedy

Bad Habits

With a Twist
Chaser
Last Call

Wasted Words

Once
Short story on Amazon

Sign up for the newsletter to receive a FREE copy of Deer in Headlights

To Kandi Steiner
For holding my hair back.
#BestieRelease #SteinHarts

CUP OF TEA

Joel

"THIS IS THE WORST IDEA you've ever had."

Shep glanced over at me, his sidelong smile mocking from behind his dark beard. "I thought you were through being salty?"

I glared at him. My shirt was too tight — the tie around my collar may as well have been a noose as we stood in our tattoo parlor that night, waiting for some hotshot producers to meet with us. The steaming heat building inside my stiff clothes ratcheted up my irritation degree by degree.

"I'll be through being salty when this show is over."

"Well, our agent said we could get signed on for years, if we're lucky."

A laugh shot out of me. "Right. Lucky. How are we supposed to work with cameras in our faces and people telling us where to stand and what to say?"

"It's reality TV. Telling us what to say would defeat the purpose, wouldn't it?"

I gave him a look. "You really think they're not going to give us some kind of objective or script or something?"

He shrugged, not seeming to mind. But that was my brother. A younger version of me without a care in the world. Not that I minded bearing the brunt of the responsibility. In exchange, he could remain carefree, though in times like these, I wished he'd had

6

an iota of self-preservation.

"Listen," he said, his voice a little softer, his smile a little less mocking. "I know you're not happy about all this, but it's going to be good for business, not bad. They're not going to follow you around at all hours, you know? There are rules, man."

The look I'd been giving him hadn't quit. He sighed and rolled his eyes.

"It's better than the show going to *Hal*, isn't it?"

The muscles in my face tensed at the sound of his name. Hal, owner of the *second* biggest parlor on the West Side — the first being mine. Hal, the current husband of my ex-wife. Hal, the burr in my ass that I could never get rid of.

I shifted, rolling my shoulders to square them as I shifted my gaze to the door. "Fuck Hal."

"Exactly," he said, his tone pleased. He had me. It was how he'd roped me into the situation in the first place.

When we'd been approached to do a show about our shop, Tonic, by a big network that mostly ran reality TV, I'd immediately said no. There was no question — not a single molecule in my body was on board with putting any part of my business or self out there for the masses to binge on Netflix. But Shep was so on board, he could have driven the train.

In fact, he did end up driving the train. He spearheaded an effort to convince me, starting with his girlfriend Regina, our piercer. She'd then gotten her two roommates, Veronica and Penny, on board, and they'd spread the excitement through the shop. They didn't see it as selling out — they all thought it would make them famous, set their careers up for life. I supposed it would, but at what cost? That was my question.

To my credit, I'd held my ground with only one person on my side — Patrick. He was as interested in exposing his personal life as he was exposing himself to chlamydia. And as outnumbered as I was, I wasn't going to budge. Shep needed my permission to do it, and I wasn't going to give it. End of story.

Until we caught wind that Hal's shop had been approached too. The last thing I wanted in the entire world, other than being on a reality show, was for Hal to be on one.

My attention snapped to the door when the ding of the bell chimed, and two pencil skirts walked into the shop. One of the women walked forward, probably near my age, with dark hair, dark eyes, and a friendly smile, though I knew better than to trust it. Laney Preston, I assumed, the creator of the show. She was beautiful, the kind of woman who was way out of my station, rich, powerful. But I could have gotten her into bed with a few words — she was the sort of woman who would only want me for a night or two, never more, which was exactly how I preferred it. I'd had my fill of relationships with Liz.

But it wasn't Laney who I couldn't take my eyes off of.

The woman at her side was tall and blond, with skin like a porcelain dish brimming with cream. Wide-set, big eyes with icy irises assessed me coolly, dark lashes long. Her nose was pert, just a button, though her lips were wide, just like her eyes. She looked like a doll, a cold, beautiful doll that belonged on a shelf where no man should touch her.

For some reason, all I could think about was whether or not her skin was cool to the touch like I imagined it would be, like a statue made of marble.

I tore my eyes away when Laney spoke.

"Joel Anderson?" she asked, her lips still smiling.

I offered my hand. "Ms. Preston?"

"Call me Laney." She took it and gave it a firm shake. "Nice to finally meet you."

"You too," I lied. I'd been putting the meeting off for weeks.

She smiled like she knew before looking over the shop. "I'm sorry we haven't been by personally before now. This space is beautiful. You've done a great job with it — it's going to film brilliantly. Is there somewhere we can sit?"

I nodded and gestured to our waiting area and the antique Victorian couches and chairs that stood there.

Laney chose the blood-red velvet couch, and the china doll sat next to her with an unreadable expression on her face, though her big eyes scanned the room like she was taking stock of her surroundings. She reached into an attaché and pulled out a folder, placing it in her boss' hand.

"I'd like you to meet our executive producer and the show runner, Annika Belousov, my right hand. We'll all be working closely, hopefully in more comfortable clothes than we're meeting in tonight."

Shep chuckled. My eyes were on Annika, who smiled, if you could call it that. Really, it was just a twitch of one corner of her lips by a millimeter, chased by a spark in her eyes as they met mine. Something about it sent my pulse racing, and a flush bloomed on her cheeks. She was as affected by me as I was by her.

It was then that I realized that her mirth was equal parts attraction and judgment. I got the impression that she thought little of us, yet her eyes scanned my arms, which were covered in tattoos, in a way I wouldn't call completely unimpressed. I wondered if she had a single mark on her perfect skin and imagined taking my needle to it, making a mark I could leave there forever.

The thought sent a rush of heat through me. Her hair was pulled into a strict bun, her skirt tight around her hips and waspish waist, everything about her severe and beautiful. I wondered what it would look like when she smiled, when she was free and happy, if she ever was. There was something more to her, but I couldn't figure out what. And I wanted to know.

I then decided two things.

One: My new mission in life was to make her laugh.

Two: I'd crack her open if it was the last thing I did.

Laney opened the folder and set it on the table, leaning over her crossed knees to sort through the papers.

"We wanted to go over some of our plans for modifying the space for the show, as well as discuss the layout for the episodes. Annika?"

Annika sat even straighter, if that were possible, making eye contact with me. "If you have a look over this, you'll find the details of the construction proposal. Cameras will be added to several points in the store, as well as some ancillary lighting. We may need to rearrange the booths to …" She kept talking, but I wasn't really listening anymore.

Her voice was low and a little raspy, the contrast to her perfect, pristine outward impression catching me off guard. I expected a cold voice to match the rest of her, but it wasn't — it was burning embers and crackling wood.

I swallowed the thought of that voice whispering my name, and then I smiled, leaned back in my chair, folded my arms across my chest, and pretended I didn't have a single worry in the world.

She stopped mid-sentence, and the temperature dropped as she threw down the iron curtain, any trace of warmth she had disappearing in a snap. "Is something amusing, Mr. Anderson?"

I shrugged. "Not particularly."

Her eyes narrowed. "Once you sign these papers, we'll have permission to come in here and modify your store. You should take it seriously."

Laney gave her a look, but Annika didn't falter.

"I don't take much seriously, if I can help it."

I got the sense that if we weren't in a business meeting, she would have rolled her eyes. Her back was ramrod straight as she directed her eyes to one of the sheets on the table and went on with her presentation. I watched her fingers, long and white as she pointed to diagrams and told us about the changes. Shep watched me, amused.

I smirked at him.

Annika went on, going over everything with a detached tone to her voice, though I could hear the tightness in the undercurrent of her words. She pushed the papers toward us when she was finished and leaned back, turning to Laney, never chancing a look at me.

The knowledge that she was avoiding eye contact was like spurs in my side. I kept my gaze on her, willing her to look at me so I could burn a hole through her.

Something about her made me feel reckless, more reckless than usual. I'd never really had trouble convincing women to spend a little time with me, but climbing over the wall of ice she'd thrown between us was a challenge I was game for. I could press her out of curiosity with one of two outcomes. She'd leave the show and take the whole thing with her, or she wouldn't. And if she didn't, maybe there was a chance that I could get catch a better glimpse of whatever I'd seen in her.

Shep cleared his throat, and I looked over to find both Laney and Shep staring at me expectantly. Annika's eyes were still on Laney.

I smirked again, not even a little ashamed of myself. "Sorry. It's chilly in here, don't you think?"

Shep tried to cover a laugh with a cough and said, "I dunno, man. Feels a little steamy to me."

I laughed. "That's just your monkey suit talking."

Laney's lips pursed once, suppressing a smile. "I was just asking whether everything looks good to you or if you need some time?"

My eyes were on Annika again, and I didn't know just why I found the whole thing so amusing. But I did. "Everything looks good to me. Real good."

Laney full-on smiled that time and pulled out some more papers. "Perfect. I'll need to have all of your employees sign these updated contracts, as well as you and Shep. This is the final version with all of the requests that your lawyer made, including the negotiated payment and reimbursement for any damages and modifications to the shop. I convinced my bosses to do the history and cultural segments you asked for, too, which you'll find in the episode packets. They love the angle of learning about the subculture — it's something we haven't seen before. They were also on board with hiring a new composer, as so not to have the—" she glanced at one of the papers in her hand, "*Cheesy TLC bullshit* soundtrack, as you called it."

I smiled and sat up in my seat. I had a list of demands in order for me to participate in the farce, and Laney had pulled through. Part of me had hoped they wouldn't so I could refuse, but at least if I had to do the damned show, it would be on my own terms.

She smiled back and shuffled through more papers. "We also have copies of all of the permits in here for your files, in case your landlord or the city needs to see them, but you can always direct any inquiries like that to us."

I nodded.

"We appreciate you meeting with us, Joel. Your brother told us that you weren't overly enthusiastic about the show, but I'm glad you came around. I hope you'll be pleasantly surprised with how we do things. It's not all fake drama and cat fights — we leave that to *Survivor* and *The Bachelor*. And if there's ever an issue, you can always come to Annika or me. We're here to ensure that things run smoothly — we're problem solvers. So if anything crops up that you're unhappy about, let us try to help fix it. Okay?"

I nodded again, uncomfortable with her hitting me in a soft spot, calling me on my fears so openly.

"Great. I just told our lead engineer that I'd take a couple of shots of the office and back room for him, some things he didn't get when he was here last week. Could one of you show me the way?"

Shep stood up as I opened my mouth to answer.

"Yeah, come on. It's just back this way," he said.

Laney stood and smiled at me like she knew what I was thinking, which was nearly full-blown giddiness at the prospect of being alone with Annika. I wanted to see her squirm. I'd see her squirm if it killed me.

Shep turned his back to the women and winked at me as he passed.

Annika recrossed her legs as they walked away — her long legs, the same creamy white as the rest of her — and brushed the backs of her fingers against her skirt with a flick before leaning forward to pick up the papers, stacking them with a click against the table.

She still wouldn't look at me.

"So, we'll be working closely, it would seem," I said.

"It would seem." The words were tight.

A smile played at my lips. "Does something about me offend you, Ms. Belousov?"

She shifted, turning her nose up, her eyes toward the window — my eyes followed the line of her jaw, which was somehow both hard and soft. "Not at all."

I chuckled. "You're a terrible liar. Has anyone ever told you that?"

Her eyes finally snapped to mine, and I tried to melt her panties off with my mind. A flush rose in her cheeks. "What is it with you?" she asked, surprising me with her directness.

I shrugged. "Not quite sure what you mean."

"Didn't anyone ever tell you it's not polite to stare?"

"Sure, but when I see a stone-cold fox such as yourself, I find it hard not to look."

She laughed, but the sound held no humor, and her eyes were hard and mocking on mine. "Yeah, I get it. I'm just the pretty face, right? Why wouldn't I want to be sexualized by strangers? Did you have any cat-calls on hand for me? Maybe it's one I haven't heard before."

One eyebrow climbed. "Touché."

She shook her head, her eyes hard on mine. "You're basically a walking cliché. Funny that you don't see women treating men like meat."

I chuffed. "Wait until you've spent a few days in the shop, sweetheart."

Her anger flared, her flush deepening."Don't call me sweetheart, asshole."

"Don't call me asshole, princess."

She glared. I smiled.

I put my hands up in surrender, finding her presumptions amusing, imagining the look on her face when she realized exactly how wrong she was. "Listen, I'm sorry, but in fairness, I'm not the one playing ice queen."

"No. You're playing the rogue, aren't you?"

I bobbled my head. "I don't really *play* the rogue. It's just my natural state. Drove my mother nuts."

"I'd have to agree with her."

"So you're admitting I drive you nuts? This has to be a new record for me. What's it been, fifteen minutes?"

She glanced at her watch. "Twelve." The word was flat and humorless, but I laughed nonetheless.

"I like you," I said. "Can't figure out exactly why."

A ghost of a smile, suppressed and gone in a millisecond. "That makes one of us."

"Well, I, for one, am looking forward to working with you, Annika."

"Ms. Belousov is preferred, thanks."

The words were brusque, and I wondered if she was already trying to figure out how to get out of the job. In that exact moment, I hoped she couldn't. I hoped she'd be stuck to me like static cling.

I leaned forward, finding myself close to her, close enough to smell her perfume, a hint of something floral and familiar, but I couldn't place it. What I *could* have done was gotten drunk off it.

"Well, *Ms. Belousov*, maybe I can change your mind."

She turned her cool eyes on me, and I found them burning like I'd hoped, though it was veiled. I found their heat all the same. "I very seriously doubt that, Mr. Anderson."

I smiled. "Oh, I dunno. I can be *very* persuasive, when I put my mind to it."

Her lips pinched and eyes narrowed by a tiny degree just as Laney and Shep walked back into the room. I sat back in my chair, absolutely pleased with myself.

"Great," Laney said as she approached, not moving to sit back down. "I think we've got what we need. Annika will be in touch regarding the schedule. If you could get these contracts back to me in the next couple of days, it would really speed things along."

Shep smiled. "We'll get you everything tomorrow."

"Perfect, then we can get our crew here to start the work Monday. It should only take a couple of days."

"That's all?" I asked, trying not to watch Annika as she stood and stepped away, taking the route that would keep her as far away from me as possible.

Laney nodded. "They've got it down to a science."

I stood and extended a hand. "Then I'll be seeing you sooner than later."

"Yes, you will," she said as she took it. "Thanks again for meeting with us, and for going for the show. It's going to do amazing things for your store, your brand."

I gave my brother a look. "So I hear."

"Good to see you, Laney," Shep said as he shook her hand. "Ms. Belousov." He shook her hand too.

Something ignited in my chest as I reached out to shake Annika's hand, knowing she couldn't refuse with Laney watching on. "Nice to meet you, Ms. Belousov."

The flush was back, just a rosy tinge to her high cheeks as she slipped her white fingers into my hand. They were soft and warm — no, they were hot — her palm pressing against mine as her fingers closed. It was only a second that we touched, but every single thing about the way she felt impressed into my mind.

I squeezed once, firm but gentle, before she pulled away, but my fingers trailed down hers like they didn't want to let her go.

She said nothing, just gave a curt nod and turned in a whoosh that left the smell of flowers in the draft, and I watched her walk out the door, narrow hips swaying in time to the click of her heels.

I slipped my hands into my pockets and watched the door for a second, my mind spinning and whirring. I wanted to figure her out. In fact, I wanted that more than I'd wanted anything in a long, long time.

After a moment of silence, Shep burst out laughing.

I glanced over at him, but he just kept laughing, the apples of his cheeks pink, his laugh big and booming.

"What?" I asked.

"Jesus Christ, Joel. It's been ages since I've seen you fuck a girl up with your eyes."

I shrugged.

He kept laughing. "Just do me a favor."

"If it involves me not sleeping with her, I'm out."

"Trust me, I know better than to try to stop you once you've set your mind to something." His smile slipped, his eyes narrowed with worry but still full of hope. "Just don't ruin this for us, okay?"

I clapped him on the shoulder and pulled him into my side. "Don't worry, little brother. I'll keep it under control." And at the time, I actually believed the words.

HAIRY

Annika

I PULLED IN A BREATH through my nose so hard, my nostrils threatened to stick closed.

That guy.

That hairy fucking guy.

That hairy fucking guy with those stupid fucking eyes that looked at me like he could see me naked.

I'd been given the label of *frigid bitch* more than a few times, a label that would make most women cringe. But not me — I embraced it. It was a mask, armor cultivated over years of practice, years of working in reality television. It protected the rest of me, the real me, from the sharp edges of my job. It made the men who I worked with in the industry take me seriously. It kept the would-be players well away from me. One pointed look would usually have them skittering away with their tail between their legs.

But not That Hairy Fucking Guy. I couldn't even bring myself to think his name, as if thinking his name would give him some kind of power over me. So Hairy Fucking Guy would have to do. Or maybe just Hairy.

I tried not to think about how he stared at me, like he would do things that would make my toes curl up and my knees buckle. Like he would fuck me up in a way that would have me begging for more. He didn't shy away from my glare — which would level most men

— instead, he met it with heat that burned through me like molten lava. Or indigestion.

I also tried not to think about how it felt to shake his hand. I'd shaken a million hands, but that? After he'd looked at me like he did? All hairy and beastly and feral and lusty? I swear, electricity shot up my arm, down my ribcage, and straight between my legs.

This fact made me very, very angry.

Our car was still waiting at the curb, and I climbed in after Laney. It wasn't until the door thumped shut, muting the sounds of the city for the soft hum of air conditioning, that she looked me dead in the face and started laughing.

I felt my face turn to stone, the pinch of my lips at the corners. "It's not funny, Laney."

"The unflappable Annika, completely flapped."

"I am not flapped. In fact, I'm the opposite of flapped."

"That's what I'm saying. Usually you smile and schmooze, but you shut down like New York during a blizzard."

I tightened my lips to stop myself from sulking and changed the subject. "He's awful."

"No, he isn't," she said as the driver took off.

"He is too. He's crass and uncouth and … hulking. He's medieval. Put a mace in his hand and point him to the Saxons."

"I think he would have been a Saxon. And anyway, he was wearing a suit, for God's sake." She watched me, and I could feel her smiling. My eyes were out the front window, chin high. "He's no worse than Cesar."

I huffed. None of the guys on our last job could have ever done what Hairy did to me — watched me in a way that made me want to deck him or rip his clothes off. Maybe both. "Please. Cesar was hulking and hairy, sure, but he was also clean and well-spoken and —"

"Gay."

"Just like almost every guy on Fashion Forward."

"Exactly. Which meant their fuck-me eyes were pointed at each other and not you."

"Which is exactly how I prefer it." My nose wrinkled. "He's

seriously so hairy, Laney. Makeup is going to freak out when they see all that …" I gestured to my face, trying not to say hair again.

"Oh, come on," she said with a chuckle. "He's a fine specimen of man who has a particularly virile, testosterone-fueled head of hair and quite possibly the most beautiful beard I've ever seen."

"Out of control. I bet his back looks like a sweater."

"It is not out of control. It's even groomed."

"His back?" I asked with a brow raised.

She gave me a look. "His beard. He didn't even have neck hair. His facial hair even looked combed, Annika."

I shrugged. "Medieval."

She sighed and settled back in her seat, looking pleased with herself. "Viewers are going to love him."

"No accounting for taste, I guess."

"Looks like you might too," she said, laughing.

My mouth popped open, and I looked at her, disgusted. "You're joking."

"I mean, I wouldn't blame you. Just remember to keep it all business or you'll end up like Tina."

I narrowed my eyes. "I'd never fall for a guy on the show, and Tina is the shining example as to why. She got all hung up over a guy and chose not to do her job because it would hurt him. Fired. *Over a guy*," I scoffed.

"What people won't do for love."

"Good for her and all, but I've worked too hard to throw it away for a guy. Especially not a big, hairy medieval guy."

"Hmm." Laney watched me for a moment like she didn't believe me.

My brows drew together. "Don't *hmm* me like you think I'm lying."

"Are you going to be able to produce him?" The question held an edge, tinged with challenge.

"Of course I'll be able to," I shot back.

But she didn't back down. "That wasn't the Annika I know. I expected smiles and arm touching and general amiability. Whether it's sincere or not doesn't matter. If you're going to have any form of influence or control over him, it's not going to happen if you repeat *that*. He shook you up. So, I don't think it's out of line as your boss to ask if you're certain you can produce him."

I thought about the way he looked at me and found myself embarrassed that I'd lost my grip on the situation. Producing, in our definition of the word, meant to manipulate. To create the environment for drama. And I should have been able to produce him even then, *handle* him, bend him. But he'd caught me off guard. I found my resolve — next time, I'd be prepared.

"Yeah. I'll be able to produce him," I answered with confidence I felt into my Manolos.

"Good," she said, satisfied, turning her dark eyes to the windshield and road beyond. "I don't want to have to step in, which means you're going to need to bring it. We left Fashion Forward for this. It's my shot to create my own reality show that people want to watch at a time when people are over reality TV. It's *your* shot to prove you can run a show on your own. If you fail, I fail. And I'm not going to fail."

"Understood." Dread snaked through my stomach at the thought of failing anything, especially this. I cut off its head with a solid, fortifying breath.

"We've got a lot to work with, a good cast full of good people who we can hopefully turn into good TV."

"So, good people who we can ruin."

She shrugged. "They know what they signed up for. But this isn't going to be like Fashion Forward. There are no sides, no winners. No villain."

"Not true." I pulled out my stack of dossiers. "We've got Hal."

"True. And the fact that he's married to Joel's ex? We've got plenty of nerves to expose. But you know what I mean. There's no villain contestant, no story manipulation, no pushing, or at least not on the competitive scale. I'm good at being a manipulative bitch, but I can't say I'm not glad to have to ruin fewer lives. Maybe we can even do some good."

I smiled. "Aww, look at you, ya big softie."

She laughed. "I like Joel and Shep. And they're going to kill it in the ratings. Let's go over everyone again."

I flipped through the folders in my lap. "Joel Anderson, thirty-eight, running Tonic for seventeen years with his brother, Shepard. Parents died a few months apart, his mother of ovarian cancer, and then his dad was in a car accident." My heart ached at the thought of losing both parents so close together. "Married for five years to Elizabeth Jackson. Volatile, physical relationship, lots of fighting. She put him in the hospital just before they were divorced."

"She sounds like a real gem. Maybe Hal's shop would have been a better choice for the show."

I chuckled. "Maybe if this were Fashion Forward, but if we want to do something different, something people will watch, we need heroes people can root for."

She sighed. "So true."

I flipped to my cheat sheet. "Shep and Ramona have been dating for a few years — she lives with the other two girls in the shop, Penny and Veronica."

"Penny's the one with the technicolor hair, right?"

"Yeah, and Veronica used to date Patrick."

"Brooding hottie?"

I smirked. "I mean, they're all gorgeous, but yeah. That's the one. Veronica broke up him and his girlfriend for a time."

"That's a great angle to play. She's single? He's back with the other girl?"

"Yup."

"Oh, that's good. Real good."

My finger ran down the list. "Max and Eli are like Tweedledee and Tweedledum."

"Except with better abs."

I laughed. "Max has a girlfriend who he has a super physical relationship with. Apparently they get caught having sex in the shop all the time."

She made a face. "Is that a health department concern?"

"They seem to keep it to closets and back rooms."

"Well, skin never hurts ratings."

"So we've got exes, horn dogs, and roommates," I recounted.

"Like you said, it's a ton of great material."

"The roommates should be able to give us some drama too. They're really close, but I've got some ideas that shouldn't ruin any relationships."

She smiled. "Of course you do. You're the best in the business, besides me."

I chuckled and closed the dossier, feeling a little better. It was so much easier when we didn't think about them like people. Not that it was always easy to do, but it was the only way to really get the job done. Although, the situation was infinitely better with the format of Tonic than it was on Fashion Forward. If anything would turn you into an incarnation of Satan himself, it was producing competitive reality television.

"Let's sit down in the morning and go over our character stories for the first half of season one and figure out our finale so we've got something to work toward. The crew will have everything moved into the apartment upstairs by tomorrow for sure, so we can start setting up the control room and our boards."

"Good. It always stresses me out to not have them. Like all the details are in my head and these files. But when they're on the board where I can see them, that's when it's real."

"Me too," Laney said as the car pulled to a stop in front of her apartment building on the East Side. "Need anything?"

I smiled as she gathered her things. "Nah, I'm good."

"Get your head on straight about Joel. If you can't handle him, we're going to have problems."

"Oh, don't worry. I'll handle him just fine."

She laughed. "I mean, if that's how you have to get it done, I'm not one to judge."

I gave her a look as she opened her door. "Bye, Laney."

"Night, Annika. See you in the morning."

I twiddled my fingers at her as she closed the door and let out a breath as the car pulled away.

"Where to, Ms. Belousov?" the driver asked.

"My parents'. Thanks."

He nodded, and I settled back into my seat for the long ride into

Brooklyn.

My parents lived in Brighton Beach in the same house where I grew up, just off the strip in Little Russia. They'd fled during World War II as children, part of a group of families, making their way through Eastern Europe to escape persecution until finally ending up in Israel. But when they went back to Russia to help my aunt escape, their papers were confiscated, and my uncle Andrei extracted them, bringing them to New York where he was, using his Bratva connections. Though being connected to the Russian mafia was never something we discussed in depth.

They settled into Brighton Beach, the home away from home, buying a house and opening a dry cleaning shop, again with the help of my uncle. And within a year, my mama got pregnant, a surprise to everyone at forty-six, especially my parents who believed they'd never be able to have children of their own.

So I grew up in the shop, helping my mother and aunt doing alterations, helping Papa press the pants for the rich men and Bratva who came into our store. It was there I learned the value of hard work. It was also there that I learned that I didn't want to stay in Brighton Beach. I didn't want the life so common for my culture — a life of not-so-quiet complacency.

Uncle Andrei had a daughter, Roksana, just a few months after I was born, whose mother died in childbirth. And when Andrei was busy with Bratva business, Roxy came to stay with us. We looked very much alike — blond hair and clear blue eyes, tall, fair — but she was the wild one, the one who would run through the rack of clothes in our store with her hands outstretched, trailing through the plastic-covered pants and shirts, giggling. She was the one who could always make me smile, who always set me free. As much as I'd allow, at least.

We moved in together after we graduated, into a brownstone in Park Slope where she had her daughter, close enough to my parents to see them, but far enough away that we were out of Little Russia.

When we both worked at Bryant Park in fashion — me on the show and her in actual fashion — the location made plenty of sense. Now that I would be in the Upper West every day? I was feeling like

I lived on Mars.

At least it would only be for six weeks. The thought made me feel better about a lot of things. Including Hairy.

I tried not to think about how broad his shoulders were in his suit, or about the juxtaposition of his tattooed skin against the crisp lines of his collar. I tried not to think of his eyes on me and how they made me hot and cold all at the same time. Or about his cheekbones or dark lashes or strong brow.

I sighed and recrossed my legs, hanging onto the dossiers. I opened his again, touched his picture. *6'4", 220lb, born August 14th, 1978. Opened Tonic with inheritance in September, 1999.* There were photos inside of his ex, Liz, and Hal, the owner of the rival shop. We had plans for him, the hot-button to rile Joel up.

A flash of foreboding ran through me, but I shook it off. This was all part of the job. They were just meat puppets, pawns in a game to move around, crash into each other, all while trying to make sure we caught it all on camera.

I reminded myself that Tonic would be so much less destructive than *Fashion Forward* as the car pulled to a stop in front of my parents' building. I thanked the driver, slipping the folders into my attaché before climbing out of the car.

A row of red brick duplexes stood in front of me, built in the thirties with awnings over the porches and flower boxes hanging on the cast iron bannisters. It looked quaint, like a snapshot from another time, even in the dark as my heels clicked on the sidewalk and up to the door to ring the bell.

I heard my parents talking and the footfalls of my mother just before she opened the door, smiling, cheeks rosy and hair twisted into a bun much like mine, though her blond locks had turned a beautiful shade of silvery-grey.

"Annika! I didn't think you'd make it tonight," she said in Russian, opening her arms to greet me.

I slipped into her arms, and they folded around me, bringing me into her soft body that smelled of rose water. I sighed, smiling. "Hi, Mama. I'm sorry I'm late."

She made a dismissive noise and pulled me inside before closing the door. "Don't be silly. We know you're busy. Come in, come in."

Papa stood from his recliner and made his way to us, smiling broadly, arms open. His beard was thick, grey and white just like his hair, which was combed with a slight wave to it. His belly was large — when I was little, I thought it was why his laugh was so big, like the sound originated from a cavern somewhere in there and echoed out joyfully.

"Ah, my little Annika. Come and give Papa a squeeze."

I slipped into his arms. "Hello, Papa."

He kissed me on the cheek, though he didn't let me go. "I missed you. I always miss you when you're gone, my star."

"I miss you too."

He held me by the shoulders and leaned back. "You look hungry. Mama made supper — come fix yourself a plate."

My stomach rumbled in response, and I breathed in the comforting smell of pastries and meat with a hint of cabbage, which was in nearly every Russian dish. He cupped my shoulder and guided me toward the kitchen, not requiring an affirmation.

"Anni!" a little voice crowed, followed by a thumping of feet as my cousin's daughter Kira bounded out of the kitchen and flew toward me.

I scooped her up when she reached me. "Hello, Bunny," I said, still speaking Russian. Roxy wanted her to learn, and I didn't have a single qualm about that.

"*Zdravstvuyte, tetushka*," she answered carefully, enunciating very slowly.

I laughed, the first truly happy sound to leave my lips all day. "Well done."

Roxy appeared in the doorframe of the kitchen, smiling. "Hey. Long day?"

I sighed, not wanting to talk about work. Not now that I was home. All I wanted was to enjoy my family. "As usual." I moved toward the kitchen, kissing Roxy's cheek as I passed. "Do I smell pelmeni?" I asked, looking for the dumplings in the dishes on the table.

Mama chuckled. "Yes, and pirog."

I spotted the meat and vegetable pie on the table, salivating as my eyes caught on the thick, fluffy crust. I set Kira down, my eyes glued to the food as I gravitated over. "Oh, thank God. I haven't eaten all day."

Mama tsked.

"What? I've been so busy with work."

Everyone took seats to keep me company while I ate, since they'd already finished.

"Your new show starts soon?" Papa asked, slipping back into Russian again.

"Hopefully next week. The crew is on standby — we just have to get the cast contracts signed and the shop modified," I answered as I loaded my plate, only satisfied when every inch of it was covered with food. "How did it go getting the papers I needed?"

Papa nodded. "Mama has them for you, everything we have for our business."

"Let me get them for you," she said and pushed away from the table.

I took a bite, nodding back. "I'm so glad you finally decided to retire."

He chuckled. "Yes, well, I might have stayed there forever, if that was what fate had in store for me. But I'll be happy to rest my bones all the same."

I smiled, shaking my head as I took another bite of the pirog — the crust melted in my mouth, and I did my best not to moan. "You deserve retirement, as hard as you've worked, as much as you've been through in your life."

"It is not our way," he said with a shrug. "We do what we must and accept what we're given. We make the best of what we have without asking for more. I would have worked until I could no longer do my job if you hadn't insisted we discuss selling the shop."

My cheeks flushed, and an exasperated sigh slipped out of me. It was always the same argument, one we'd had a thousand times. "Papa, you can make your own fate. That's what I've done. If you can sell the shop and make enough, along with the money you've been saving for years? Why not enjoy the rest of your days in leisure?"

But he only smiled. If I didn't know him so well, I'd think he was patronizing me. "Of course, little star. You want to take care of us, help us, and we appreciate all you've done to do so. I haven't even complained, have I?" he asked, teasing.

"No, you haven't." Which was true. They'd let me put their savings into high-yield accounts and IRAs, plus I'd set up a 401K for them. And they'd given me permission to help them sort out their books to determine whether or not they could sell, and if so, how much they could make. Their expenses were low — no car, their house paid off, and they were legitimate citizens, granted by the government when they immigrated, which gave them access to Medicare. It wouldn't take much to sustain them, and I was sure I could find a way. They'd earned it.

His smile widened, his eyes full of adoration. I melted like a snow cone in August.

Mama reappeared in the entryway with a bankers box, setting it on the table next to me. "Here you are."

I set down my fork and wiped my lips before removing the lid, unsure what I'd find, not entirely terrified once I saw the contents.

Folder upon folder of receipts and ledgers lay inside, a massive stack of paper and numbers that nearly made my head spin. I let out an involuntary breath, my eyes combing over the pile, wondering what I'd gotten myself into.

"Okay," I finally said with an air of determination. The only way out was through. One bite at a time. All that jazz.

Mama twisted her hands before slipping them into her apron pockets to keep them busy, I suspected. "Are you sure you want to do this, Annika? You are so busy already. I don't want to burden you."

I smiled at her and cupped her soft elbow. "It's no burden, Mama."

"I can help, too, Dina," Roxy said.

"Me too!" Kira chimed.

I laughed. "See? We'll get it sorted."

She relaxed, smiling. "All right."

I put the lid on the box and set it on the ground next to me before tucking into my dinner, listening to the easy chatter of my family. That was the best thing about being with them — it was always easy, where everything else in my life was a battle, uphill, in the snow and sleet and rain. The Industry was a place of lies and illusions, a city built on shifting sands, and the only way to survive was to know your enemy. And everyone was your enemy.

VODKA DRAWERS

Annika

I DREW IN A SLEEPY breath when my alarm chimed. It was already light out, thanks to the long summer days, and my eyelids resisted subjecting me to the sunshine. I reached blindly for my phone, sighing once I unlocked it and the alarm stopped.

It had been late when I finally fell asleep — I'd spent hours staring at my ceiling, thinking about how I'd failed my first interaction with Hairy, considering plans to course-correct. I didn't have a lot of options, but they included:

1) Apologizing and pretending we were friends, which made my stomach turn.

2) Telling him straight up how I felt and calling for a truce, of sorts.

I imagined meeting him again, thought through all the potential conversations we'd have, including a few possibilities that ended with a hot and heavy make-out session and some ripped clothing. I don't know why the thought occurred to me, exactly — he was the polar opposite of any man I'd ever dated. I had requirements, such as: clean cut, ambitious, professional, refined. A man who was my equal, a match wherein we had the same goals, the same perspective, the same foundation. Guys like Hairy were the kind you met at a bar or a concert and let ravage you, do all those things you wouldn't expect from a respectable guy. Let him own you, for a moment, at least. But they're not the kind you keep around.

And that was all there was to it. He was a fantasy, not a *real* prospect. So of course the idea of him was enticing. It was enticing because it was imagined.

I sighed, having convinced myself I was right, and flipped off my covers before padding into the bathroom. I stopped at the sink, pausing in front of the mirror. I looked a little wild, for me — blond waves loose and framing my face, just brushing the tops of my shoulders, my eyes wide and blue, cheeks rosy, like they'd been pinched, white cotton sleep shorts and top, almost transparent.

Sometimes I didn't even recognize myself. It was like looking into a mirror at my past to find the old version of myself. The quiet girl who walked wide-eyed into the television industry, naively thinking it was pure and good. But it wasn't. At the time, I'd been assigned to Laney as her PA. She was my friend and my enemy, teaching me what it took to navigate our careers through tough love and hard choices, putting me on the spot whenever she could to keep me on my toes. She was just a producer then, and we struck a quick friendship, one that evolved into a mentorship, and slowly, I'd turned into a version of her — a cold-blooded shark with a lying smile full of teeth. It was how we produced. It was how we survived. And that was how the dichotomy of my life was born.

The old version of me disappeared unless I was with my family, and the new version was the dictator of every other aspect of my life. Every man I'd dated as an adult matched that new outlook — I'd adopted it so deeply that I could hardly remember being any other way. And they'd all been perfectly fine. I just didn't really want *fine*. On top of that, I was married to my job, and that relationship was demanding, intense, and everything I'd ever wanted.

By the time I was finished getting ready, I looked more like myself — hair tight and tidy, black cigarette pants and white silk tank, black oxfords, red lipstick. Together. Tailored. Controlled.

I smiled at my reflection, red lips curling, ready to take over the world. Or the Upper West. Or Hairy. Whatever.

I made my way into the kitchen, finding Roxy pouring coffee and Kira at the table watching cartoons on her tablet while she ate cereal. Her little feet swung in bobby socks and saddle shoes, plaid uniform skirt fanned out on the seat around her, blond hair neatly braided.

"Morning," I said, still smiling.

Roxy smiled back, looking hideously unfashionable, for a fashion designer. Her bathrobe was pink, furry chenille — a relic of her mother's — and she wore slippers that were basically stuffed monkeys with holes in their bellies to stuff her feet into. She also had on banana pajama pants and a tank top, her blond hair in a topknot.

This was not an unusual outfit for her. At that hour, at least.

"Ugh, not the monkey getup again, Roxy."

"And a lovely day to you, too," she said snidely and reached for another coffee cup. "Don't dis my thing."

I laughed as she poured, stopping next to her, leaning my hip on the counter. "It was a perfectly normal thing when we were twelve."

She shrugged and passed my coffee over. "Listen — it's not my fault that my face happens to contort into a monkey face worthy of stupid human contest blue ribbons. Everyone made it a thing. It was literally all I got for my birthday and Hanukkah for like … well, I still get monkey stuff for my birthday and Hanukkah. Anyway, monkeys are cute."

I shook my head and took a sip, glancing over at Kira as I swallowed. "She's growing up so fast."

Roxy sighed and folded her arms across her chest, eyes on her daughter. "I know. She's so excited about Kindergarten starting that she insists on wearing her new uniform every day. I've got her talked down to Mondays, Wednesdays, and Fridays, so that's something."

"It doesn't start for months!"

"I know, which is why I've got to put the lid on it now or else they'll be tatters by the time the first day rolls around."

I chuckled. "At least we know someone in the alterations and dry cleaning business."

"Very true. I'm dropping her off there in a bit. Thank God Dina and Max don't mind her there all day."

"No way. Papa's going to be a mopey old grump when she isn't at the shop with him every day."

"Max? A grump?" She laughed. "That's funny, Annika."

"What can I say? I'm a riot."

"I've always wondered where you got your grump from. It has to be genetic somewhere, but there isn't a single member of our family who's as serious as you."

I shrugged. "Maybe I'm adopted."

"Ha. That'd be a neat trick since we're very clearly related." She motioned to our faces, which looked so much alike.

I sighed, cupping my mug in my hands. "Sometimes I feel like I'm the only one who takes things seriously. But honestly, I don't mind. I like taking care of all you ragamuffins."

She snickered.

"Honestly, I think I just have Resting Bitch Face."

"RBF? Yeah, sorta, but only sometimes."

"At work it's always on. Because bitches get shit done."

She held up her hand with a laugh. "Hear, hear."

I slapped her palm and took a deep pull of my coffee. "I've gotta run. I'm supposed to meet Laney at the apartment we rented for production. Wish me luck."

"Psh. What do you need luck for?"

"Dealing with Hairy."

Her face contorted. "What?"

Instant regret. "That Hairy Fucking Guy that runs the tattoo parlor."

She didn't look any less confused. I sighed.

"He's just one of those guys, you know? Like he's smarmy and hairy and thinks he's hot shit."

One eyebrow rose. "Is he hot shit?"

My cheeks warmed up. Traitors. "I don't know, Roxy. He's big and hairy and maybe has X-ray vision."

"As in …"

"As in, I'm pretty sure he knows what I look like naked without having seen it with his own eyes."

She still looked a little confused. "Okay, so he's a creep?"

I huffed. "No. Yes. I mean, he is and he isn't, you know?"

"No."

My eyes rolled far enough into my skull that I could see the clock behind me, and it was time to get the hell out of that kitchen. "Yeah, you do." I kissed her on the cheek. "I'll see you later," I called as I walked away.

"This isn't over."

"'Kay," I sang cheerily.

"Bye, Anni!" Kira finally said, tearing her eyes away from the screen.

"Bye, Bunny." I kissed her head and grabbed my Tom Ford purse, flying out the door before I could answer any more questions.

The real question was, why was he even on my mind? Which happened to be the question I *definitely* didn't want the answer to.

The driver — a different one every day — dropped me off outside of Tonic, and I climbed out, coffees in hand. I tried not to stare into the windows of the shop to see if Hairy was there as I walked by — his chair was in front by one of the windows, I knew, but it sat empty. An unfamiliar feeling sank through me and disappeared. Disappointment? I almost laughed at the absurdity.

I grabbed both cups with one hand like I'd learned waiting tables in college and pulled open the door to the stairwell that would take me to the apartments. We'd rented one to use as our office and control room while filming, a place to store extra gear, with a green screen room to film interviews and catch a little rest.

At the second floor landing, I passed Joel and Shep's apartment, where he'd lived since they'd opened the shop in the nineties. It was crazy to think that when I was nine and playing in my parents' store, he had lost both of his parents and started his own business. He'd even been married then, for God's sake. The thought unnerved me — I became acutely aware of how very different our lives had been.

I kept walking, climbing another two flights to get to the control room. The long wall of the living room was set up with a dozen monitors on utility shelving. Two rows of tables faced them, with our whiteboard standing in the back, complete with head shots of our cast, though otherwise they were blank, for now.

Engineers bustled around, working on connecting playback equipment and testing the cameras. Another group sat at the tables, going over plans for construction, and I walked past, straight to the bedrooms. One room was set up for filming one-on-ones, and the other contained fully decorated room which included a couch and two desks — mine and Laney's. My own desk. Executive producer of my own show.

I couldn't help but smile.

Laney looked up from the papers on her desk as I approached, setting her coffee down next to her. "Morning."

She picked up her drink and took a sip. "You know we have PAs for this, right?"

I shrugged. "Old habits, I guess." I took a seat across from her and sat back in my chair with a sigh, panning the room once more.

"Not too bad, huh?" she asked, looking around with a smile.

"Not bad at all. I can't believe they hung paintings and mirrors in here. I mean, there's a rug. Who got a rug?"

"It was of my demands — an office where I could spend all day, every day, happily. Relatively, at least."

I chuckled. "Yeah, well, it's not like our jobs are very Zen."

"Not at all, which is why we deserve a sanctuary. How are your parents?" She folded her arms on the table, and her dark hair swung over her shoulder, framing her face.

"Good. They gave a giant box of ledgers to go through so I can figure out how they can retire, so that should be fun in all my spare time."

"Ha."

"Exactly." I sat up and leaned on my desk. "So, what's first on the agenda?"

"Well," she started, scanning her computer screen, "the first thing I need are those contracts. If we can get construction going tomorrow, we could be ready to roll Sunday for filming."

"Excellent."

"Why don't you go down there and grab them?" There was a sly undertone to her words I didn't trust.

"Can't we send a PA?" My eyes narrowed.

"Nope. They're not all here yet. Besides, you may need to talk someone into signing still. So, scoot."

I didn't move to stand, just kept eyeing her.

"Joel's not down there, if that's what you're worried about."

"It's not," I lied. Plans or no plans, I wasn't ready to see him just yet. Too much pressure not to buckle like I had last night.

"Seriously, he's not there. Just go talk to Shep. He doesn't bite."

I rolled my eyes and pushed away from the desk. "Fine."

"Oh," she said as I walked past, "be sure to ask him to close the store tomorrow for construction, would you?"

"I'm sure he'll take that well."

She shrugged. "Like I said — they know what they signed up for. Good luck."

"We don't happen to have any beer or whiskey or anything to bribe them with, do we?"

Laney laughed. "You don't need it. *Bye*, Annika," she said pointedly.

I planned out my attack as I descended the stairs, and by the time I pulled open the door, I was prepped and ready. Until I looked up and saw not-Shep behind the counter.

Hairy was smirking, shoulders broad and muscular in a white T-shirt that was tight in all the right places, or wrong, depending on your angle. The sleeves were tight around his biceps, which were covered in ink, the crisp, clean whiteness of the fabric against the dark ink in his skin calling my eyes to it, a harsh line of contrast that demanded attention. He leaned on the counter, palms flat on the surface, the apples of his cheeks tight with his smile.

"Well, well, well. Morning, princess. Didn't expect to see you again so soon."

I kept walking, keeping my face still as I approached him, all business on the outside. "Good morning. Laney sent me down for the contracts. Did you have them ready? Or should I come back later?"

"I've got them," he answered, still with that smirk on his face as he reached under the counter and retrieved a folder.

"All of them?"

He held them out for me to take. "All of them."

"Thank you," I said tightly and reached for them, but he snatched them back before I had a chance to grab them.

"Ah, ah, ah. How come you came down to get these?"

A flush crept up my neck, feeling foolish that he'd tricked me. "I told you, Laney sent me."

His eyes sparked, the greens and browns and golds of his irises twinkling with amusement as he leaned on the counter. "What, you didn't want to see me? I'm hurt."

I let out a controlled breath. *Handle him.* "Listen. I think we got off on the wrong foot last night. I'm sorry I called you an asshole—"

"No, you're not."

My lips tightened. "All right, I'm not. I don't like being ogled or spoken to like a good-time girl. That's not what I am. I'd like to make that perfectly clear."

"Trust me, princess. It's perfectly clear."

I leveled my eyes at him. "But my distaste for you doesn't affect my ability to do my job. So, I want to call a truce."

"A truce? I didn't realize we were at war."

"Didn't you? Seems to me like you've got your cannon loaded."

He laughed, a big, happy sound that might have made me smile, if I hadn't been so pissed off.

"You know what I mean," I snapped.

"Yeah, I'm pretty sure I know exactly what you mean," he quipped back, that smug bastard. "So, what are your terms?"

"Stop trying to pick me up."

He measured me with his eyes. "Oh, I'm sure I could pick you up. You weigh, what, one-twenty-five?"

I turned on my laser beams and tried to flatten him with them. "Mr. Anderson. Stop hitting on me. You realize this is sexual harassment?"

"Psh, I'm not even your boss."

"That doesn't matter, you're still harassing me."

He watched me for a second, his smile finally faltering. "You're serious."

"Of course I'm serious. Wait, you're not one of those *No means yes* guys, are you?"

He made a face. "No. Believe it or not, I don't typically have a problem picking up women."

I made a face back that said I thought he was vain, and his face fell. He looked cowed, his full lips turned down at the corners.

"Listen, I'm sorry, An—" he cleared his throat, "—Ms. Belousov. It really was all in good fun."

Somehow, I felt like a bitch for forcing him to apologize, like I didn't know he was toying with me. But I reminded myself of my discomfort. I had every right to ask for what I wanted from him, and that was for him to leave me alone.

I thought it was, at least. With him looking all sorry, I almost backed down. But I didn't because I'm probably one of the most stubborn people on the planet.

"Thank you," I said after a moment.

He nodded once. "You're welcome."

I relaxed a little. "Are you able to close the shop tomorrow for construction?"

He full-on frowned at that. "It's Saturday. We've got a full day booked for almost our entire staff."

"I understand, but the sooner we get it done, the better. We'll reimburse you for any money lost, per the contract."

"I'm not worried about the money, I'm worried about my reputation." The words were sharp and low, his face tightening as he spoke.

"I understand, Mr. Anderson, but we've got to get this construction completed so we can begin filming."

He scowled at me.

I paused, then offered, "The sooner we start filming, the sooner we're finished."

The scowl continued for a beat before he growled out the word, "Fine."

"I'll let Laney know."

"Good," he snapped.

"Great," I snapped back and held out my hand. "Contracts,

please?"

He set them in my waiting palm, still giving me the hairy eyeball.

I tucked them under my arm and stood there for a second. "I'd better get these upstairs."

"Hmph," he answered noncommittally, and I walked out of the shop, feeling his eyes on me until I was out of sight.

I stormed up the stairs and into our apartment, feeling set up and annoyed. God, he got under my skin like a freaking chemical burn, and there was nothing that could help except vodka. Lots of vodka.

Laney looked up when I slapped the folder on her desk.

"You knew he was going to be there, didn't you?"

She sat back, watching me. "Maybe."

"Goddammit, Laney. I don't appreciate being played."

She shrugged. "You needed to be the one to talk to him, not me, and you've got to get used to the idea of working with him. Neither of you are going anywhere."

I didn't respond.

"I mean, *he's* definitely not going anywhere, so unless you have big plans to walk out on the show, then you've got to find a way to play nice. I just provided you an opportunity."

I pursed my lips, biting down on them to shut me up.

"So, are you still in?"

I eyed her for a heartbeat and said, "Where's the vodka?"

"That's the spirit." She laughed. "In your bottom right drawer. Glad we're on the same page."

I sat down and opened the drawer to find a bottle of Grey Goose and a shot glass — the only contents of the drawer. "Yeah," was the only response I could muster as I poured a shot and kicked it back, effectively burning the taste of Joel away.

UBLYUDOK

Joel

I WOKE ON MY OWN the next morning, stretching slowly in the morning light. It was early, which was nothing new. My alarm hadn't beaten me to the punch in years.

Annika almost immediately found her way into my thoughts. Not surprising, since she was the last thing I'd been thinking about before I'd fallen asleep. And maybe a good portion of the day before.

I tucked my hands behind my head, smiling up at my ceiling. She was an enigma, a puzzle I found myself itching to figure out. I wanted to take her apart, find out what made her tick. I didn't know why, exactly. Maybe because she seemed so intent on ignoring me. The thrill of the chase, and all that.

But something was different about her — it wasn't just a simple tail chase. I'd done that plenty, and I recognized the difference easily. I just couldn't explain it.

I'd only seen her that one time the day before, when she came to get the contracts. The look on her face when she saw me behind the counter was cold, but her eyes were all fire. She called a truce, told me to back off. Maybe she really wasn't interested. Maybe she really did feel violated in some way.

My smile fell, slipping into a frown.

I liked to think I had a knack for reading signals, and Annika's signals didn't tell me the same things her words did. I could *feel* it, feel her attraction to me just as strong as mine was to her. But she called me out and asked me to stop. So I'd have to stop. There was nothing else to be done.

No more squirmy Annika.

My frown deepened.

Then I remembered that the shop was closed today. I groaned and ran my hand down my face and across my beard. Shep and I spent all yesterday calling clients, many who had waited for months to get Saturday appointments, and reschedule them. I'd lose money, that was for sure — I'd ended offering deep discounts on a lot of those jobs just to keep the customers happy, but no one seemed too upset. Mentioning the show helped raise spirits too.

Fame. Something I'd never be ready for. Dread slipped over me like it always did when I thought about that part of it. Being on TV. Strangers knowing your name. And with that dread came the familiar feeling of regret for agreeing to the whole circus.

I climbed out of bed, heading to the shower to try to wash the doubt away. Shep would say I'm a cynic, but he's the blind optimist, and somehow us *compromising* ended up with *us* in a reality TV show.

I shook my head, disgusted with myself for caving for Hal, the scum of all scum. He wasn't worth the potential disaster hanging over us, but I couldn't even handle the challenge — Hal couldn't win.

I cranked the water to hot and dropped my boxer-briefs before looking in the mirror as I waited for the shower to warm up. My beard was a little too long — I ran my hand over it, angling my head to get a good look. I could have used a haircut too. It was impossible to keep in place when it was any longer than it was. My eyes were a mixture of green, brown, and gold, changing colors with whatever I was wearing, which, at the moment, was absolutely nothing. They were the same eyes my mom had, the same eyes Shep had.

I thought about Mom as I stepped into the shower, hissing when the scalding water hit my back. She'd been gone seventeen years, and I still thought about her every day. I remembered sitting in the hospital for hours watching old movies with her thin hand in mine.

Remembered when we shaved her head before chemo, because she wanted to make the choice herself. Remembered when her lips were pale, her breath labored as her lungs expanded and contracted, a countdown to the end.

Then Dad just after her, the phone call in the middle of the night. The accident. And just like that, he was gone too, leaving Shep and me alone.

Everything changed overnight. Money. Family. They were part of the reason I married Liz, if I was being honest, chasing the dream of a family to replace the one I'd lost. I was my brother's keeper — he became my responsibility more than ever, and I'd always felt responsible for him.

Part of me wondered what I'd do when he married Ramona — I knew for a fact he was planning on it. But he didn't even live with her, and I silently suspected it was because of me. I never let him think anything different because it had always been him and me. Without him, I'd be well and truly alone.

I pushed the thought away. I could be alone, and I'd be fine, somehow. Lonely, maybe. But I'd survive.

I lathered and washed, scrubbed and rinsed, dried and dressed, and within a few minutes of turning on the coffee pot, Shep shuffled out of his room, yawning.

"Mornin'," I said.

"Morning," he answered, scratching at his beard. "Sleep okay?" I shrugged. "Fine. You?"

He rolled his eyes as he sat down at the small table. "No. I was up all night thinking about the show. It's really happening," he said with the shake of his head. "I can't believe you got them to agree to all the history and art stuff you wanted to do."

I smirked and folded my arms across my chest. "I had terms, that's all. They're fixers, remember?"

He snorted. "Yeah, I think you could use a little fixing. What's with you and the ice queen? She's not your usual flavor."

"No, she isn't. I don't know what it is about her. I find her … intriguing."

He laughed. "Stroke your beard when you say that."

I exaggerated a frown and raised a brow. "Intriguing," I said, hoping I sounded British.

"There it is." Shep shook his head. "I dunno, man. Like, I feel like she's got a thing for you by the vibes she puts out around you, but she's ..." he paused, thinking.

"Uptight? Snobby? Aggressive?"

"I was gonna say tall."

I laughed. "Yes, she is tall, and maybe all of the rest of it too. But there's more to her."

"And you're gonna figure out what."

"Yes, I am."

He sighed. "I'm sure that'll end real well. We have to work with her, don't forget that. So when you bang and bail, you'd better have a plan."

I gave him a flat look. "Please. I always have a plan."

He mirrored my face, beard and eyes and all.

I put up my dukes, flashing the words *THIS* and *THAT* tattooed on my fingers. "Never underestimate the power of *THIS* and *THAT*." I made waves like the curves of a woman. "They always get their way."

He rolled his eyes again like a teenage girl. "That joke is so old, man."

"Psh. That joke never gets old. Besides, it's the truth."

"I'm serious, Joel. You can't just sleep with her."

I frowned.

"And you can't date her."

A shock of aversion burst through me. "Date her? I haven't dated in ..." I did some quick math but didn't say the number out loud.

"Exactly. Just stay away from her if you don't have a plan. A *real* plan."

"I'll tell you what. Let's just see what happens."

He sighed and shook his head. "And you're supposed to be the responsible one."

My brow dropped. "Listen, I'm not gonna fuck up your precious show, okay? I'm not an idiot, and I know what I'm doing."

"Which is?"

"Which is to leave her alone, per her request. *For now,*" I tacked onto the end.

"Until when?"

I shrugged. "Until I can melt the wall at Castle Black."

He gave me a weird look before it dawned on him. "Oh, Game of Thrones. Nerd."

"Whatever, you love that show."

"Yeah, but you read all those gigantic books. That last one looked like a goddamn dictionary."

"Chicks think reading is sexy."

"Not Ramona. She doesn't like me to challenge her intelligence."

I laughed, shaking my head. "So, what are you guys doing today now that the shop is closed?"

"No idea. Nothing, hopefully. I'd like to just sit around all day like a slob. You?"

"Oh, I'm still going down there."

He frowned. "We're not supposed to be down there when they're working."

"They're down there, in my shop, with power tools. They can try to stop me, but I'm gonna sit down there behind the register and watch their asses all day, if I have to."

"And look out for your girlfriend."

"Hey," I said with a smirk, "if she shows up, it wouldn't be the end of the world."

An hour later, I made my way downstairs to find Tonic's door wide open, with workers in coveralls everywhere. Plastic sheeting covered all the furniture, and a crew of people were installing extra lights, cameras. It was almost unrecognizable, everything muted by the foggy plastic — the antique chests at each station full of supplies, the Victorian art and gilded mirrors on the walls, the cases of balms and salves and apothecary jars.

A few of the crew glanced over at me as I walked through the door, and a skinny little hipster dude walked over with a clipboard and a tentative smile.

"Uh, hey. Joel, right?"

"That's right." I folded my arms, fanning my biceps against my chest, and stood up straighter, looking down at him.

He laughed nervously. "Ah, uh, great to meet you. I'm Mark, the head PA. Did, ah, Laney let you know we needed the space clear of any cast today?"

"She did." I didn't move.

"Cool. Cool," he said, looking around before meeting my eyes again. "So, um, did you need anything?"

"Yeah. I have some stuff to do."

He waited for me to give him an explanation.

I didn't.

"Sweet, okay," he finally said and laughed again. "Well, um, great. Let me know if you need anything."

"I'll be sure to."

He scurried off, and I took a seat behind the register, arms still folded, eyes narrowed.

It was mostly for show — I just really wanted them to worry I'd murder anyone who fucked up my parlor. The good news was, it seemed to work.

I had a sketchbook stashed under the register and broke it out, opening it to a blank page. My thoughts slipped to Annika, and my pencil took on a mind of its own. Her long neck. The small tip of her nose, turned up just at the end, just a touch. She was all eyes and lips and a story I wanted to know. I needed to know.

It wasn't long before I had her drawn down to the shoulders, stylized. Flowers in her hair, down and messy, something I didn't know that she would ever do on her own. But I wanted to see her like that. Free.

I wondered if that version of her even existed.

I caught a column of black in my periphery and looked up to find Annika walking in, looking annoyed. My hand slipped under the cover of the book and closed it as she approached. Since I wasn't supposed to be harassing her and all.

"Ms. Belousov."

"Mr. Anderson," she answered. "What's up?"

I shrugged. "Just getting a little work done." I held up the sketchbook in display.

"And you need to be down here to do that work?"

"Not really."

She took a controlled breath. "We needed the space clear today for construction."

I looked around. "I don't seem to be in the way."

"You're not. It's a liability thing."

"Need me to sign a waiver?"

"I need you to leave the store."

I folded my arms across my chest. "Not happening."

She folded her arms right back at me. "Are you worried about what we're doing here? Because I assure you, we won't do any damage."

"I'll stay right here and make sure of that myself."

"Joel—"

My heart jolted at the sound of my name from her lips, but I still cut her off. "Listen. Hand me a liability release waiver and I'll sign it. I'm sure you have a dozen on hand. I'm not leaving this store until it's done, not when every penny I have is tied up in it. This is my home, and you're all strangers here. So at least give me the courtesy of being present while your team drills into it."

Something about her face softened, her eyes I think, though the shift was almost imperceptible. "Fair enough," she said, the venom gone, but the cold steel was ever-present. "But I'm staying with you."

I raised a brow. "You don't have something more important to do?"

"Other than make sure you don't get brained by a light fixture? No." She stepped behind the counter, and I shifted so she could squeeze past and sit on the other stool. The scent of her — jasmine, maybe? — slipped over me as she moved by. Once in her seat, she turned her attention to her phone.

I made no move to open my sketchbook, just turned on the stool and leaned against the counter. "So, that's it? We sit here in silence while you jack around on Facebook?"

She glanced up. "I'm not on Facebook. I'm reading."

"As in, a book?" I asked, surprised.

"No, a census report." She shook her head. "Yes, a book."

"Hey, it could have been an article or an email or something."

I thought I caught a hint of a smile. "Sorry. Yeah, I'm reading *Persuasion* by Jane Austen."

"Romance?" The question was flat.

"Romance. I know it's not the latest edition of *Bros and Beers*, or whatever you read, but I think it's all right."

I snorted and reached under the counter for my book, setting it on top of the counter. "I read a lot of sci-fi. This is my desk book."

She picked it up. "Ursula K. Le Guin? I've never heard of her."

"I'm not surprised. She's pretty obscure and was out of print for a while, but her writing … I don't know what it is about it. It's dark, haunting. When you read her words, they stay with you."

"I really only read historical fiction, the classics, usually nothing post-mid-century in time period," she offered. "Although, I do love Margaret Atwood."

I perked up. "Have you read her MaddAddam series?"

"No, I haven't. It's sci-fi?"

"Dystopic, as is her specialty. It's dark and genius, per her usual."

The shadow of a smile found her lips again. "I will. Thanks."

"You're welcome."

She glanced away toward the workers, forcing a lull in the conversation, and I scrambled to keep it going.

"So, I've been wondering about your name. Eastern European?"

"Russian," she answered, still looking away, giving me nothing more.

"Are you from Russia?"

"My parents are. They fled during World War II, ended up bouncing all over the place before ending up here just before I was born."

"Do you speak Russian?"

Icy eyes locked on mine. "*Da.*"

I smirked. "Say, *Joel is an impossibly handsome bastard.*"

She mirrored me. "*Joel nevozmozhny ublyudok.*" The words rolled off her tongue and past her lips, powerful, her voice smoky but with the edge all her words seemed to possess. I found myself full-on smiling.

"You didn't say what I asked, did you?"

"I might have left a word out." She actually smiled back, the corners of her lips rising, eyes lighting with mischief. It changed her face, her air, *her.*

"Bastard?"

"Handsome."

I laughed, a big sound, the kind that came from deep in my belly. Her smile stayed put, though a flush brightened her cheeks.

"I like you," I said simply.

"Really? I couldn't tell."

We were both smirking again. "And here I thought I was being discreet."

"About as discreet as a bullhorn. You know, you're much more pleasant when you're not hosing me down with testosterone."

"Well, you asked me to stop, and I'm not one to hose anyone down with testosterone unwilling. Not when I have plenty of volunteers. It's a veritable wet T-shirt contest when it comes to my testosterone-hosing."

She shook her head.

"Too far?"

She almost laughed, I could feel it. It was all of a sudden the single thing I wanted from the universe. She shook her head again and slipped off the stool, taking my chance with her.

"The bathroom is this way, right?" She pointed to the back of the shop.

"It is. Second door on the right."

"Thanks."

She touched my back as she slipped past me, a simple gesture, one that probably meant nothing, but I felt it, felt her through the pads of her fingertips, through the cotton of my shirt. I'd never thought that chemistry between two people could be tangible. But there was also something strangely deeper than just the physical. Don't get me wrong — I wanted her, bad. But it was more than just the itch, the opportunity, more than something that would pass once acted upon. I had a feeling once I got a taste, I wouldn't be able to get her out of my system for a long, long time.

The thought gave me pause.

I hadn't been so attracted to someone in ages. In fact, I never remembered even being this attracted to Liz, not like this. Like I was fire and she was crisp, clean air, and if I couldn't breathe her in, I'd disappear.

I had no idea what had come over me.

I pulled in a deep breath to clear my head, watching her as she walked past, pretty sure she was intentionally avoiding looking at me and fully aware that my eyes were on her. But just as she passed under a strip of lighting, one of the canisters slipped loose and fell, hitting her squarely in the head.

I was out of my seat and halfway to her before she hit the ground.

Annika

One minute, I'm fleeing the clutches of Hairy, and the next, I'm dead.

No, not dead, I realized as my head thumped low and dull, though everything was still black. I groaned and peeled my heavy eyelids back to find myself in the clutches of Hairy anyway.

Worry creased his brow, which was low, his eyes green and dark and fierce. His face was close to mine, closer than we'd been before, and I realized his arms were around me. His very large arms.

"Oh, thank God," he muttered. "Annika?"

He'd said my first name again, and with his arms around me, with the smell of him in my nose, I felt dizzy. So dizzy.

I groaned again — I couldn't speak. His hand was in my hair, inspecting the side of my head, and I realized I'd been hit.

"Are you all right?"

"Did I get brained by a light fixture?"

His worry softened as he smiled, just a little. "You did. Hopefully you signed that liability waiver."

"Ha," I breathed roughly. "Better me than you."

And just like that, the smile was gone. "Don't say that. Can you sit up?"

"I …" I assessed my body and thought I could, but I didn't want to answer. I didn't want him to let me go. I was so tired, and his arms were so big and strong, and he smelled like soap and laundry and— "Yeah, I'm fine," I said, pushing him away gently before I lost my mind completely and kissed him or something. I hadn't noticed before how full his lips were, and I wondered absently if he was a good kisser.

I sat all the way up, but pinched my eyes closed when I got the spins.

"You okay? Somebody get her some water," he called out to the peanut gallery of crew members, the timbre of his voice low and annoyed at the necessity of the command, it would seem.

I pressed the heel of my palm into my eye socket and pulled in a long breath. "I'm okay, I think."

He cupped my face. "Open your eyes, Annika."

I did as I was told, and he was close again, even closer than before, and he searched my eyes, tilting my face up toward the lights.

"Your pupils aren't dilated, so that's good. Feel woozy?"

"Uh-huh," I breathed in affirmation, my eyes on his, and I felt hypnotized, like a snake charmer and a cobra. I giggled, glad I was the cobra.

He frowned, brow dropping. "Are you sure you're all right?"

I frowned right back, annoyed. "I said I was, didn't I?"

He shook his head. "Stubborn."

I moved to try to get up, and he grabbed my elbow. When I was on my feet, I pulled away, but the second the support was gone, I wobbled.

He caught me again. "We need to get you to a doctor."

"I said I'm *fine*. God, are you always this pushy?"

"Yes," he said, still looking all broody. "Come on, we're going to talk to your boss."

"Jeez, fine," I conceded, since my head was ringing like the Liberty Bell. I even leaned on him a little as we made our way upstairs, past his apartment and into the control room. You know, for balance. Not because he smelled good and clean and *good*. Or because he was big and strong and burly.

It was then that I realized that I most definitely had a head injury.

Laney looked up from her computer, her eyes bouncing between us.

"A light canister knocked her out, and I think she might have a concussion." Joel said, his words rumbling through his chest and into me like an earthquake. I giggled again at the thought, wondering where Joel would rank on the Richter scale.

Laney's eyebrows rose. "I think you might be right."

The room started to spin again, and my stomach clenched, sending my breakfast charging up my esophagus.

"Oh, God," was all I managed as I pushed away from Joel, launching myself toward the tiny trashcan next to Laney's desk. And then, I hurled.

When it had passed, I looked up to find Laney gaping. She handed me a tissue.

"Thanks," I croaked as I took it and wiped my lips, swiping the involuntary tears from my cheeks.

"Head to the doctor and get yourself home."

I nodded, knowing there'd be no arguing with the contents of my stomach in the trashcan between us.

"You're just gonna send her by herself?" Joel shot, clearly upset at the idea.

"She has a driver."

"Is there anyone you can call?" he asked me.

I shook my head, not wanting to bother anyone with something so stupid.

"I'm going with you."

Both Laney and I swung our heads in his direction. "Oh?" I

said.

"I think it's a great idea," Laney said, and my head pivoted again so I could stare her down. She smiled, looking like a traitor if I ever saw one. "Thanks, Joel. Just keep any receipts for anything you buy and I'll reimburse you."

I looked back to Joel, annoyed and cagey and woozy. "I thought you had *stuff* to do today?"

He shrugged and knelt, taking my arm and hand to help me up. "I'm not supposed to be in the shop today. Seems there may be some potential hazards I wasn't aware of before this morning."

"Convenient." Once up, I leaned into him again, grateful to have him solidly next to me.

"Can you call your … driver, or whatever?"

"I've got it," Laney answered for me and handed over my purse, which Joel took. "Take care of our girl."

"I will," he answered, and the resoluteness in his voice did something to my uterus. My brain shouted at me to stop being such a freaking ninny. I didn't need anyone to take care of me.

So I said, sounding way more bratty than I meant to, "I don't need anyone to take care of me."

I nearly missed the first step, and he caught me, squeezing me in his grip before I'd moved much more than my feet. "Right, princess. You're doing just fine on your own."

I made a noise in dissent but let him guide me down the stairs anyway.

Within a few minutes we were in the car — Joel ran back into the shop to get a couple bottles of water. Literally ran, or jogged, I guess. I watched his broad shoulders, muscles bulging as they expanded and contracted, then the serious bend of his brow as he slipped in next to me. I thought it was funny — Joel, serious — and stifled another giggle. He didn't take anything seriously. His serious face looked more grumpy than anything.

I leaned back in the seat, chin lifted, eyes closed, trying to get a grip on my brain.

"Want some water?"

I didn't open my eyes, but extended a hand, closing my fingers around the cold plastic when it touched my palm. "Thanks." I twisted off the cap and took a drink.

"Gonna puke again?"

"No promises either way."

"Gonna keep fighting my help?"

"Probably."

He chuckled, and I cracked my lids, turning my head to look at him. He really was handsome underneath all that hair and ink. I knew in my head that he was much older than me, twelve years older, in fact. But he didn't look older. I mean, he looked older, but not *older*. The only indication that he was a couple years shy of forty were the smallest of creases next to his eyes, lines that said he laughed, and often.

I found myself smiling, and he looked over, smirking when he caught me.

"You're pretty funny when your brain's furry, you know that?" he asked.

I shrugged.

"I bet you're a riot when you're drunk."

I shrugged again. "I only drink vodka. Pretty much all other liquor makes me take my clothes off."

One of his dark eyebrows rose. "I'll be sure to stock up on whiskey, in that case."

"Okay, first — stock up all you want because I won't drink it. Second, stop hitting on me."

"Whatever you want, princess."

"And stop calling me princess."

"Sorry, that one's non-negotiable."

I huffed and fixed my head back where it had been, closing my eyes again, knowing it was useless to argue, even if I had the energy for it. I really did feel terrible. Not to mention confused — I wasn't mad at him at all. Mostly I just thought he was funny and cute. *Obviously you have a head injury*, I told myself. But I liked that he pushed back, didn't back down, didn't run away. He stepped right up, spit in his hand, and got ready for the fast pitch.

Baseball metaphors. That's how you know you've got a

concussion. I don't even like baseball.

It was just because he was being nice, going all caveman to take care of me. Pretty sure it was an autonomous response, something my genetics screamed for like fangirls. Double-crossing, anti-feminist DNA.

We hit a pothole, and I groaned when my head bounced against the headrest.

"Drink some more water," he said, not asking.

I sighed and obliged.

"And try to stay awake."

"That's a myth," I mumbled.

"What is?"

I opened my eyes and lolled my head over to look at him again. "Not letting someone sleep when they have a concussion. It's a myth. Sleep is good for healing, so long as there aren't any other major symptoms, like dilated pupils."

"How about barfing?" It was a challenge.

I gave him a flat look.

"I'm just saying. Try to stay awake."

My head thrummed, but I didn't feel nauseated anymore. I was tired though, my body heavy and mind slow, that kind of tired that could let you sleep anywhere. I breathed slow, hands in my lap, telling myself to stay awake or have to converse with Hairy. But I felt myself drift away, unwilling, unable to stop myself.

52

CLEOPATRA, QUEEN OF DENIAL

Joel

I WATCHED HER FROM ACROSS the bench seat, studying her breathing, but when her hand slipped off her lap and into the seat, I knew she was out.

I reached for her, clasping her hand in mine. "Annika. Wake up." My other hand slipped into the curve of her neck.

Her eyes opened slowly. "Hmmm?"

"Come on, princess. Stay awake. Don't make me resort to singing show tunes."

She smiled faintly. "You know show tunes?"

"Do I know show tunes," I said with a laugh before clearing my throat. "*Ohhhhhhhhhhhh-klahoma where the wind goes sweepin' down the plainnnnn. Where the wavin' wheat can sure smell sweet, where the wind comes right behind the raaaaaaaaain.*" I bellowed the lyrics, knowing full well I was tone deaf.

She gaped, eyes bright for the first time since she'd been knocked out. "Oh, my God."

It took all I had not to laugh. "*Ohhhhhhhhhhhh-klahoma, Ev'ry night my honey lamb and I, sit alone and talk and watch a hawk makin' lazy circles in the skyyyyyyyyyy.*"

And then, she laughed. It was a glorious sound, rough and raw, unbridled. The gift was one I knew not many received. I checked off the box next to making her laugh and made a new mental checkbox — make her do it again.

"I cannot believe you."

I shrugged, realizing then that her hand was still in mine, her long, white fingers draped over my palm. "My mom loved old musicals. I've seen a million of them, watched them with her ever since I was a kid. I think that's where I learned to really love music, honestly. Or not. I dunno. Our house was never quiet, Mom couldn't stand it. She always had something on, classic rock from the 70s, they'd say now. At the time, it was just the radio."

"You're just full of surprises, aren't you?"

I smirked. "You have no idea."

"Except that you're tone deaf. I would have guessed that."

I sighed. "I wish I wasn't. My mom could sing like an angel."

Her face softened at the mention of my mother. "I can't imagine losing my mama. I know it'll happen — they're already in their seventies. I'm trying to convince them to retire, but it's no easy task. They never planned for much of anything."

I didn't question her openness, assuming it was her concussion. "You're close?"

She nodded, eyes closed. "They're my safe place. I don't have to be anyone but me when I'm around them."

I didn't press her, sensing that if I pushed, she'd lock it down again. I squeezed her hand. "Stay awake, or I'm switching to *Music Man*."

That elicited a soft laugh as the car came to a stop. I glanced out the window and saw we'd reached the hospital.

"Thanks," she said to the driver as I opened the door and helped her out, slipping an arm around her waist.

I tucked her into my side, and it felt good, taking care of someone. It had been a long time. A very long time. Liz and I were rarely tender, more intent on destroying each other than taking care of one another. I wondered if this was what everyone else felt in their relationships. Not like they were a dead end, a brick wall, but an open road. If it was possible to really be in it together.

I saw my brother and Ramona together and knew it was. Or Patrick and his girlfriend, Rose.

Maybe I just thought it wasn't for me. That it couldn't be me. That I wasn't made for it. But if I were being honest with myself, I'd admit that the idea of repeating what I went through with Liz scared the hell out of me.

But for the first time in more than a decade, I felt the desire to try. Whether it was with the girl pressed into my side, I didn't know. But I was starting to hope it would be.

Two hours later, we pulled up to her brownstone in Park Slope, a ritzy neighborhood in Brooklyn. I couldn't help but gape at the beautiful old building, wondering how she could afford such a place, then wondering exactly how much television producers made. She was able to walk on her own at that point, and was sure to tell me so as she climbed out.

"Seriously," she insisted. "I'm fine. My driver can take you back to Tonic."

I slid across the bench to get out, but she barred my way. "Is anyone home to take care of you?"

"My cousin and her daughter will be home in a few hours."

"A few? What time?"

"Six."

I gave her a look. "That's five hours from now. The doctor said someone has to wake you up every few hours if you go to sleep."

"I'll set an alarm." The words were firm.

"I'm staying."

Her jaw clenched, and she let out a breath. "I really appreciate all your help today, honestly, but I'm fine. I can take care of myself."

"I'm sure you can," I said as I slid back to my door and climbed out, smiling at her over the roof of the car, in part because she looked so pissed.

"What the hell are you going to do in my apartment for five hours?"

"Make sure you don't have a subdural hematoma. Maybe read.

Probably go through your medicine cabinet."

"Joel," she warned.

I walked around the car to the sidewalk where she stood. "Listen, if something were to happen to you when I could have stayed, I'd never forgive myself. That's the honest truth. So, for my own lousy peace of mind, can I please sit on your couch while you sleep until your cousin gets home?"

She was quiet while she thought it over, her eyes cool and hard. "All right."

"Thank you." I relaxed considerably.

She sighed and turned for the stairs to her building, fishing in her bag for her keys.

"Nice place," I said, following.

"Thanks. My uncle owns a bunch of properties and lets us stay here for free."

"Must be nice."

She smirked over her shoulder at me. "It is."

When she opened the door, I was even more surprised. The house was gorgeous — dark hardwood, crisp, white walls, what looked like it might have been original crown molding. The property had to be worth a couple million at least, a mind-blowing amount of money in my world. After living for seventeen years in the same apartment — and in a different apartment my entire life before that — living in this sort of luxury felt mythical.

I closed the door and locked it behind me as Annika set her bag on the hall table and kicked off her shoes. She looked exhausted.

"I'm exhausted," she said, and I smiled.

"Get some rest. I'll wake you up in two hours."

She nodded and headed for the stairs.

"Which room is yours?" I asked.

"Top of the stairs, next to the bathroom. Help yourself to anything in the fridge, and most of my paperbacks are on the bookshelf in the living room. Or you can watch TV, whatever."

"Thanks."

She paused with her hand on the rail, her face soft. "No, thank you. I really do appreciate it."

"Don't mention it."

"Even if I didn't actually want your help," she added with a smile.

"That's me. Helping out even when it's unsolicited. What can I say? I'm a hero like that."

She snorted and rolled her eyes, the sound crass and very unrefined. I loved it.

"Sleep tight, Annika."

She smiled. "Thanks, Joel." And then she turned and walked up the stairs.

Not even going to deny that I watched until she was out of sight.

I sighed and turned for the living room, taking stock. All the furniture was a mixture of modern and vintage, an eclectic collection. I'd figured her place would be sterile, clean and white, no color, but this place was soft and colorful without being loud. It looked lived in, comfortable. I remembered her saying that her cousin and her daughter lived with her. I wondered how old the little girl was until I saw a stuffed bunny on the couch. I couldn't help but pick it up, the soft, wide corduroy a creamy grey, its button eyes stitched on and pink velvet ears worn with love.

I set it back down and looked around for the bookshelf, making my way over to kneel in front of the rows and rows of books. They were full of classics, a lot of hardbacks, from Ayn Rand to Dickens. But on their own shelf held standing by agate bookends, the swirl of the stone geometric and organic, stood her collection of hardback Jane Austen novels. I trailed my fingers over the spines, which were stamped in gold or silver with the titles. *Pride and Prejudice* was the one I knew everyone went for, but I decided on *Persuasion,* curious about a book that touched her, that shaped her.

I glanced at my watch and noted the time, settling into the couch to read, trying not to think about her sleeping just upstairs.

A very fat, very old calico appeared silently next to my legs, peering up at me with yellow eyes. Patches of orange and black were surrounded by white fur, and it had a black stripe on its face through its eye, which made it look like the Scarface of cats.

"Hey, there."

It gave me a single *meow* and blinked, watching me.

I reached down and scratched its jaw, rubbing my thumb against its ear, and it leaned in. "Wonder what your name is."

Meow, it said in response. I smiled and leaned back, and the cat hopped up, stretched out next to me, and went to sleep, purring.

I chuckled, comforted by the warm presence, and cracked open the book.

Hours went by, and I reveled in the absolute quiet, the city seeming far away from where I sat in Annika's living room, insulated in the brownstone. I'd woken her once a few hours before — she was nestled in her bed with the curtains drawn, her face slack and soft. She looked like a girl like that, the hardness gone, her hair out of its tight bun and spread across her pillow like spun gold.

I'd almost touched her face, realizing at the last second just how intimate the gesture was, but I barely stopped myself, as if her skin begged to be touched. Instead I touched her arm, and she opened her eyes sleepily, said she felt fine, other than being tired still, and asked to sleep some more. So I obliged.

I checked my watch — it was time to wake her again, and this time I thought it might be best if she stay awake for a stretch, especially if she wanted to sleep that night. So I headed into the kitchen, looking around for the coffee pot, or a tea pot. They were right next to each other, along with a small box of tea, so I took it as a sign that it was a regular thing and filled up the electric teapot.

It was old and loud, the water hissing and bubbling as I searched for a coffee cup.

"Stop right there," a hard, cautious, female voice said from behind me.

I put my hands up, though a mug with an illustrated monkey hung on my pointer finger. When I turned, I found a woman who looked like she could be Annika's sister, leaning toward me with an outstretched hand wielding mace. A little girl peeked out from behind her with golden hair just like her mother, and blue eyes like ping pong balls, widened in fear.

"Who the fuck are you, and what the fuck are you doing in my kitchen?"

My hands were still up. "I'm Joel. Annika didn't text you?"

Her brow dropped, but her hand didn't. "No. Why?"

"She got a concussion at work."

Her eyes widened. "Oh, my God. Is she okay?"

"She's fine, upstairs sleeping. Could you maybe lower the mace? I dunno if you've ever been maced, but it's what I imagine hell feels like."

"Oh, sorry." She lowered the spray and extending her hand for a shake. "This is Kira, and I'm Roxy, Annika's cousin."

I took her hand. "Nice to meet you. Sorry for the confusion."

She waved a hand and wrapped it around the little girl's shoulders. "No, it's okay. I'm glad you were here. I wonder why she didn't call me?"

"Said she didn't want to be a bother."

Roxy rolled her eyes. "Of course she did. I'm surprised she even let you stay here with her."

I smirked. "Me too, but I'm persistent."

"You have to be, with her."

The teapot dinged, and I turned to pour out a cup. "She drinks tea, yeah?"

"Yeah, she does. How long have you been here?"

I shrugged. "Since one or so, when we got back from the hospital."

"And you've just been sitting here?"

"Reading, but yeah. Met your cat."

One blond eyebrow rose. "Kaz?"

"That's his name? I was wondering. He kept me company all day. Sweet cat."

"*Kazimir?* Destroyer of peace? That cat is pure evil and hates everyone."

I frowned. "Seriously? Because he just laid on me and purred for hours."

She shook her head. "You must have some weird voodoo on you because the only people that old cat loves are Annika and Kira."

The little girl nodded. "He wears dolly dresses for tea parties."

Roxy made a face. "Yeah, and he pees in my closet. Oh, once? I came home and he'd shredded my feather pillow. He was sitting on my bed like a goddamn prince surrounded in goose down. *Ublyudok.*"

I recognized the word. "Bastard?"

She smirked. "She told you?"

"Lucky guess." I picked up Annika's tea. "Mind if I take this up to her?"

"Be my guest."

"Thanks," I said as I passed, though when I rounded the corner, I found a sleepy Annika shuffling down the stairs, hand pressed to her temple, wearing long sleeved button down white satin pajamas. She blinked at me and yawned.

"Nice jammies. Not a princess, huh?"

She made a face at me.

I approached her, meeting her at the foot of the stairs. "Made you some tea. Was just coming up to check on you."

She smiled, but it was small, more closed than it had been before she'd gone up. "Thanks," she said as she took the mug.

"So, Roxy came home just now and tried to mace me."

Her eyes flew wide. "Oh, my God. I forgot to call her and tell her. I'm so sorry."

"No worries, no harm done."

"Good," she said. We stood in silence for a moment.

"So, I should probably be going," I said just as she said, "Well, thanks a lot for your help today."

We both chuckled.

"I'm heading out. Let me know if you need anything, okay? You have my number."

"Thanks, Joel."

I smiled. "Sure thing. Glad you're feeling better." I turned to go, but stopped. "Oh, mind if I borrow *Persuasion*? I started reading it and thought, if it was okay, that I could hang on to it for a couple of days."

She didn't mask her surprise. "Yeah, of course," she said,

disbelieving.

"Thanks." I made my way into the living room, grabbed the book from the couch, and walked back by. "See you tomorrow," I said as I passed her, reaching for the door.

"Bye." The word was unsure, and I couldn't help but smile to myself as I pulled open the door and stepped into the New York dusk. Because I had a feeling that single word meant I actually had a chance.

Annika

Joel disappeared with the click of the front door, and when I stepped around the banister, I was met with Roxy's smirk, which was practically accusing.

I wrapped my free hand around the warm mug and narrowed my eyes as I headed for the couch. "Don't."

"Don't what?" she feigned innocence.

"Don't start."

"So I shouldn't ask any questions about Tattoo Tommy and the Bearded Gun Show that just happened?"

I sat down and propped my feet on the coffee table. "I had a concussion, and he wouldn't leave until you were home."

"Chivalrous," she said as she sat down next to me. "Who is he?"

"One of the shop owners. Hairy."

Her face lit up. "Wait, *that* was Hairy? I pictured some balding guy with a ponytail and beer gut."

"Nope, and that somehow makes it that much harder to hate him."

"So is he the older brother or younger?"

"Older."

"Is his brother as hot as he is?"

"If you think hairy, bearded, pushy scoundrels are hot, then yeah."

She snorted. "Scoundrel. You've got to read something that

takes place past the 19th century. Does he have a girlfriend?"

I glared at her, wondering why the thought made me want to pull her hair. "Who, Joel?"

Roxy laughed. "No, the brother. Joel's clearly already spoken for."

I frowned. "Shep has a girlfriend, yeah. And what do you mean spoken for?"

"God, for a smart person, you're really dense. Why didn't you tell me you had a thing for him?"

I huffed like a teapot. "I don't have a 'thing' for him, Roxy."

"Right, and having kids doesn't ruin your boobs." She gestured to her rack to illustrate.

"You're one hundred percent wrong, Rox. I'm sure he's a nice enough guy, but he's not my type."

"Exactly, which is what you need. Your type is boring. Safe."

"What's wrong with making safe choices? I don't have a single thing in common with Joel Anderson."

"Since when does that matter? I saw you looking at him, and I saw him looking at you — you practically set the curtains on fire. So don't tell me you're not into him because it's a goddamn lie."

I felt heat crawl up my neck and across my cheeks. "Would I bang him? Yes, I would. But I'm not going to because A: I'm his producer," I ticked off on my fingers, "B: I'm not interested in a relationship with him, C: I'm not interested in ruining my career, and D …" I trailed off, still mad but unable to think of a fourth point.

She waggled her brows. "The D is the single reason why you *will* bang him."

I fumed. "I'm not having sex with him, Roxy! Why are we even talking about this?"

"Because you're in denial, Cleopatra. I've been there, where you are. You can't ignore that kind of physical attraction, even if that's all it is. I tried, which resulted in me getting knocked up."

I opened my mouth to ask her who Kira's father was, a secret guarded with her life apparently, in part because it kept me up nights wondering, but mostly to do whatever I could to take the heat off me.

She waved me off before I could speak. "Don't even ask. We're talking about you. You like him. Why won't you admit it?"

"I just fucking did!" I almost yelled it, and Roxy made a face before looking over at Kira, who sat coloring at the table with her stuffed bunny sitting in her lap like he was watching.

"I just don't get it. He's obviously into you if he sat here all day with only Kaz to keep him company while he read a romance novel."

"For the last time. I'm not interested in hooking up with him or dating him or even thinking about him outside of work. I didn't ask him to stay. I didn't want him here. I don't want him to be into me, and I'm not into him. Okay?" I found that I was trying to convince myself just as much as I wanted to convince Roxy.

She was almost pouting, but in an angry way.

"End of story." And I felt that was the absolute truth. I felt the desire for separation seep from my head down into my heart like roots of a tree. I was resolute, and when I made a decision like this, when I dug in my heels, I wouldn't change my mind.

Roxy knew this, and said, frustrated, "If you say so."

"I say so."

"Then that's that."

"Yes, it is."

"By the way," she started before punching me in the arm.

"Ow—" I cried, but she was already talking.

"Why didn't you call me? If you really didn't want Hairy here, I could have come over."

"Because you're busy and I didn't want to bother you." I rubbed my arm. "That hurt."

"Good. That's for being presumptuous. Always call me, okay? You had a concussion for God's sake, not period cramps."

I chuckled. "All right. I'm sorry."

"Me too," she said, not elaborating, not needing to. I reached for her hand.

"I'm glad you're okay and that Hairy was here to take care of you."

"Thanks. Me too."

"So, are you feeling okay now?"

"Better than earlier for sure. I feel like I should be hungry, but my stomach is a little tender. I just came down to see if Joel was still here and to try to get him to leave again."

"I don't think he would have."

I sighed. "Me neither. You're right about him being into me, and it's not that he's not … I mean, you've seen him."

She laughed.

"But it's just a bad idea." My stomach clenched, though I pinned it on the concussion, not the thought of him and me doing the naked tango. "It can't happen, and it won't. But he's … persistent."

"Well, so are you, so I don't doubt you'll remain at an impasse forever. A couple of gluttons for punishment, if you ask me."

"I didn't ask you, so feel free to keep it to yourself," I half-joked.

She rolled her eyes. "Fine, fine. Want to watch TV?"

I yawned, surprised that I somehow still felt sleepy. "I think I'll head back up and read for a bit before sleeping some more. I feel like I could sleep for a week, honestly." I hauled myself off the couch and yawned again.

"Don't forget your tea."

I picked up the monkey mug and found myself smiling down at it. "Thanks."

"You're welcome. Just text me if you need anything and I'll bring it up."

"Really, thanks, Rox."

"Anything for you. Now go get yourself better, okay?"

I smiled a little wider. "Okay."

The stairs creaked under my feet as I climbed them, and within a minute, I slipped back into bed, tea still steaming. He'd picked my favorite, jasmine tea, and I wondered if it was a coincidence or if he somehow knew I'd like it. I shouldn't have been wondering about him at all. But I was. I wondered what he'd done all that time. Kaz jumped onto the bed and into my lap, curling up into a purring ball, and I wondered about that too, how Kaz, the spawn of the Devil, would have befriended Joel. I wondered what Joel was doing just then, what he'd do for the rest of the night, when I'd see him again.

But those roots of decision wound around my heart and squeezed. Joel and I made no sense. He was charming and annoying and bossy and hairy and *all wrong.* He was everything I wasn't. He was everything I'd tried to avoid in my life. He was the opposite of what I needed, of what fit into my plan. And that was exactly why I had to put him out of my mind, put him into a safe, lock it up, and throw away the key.

But even though my mind tightened up the reins, my heart whispered the assent, too soft for my mind to notice.

WANG FEAST

Joel

"HOW DO MY BOOBS LOOK?"

I glanced over my shoulder with one eyebrow cocked, but Penny wasn't talking to me. Her hair was hot pink this month, and it was all done up like a pinup girl. She shimmied around her breasts in her bustier, and Veronica laughed from the chair next to me in makeup, which *used* to be my stock room.

"They look perfect. Stop worrying."

My makeup artist turned my face toward her and kept dabbing at me with a makeup brush.

"You have great eyes," she said.

"Thanks. It's genetic."

She chuckled.

"I'm not really worried," Penny continued. "Mostly excited. We're gonna be on *TV*, Ronnie. Like, you realize we're about to become a household name?"

I found myself frowning, that familiar apprehension winding through my guts.

"Maybe I'll get a deal for my own line of makeup, like Kat Von D," Penny mused. "Or hair dyes. You should get one for eyeliner, Ronnie. Nobody rules the cat-eye like you."

Veronica chuckled. "One thing at a time, all right? We haven't even started filming yet."

"But we will today," Penny sang. "Man, you also realize we're about to have access to pretty much any man we want? It's going to be a freaking man-buffet. A shlong smorgasbord. All-you-can-eat wang feast."

"And what makes you think all those men are going to come running?" I teased.

She gave me a look. "Have you met me?"

I couldn't help but laugh. I'd seen hordes of men trip over themselves for Penny, pretty much since the second I'd met her. But she was about as attainable as world peace. "Bunch of suckers. Always wanting what they can't have."

She shrugged. "That's on them. I don't make promises I can't keep." She smiled at that and winked at me, and I shook my head.

Penny and Veronica kept talking, but I zoned out, my eyes fixed on a point across the room where shelves used to be. Luckily, we stored most of our supplies at our stations, but it peeved me to have *my* space packed with mirrors and makeup and lights, making it unfamiliar to me, changing the space I'd practically lived in every day for the majority of my life to something unrecognizable.

Better this than Hal, I told myself for the eleventy trillionth time. So many times, in fact, that it had nearly lost its effect all together.

I heard a voice in the front of the shop and turned my head, certain it was Annika. The makeup artist guided my head back toward her with the patience of a saint, but my heart ticked up just a notch, just enough to notice.

I hadn't seen her since I'd left her house on Saturday. It was Monday. It could have been a month, as much as I'd thought about her. I spent all Sunday working, replaying the day before to the steady hum of my tattoo gun, the vibrating of it in my hand comforting, hypnotizing. The motions were automatic, as easy as remembering to blink or breathe. But she was on my mind all day.

To see her soft, almost silly. To hear her laugh. The feel of her against me, leaning into me. The vision of her lying in bed with her hair around her like a veil.

I'd figured I wouldn't see her Sunday, but every time the bell over the door rang, I whipped my head toward the sound, ripped from the trance like a that bell was a bucket of ice water. I worried about her, too, hoped she was all right. But I knew I'd see her today, and even though I tried to play it cool, I'd found myself counting down to it, even waking an hour earlier than usual, which left me early enough to have nothing to do. I felt like a kid waiting on my front porch, fully dressed and ready to go.

So, I'd spent the early morning reading *Persuasion,* which I found myself enjoying more than I thought I would. Getting into the way they speak was the hardest part, but once I got past that, it was easy. It was a story of two people finding their way back to each other, of finding the way to themselves after being lost. I found I could relate to the sentiment.

I'd killed time waiting for the hour when we'd all file upstairs and into the green room for one-on-ones with Annika. We only had a few hours, and then we'd resume our regularly scheduled clients, with more to film tonight after we closed the shop. Days were going to be long, and we'd need to be 'on' for all of it, which wasn't something we were used to. I just hoped everyone held up without cracking.

Believe it or not, most tattoo parlors are pretty boring, day to day. We sit in a chair with flesh and ink under our hands, mostly in silence, other than the music that plays and the buzz of the gun in our hand.

I heard her voice again, closer this time, and forced myself to sit still. I'd see her when I saw her, I told myself. But my nerves buzzed just like a tattoo gun with nothing but a rubber band to hold everything in place. Because something had shifted between us, and I wanted to find out if she felt it too.

But she never came back to us. My makeup artist dabbed a little more goop on my nose and leaned back to look at me. Her eyes darted over to one side, and she froze like she was listening to something. She smiled at me.

"They're ready for you in the shop," she said, and at my confused face, she pointed to her ear where a monitor sat nestled.

"Thanks …" I started, searching for her name as a PA appeared at my elbow to mic me.

"Kyla."

I smiled. "Thanks, Kyla."

"You're very welcome," she said with a smile as she slipped the brush into her apron.

I climbed out of my chair and headed out and upstairs to the interview room. A chair stood in the middle of the room with lights and reflectors all pointed at it, and a cameraman and boom operator fiddled with their equipment, but I barely noticed them.

Annika sat on a stool next to them, smiling up at me. She looked fresh and recharged, though still cool and collected. The animosity seemed to be mostly gone, if I wasn't making up the notion.

"Hey," she said as I approached, standing to greet me.

"Hey," I smiled back at her.

She hitched a thumb over her shoulder. "Can I have a word while we finish getting set up?"

"Of course," I answered, feeling a little nervous, playing it off completely as I followed her out and into the hallway.

She reached for my hip, and I froze, too caught off guard to react. But her fingers closed over my mic battery and clicked it off with a snick. She popped her own monitor out of her ear, leaving it dangling over her shoulder.

Her face was calm, masked, cast from marble, but she smiled, which gave me the tiniest modicum of hope. "I just wanted to thank you again for taking care of me the other day. It was really great of you, and I appreciated it a lot."

Great. Appreciated. These were not the words of a woman head over heels in love with me, and I felt my smile fall. "Yeah, sure. I wouldn't have left you on your own like you were."

"It was so nice of you."

I almost flinched at the least productive adjective in the English language. "Well, you know me. I'm just a *nice* guy."

"I just hope I didn't give you the wrong impression. I know I can come off as a little … *frosty*, but I like to think that I'm not a terrible person. I'm just cautious, is all. And I know yesterday my guard was down, so I just didn't want you to think I was …" she trailed off, and I picked it right up.

"Into me? Defrosting your cold, black soul?" I inched closer, and she leaned toward me just a degree, just enough to give me permission. I pressed the opening. "Waiting for me to kiss you?"

"Joel," she said, her voice layered with warning and yearning, and I couldn't help myself. I leaned in closer still.

"Or were you waiting on this? Were you waiting on me?" I breathed the words, my nose filled with the scent of her — honeysuckle? No, that wasn't it either—

She put a hand on my chest, her face hardening. "Stop."

The word was a punch in the gut, stopping me immediately, and I drew a breath at the sting. I stepped back.

"I was concussed. Whatever I said or did the other day, I wasn't in my right mind. Literally. Nothing has changed. I still don't want you hit on me. *This* isn't going to happen, okay?"

But her eyes — her eyes, her tone of voice, her hand on my chest like it was connected to me rather than trying to push me away — they told me a different story than her words. So I put on my best smirk, because she could say she didn't want me all day long, but that wouldn't make it true. "Okay, Annika. Whatever you say."

Her brows dropped, the tension broken. "Don't say that like I just challenged you."

I shrugged. "You're the boss, boss."

She rolled her eyes and huffed, reaching for my hip again. I resisted the urge to lean into her hand as she turned my battery pack on and brushed past me. I turned and followed, taking my seat in front of her. She wanted to play it this way? I'd play along, back down, let her be the boss. Let her take the lead.

I had a feeling that if I did, the payoff would be well worth the wait.

Annika

I sat in my chair across from Joel, clipboard in my lap, heart thumping like a kick drum against my ribs.

That hairy bastard smirked at me from his chair like he knew a secret. I could practically hear him singing *neener-neener-neeeee-ner* like a child, hands clasped between his parted thighs, like he knew exactly how sexy he was, how right he was.

What a dick.

I slipped my pen out of the clipboard's clip and smiled as Randy nodded to me from behind the camera.

"So, Joel," I started, "have you always been an insufferable horse's ass, or is it a more recent development? Something acquired in your old age?"

He laughed, and the sound was so hearty, so full of life and pleasure that I pursed my lips, determined not to laugh back.

"Oh, no. I've been insufferable since my exit from the womb. It's only sweetened with age."

I'd been doodling absently on my blank page and realized with a smile that I was drawing a dick as I thought through my questions.

"Noted. So, tell me a bit about how you got started in art and tattooing."

He began to talk, his eyes taking a far-away look back into his life, and I listened, making notes, drawing what looked like scratchy pubes on the balls of the dick, giving the crown a beard and a smirk, trying not to listen too deeply. Because everything I learned about him piqued my interest even more. And that stupid interest pissed me off. I didn't *want* to be interested, but there I was, listening to it all, trying not to think about how he'd almost kissed me. How much I'd wanted him to.

He told me about how his parents had always encouraged his drawing and sketching, even his tattooing, which, he explained, most of his companions didn't have growing up. They were a rag-tag band of misfits, finding home in their culture, in their jobs. They were their own family, especially once Joel and Shep lost their parents.

I wrote the word *Hairy* at the top of the page, tracing it over and over again as we volleyed questions and answers back and forth to each other, digging deeper into his life. What started off fluffy had delved a little deeper than I suspected he was comfortable with, but part of my job was to push the boundaries. Make people cry like Barbara Walters or Oprah. Get them to open up. So I asked a question I shouldn't have, only in part for my job.

"Tell me about your ex-wife, Liz."

I might have just imagined it, but I swear he flinched a millimeter when I said her name. "What do you want to know?"

Everything. "Where did you two meet?"

"A bar."

"What did you think of her the first time you saw her?"

His eyes narrowed. "That she was somebody I'd like to know."

I nodded, annoyed that he wouldn't answer me as I added more pubes to the balls. "Sure. I heard she's beautiful. I saw some pictures from her wedding day when we were vetting Hal for the show."

Somehow, his eyes narrowed even more.

"She and Hal looked really happy. That was, what, a few months after your divorce was finalized?"

He stood up and pulled off his monitor, refusing to look at me. "We're done here."

My stomach fell into my shoes as I realized what I'd done, and I stood as he passed me, leaving my clipboard on the stool. He stormed out the door, and I followed. The control room came to a silent stop, including Penny and Ramona, who were waiting for their turn.

"Joel, I—"

He whirled around, wounded and angry. "What the fuck was that, Annika?"

"I'm sorry. I didn't mean to upset you—"

"Like hell you didn't."

I took a breath. "You're right, but I didn't mean to hurt you. It's easy to forget that you have feelings when you disregard mine."

His nostrils flared. "That's all well and good, but you're not the one being filmed."

My mouth opened to speak, but he headed me off.

"Don't bait me. Don't push me. This show isn't about Hal and Liz. This is about my shop, about our culture, about art and history and *people*. I'm not a fucking puff piece or a puppet for you to dick around with. I'm a human fucking being with baggage just like everybody, and I don't appreciate that being exploited on national fucking television."

"I know," I started, hoping he'd let me finish. "But people are going to want to know about you, about your past. The women are going to want to hear about why you're single, imagine themselves with you."

He took a deep breath, his chest rising and falling slowly, lips a thin line. "I don't give a shit, Annika. This is my life, and there's a time, a place, and a way to talk about it. But that—" he pointed toward the front of the shop where we'd been sitting, arching over me, "—is not the way. Have some fucking respect."

I blinked at him, my mouth open at his proximity, as close as he'd been earlier. But now he breathed hot anger and hurt instead of the heat of desire. My thoughts swam as he spun around and marched out the door, leaving me standing in the middle of the room with a dozen sets of eyes on me. So I did what any good producer would do.

I looked to Penny. "You're up. This way, please," I said with my voice cold, carrying a calm I didn't feel.

The interviews went on for a few hours, and we got through the first half of the staff. I couldn't stop thinking about Joel, about the anger in his face, in his words. But I kept smiling, kept talking, kept going. It didn't stop me from feeling like I'd done real damage. It didn't stop me from feeling all sorts of things.

I found myself asking the artists about him under the guise of looking for material, telling myself I was looking for chinks in the armor. But really, I found their stories and words about him a testament to the kind of man he was. Everyone I interviewed spoke of him with admiration and respect, with smiles on their faces and eyes full of love. Because they did — they loved him with something close to worship.

All of this did absolutely nothing to make me feel better about pushing him so hard.

He was angry, and he had every right to be. I was out of line, and I'd hurt him, going too far because he'd pushed me by almost kissing me. He made me uncomfortable, not because I didn't want him, but because I did. And that fact scared me enough that I'd keep pushing the notion away in the hopes that it would disappear.

But that was no excuse. He stopped when I asked him to, even though I didn't necessarily want him to. He'd done exactly what I'd asked of him, and then I turned around and pulled the trigger on him.

No one held the ability to press my buttons like Joel Anderson did. He could see through my façade like he had X-ray vision.

Once we wrapped, everyone dispersed, moving downstairs to get ready to film for the day. But Joel wasn't there, and I found myself a little sad and a little relieved, because I needed to talk to him, and I didn't want to do it with an audience.

I made my way outside and through Tonic's door, up the stairs and to his apartment, where I took a breath, smoothing my skirt. And I rapped on the door, waiting only through a couple of heartbeats before he answered, brow low.

"Yeah?" was all he offered.

"Do you have a second?"

He seemed to think on it for a moment before stepping back, opening the door to make room for me.

I took a few steps in, not feeling welcome enough to venture any farther in, though I did sweep the space quickly out of habit. It was clean and homey, with couches that looked worn without being worn out, furniture that felt old without feeling outdated. It felt comfortable.

He closed the door and stood expectantly in the small entryway.

"I …" I started, feeling unsure of myself, of what I wanted to say. It was impossible to think with him standing there, looking angry and hurt. But I found myself, somehow, and swallowed the rest like a lump of sawdust in my throat. "Joel, I really am sorry about earlier."

He didn't say anything, just folded his arms across his chest.

So I kept going. "All I have to offer are a string of excuses, and I'm not sure any of them matter."

"Try me," he said.

I took a breath. "Well, we've made a habit out of having a go at each other, you and I. And when you came at me, came on to me, pushed me, I pushed back. I just … I pushed too hard."

He didn't say anything, but his face changed almost imperceptibly, just a little softer around the edges.

"Do you know much about where I worked before this?"

He shook his head.

"I was a producer for Fashion Forward. Have you heard of it?"

His eyes narrowed, and he nodded once. "The fashion designer show? Big competition?"

I nodded back. "That show … well, it wasn't like this show will be. That show was built around drama, from the timelines and materials they could use to their relationships with each other. We'd put them all in this pressure cooker and crank up the heat until the lid flew off. And my job was to push people together and apart, to manipulate them. To make them fight or make them friends or make them kiss or whatever the show called for. To make it *interesting*."

He shook his head, brows furrowed. "Jesus."

"When I started there, I was naive. I thought I was walking into a musical, when really I was walking into a meat grinder. Within the first year, I realized what it would take to be successful, and for me to be successful, I had to check my conscience at the door. It changed me, it almost … split me in two — the old me and the soulless me," I admitted, wondering why I was telling him so much, feeling like he understood, like he wouldn't judge me. "Laney was my mentor, and Laney is a shark. It's how she's gotten ahead — being ruthless." I thought back to the years I worked on the show, years of lying, exploiting, and I didn't want to admit any of the specifics to him, not in that moment. "Joel, I've been trained to push buttons, and old habits die hard. But I crossed the line today, and I'm sorry. You're right. I'm not being filmed. I put you on the spot, on camera. On your *first time* on camera. It was a dick move."

"Damn right." His arms were still folded, biceps fanned out, covered in ink. I caught myself looking and averted my eyes.

"So, what can I do to make it up to you?"

His frown shifted into a smirk. "So many answers to that question."

I huffed. "Seriously, Joel?"

But he put his hands up and laughed. "I'm sorry. It's just too easy."

I chuffed. "Why's that?"

He smirked. "You set yourself up for it, and you get too mad. Mad in a way you can't hide. That blush of yours — it's just about your only tell."

The offending blush reared its head at that. "Good to know."

"Anyway, I get it, about pushing buttons and all." His face hardened a little. "You wanted to know about Liz? Well, that's all she and I did — push each other. We pushed each other until we self-destructed, taking everything down with us. I don't want to talk about her on camera, Annika. It's not fair."

I nodded and swallowed hard, feeling worse. "I get it. I do. But just know that it's not something you can avoid forever. I'll be more careful with my words, with how we talk about it on camera, but just know that Laney won't let it go. And you'd rather have me asking the questions than her. So, think about it. Work with me, and I promise we'll work together. Okay?"

He watched me — sometimes I thought his eyes were brown, but they looked green occasionally too, always with flecks of gold and blue, like in that moment as he assessed me. "I'll think it over."

"Thank you." I felt the pressure in my chest release, pressure I hadn't realized was there until it was gone. "So, are we good?"

"Yeah, we're good," he said, his voice light, the smirk back, shoulders squared.

I found myself smiling at him, wondering how he managed to affect me like he did. I ate most men for breakfast — they never stood a chance. But Hairy could smirk at me and pop off a snarky line and BLAMO. Involuntary bodily reactions like blushing and thigh clenching. I secretly hoped there was something about me that affected him like that. I then made a mental note to look for his tell, because if there *was* something I did, I needed to know what it was and what it did to him so I could exploit the hell out of it.

"Well, I'll leave you to it. They're just straightening the shop up and you guys will be ready to roll. I've got a PA down there all day to help you guys remember to get waivers from all your customers, and if they don't want to sign one, they'll need to be tattooed in one of the private rooms. If you have any questions or anything, just let your PA know and they'll come get us, or you can come up. We'll be in the office."

He nodded. "All right." He pulled open the door and leaned on it in a way that was effortlessly cool. "I'll see you when we close up tonight."

I walked past. "Sounds good," was the coolest thing I could manage, which wasn't really cool at all, and he smirked one last time before closing the door behind me.

I decided then that maybe I wasn't fully recovered from my concussion after all.

Composing myself became my number one priority as I climbed the stairs to the control room apartment. The crew bustled around, some already working on editing what we'd gotten that morning. Joel was on one of the screens, pulling his monitor out of his ear, and my stomach clenched, hoping to God they didn't choose to use that for anything. Ever.

We call it Frankenbiting — taking sound clips and video, chopping them up, then splicing them together to make it look like what we want. Whether or not it was in context didn't matter, so long as the end result worked for the story we were trying to tell. And the thought of Joel being misconstrued sent an unfamiliar feeling of unease through me. I felt *protective* over him, and found myself frowning as I walked into the office.

Laney was on the phone, her tone firm — though I didn't register who she was talking to or what they were talking about as I sat down across from her, opening my laptop to stare blankly at my spreadsheet for that night's schedule.

I wasn't really sure how it had all come about, all the feelings I was having, all the things Joel seemed to bring out in me. Frustration. Annoyance. Amusement. Caring. I typically prided myself on *not* caring, keeping myself purposely separate. I'd venture to say that I hadn't even let the men I'd dated all the way in. I didn't trust them to show them all of me, and the only people who did know that part of me was my family. But somehow, I trusted Joel enough to *care*.

I mean, don't get me wrong. I didn't know him, and he didn't know me. He'd done nothing to earn my trust other than be unabashedly honest and open. Truth be told, I saw a bit of myself in him, which wasn't necessarily a good thing. But he was somehow a kindred spirit, and I recognized that. And that recognition was mystifying and terrifying and almost unfathomable, mostly because it had occurred so naturally.

"—said everything is on track though." Laney paused. "Are you listening to me?"

My eyes snapped back into focus, and I looked up at her. "Sorry. Weird morning."

She smiled as she shuffled through the papers on her desk. "Yeah, I heard. Day one, and you've already had a blow up. Not bad."

Inside, I cringed. Outside, I kept my face still. "It was too soon to push him about Liz."

"Probably. Everything okay now?"

"Yeah, I just spoke to him about it all and apologized."

"Whatever you have to do to get the job done. Keep him happy. Pump the breaks on Liz for now. You can find the cracks later and stuff them full of dynamite." Laney leaned back in her seat. "So, what happened when he took you home the other day?"

I shook my head. "Nothing. He just got me home and that was that."

"That's all? I'm surprised he didn't try to make a move on you."

"Was that your plan all along? Is that why you pushed me off on him?"

"Honestly? I just wanted to see what would happen, how you would handle it."

I gave her a look. "What's your deal?" I asked, feeling prickly. "I'm not interested in him."

Her smile faded. "He's into you, and if you hook up with him, it can go one of two ways. Either you can use your lady bits to control him, or your lady bits will implode the whole thing. I want to know which path you're going to choose."

I fumed. "Neither. The lady bits are locked up and out of commission when it comes to Joel."

She inspected her nails. "Yeah, I don't believe that."

"Yeah, well, neither does he, and you're both assholes for it."

"Listen, I'm only saying you need to be smart. If you're going to cave, have a purpose, a plan. Because if you go into anything with him blind, you could take the entire show down with you. It wouldn't be the first time, either. Remember Tina?"

Cold slid down my back. "Yeah, I remember Tina."

"She couldn't keep her shit together, and we almost lost the show. You're not allowed to have feelings for him."

"Oh, so now you're telling me what to feel?"

She looked up, leveling her eyes at me. "Who even are you right now? He's a *meat puppet*, Annika. You can't have feelings for him, or you'll fuck us all over, Joel included. Use your brain. If you want to fuck him, be my guest. But don't go falling for him or *we're* screwed." She pointed at her desk, leaning forward as she said the word.

I broke her gaze and opened my vodka drawer, unable to really be mad. Because if the tables were turned, I'd be doing the exact same thing to her. So instead, I poured a shot and said, "Got it, boss."

NO RAGRETS

Joel

THE SHOP SEEMED TO BUZZ all day, even though the crew was gone, save a lone PA who sat behind the desk on his phone. Everyone who'd had an interview that morning was zinging, high off it, and the ones who were interviewing that night seemed full of nerves. But I sat in my chair, mostly quiet, spending the day working, blaring The Black Keys' discography on repeat as I thought about her.

Everyone was talking about my blow up, since half the shop and crew had been present for the outburst, but I wasn't sorry. She was out of line, and I'd been so pissed, I'd barely been able to see as I flew out of the shop and upstairs. I'd planned on watching everyone's interviews to be certain everyone felt comfortable and that no one was taken advantage of under my roof. But they were on their own after what she'd said. There was no way I could have sat there next to her all morning and pretended what she'd done was okay.

I thought about Liz and Hal, my past that I rarely revisited, never mind talked about, getting dragged out into the daylight for Annika to kick and prod. Especially since she was the last person I wanted to talk to about it all. In front of a camera, no less.

See, when my parents died years ago, they left Shep and I everything they had, which wasn't a lot, but it was enough to start our own shop. We were kids at that time, Shep eighteen and just coming out of apprenticing, me twenty-one, married to Liz, and sure I had all the answers. Hal had worked with us at the shop we were at, and when we came into the money and opened Tonic, he came with us. We were friends, though the kind of friends based more on proximity than brotherhood. But we were friends.

I thought, at least.

The bigger we got, the worse he behaved. You know the type. The one who thinks he's the best at everything and jumps at the chance to tell you all about it. The kind who drops names and gloms onto someone he thinks might take him somewhere.

Honestly, I thought Liz had better taste. She and I met when I'd only just moved out of my parents' house at nineteen and I'd landed my first job at a shop. Liz and I excelled at two things: fighting and fucking. Typically while drinking. I asked her to marry me after a month of dating — pre-fighting. At that point, we excelled at fucking, which was spectacular. So we flew to Vegas and got married in the Chapel O' Love by a drag queen.

Thus began the longest five years of my life.

Days were long at work, nights were long with cycle of drinking, followed by the fighting, then fucking. When my parents died, everything intensified until the heat of it was almost all I could bear. Shep moved in, and we opened the shop, and the stress compiled, making the days seem even longer until I felt grey and deflated. The fucking stopped. The fighting didn't, made worse by the drinking.

The night she sent me to the hospital after knocking me out with a bottle of Jack Daniel's was the last. I kicked her out and filed for divorce. She went to stay with Hal.

Smug didn't begin to cover it. Hal had always been so sure he could do everything better than me. Run a shop. Handle Liz. So when he walked out the door, taking my baggage with him, I waved goodbye without a regret. I just didn't know he'd be my shadow for the rest of my days.

It started with him opening his shop, modeling nearly everything after mine. He tried to shark my artists. Tried to copy my life. But in the end, a copy of an original is never as good. Like a fax, distorted by perception, made grainy by misinterpretation.

And now, here I was. I'd have to talk about Liz. On camera. I'd been warned, and I believed every word Annika said.

Annika.

I was still chewing on the exchange, just as I had been all day. We'd been having a go at each other, all right. And at the mention of it, I couldn't help but think of Liz again in comparison. I'd done this before, survived a relationship fueled by gasoline and a hot match. Barely survived. And now, after all this time, the first girl to wake me up wasn't much different.

Part of me wanted to justify their differences. Annika wasn't Liz, not by a long shot. We pushed each other, but it wasn't destructive. Was it?

After her display that morning, I wasn't so sure.

The difference between Annika and Liz was that Annika was sorry. She apologized and meant it, I thought, at least. Liz and I would just wake up and pretend like nothing had happened. Nothing was ever solved, and so the wheel would turn again and again, over and over, to no end.

But I didn't want to fight. I didn't want to push. I just wanted to be happy.

My head ached, and I popped some ibuprofen between clients, wishing there were a pill to set the rest of me to rights. Annika said she wasn't interested in me, and that was probably for the best. The whole ordeal was doing its best to remind me why I'd been single for so long, resigned to be alone, maybe forever.

I took a long pull from my water bottle as I waited for my next job to walk in, and Patrick rolled his chair over to the short wall between our stations, his eyes somehow bright and dark, searching mine.

See, Patrick knew me, and he knew me well. He'd come into the shop near ten years before, all arms and legs, eyes sunken into his head, with a sketchbook under his arm packed cover-to-cover in promise. So I hired him, the quiet boy, the drug addict, and I gave him a place to stay, a place to work, a place to call home, which wasn't something he'd had much of in his life. And in doing that, he became like a brother to me and to Shep.

I smiled at him to cover for the fact that I was broody. "Going okay over there?"

He nodded and leaned on the wall. "How about you? Doing okay?"

"Never better, man. Never better."

He jacked a dark eyebrow. "That so? Penny spilled the beans about earlier with Annika."

I chuffed. "She would. It really wasn't anything to talk about."

"You cussed her out in front of half the crew."

I shrugged. "She had it coming."

He laughed at that. "I'm sure she did."

"Really, it's fine," I reassured him. "She just hit a soft spot, that's all. Wanted to talk about Liz and did it in a way that wasn't copasetic. But she came up after and apologized, so we're good. And that's all there is to tell."

"What's going on with you two? There's been a lot of talk that you two have a thing going."

I wasn't sure if I could evade him, so I only gave it a half-assed attempt. I sighed. "There's nothing going on."

"But you want there to be something going on."

I sniffed and scratched at my beard. "Doesn't really matter what I want."

He made a face. "Why are you being like this? It's not like you to make me drag details out of you."

I sighed again and pulled up a little closer, hanging my arms on the wall next to his. "I don't know, Tricky. I really don't. It's just that from the second she walked through that door, she's been under my skin, and I can't shake her."

He nodded. "I know how that goes. What's the deal with her?"

"She's resisted my charms on all fronts. Asked me to stop, told me she wasn't interested."

His brow dropped at that. "Yeah, that's final."

"And she gives me the signals, but I'm not about to chase down a chick who's telling me no. It's just that … I dunno. I can't help it, man." I sighed one more time, promising myself it would be the last, feeling heavy pressure in my ribs. "She's smart, sharp as a fucking switchblade and gorgeous. I'm interested in her, undeniably. But we aren't getting along, and I can't figure out if it's by design or by accident."

"Maybe there's just something else going on with her. Can you just give her space?"

"That's all I can do. And it's stupid."

He chuckled. "Yeah, waiting isn't your scene. That's more mine. But you're a go-getter."

I shook my head. "It's not the end of the world. She makes me feel a little like Liz did. Like I'd drown myself in her, sink until I disappeared. I don't want to do that again, Tricky. I can't."

He watched me, offering a nod. "I get it. I do. Maybe it is for the best then."

"Doesn't feel like it. But to quote a great man, *Heads and hearts are connected by threads impossible to cut completely.*"

Patrick narrowed his eyes in thought. "Paolo Coelho?"

I smiled. "Joel Anderson."

A single laugh burst out of him.

"Your interview is tonight, right?"

"Yeah. Not looking forward to it."

I waved a hand. "It's not so bad. Just don't let her strong-arm you into anything, okay?"

"Okay. Ronnie said Annika asked her about me and Rose." His brand of the brood — something he could have copyrighted — passed over his face.

"Well, you had to figure they'd want to talk about Veronica's big crush on you, how she broke you and Rose up the first time."

The brood set even deeper into his face. "She didn't break us up. I broke us up."

"And then you took Ronnie to the bar where Rose was bartending, thus barring you from getting back with her when you realized what a dumbass you'd been."

He huffed. "Still. It's low. There's no story there — that whole thing is old and worn out, and I'm with Rose. For good."

"Hey, *I* know that. You don't have to convince me. Just convince

Annika and maybe she'll move down her list until she finds something that sticks."

"You really don't think she's going to try to press the topic with Veronica and me? Try to make some storyline out of it? Because I don't believe that for a fucking minute." He shook his head and raked his black hair back with his hand. "If this fucks something up with Rose and me, I swear to God, I'll lose my shit."

I angled to face him, looking him square in the eye. "I won't let that happen. Okay?"

"You can't stop it if it does. We've signed our lives away for this show, and you and I are the only ones who know it."

I wished I could say he was wrong, but I couldn't. "This was a bad idea, Tricky. Maybe the worst idea. I just really fucking hope we can make something good of this. In the meantime, talk to Rose and tell her everything. Be honest with her. Keep her in the loop. She'll be all right and so will you."

He sighed. "I hope you're right."

As I turned back to my station, I hoped I was too.

Annika

That night, Joel handed a girl in his chair the mirror, trying to keep a straight face as the cameras rolled. I was too, pen between my teeth to give my mouth something to do besides laugh.

She looked over her shoulder into the mirror at her new tattoo: a Cupie doll on her right shoulder with a banner up top that said *No Ragrets* and one below that said *#YOLO*.

"Oh, my God. It's perfect." She smiled in the mirror and beamed at all of us. "It's ironic."

He smiled like he was thinking a thousand things, and I wanted to know every one.

"Thanks, man. Seriously," she said, still beaming.

Joel chuckled as he reached for the plastic sheeting to cover it up with. "Anytime."

He taped up the sheet and gave her a piece of paper with

instructions, rattling off tips for her like he had a million times. She tipped him mightily and practically bounded out of the shop after Shep rang her up.

The cameras were still rolling, and Joel sighed, shaking his head as he began to break down his station, pulling the plastic wrap off his tray and disassembling his gun.

"So," I started, "do you get a lot of tattoos like that?"

He looked up, his hands busy as he answered. "We get all types, you know? Most people want art, something meaningful to carry around with them every day, reminders, that sort of thing."

"Do you get a lot of hipsters coming in?"

He glanced up at me and then back down. "I try not to judge. If someone wants to come in here and get a hashtag tattooed on them, who am I to ask questions? They get what they want, something that makes them happy. That's part of the problem with the culture sometimes. No one is more or less legitimate than someone else just because of how they choose to tattoo themselves. It's just another way for people who historically have been persecuted for their choice to get tattooed to persecute someone else. None of us own the culture, and the people who judge are the worst kind of assholes."

I smiled. "So everyone's included?"

He shrugged and tossed a wad of plastic and paper towel in the trash under his desk. "That's the idea."

"I like it."

He finally looked up at me and smiled, though there was something else behind his eyes, the same something that had been there for the last few days, ever since that first day of filming. He made me hot and cold, furious and fevered, and everything I learned about him, every time we spoke, the want to know more built until I couldn't help myself, disarmed by him completely.

It was late, the last segment of the night, and we were set to shut down. So as Joel finished breaking down his station, the camera crew broke down their equipment and PA's swarmed, grabbing film and hard drives to take upstairs to start editing. I took a seat in his tattoo chair while his back was turned, and when he looked back and found me sitting there, that something in his eyes was gone, replaced with something else entirely, something that made my breath catch.

He had frozen — I didn't notice until he snapped back into action, moving to his desk to put his machine parts away, and I couldn't help but watch his muscles and tendons flutter in his tattooed forearms as he arranged the pieces.

"That was a great piece. Good shoot tonight."

He made a sort of *humph* sound, but it was amused. "Just doing my job." He closed the drawer and sat on the surface, leaving one foot on the ground, his other thigh on the desk, elbow resting on it. He looked casual, easy, like your favorite pair of jeans, the ones that made your butt look amazing. That pretty much summed Joel up.

I realized then that I'd missed flirting with him, and I felt like an asshole for turning him out like I had. He just made me so uncomfortable that shutting him out was my only defense against him.

The realization made me even more uncomfortable than his flirting had.

"You looking to get some work done?" he asked, nodding to the chair.

I laughed softly. "No. If you couldn't tell, I'm not exactly the alternative type of girl."

"You don't say?"

I smiled. "I know. Shocker, right?"

"So, you don't even have one tattoo? I mean, almost everyone has at least one that they got when they turned eighteen."

I wrinkled my nose and inspected the black vinyl of the arm rest.

He laughed, the sound full and easy, just like the rest of him. That sound had me wondering again what my hangup with him was. "You do. Is it bad?"

"Define bad?"

"Bad as in you don't want to tell me because it's that bad."

"Then yeah. It's bad."

He was smirking now, and I felt myself smiling back. "Tell me the story."

"How do you know there's a story?"

"Princess, there's *always* a story."

I rolled my eyes, giving only a superficial impression of actually being annoyed. "Well, you've met Roxy."

"I have."

"So, our birthdays are only a month apart, and when we turned eighteen, she got me drunk on Stoli and dragged me to a tattoo parlor."

He ran a hand through his hair. "Oh, God. Maybe I don't want to know."

I laughed. "I'll gladly stop there."

"No, I won't be able to sleep not knowing. Lay it on me."

One of my brows rose. "Hmm. Well, now I don't know if I want to tell you. The thought of keeping you up at night sounds really appealing."

That something was back behind his eyes, and his smile fell. "Not fair."

I smiled apologetically. "I really didn't mean it like that — I'm sorry. More in the way that it would be fun to torture you."

He leaned toward me a bit. "So where is it?"

I felt my stupid flush bloom across my cheeks. "Well, I knew I wouldn't want it somewhere I could see it, where anyone could see it."

"Hip?"

I bit my lip before answering. "Lower back."

He laughed again, teeth flashing from behind his dark beard. "No."

"Yes."

"What is it?"

My cheeks could have been steaming, they were so hot. "A Chinese character."

He shook his head, still laughing. "Oh, Annika."

I made a face at him. "What happened to accepting everyone?"

He made a face right back at me. "Did it make you happy?"

"No," I conceded.

"Then it wasn't the right piece for you. Did you see that girl when she left? You thought her tattoo was stupid, but she left here ready to fly. What you think doesn't matter to her. But you can barely even tell me what you have tattooed on your body because you're so embarrassed."

I didn't want to admit how right he was. He didn't wait for me to — he probably knew he had me.

"What character did you get? Did it mean something to you?"

"It does mean something to me," I said, wanting to defend myself, but I was without a single bit of traction, except this. "It's the symbol for ice."

Joel watched me for a long, quiet moment. "Tell me what it means."

I swallowed, feeling the weight of his eyes on me, my own eyes on my fingers as they traced a small split in the vinyl of the arm of the chair. "Ever since I was a little girl, I was serious. Roxy was the sun and I was the moon. She was the spring and I was the winter. She was the fire and I was the ice. Cold, just like the place where my ancestors were born. *Led*, ice. Hard and harsh and sharp. I've always been this way," I said, as if I were trying to convince myself that it was all right just as much as I wanted to convince him.

He watched me in a way that made my heart speed up. "That's not what I see."

I met his eyes. "What do you see?"

"Snow. Cold and soft, the sum of an infinite number of beautiful pieces. And when the light hits just right, you shine."

I had no words, my mind blank as my eyes hung on to his like a lifeline.

He broke our gaze and moved to stand. "Let me see it."

"What?" I blustered, caught off guard.

"Stand up and turn around. I want to see it."

I was too surprised and caught up in the moment to refuse, so I stood and turned, laying my palms on the armrests as I faced the back of the chair.

One hand rested on my hip.

My heart stopped as I wondered what the hell I'd gotten myself into.

I glanced over my shoulder, my gaze bouncing between his face — turned down too much to read — and his reflection in the speckled, antique mirror, which I couldn't see much of either. His free hand moved to the waistband of my tailored pants, and his fingers hooked and tugged, pulling the band down low.

His thumb ran over where I knew the tattoo was, and I felt his breath. Every place where we connected spoke to me of ownership.

"You got this done here? In New York?" His voice was rough.

Mine wasn't much better. "Yeah. In Brooklyn."

"Let me cover it up for you. Give you something you're proud of. Your skin …" He paused, and I wished I could see his face, read his mind. "This shouldn't be here, not on you. Let me … I want to …" He had moved closer, his hand on my hip pulling me back into him slightly enough for me to not have noticed that the backs of my thighs were touching his, my back arched just enough, his breath hot.

And then, he disappeared. I stood, finding my hands were trembling, wondering where I was and how I'd gotten there. The shop was mostly empty — no one had seen, not that it would have looked like much from the outside. But from where I stood, I felt every single deliberate move like a telegraph, telling me exactly what he wanted to do without him having to finish the sentence.

His back was to me when I turned around, his face down — I couldn't see it in the mirror over his cabinet of ink and needles as he dug around in the drawers, seemingly for nothing in particular.

"Let me know if you want me to draw something up."

"Okay, I will." I paused, not knowing what else to say, feeling like I should say something. But there was nothing that I *could* say. "Well, have a good night, Joel. I'll see you tomorrow."

He nodded, glancing at me in the mirror. "See you, Annika."

I tried not to bolt out of the shop, but once outside, I admit it — I took off. I hauled up the stairs and into the office to grab my bag, grateful that Laney was already gone, and I texted my driver, asking him to pick me up a few blocks away so I could walk, put some distance between me and Joel, get the energy out of my body,

Tonic

through my legs and feet, into the pavement.

ICE QUEEN

Annika

THE CITY PASSED BY OUTSIDE my window as we drove to Brooklyn, the lights zipping past in streaks, my eyes focused on a fleck of mud on the glass.

Nothing made sense.

It was pretty clear to me that I wanted more from Joel than I'd admitted to myself before, and I felt like an asshole for the amount of pushback I'd given to him for coming on to me. All because the idea of him and me freaked me out on multiple levels. I wasn't sure what I even wanted from him. Sex? Definitely. The way he touched my skin, as simple as the motion was, it was undeniable — my body wanted his body.

Past that?

I sighed, unable to even imagine what went past that. Dinner with Joel? I didn't think he'd like the idea of a nice dinner at the restaurants I frequented. Joel in a suit. My thighs squeezed together remembering him in the suit that first night, imagining him in one again, sitting across from me at a candlelit table, or in my room, my hands under his jacket, pushing it over his shoulder—

Stop it, I told myself. We had nothing in common. What would we even talk about? My heart argued that we hadn't lacked for conversation up to that point. My head told my heart to sit down and shut up.

Indecision swarmed through me like evil bees, but in the center of that was the honeycomb — the knowledge that I wanted more from Joel, though I wasn't ready to define was *more* was. That knowledge, at least, was comforting, the release of the levy I'd been doing my damnedest to keep standing, and I was flooded with relief.

More relief came as we pulled up in front of my house — Roxy would know what to do.

I thanked my driver, climbed out of the car, walked across the sidewalk and into the house, ready to spill it all.

The house was dimly lit, having wound down from the day, and Roxy sat on the couch, humming along to The Lumineers as the soft, folky sounds filled the room. She looked up from her sketchbook and smiled.

"Hey."

I set my bag down on the hall table. "Hey."

Her smile fell a hair. "You okay?"

I sipped in a deep breath. "Yes and no."

She full-on frowned and set the drawing of a garment on the coffee table. "What's going on?"

"Anni!" Kira squealed and bounded down the stairs and into my legs, which she wrapped her little arms around.

I smoothed her hair, looking down at her. "Hey, Bunny. What are you still doing up?"

"Mama said I could wait up so we could play."

Roxy stood. "Baby, I said *maybe*, but I think Anni's tired."

I waved her off. "No, it's okay. I promised her yesterday."

Kira beamed, and I took her hand.

"Come on, let's go. What are we playing?"

"Anna and Elsa," she said definitively and to no surprise to me.

I laughed. "So I'm Anna?"

Kira gave me a look like I was crazy as we climbed the stairs with Roxy in our wake. "You're *Elsa*. You're always Elsa."

"Oh, of course. I thought maybe we were switching it up. Looks like Mama's going to play too. Who will she be?"

"Sven. And Kaz will be Kristoff"

Roxy rolled her eyes. "How come I always have to be the

moose?"

"*Reindeer*," Kira huffed, impatient as we turned into her room.

"He has no lines! I just end up giving Kira rides around her bedroom."

"Well, Mama, you're not a good singer like Anni and me," she said matter-of-factly.

Roxy laughed. "I guess that's true. But I could at least get to be Olaf."

"Okay," Kira started once we reached her room, straight to business. "Anni, you sit here. Mama, you sit there. Kaz will go here." He was already in her room, asleep on the rug, and she picked him up under the arms, moving him to the bed. He looked apathetic at best. "Okay, lemme get your costumes." She turned for her closet to rummage through a trunk full of dress-up clothes.

We sat, and I unbound my hair, shaking it out before getting started on a French braid that sadly lacked the length or girth of Elsa's. Roxy leaned in. "What's going on?"

My fingers wound my hair around and around. "Hairy."

Her brows rose. "Good or bad?"

"Both," I said as I wrapped the hair tie around the end.

Dresses flew over Kira's shoulder as she kept digging.

"Well, what happened?" Roxy asked.

"I think I like him."

She opened her mouth to say something snarky — I could tell by her face — when Kira cheered and ran over with two dresses in hand.

"This one's for you, Anni." She extended the blue-and-white sparkly costume, adult sized, which I took. "And this one's for me." She clutched the darker dress to her chest.

"What about me?" Roxy asked.

"Oh!" She bounced off, and Roxy turned to me.

"I'm glad you finally figured it out. But what *happened*?"

Before I could answer, Kira was back, wiggling an antler headband in Roxy's face. Roxy leaned back to avoid getting speared in the eye and situated the headband on her head.

"Okay," she said as she wiggled into her dress, and I pulled mine over my head, an adult-sized costume copy of Elsa's gown. "Let's start with me looking for you. You go sit up there in the ice castle, Anni." She pointed to her bed, and I did as I was told. "Come on, Mama. I mean, Sven. Let's go find Elsa."

Roxy got on all fours, and Kira climbed onto her back, humming as Sven crawled in circles on the rug. "Was there k-i-s-s-i-n-g?" she asked.

"No," I answered. "But I think I want there to be."

"And you really just figured this out?"

"No, I mean, I knew, but I didn't want it to be true. After today though, I don't think I can hold off. I don't think I should. In fact, I don't know what was stopping me in the first place."

"Well," she said, circling the rug again as Kira pointed to her closet and said *over there!* Roxy headed in that direction. "You gave me the list the other night, but it all sounded like BS to me."

"BS, BS, BS," Kira sang, then said, "Oh, no! It's Marshmallow the snow monster!"

"*Rawr,*" Roxy growled and reared back, and Kira squealed as she held onto Roxy's neck. "Whew, we made it," Roxy said as she continued on and began to circle the rug again.

"I don't know, Rox. I don't know anything right now."

She gave me a sympathetic look.

"There she is!" Kira pointed at me, and Roxy gave her a lift to the bed.

"Sister!" I cried, opening my arms.

She climbed into my lap. "I missed you. Me and Sven looked all over the forest and almost got eaten by Marshmallow!"

I gasped dramatically. "But my monster wouldn't hurt a fly!"

She giggled. "I know, but he growls scary. Okay, now it's time to sing 'Let It Go.'"

I laughed. "Oh, it's already that time? Will you sing with me?"
"Yes!"

And that began our musical interlude, wherein my little cousin and I sang "Let It Go" for the eighteen thousandth time. I'd learned all the lyrics like a good auntie and sang them almost daily. Halfway through the song, Kira stopped singing, leaning into the crook of my arm so she could look up at me with wide eyes. Even Roxy looked dreamy as she listened, and I sang through to the end.

They paused for a second when I was finished before cheering, clapping and squealing or whistling, depending on age and ability. I bowed my head, smiling.

"Thank you, thank you."

Roxy sighed. "You have the most beautiful voice I've ever heard. I wish you weren't such a fuddy-duddy about karaoke."

"Please. Embarrassing myself in front of you two is nothing, but bar full of strangers? No thanks."

"You're crazy," Roxy said.

Kira squished my face. "You sound like an angel," she said, triggering the memory of Joel saying the same thing about his mother.

I kissed her nose. "Thanks, Bunny."

"Okay," Roxy started, "I hate to cut this short, but it's super late, kiddo."

Groans of dissent filled the room.

Roxy got back on all fours. "Come on. I'll still be Sven until after teeth are brushed."

That perked Kira up, and she slid off my lap and onto her mother's back.

"Go pour us drinks. I'll meet you downstairs in ten," Roxy said as she adjusted Kira.

"Deal." I pulled off my costume as they made their way down the hall, packing the abandoned dresses back in their chest before heading downstairs.

I smiled to myself, listening to my cousins upstairs laughing as Roxy read her daughter a story, and I settled into the couch with a bottle of Russian Standard, pouring a finger of liquor into a rocks glass. Kaz jumped up and lay down next to me as I knocked back the shot. I was just pouring another when Roxy came down.

She climbed onto the couch next to me and picked up her drink. Her feet brushed Kaz, and he bit her toe, swatting at her foot with his paw. "Ouch!" she shouted, jerking away from him with a furrowed brow and red cheeks. "Screw you too, you mean old son of a bitch."

I laughed, chiding the old cat half-heartedly.

She settled in, still eyeing him. "All right. What's the deal? You and Joel?"

I took a sip, buying a second before answering. "I don't know what the deal is with us. I mean, I've been telling him absolutely never for the last week, and now …" I sighed. "I don't know anything past the fact that I want him to kiss me. And that seems like a terrible idea. There are still reasons why I shouldn't, but they all seem stupid now that I've admitted to myself that I like him."

"Okay, so tell me again for real — why can't you let him kiss you?"

"Because I already told him he's not allowed to. Because he's not the kind of guy I usually picture myself with. Because we work together, and me getting emotionally involved with one of the cast members could affect my ability to be objective. Because he makes me uncomfortable. Because he scares me."

"Scares you?"

"Roxy, he is the literal unknown, in the flesh. I'm not the one to throw caution to the wind."

She chuckled. "No, you are the last one to disrespect caution so openly."

"But he's just so different from anyone I've ever been with. He's not like me."

"Annika, listen to me."

I looked up to meet her eyes, eyes that were so much like mine.

"You're smart. You know yourself, and you know your limits. You're not going to fuck up."

"I don't even know why I'm entertaining this, honestly. He's not the first guy I've been attracted to, and that isn't really a reason to potentially put my career on the line."

"Is there anything that expressly forbids you being with him?"

I shook my head. "No, but Laney made it pretty clear that she's onto me and that it could end in disaster. I've worked too hard to throw it all away just because I'm hot for a guy."

She took a sip of her vodka, watching me over the rim of her glass.

"I mean, what am I even doing? I swear to God, Rox. I showed him my tattoo tonight—"

Her eyes widened.

"—and when he touched it … he could have done anything he wanted in that moment and I would have let him."

She sighed. "The thought of you not acting on something that intense makes me itchy."

"Me too." I knocked back my drink and poured another.

"Do you think a taste would be enough to satisfy the thirst?"

I chuffed. "I don't think a five-gallon tank would satisfy that thirst. But even worse than that — what if it turns into more? What if he wants more and I don't? What if I want more and he doesn't? What if I have to do something … lie to him or manipulate him? This is my *job*, and he's the star of the show. It can't end well." Futile resolution washed over me, cold and steely. "It can't happen, Roxy. I could ruin my career or his heart or my heart or all of the above. It's not worth it."

She reached for my hand. "I hate to say you're right, especially about this, especially knowing how much you like him, but I think you might be right."

"Maybe after we're finished filming. It's just a few weeks. Maybe there's a way later, but not now, not yet. Maybe not ever." The sadness in my voice pissed me off, and I took a long pull of my vodka, hating myself for the position I found myself in, which was, in the end, not under Joel where I wanted to be.

PLAYED

Joel

THE NEXT DAY, I FOUND myself sitting behind the counter in the shop watching Annika, as I had since she'd walked through the doors of the shop that morning. They were filming Patrick as he worked on a client's back, a piece he would work on throughout the course of the season. The idea was to show the progress, give the viewers some insight into the work that goes into art that big, that detailed, and Patrick was the one to watch. He was one of my most talented artists.

But I didn't pay him much mind, just snuck glances at Annika over the top of *Persuasion*.

I felt like I'd snapped the night before, seeing that mark on her skin, touching it, feeling the heat of her under my palm, against my thighs. I knew she felt it too. She had to — she was practically calling my name with every breath she took.

That tattoo shouldn't have been there, a tacky slash on her perfect skin. If anyone was ever to mark her, it should have been me. It should have been something beautiful, something to complement her own beauty.

The thought that I wasn't the first to mark her made me furious. Unreasonably furious.

I shook my head and tried to turn my attention to my book, which had been a lost cause since I'd picked it up that day. The words all blurred together, my mind comprehending nothing, still somehow tuned to her.

She said doesn't want you, I told myself. I reminded myself to take the hint, which wasn't even a hint — it was a flat-out demand. It didn't matter what I thought she wanted or what I felt. I didn't want someone who didn't want me any more than I wanted someone who would ruin me like Liz did. And Annika seemed to fit into both of those categories.

The bell on the door rang, and what I saw when I looked over sent an icy hot shot of adrenaline through my veins.

Hal strode into *my* shop — a threshold he hadn't crossed since he'd walked out the door almost fifteen years ago. And yet, there he stood, looking smug.

I hated his beard. I hated his undercut. I hated his stupid fucking face and his stupid fucking smile and all of him. I hated him.

My fists clenched, and I wondered what I'd hit him with first, *THIS* or *THAT.*

"What the fuck are you doing here?" I asked as I stormed around the counter.

Hal smiled. "Good to see you, brother," he said as he approached, hand extended.

I slapped the back of his hand. "I'm not your brother. Answer my question."

He shrugged, seeming unfazed. "Just wanted to swing in, see how the show was going."

My eyes narrowed to slits. "You thought you'd just *drop in*, huh? You haven't been welcome in this shop in more than a decade."

"Come on, man. It's been years. Water under the bridge, right?"

I arched over him. "Fuck you, you little punk. *Water under the bridge*," I scoffed. "The bridge *you* blew up the last time you walked through those doors. Now tell me why you're here."

"I got a call. They asked me to come."

My nostrils flared, my vision dimming with the pressure of my pumping heart. My eyes swept across the crew, coming to rest on Annika, registering distantly that all of the cameras were pointed at me.

"Everybody, get the fuck out of my shop."

No one moved. My eyes were still on her — she was still as stone other than her eyes, which darted between me and Hal.

"*Did I stutter?*" I roared, and she flinched. "All of you, get the fuck out. *Now.*"

The cameras hadn't stopped rolling. Patrick's hands were still, his client looking over his shoulder, everyone staring at me. Two steps and I had my hand on the hood of a camera lens, pointing it to the ground. "Out." I pushed a sound engineer toward the door. "Out!" I bent to level my eyes at a PA as I pointed at the door and yelled, "*Out!*"

They finally got the hint and began filing toward the door, including Annika.

I grabbed her arm. "Not you. You stay right where you fucking are. And you," I whirled around, stepping into Hal until our noses were nearly touching. "Don't show your face here again, or I'll fuck it up beyond repair. Got me, *Hal?*" I spit the words at him, my lip curling.

But he didn't back down. "Get over it, Joel. You always were a fucking baby about shit like this. Look at you. You can't even have a civil conversation with me."

I was shaking all over, including my breath as I whispered. "Leave before I do something that'll put me in jail."

He shook his head, his face hard. "Whatever, man. Whatever." He looked over at Annika. "Next time you need a stooge to piss him off, call somebody else."

And with that, he turned and walked out the door. It took every ounce of willpower I had not to reach for his shirt and hit him, my fists clenched so tight they ached from the pressure.

As the bell over the door chimed to mark his exit — the only sound in the silent room — I turned to Annika.

"*You.*"

Annika

His eyes were wild as he stepped toward me, grabbing me by the arm while Patrick and the client filed out behind us. Joel said nothing, though he huffed like a bull as he dragged me toward the back of the shop, his fingers digging into my arms almost hard enough to hurt.

He tossed me into a private room, one of the rooms with no cameras, and slammed the door behind him.

"Turn off your monitor," he barked, and I nodded with shaking hands, pulling it from my ear, unclipping my battery and flipping the switch. I almost hesitated, almost left it on, but something stopped me. I set it next to the sink on the back wall, putting the chair between us. In part, because I was terrified. In another part because I was somehow turned all the way on and overheating.

"What the fuck, Annika? Why? *Why would you do this?* Why would you bring *him* here with the cameras rolling? Is it just good TV for you? Do you give a fuck about *anybody?* I want to know *why. Tell me why.*"

"I … I didn't know," I stammered, hands still shaking. "Joel, I didn't have anything to do with this."

He leaned on the chair, eyes narrowed. "Why don't I believe you?"

I jerked back like he'd slapped me. "Why would I lie to you?"

"Because that's what you do, isn't it? Lie? Manipulate? Push every button to get a reaction on camera? Well, fuck you, princess. I'm not a goddamn toy. I'm not a fucking joke. I'm not a pawn you can push around your board like I don't fucking matter."

My brow dropped, the heat rising up my neck, across my cheeks. "I've never lied to you, not once, and I'm not playing games with you."

He laughed, a sound that didn't hold an iota of joy. "Right. Just like how you keep telling me I'm harassing you, how you don't want anything to do with me, but then you look at me, show me your tattoo like—"

"You asked to see my tattoo. I didn't throw myself at you, and I'm not toying with you, for God's sake. Don't you get it? They're playing games with *me* too. You're not the only one being manipulated. For the last time, I wasn't told that Hal would be here today. I had *nothing* to do with that."

His chest rose and fell, breath shallow. "But isn't that just the way it's going to go?" His voice was lower, quieter, but less calm, somehow, and I almost took a step back as he walked around the chair. "You exploit me. You stick your pretty long finger in my wounds and twist, making sure your camera is rolling when you do it. You tell me with your pretty lips that you don't want me, but your eyes tell me something else. I don't trust you. How could I?"

"Because I'm telling the truth." He was close — too close, not close enough. "I'm not supposed to want you. You … you make me mad and you make me laugh and you make me *crazy*, and I'm not supposed to want you, but I do. What am I supposed to do? What do you want? You want me to throw away my career? How about you? Should I use you up and toss you out too? Or maybe you'll do the same to me. I don't know, because I don't know you. But that hasn't stopped me from wanting you, not since the first time I ever saw your stupid, hairy face. I hate you, and I want you, and I hate that I want you. But I do."

It was too much, the admission pouring out of me too fast to stop. I had to get out of there, needed to run. I sidestepped to move past him, but he shifted.

"Is that really the truth?" His voice was low, rough, and I was assaulted by his proximity, the smell of him, sensing his body, even though we weren't touching. It was dizzying.

"That's the truth."

"Annika." The word was tortured and elated. His hand was on my arm. My heart was in my throat.

"Don't," I said, terrified, and he froze where he was, just like I'd asked. I stepped around him and put my hand on the doorknob, fully intending to leave, running somewhere, anywhere safe. But my hand was on that cold, metal doorknob, and he was still just where I'd left him, doing exactly what I asked, even though he knew I wanted more.

And then I did the unthinkable. I pushed my brain down the trash chute, let go of that doorknob, and spun around.

Three steps and I was in his arms.

Two heartbeats and I looked into his eyes.

One breath and I kissed him.

It was sweet relief, his lips against mine, lush and firm, his breath my breath. His tongue swept my bottom lip, and I let him in, wrapped my arms around his neck. I was surrounded by him, his arms around me, hands splayed across my back, clutching me into his hard chest, our lips a hard seam.

I felt helpless and powerful, like I couldn't stop whatever I'd started by kissing him, but like I could own him just as easily as I wanted him to own me.

I didn't know when he laid me down, but I was in the tattoo chair and he was on top of me. I felt the chair move, the back reclining until I was flat on my back, under Joel after all. The weight of him against me sent a moan past my lips, lips he nipped and sucked as his hands moved up my body and down, back up, into my hair, tugging at my bun. He hummed into my mouth when he slipped his fingers into the loosened strands, pressing his hips into mine.

"Skin," I muttered, fumbling for the hem of his shirt. "Give me skin."

He knelt on the bench, reaching between his shoulder blades for a fistful of cotton jersey, pulling it off so fast, I barely had time to get mine off. His hair had been knocked loose, his chest broad, waist narrow, every inch of skin covered in art. And then his hand cupped my cheek, and his lips were against mine, and I was lost, frantic, needing him, all of him, just as badly as I needed air. Like if I didn't have him, I'd suffocate.

His hot skin pressed against mine, our hips moving together in a long tease. There was only decision, a silent agreement that we wouldn't stop. I couldn't stop, not my hands that found the button of his jeans, then the zipper, not my hungry fingers as they slipped into his pants and closed around him. I couldn't stop my lips as they flexed and eased, not my tongue as it tasted him, the sweetness of him. I couldn't stop my hips from rolling against his.

He flicked the button of my pants open with two fingers and dropped my zipper, sliding his hands into my panties to palm me, to drag his finger up the center of me, to slip his finger inside.

I gasped, my hand flying to his wrist, bracing myself against him, urging him on. I couldn't think, my eyelids fluttering, neck arching. It had been so long since I'd been touched that, I'd forgotten just how much I needed it.

My hands slipped into the back of his pants, thumbs hooking over the band, inching them over his ass, and he pulled back, chest heaving as he stood and dropped them. He grabbed my pants as I lay panting on the tattoo chair, yanked until they were a pile on the floor, and I unhooked my bra and threw it. The only thing left were my panties.

"Off," he growled as he picked up his pants and searched for his wallet, pulled out a condom, and threw the rest to leave it all abandoned on the floor, his eyes between my legs as I slid my black panties down until they fell next to his feet.

For one long moment, we stared at each other — me stretched out on the chair, naked, exposed, him gripping his cock, eyes drinking me in. And then he sprang into motion, and before I could even react, he was kneeling in front of me, hands on my hips, sliding me down to crash into his mouth.

I gasped, back snapping off the chair, eyes slamming shut as his mouth covered me, sucked, teased me with the flat of his tongue running up the line at my core, devouring me like I was the last he'd ever taste.

I couldn't breathe, my body no longer my own, but his. But I wanted more, I wanted it all.

My hands were in his hair — I hadn't realized I'd done it, but my fingers were twisted in his dark hair like reins. I relaxed them, pausing when he sucked again, pulling me into his mouth, demanding that I give him whatever he wanted.

"Joel," I breathed, and his eyes flew open at the sound of his name, though his lids were heavy. He let me go, climbed up my body, pausing over my breasts. I watched his hand, his dark skin against my white, the ink of him against the cream of me, the marked and the blank, and was overcome with need, with emotion that sprang from somewhere locked away. His thumb brushed my nipple, and he bowed his head, bringing his lips to the rosy skin, closing them to kiss me with an air of worship, and when he met my eyes, they were on fire.

I felt him against me and spread my legs, needing him, waiting for him as he caged me in his arms, his lips a millimeter from mine, his crown a millimeter from pressing into me, and in the space of a breath, we connected. He filled me with the flex of his hips, his lips taking mine with the same motion, his tongue slipping deep into me just as the rest of him did.

Release and flex. Then harder. Then it was desperate, our bodies waving together, our hands searching for something to hold on to. Another flex. Then again as my heart rushed in my ears, my breath shallow, my eyes closed as he pushed me faster, harder, my hips rebounding, pushing me into him by sheer force of gravity, of *his* gravity. And he moaned my name, filled me until he hit the end, rolled his hips against me, and I fell apart, gasping for breath, nails against his back like they'd stop me from falling.

But it was too late. I'd already fallen, and there was no going back.

PROMISES, PROMISES

Joel

I SLOWED MY BODY, AND she met my pace as I pressed my lips to hers, my hand finding the crook of her long neck, the skin so soft against the rough skin of my fingers. It was a deep kiss, a kiss that said it wasn't a mistake, a kiss that sealed the deal on my heart.

I pulled away after a moment so I could look into her eyes, and her lids opened slowly. The soft heat I found there didn't last long enough, hardening and cooling as my brow dropped.

She ran a hand down my chest and shifted, pressing gently, and I moved as much as I could in the chair, knowing she wanted up. And she bolted the second she was able.

I lay in the chair, watching her bend to gather her clothes, watching her.

"So …"

She stepped into her panties, saying nothing.

I waited all the same until she had on her bra and was scanning the floor for her pants.

"Are we really not going to talk about this?"

She picked up the black slacks and pulled them on, one leg at a time. "Not right now, no."

My eyes narrowed. I didn't respond otherwise.

She finally looked at me, her face still, hard, the mask in place. "I've got the crew standing outside on the sidewalk, that is, assuming they didn't come back inside and hear what just happened. I've got to take care of my shit right now," she said as she buttoned her pants and picked up her top.

"But we will talk."

"Is there any other way with you?" She pulled her top over her head and combed her hands through her hair.

I smirked at that. "No."

She almost smiled as she twisted her hair into a fresh bun. "Didn't think so." Her eyes moved down my body. "Planning on getting dressed?"

I shrugged. "Think they'd suspect something happened if I walk out there like this?"

"Hang on. Let me at least get the cameras rolling first," she said, a smile playing on her lips again as she walked around the chair.

I reached for her arm, sliding my fingers down her soft skin until they reached hers. "Promise me we'll talk."

She took a breath, the ice in her eyes cracking for only a moment, her fingers flexing to squeeze mine. "Promise."

She let me go, and I felt the loss of the connection almost immediately.

Her eyes ran over me again with a spark of admiration behind them. "You really should get dressed. If we don't go out there together, they really will suspect something."

I smirked and stood, making sure she could catch all my good angles as I dressed, and once I pulled my boots on — I never really laced them up, something I was thankful for, given the urgency for needing to be naked a few minutes earlier. And with that, we walked out of the room together.

The shop was still empty, and to Annika's credit, she was unfazed, her face hard and eyes steady. There was no smoothing of clothes or hair, no tell that she was uncomfortable. And maybe she wasn't. There were two signs that reminded me of just how I'd taken her in the back of my shop. The pink in her cheeks, which had begun to ebb, a sight I was sorry to lose. And the other sign was one that I didn't know if anyone else would recognize — a nearly imperceptible inclination to me, as if she were tuned into me, and I was tuned into her, like we were on a frequency all our own now. She walked a little closer than usual, and I could *feel* her in a way I hadn't been able to before I'd tasted her, touched her.

Now? Now I just needed to touch her again.

But not yet.

We walked out the front door to find everyone still on the sidewalk, except Patrick's client. He gave me a look that said he'd explain later, and I nodded my understanding.

Annika was all business, directing the crew, telling them to pack up for the night and take their film upstairs to start cutting. Anger flared in my chest at the realization that she was still going to use it. Of course she was. It was her job, after all. I pushed past the betrayal, reminding myself that she hadn't known either, hoping she was telling me the truth. I honestly had no way of knowing, other than the look in her eyes. I trusted her that much, at least.

The crew made their way into the shop with Patrick and I in their wake, Annika leading the charge. She directed them on what they should take, even though they probably already knew — it was something she could control, I sensed, something for her to do that displayed her power. I was sure she felt the eyes darting between us just as much as I did while I helped Patrick break down his station. I needed to keep my hands busy just as much as Annika needed to keep her mouth busy.

I smirked at the thought of busy mouths and hands, and my worry about the situation dissipated.

Once the crew had filed out, Annika apologized again brusquely, seeming to be for show in front of Patrick, but her eyes met mine for a long moment before she turned and left. I tried to see behind the veil, tried to guess what she was thinking, but it was lost on me. She told me she'd see me tomorrow and walked out, and all I could do was watch her go.

Patrick turned to me the second the bell chimed, marking the closing of the door.

"What the fuck, man?" he asked.

I rubbed the back of my neck. "I don't even know."

"Did you—"

"Yeah."

He gave me a look that was equal parts annoyance and understanding. "So what's the deal?"

"No idea. She didn't hang around long enough to figure it out."

He flinched. "Ouch."

"I mean, there wasn't much to be done just then, not with everyone standing outside waiting."

"True. Not gonna lie — it was an awkward ten minutes."

"Is that all it was?" I asked. "Huh. Felt longer."

He smirked. "I'm sure it did. I snuck in and grabbed Tony's stuff, told him we'd just finish up next round."

"I'm sorry. I didn't set you back too far, did I?"

"Nah, we were almost finished. And anyway, *you* didn't do anything."

"Well, I *did*, but I get your meaning. Hal."

"Hal," Patrick echoed. "Did she set this up?"

"She says she didn't."

"And you believe her?"

I shrugged. "I guess I do. Don't really have a choice at this point but to have a little faith."

"A little faith is fine. A lot of faith could be a problem."

I took a heavy breath and let it out. "Guess we'll see."

"You like her." It wasn't a question, just a statement of fact as he saw it.

"I do."

"That's kind of a big deal."

I frowned. "I know. But it's what it is." I ran a hand through my hair, wondering what I was doing. "I'm not sure if I even know how to do this anymore."

He chuckled and clapped me on the shoulder. "It's like riding a bike, Joel. You'll get the hang of it."

I smiled, shaking my head, and we walked through the shop, shutting it down for the night. Patrick and I said goodnight on the sidewalk outside, and I turned for the short walk up the stairs to my apartment.

I could still smell the sweetness of her perfume on me — honeysuckle? No, too sweet — and she filled my thoughts. The softness of her skin. Her face — no longer hard, but soft, open. There was another version of her, the one I'd only caught glimpses of, and it was more enticing that I could have imagined.

Tomorrow.

It was the soonest that we could talk, and the words were already scratching at my throat to get out.

I paused at my door and glanced up, wondering if she was up there or if she'd gone home. Because if she were up there, we could talk tonight.

But I sighed and unlocked my door, stepping into the dark apartment instead of climbing another flight to knock on the door. It wasn't the time or place, and I wondered at what point we'd have an opportunity to talk as I tossed my keys on the table. I wouldn't let it go too long — it was like a disease sometimes, my mouth, and it had a mind of its own. Ignoring it wasn't an option.

Shep wasn't home — staying at Ramona's for the night, I figured — and I walked through the quiet, dark room and into the bathroom without needing to see. I could have told you how many steps it was from my bed to the fridge (sixteen), the couch to the door (eight), the door to the bathroom (twenty-one), and when I clicked on the light, I found nothing new, except my reflection.

I don't know what it was, exactly, that was different. My eyes, maybe, which held a fire that hadn't been there earlier. Or maybe it was the set of my jaw, somehow more determined than usual, or the little bit of flush in my cheeks that breathed an extra spark of life into my face. But it was there, all of it, the different-ness of it catching me by surprise.

I looked away from the mirror and stripped down, turned on the shower and stepped in once it steamed. But I couldn't wash her away — not even her scent, which somehow followed me through my apartment and into bed.

And somewhere deep down, I knew it would be just as hard to shake her.

LIZARD BRAIN

Annika

WHAT HAVE YOU DONE?

IF only my reflection could answer with the truth.

I'd barely slept the night before, my brain whirring with questions and playbacks of what had gone down. Namely Joel.

After I walked out of the shop, I climbed the stairs to the control room to get everyone going on editing. But the minute I saw him on film, his eyes full of fire as he got in Hal's face, I had to get out of there. I was down the stairs in a flash, though I paused on the landing where his apartment was, momentarily caught in indecision as the urge to knock on his door overwhelmed me. He was in there, I knew it as much as I knew my own name, but if I put my knuckles to his door, we'd have to talk. And I wasn't ready to talk.

So I went home. I showered, scrubbing my skin as if it would bring me clarity. But it didn't.

As I lay in bed, staring at my ceiling, I tried to collect my thoughts as they skittered around my head like pinballs, making noise every time they touched something.

1) I made a mistake that could cost me my career. *Ding da-ding.*

2) I didn't regret it nearly as much as I should. *Da-ding ding.*

3) His lips were the most fascinating things on the planet. *Ding, ding, ding.*

4) I wanted those lips, that body, all of him again, as soon as

possible. *DING-DIDDLY-DING, HI-SCORE.*

As all the bells and lights went off in my brain, I felt sour, not elated. This wasn't supposed to happen. *Joel* wasn't supposed to happen, not only for myself, but for the show. I stood by the fact that he didn't make any sense for me, not long term. But could I have something short term? Could I just leave any other feelings out of it? Did I have any other feelings about him now?

I searched my thoughts and realized that I did. I just didn't know to what extent. I didn't think of him as a boy-toy, with detached pleasure. The way he touched me, the way he looked at me — they hit me in a deep place in my heart.

That realization scared me the most.

I wanted to think this was just my lizard brain telling me to copulate with a male who was a genetic powerhouse. But it was more than that. And that was bad.

Very bad.

I also spent quite a bit of time wondering if the cameras set up in the shop had picked up any sounds of the foray. We hadn't been overly loud, although I'd replayed our conversation before I kissed him — which wasn't so quiet — and knew that if anyone could have heard that, they would have been able to deduce what had come after.

But as I stood in front of my mirror that next morning, I didn't have any answers, and I wasn't ready to find them. I owed him a conversation I wasn't ready to have. Because I didn't know what to do with him, with us, and I knew he'd want answers. Joel was the kind of guy who *had* to have answers, which was especially annoying because, not surprisingly, I was exactly the opposite. I could go days without answers. Months even. But he'd never let me get away with it.

I brushed my hair and parted it before pulling it into a low bun as Laney crossed my mind. She'd set Joel up, and she'd set me up by not telling me what was going on. I had no idea what the conversation I was about to have with her was going to look like, but I was pissed. She'd never done something like this before, but then again, she'd never had this much power before. I felt like another version of a meat puppet, and it didn't feel good.

Her words of warning about Joel rang in my ears — they were true. Eventually, there would come a time for me to choose, and I had a feeling that choice wouldn't be easy or simple. What would I lose? Because I couldn't have it all.

I took a deep breath and smoothed a hand over my hair, chiding myself for putting the cart before the horse. Maybe it wouldn't come to that. If I shut Joel out, that would be the end of it.

The thought made my stomach turn.

I chalked it up to not having eaten and left the bathroom, trying to leave my feelings behind me. Brick by brick I built a little wall, sloppy though it may have been, to shield my heart from my head, at least for the day. And up went the mask of indifference as I descended the stairs and stepped into the kitchen.

Roxy sat at the table in her pink chenille bathrobe, sipping her coffee, and Kira was nowhere to be seen.

"Where's Bunny?" I asked as I popped a bagel into the toaster oven.

"Still sleeping. Soon she'll start school and will have to wake up early, so I'm giving her a break. What's up?"

I turned as I poured coffee so she couldn't see my face — she knew me too well to let the mask fool her. "Nothing much. You?"

She didn't answer, and when I turned with my brows up expectantly, her eyes were narrowed. "Hang on, seriously. What's going on?"

I rolled my eyes. "Jesus, Roxy. Nothing."

"Is it Hairy?"

I felt the flush and knew there was no hiding it. But I didn't have to tell her the whole truth. "Maybe. We got into a fight last night after Laney sent his nemesis into the shop without telling any of us."

She flinched. "Cold."

I ground my teeth. "Yeah. We'll have words when I get to work. She set me up to executive produce this show and is undermining my authority, which makes me look bad in front of the entire crew. I don't know what game she's playing, but I don't like it."

Roxy blew out a breath. "Man, what I wouldn't give to hear that conversation."

"Oh, you will. Over vodka tonight?"

"Deal."

The timer on the toaster oven dinged, and I slathered the bagel with cream cheese before wrapping it in wax paper. "I've got to run, my car is waiting. Have a good day, Rox." I bent to press my cheek to hers.

"You too. Don't let Hairy get you down."

I smiled. "I'll try. No promises."

She twiddled her fingers at me before I turned and walked out, bag in the crook of my elbow, coffee and bagel in hand. The driver hopped out and opened the door for me, and I slipped into the back seat, setting my coffee in the cup holder so I could pick at my breakfast. Because I suddenly wasn't hungry at all, not with the prospect of Joel and Laney less than an hour away. Instead, I worked on adding more bricks to the wall, fortifying myself, filling my belly with ice so I could freeze all of them out, *after* I breathed fire all over Laney.

By the time we got to Tonic, I was properly riled, my fury punctuated by my footsteps on the stairs like an angry metronome. When I opened the door to the apartment, Laney stood behind an editor, watching back the footage of Joel in Hal's face.

She looked over at me and smiled. "You're welcome. This is *fantastic.*"

My eyes narrowed. "A word, please?"

Her head tilted as she assessed me, amused. "Sure."

I followed her into the office with all eyes on us and closed the door behind me.

Laney sat on the edge of her desk and crossed her arms. "Yes?"

"Don't give me that, Laney. You chose me to be the EP for this show, and then you undermine me at every opportunity. What gives?"

"Would you have put Hal on the show if I'd suggested it?"

I frowned. "What kind of question is that? This is my job, isn't it?"

"Last I checked, but you wouldn't have done it."

I evaded the accusation. "Not that you even respected me enough to tell me. You blindsided me instead. I was saving Hal for later in the season. It's too soon — we've barely gotten started and you're going to throw the ace in the hole at Joel? You showed your hand too soon, Laney. And now? Now he's pissed and doesn't trust us. You made me look like an asshole in front of everyone, and you undermined me. How am I supposed to produce people who don't trust or respect me?"

"I'm sure you'll figure something out. Did you fuck him when you went into the back room?"

I kept my face still, though the traitorous flush flared up my neck. She didn't know for sure, which was a good thing. "No. I let him yell at me, and I yelled at him." *And then he went down on me like a rock star and laid his naked body all over me, but whatever.*

She watched me as she dragged in a breath and let it out in speculation. "Well, I'm sorry to blindside you, but at present, I don't trust your ability to make decisions when it comes to Joel."

The flush was now accompanied by the tingling of fear and anger. "Are you serious?"

"If you can't do your job, then I have to do your job. We can't fail, Annika. This has to be an instant hit, and I need you on point to get it there. I want you to succeed. I want all of this to be yours some day. I want to give you the opportunities that I had to work and hustle and climb for. But you have to be on board utterly and completely. Otherwise, you'll be washing some slob's dishes in Hoboken for the rest of your life. Got it?"

My jaw clenched, though I knew it wasn't a threat — it was a truth. "Got it."

She smiled at me sadly and stood. "I get it. I do. But you've got to play this smart. Don't throw it away. Okay?"

I tried to smile back as my fears climbed up my throat. "Okay."

Joel

The shop bustled with action as the crew set up for the day, and I leaned my chair back, boot propping me up, as I doodled absently on a legal pad, trying not to watch the door for Annika.

I had no chill, not when it came to her. Not as the seconds ticked down to when we could be alone to talk.

The bell dinged, and my eyes shot to the door, but it was just Shep and Ramona. They waved as they headed back to makeup, and I jerked a chin in lieu of a greeting, my nerves jacked to the point of no return.

I was just contemplating a shot of Makers when she walked in. Her face gave nothing away — the cold, blue eyes and stern line of her lush, red lips — as she greeted the people she passed, actively avoiding making eye contact with me. She jumped straight in, talking with the main camera man — I didn't have all the lingo down for their jobs yet — then I watched as she walked back to makeup.

I relaxed my knee until the legs of my chair were all on the ground, stashed the notepad and stood, not ready to take no for an answer. But I stopped myself from following her, practicing restraint, walking instead into my booth and to my desk. What did I expect? Did I want her to run through the doors and bound into my arms? Swing by and give me a kiss? Lean on the counter and bat her lashes at me?

It was what I wanted, but I knew better. Generally, I was smarter than this, but I found myself twisted up by the drive to talk to her, touch her, kiss her again. The drive to know that it wasn't the only time I'd get to have her for my own. Because there were so many things I wanted to do to her still. So many things, and I couldn't stand the thought of not being able to.

So, I resolved myself to being patient, and for the first half of the day, it wasn't too hard. But with every avoided glance, with every time she dipped out of the room or the conversation when I entered, my patience thinned, and by the end of the day, I was ready to blow.

I was on my way to find her after she'd disappeared into the back, and when I entered the hallway, she tried to step past me, but I wouldn't let her pass.

"Excuse me," she said, her eyes over my shoulder.

"I wanted to talk to you about the Samoan tattoo segment for next week." It was the best excuse I could come up with after thinking about it quite literally all day.

She gave me a tight smile, though she still wouldn't meet my eyes. "Let's talk about it later," she said, trying to move around me again.

I put my hand on the wall next to her head and leaned in just enough. "This can't really wait."

I saw her swallow, the humorless smile still on her face, but her eyes were wild. "Okay, then."

"This way." It was a gruff command, and I grabbed her arm gently, guiding her toward my office, closing the door behind me.

She stood against the far wall with an office chair between us, and I smirked, envisioning her just like this the night before.

"You keep doing that."

"What?"

"Trying to put something between us. Why is that?"

"It's safer that way."

I stepped around the chair. "For you or for me?"

Her eyes finally met mine, piercing my heart, stopping me in my tracks. "For both of us."

"Tell me what's going on."

She stood up a little straighter, squaring her shoulders in preparation, like she'd been planning the speech all day. "Last night was … well, it happened, but it can't happen again."

I laughed — I couldn't help it. "And why not?" I stepped closer, closer enough to smell the flowers again, nearly driven mad with curiosity as to what they were. "Because you told me last night that you wanted me. That you wanted this." I slipped a hand into the curve of her neck, running by thumb against her jaw. "Tell me I'm wrong," I said as I leaned in, my lips on a track for hers. But just as they were about to connect, she sucked in a breath and laid a hand on my chest, dipping her chin to stonewall me.

"Joel …"

I tilted her face so she'd meet my eyes again. "What's stopping you?"

Her lips parted to speak, but she said nothing at first, her eyes searching mine. "This is my job. I can't get ... *involved* with you or it could impede my judgement, and I've worked too hard to throw that away just because I'm hot for you."

My smirk was back. "You're hot for me?"

She gave a smile in return. "Just as hot for you as you are for me."

My tongue wet my bottom lip, and her eyes darted to my mouth, lingering there for a moment. And I knew she wanted me. To what degree, I had yet to determine. So, I lied for the sake of getting what I wanted.

"This doesn't have to be complicated, Annika. It can be simple." My thumb found the hollow behind her ear. "It can be easy," I said as I leaned in, my hot breath rebounding off her lips. "You're here. I'm here. And when this is over, you'll leave, and I'll be right here. It'll be like nothing ever happened." I closed my mouth over the swell of her bottom lip gently, sweeping my tongue across it.

Her lids fluttered as she sighed, and I felt a hundred feet tall and bulletproof.

"What do you say? Give me a shot. I won't disappoint you."

A flicker of fear lit in her eyes. "I know. But how do you know I won't disappoint you?"

"I don't. But that's part of the fun, isn't it?"

She tried to look away again, but I held her face.

"Tell me you don't want me, and I'll walk away."

Her eyes bounced between mine again, and she swallowed as I waited, the moment stretching on and on and on until finally, she spoke, her voice smoke and fire. "I could say it, but it would be a lie."

Sweet relief and a smile on my lips were my body's answers. "Then it's settled. We'll keep it on the low. You do what you have to for your job."

"Even if it means hurting you?" she asked quietly.

My heart lurched, but I smiled. "Don't worry, princess. I don't break easy." And then I pressed my lips to hers, feeling her relief and my own at the contact. She melted into me as I pressed her into the wall with my body, and I wondered way in the back of my mind just what I'd gotten myself into.

LADY BOSS

Annika

BREATHLESS.

WHEN HE STEPPED BACK, he actually took my breath with him.

I had no idea what exactly had taken over my body, but I was drunk off it. My hands were still on his chest.

"Okay," I muttered.

"Okay." He smiled, and I resisted the urge to slip my fingers into his beard and pull him in for another kiss. "Tonight. Come to my place when you're finished working. I'll leave the door unlocked."

"Deal."

"Oh, and before you go, I need something from you."

My brow rose. "Oh?"

"Your panties."

A laugh burst out of me. "That's so cliché, Joel."

He shrugged and extended a hand, palm up. "Don't care. Hand them over."

I folded my arms, only partly in protest. "Why should I?"

"Let's just say you'll thank me later."

"And who's to say I'm wearing any panties?"

His smile rose on one side. "Should I make sure myself?"

I shook my head and rolled my eyes, almost annoyed at how

amused and fluttery I was. But he wanted to play, so I'd just have to play harder.

I turned so my back was to him and hiked up my skirt, looking over my shoulder with my bottom lip between my teeth and big eyes. But his eyes, dark and hot, were on my hands as they exposed my ass and the black thong I was grateful to have put on that morning rather than granny panties. His jaw was set, chest rising and falling as he took shallow breaths, which turned me on more than I could verbalize. But instead of talking, I hooked my thumbs into the band and bent over at the waist, dragging my panties down my legs, stepping out of them slowly to make sure he got his fill of the view.

I almost jumped when I felt his hands on my hips, but I stood straight and leaned back into him, feeling him hard against me. His lips were at my ear.

"I'm gonna fuck you up so bad, Ms. Belousov."

My breath caught. "Good," I whispered back before pulling away. I righted my skirt, panties still in hand, and turned, trying to slow my chugging heart, smiling at him like I knew all his secrets. I stepped into him, stuffing the satin thong into his pocket as I leaned into his ear. "See you tonight, Joel."

And then I walked out of the office like the lady-boss I was.

By the end of the day, I realized something very important.

Joel's knowledge that I wasn't wearing panties made me hotter than the fire of a thousand suns.

No lie, by the time the sun went down, I was aching for him. The way he looked at me — like he was actually going to nail me into oblivion — had my thighs tight as rubber bands all day. Watching him work, his hands as they held that tattoo gun, the fluttering of his forearms as he drew and shaded ... they all spoke to me of latent power. Even when he walked, he seemed to have his own gravity, catching everyone's attention like they didn't have a choice in the matter. He was a force of nature, a force that had sucked me in like a black hole.

Somehow I'd let him convince me. Like I could say no to him with his lips so close to mine and his hips pressed against me. I most definitely wouldn't say no tonight, not after the long tease we'd been playing at all day. No, tonight he could do whatever he wanted to me. I needed him to.

There came a time where he was finished with work and out of excuses to hang around, but he caught my eye as he walked past me for the door and slipped a hand in his pocket, the one where my panties were.

I smiled despite the knowledge that I was supposed to be secretive. As wound up as I was, we were all lucky I didn't bolt after him and take him on the sidewalk. But not long after, I was finished with my work and antsy to get to him. So I followed the crew upstairs and gave them instructions. Laney was gone, as usual — my job was to stay and oversee everything. Hers was to work typical hours and leave me in charge, and every night I was thankful for the office to myself. Particularly that night.

I told everyone goodnight and headed down the stairs, pausing in front of his door as I listened and watched for any lingering crew members. When I was sure no one was around, I slipped into his apartment, closing the door softly behind me.

He bolted out of his chair at the kitchen table, and I was disarmed by the raw surprise and uncertainty I found in his face, though it was quickly gone, replaced by smoldering fire. We moved for each other, crashing together in the middle of the room, his lips, my lips, our bodies tangled up as we reveled in the contact we'd been waiting for all day.

His hands were at the hem of my skirt, tugging it up and over my hips, and he broke the kiss to bury his face in my neck as he wrapped an arm around my back, slipping his free hand up my thigh and between my ass, his finger grazing the slick line at my core.

My arms wound around his neck, and I stretched up on my tip-toes, willing him to touch me more, touch me deeper, the burning at the tips of his fingers almost unbearable.

"Joel," I begged, my voice rough, my fingers twisted in his hair, clutching him to me.

His big hand squeezed, cupping me from behind, the tips of

two fingers barely slipping into me, and I whimpered. With a growl, he lifted me up by the ass, and my legs wound around his waist as he spun us around to move us God knew where. I didn't care. I just needed him inside of me.

Now.

I'd said the last word aloud without realizing it, and he rumbled against me as gravity shifted. He laid me on his bed and kissed me so hard, it left my heart aching, my ribs burning. One of his hands disappeared, and I heard the clinking of his belt, the sound of his zipper, and I briefly had the irrational, frantic thought that I didn't have patience for a condom — I was on birth control, which almost seemed like enough in the moment. But he disappeared, and I cracked my eyelids to find him rummaging in his nightstand, then the rip of the foil packet, the sound of the rubber unrolling, which got my lids open completely. I wanted to watch him, wanted to see him touch himself, but he was already descending on me, his hand on the base of his cock, and in a breath, before I even realized what he was doing, he filled me completely, to the hilt.

I struggled for a breath, my back arched as he pulled out and slammed into me. He was everywhere, kissing me, touching me, in me, around me, moving so hard, so fast that I couldn't hold on. My body pulsed, his name on my lips as he flexed his hips, hitting the end of me with a moan, and my heart stopped as I came, gripping him with all of me, pulling him deeper with every heartbeat.

He came right behind me, throbbing and hot, grunting in a way that hit me deep in my stomach as he pumped his hips.

We were both panting as he collapsed on top of me, and I wound my arms around his neck and cupped the back of his head, my fingers in his silky hair, his breath against my skin hot and huffing. I could feel his heart hammering through his shirt, through my shirt, through my ribs and into my own, which matched his pace, beat for beat.

"Mmm," he hummed and kissed my collarbone.

"Mmm," I echoed and shifted my fingers in his hair.

"I told you you'd thank me later."

I chuckled. "I didn't thank you."

I could feel him smiling against my skin. "Yeah, you did." He rolled over, pulling me with him by way of a strong hand on my hip. "Come on. You hungry?"

I found myself frowning. Okay, maybe I was pouting a little. "Wait, was that it?"

He laughed at that, the flash of his white teeth and boom of the sound making me smile, despite my disappointment. When he'd finished, he popped me on the bare ass, and I yelped.

"Princess, that was just the warm up."

Joel

I climbed off the bed, the smile on my face threatening permanence as I kicked off my boots and dropped my pants, then pulled off my shirt. I glanced over my shoulder and caught her looking, watching me with admiration, her eyes scanning my body, and I winked before walking out of that room stark naked and a few inches taller than usual. The lights in the bathroom were off, and I left them that way, cleaning up quickly and anxious to get back to her. As if I would go back to my room and she'd already be gone.

But she was there, her silk shirt untucked and skirt back in place, sadly. Her heels stood next to the bed, and I realized she'd re-twisted her bun, setting herself to rights.

Too bad I wasn't going to leave it twisted for long. No, I wanted it down, brushing her shoulders, fanned out around her. Free.

Her cheeks flushed, and she smiled knowingly — I hadn't realized I'd paused in the doorway as I looked her over. So I snapped into action, moving for my dresser.

"I'm glad you decided to come over," I said as I rummaged through my drawer for a pair of jersey pants.

"Me too," she answered, though she didn't offer anything else.

I couldn't help but wonder what she was thinking about as I tugged on my pants, but I was too afraid to ask. So I turned to her and smiled, reaching for her hand.

"Come on. Let's get you something to eat."

She smiled and slipped her soft, long fingers into my hand. "You cook?" she asked as she stood.

"I wouldn't call eggs 'cooking.'"

She laughed and followed me into the kitchen, her hand still in mine until she sat at the kitchen table, crossing her long legs underneath. I moved around the kitchen, gathering supplies and utensils. I'd never been comfortable with silence — I was much more at home talking, telling stories or jokes — but there I was, with the girl to end all girls, and I had nothing to say. The silence was deafening, and I scrambled, deciding to hit the classics.

"So, I've been wondering, have you ever lived in Russia? Like, are you *from* there?" I already felt a little better, and cracked an egg on the side of the pan, satisfied with the sound it made.

"No, my parents are."

I nodded and cracked another egg. "How long have they lived here?"

"Since '89. They settled in Brighton Beach." She let out a sigh when I didn't ask another question, continuing on. "They were … extracted by my uncle, who's been here since the 70s. They couldn't get out on their own. The whole *Russian Jew* thing."

I frowned as I popped some bread into the toaster. "I'm not overly familiar with Russia's history."

She chuckled. "It's okay. Russian Jews have been the most persecuted group of people in just about all of history. It was hundreds of years in the making, the Russian government moving toward communism, uniformity, including religion. During World War II, millions fled into Eastern Europe, the Middle East, and some to America. My parents were small children during the war, and their families were friends, leaving Russia in a group. My grandparents were freedom fighters in Hungary during the revolution in the 50s. They eventually ended up in Israel, but went back to Russia to try to help my aunt. Their papers were confiscated."

I listened soberly, trying to imagine a life of running, of persecution. I couldn't grasp it. "That's incredible."

"It is. We're survivors."

"I'll say."

"So when they were stuck in Russia, Papa called my uncle in America, Roxy's dad. He has connections and was able to get them all out, set them up in Brooklyn, help them buy a house and start their business."

"What do they do?" I stirred the eggs, fascinated.

"They run a dry cleaning shop. I'm actually trying to get them to retire — they're not young. They didn't think they could have kids — they were both forty-six, and it had never happened before. But just after they moved here, whamo. Guess it just took them not being afraid for their lives for it to happen." She chuckled softly, and I glanced back at her. Her chin was propped on the heel of her hand, fingers on her cheek. She looked young, soft and innocent, the chill gone, melted. For the moment, at least.

"Anyway," she continued, "I've got this massive box of paper ledgers to go through in an attempt to figure out how much the business is worth so they can sell it and hopefully use the money to invest and retire. They've earned it, as hard as they've worked, as much as they've been through. Papa would work until his last breath without thinking twice about it, but I want more for him. For both of them. So, I've just got to puzzle through these ledgers, but I have no idea what I'm doing."

"I can help," I said as I plated the eggs and grabbed the toast. "I've been running the shop for almost twenty years, and I started back before we had QuickBooks. Ledgers and paper receipts used to be the only way." I set her plate in front of her and sat down across from her with mine.

"I couldn't bother you with that, Joel. You're so busy with the show."

I shrugged and picked up my toast. "So are you. We can work on it together." I took a bite.

She laughed, the flush in her cheeks back, turning her eyes an electric shade of blue in comparison. "I'm not sure how much work we'll get done."

I smirked. "We'll set a timer. One hour of work for an hour of play."

"At that rate, it'll take us a year to get through the paperwork."

"But just think of all that playing. I'm just saying, pretty sure it'd be worth it."

She laughed again, shaking her head as she picked up her toast and took a bite. Somehow, she made it look elegant, delicate, even with the harsh crunch of the bread between her teeth.

"Seriously, Annika. Let me help you."

She set the bread down as she chewed, rolling the crumbs between her fingers, and they fell like snowflakes on her plate. "You'd really do that?" she asked once she'd swallowed.

"Of course. It would take me a fraction of the time it would take you. I bought a business — I know how this works and what an inspector and loan officer will be looking for. I'd be happy to pass some of that knowledge on. Plus, it's not like I don't have otherwise selfish intentions."

One brow rose. "Oh?"

"Play time. Remember?"

More laughing. The sound was maybe one of my favorite sounds in the world, just as light and free as I hoped it would be. She was a woman with two sides, behind a wall of determination. I'd just had to scale the wall to see it, and what I found was the valley of the promised land, green and lush and full of sunshine.

"So, when do you want to start?" She slipped her fork into her mouth, and I watched her lips as she pulled the fork out clean.

"You say when. I'm around."

"Tomorrow, then. It'll give me a good excuse to come over without having to sneak, too."

Worry niggled the back of my mind, knowing she was putting herself at risk. "What happens if someone finds out?"

She shrugged and took another bite, buying time to respond. "Technically, nothing. Laney suspects something, and it's not forbidden, as long as I do my job."

"Which means potentially manipulating me."

She nodded. "It's why she didn't tell me about Hal. She didn't think I'd pull the trigger on bringing him in."

The memory burned in my chest. "Would you have?"

She didn't answer right away, but looked me in the eyes. "I don't know for sure. But I think I would have come up with an excuse to postpone it."

The thought gave me comfort. "I guess I should have known he'd be used as a match to strike. But please, tell me you're not dragging Liz into this."

Her face was still open, honest. "I have no plans to."

I drew a breath and let it out slow.

"Tell me about her."

I rested my forearms on the table and shifted in my seat. "Off the record?"

"Of course," she said, looking surprised.

I brought my fingers up to touch my beard. "We were so young. I was on my own for the first time and I met her and it was like … I don't know. We were inseparable. She was crazy. I was crazy. We got married in Vegas a month after we met."

She didn't respond, but watched me in a way that told me she wanted to know more.

I sighed. "I don't really talk about it a lot because it wasn't pretty. My parents died back to back in the middle of it all, and we took Shep in. The stress of everything just imploded something that was already burning down."

"She was almost charged with assault, right?"

I nodded, hating that she'd dug around on me when I knew virtually nothing about her. "It used to get physical a lot. With her, not me. I just want you to know that. I never laid a hand on her in anger."

"I believe you," she said quietly.

"I mean, I wrecked shit, it stands to note. Many a lamp, a couple TVs, and a damn good couch were sacrificed to our fights. But I never touched her. I'd wreck the apartment instead. We'd drink, and she'd come at me, ready to fight. She'd push every button, point at every flaw, tear me down. But don't look at me like that," I said when I saw the trademark pity that accompanied this story. "I wasn't any better. We'd yell, scream, hurt each other with our words. She'd slap and scratch and throw things at me. Once, she came at me with a baseball bat."

Annika was still. I smiled, trying to lighten the mood.

"Don't worry. She didn't get a shot off. I caught it and threw it off the fire escape."

"I don't even know how I'd handle that."

"I dunno. We were married. It wasn't simple — she was there for everything, a part of me. A part I hated, sure, but she was a part of my life. Sometimes I just had to get her still long enough, and she'd kiss me, or I'd kiss her. It was the easy way to switch gears, put all that adrenaline into something less destructive. But it was hell for both of us, this cycle we found ourselves in."

"I'm so sorry, Joel."

I realized my smile had fallen and resurrected it. "Don't be. I learned a lot about what I want, about who I am and what I want out of a relationship."

"Which is?"

I shrugged. "Nothing. I haven't had a girlfriend since."

Her mouth fell open a hair, her brow dropping as she did the math. "Fourteen years?"

I nodded.

"I mean, certainly you've—"

I laughed. "Oh, yeah. I've done plenty of that."

She didn't look overly amused.

"I just haven't been interested in anything deeper. I'm not going to say Liz ruined me for that, but ..."

"Yeah. I can imagine."

And I lied again, carefully cultivating the words, slipping them into her brain. It was the only way I knew to keep her coming back to me until I figured out what to do next. "This is why what you and I have here is perfect. You do your job. Come here when you want me and I'll take you when I want. And when it's over, it's over. That's the deal, right?"

Something flitted behind her eyes, but was gone just as soon as it appeared. "Exactly."

I smiled. "I'm glad we're in agreement. Now, tell me you're finished eating."

She laid her hands in her lap. "I am, thank you."

"Good," I said as I stood, and so did she. But when I stepped into her, she turned her head.

"Wait," she said softly, and I froze.

"What's wrong?"

Her cheeks flushed. "I ... this is weird, but ..." she paused and pursed her lips. "Can I, um, use your toothbrush?"

I laughed a little louder than I meant to. "I didn't peg you for the type to share toothbrushes with anyone."

The flush deepened. "I have egg breath. Egg breath trumps germ sharing. Plus, it's not like your mouth germs aren't already well acquainted with mine."

I leaned in, wrapping my arms around her waist, running my nose against her temple before kissing it. "Sure. Mine's the purple one."

"You have a purple toothbrush?"

"Asks the girl who's worried about egg breath."

She chuckled. "Thank you."

I let her go. "You're welcome."

"Maybe you should brush yours too," she said as she turned for the bathroom. "Just saying."

"Why, does your pussy care?"

Her jaw popped open, and she laughed, the sound full of embarrassment, tinged with amusement and shock. "Joel!"

I shrugged. "That was my intended destination, so if your little lady doesn't care, you shouldn't either."

"Oh, my God. Please don't call it that ever again." She stepped into the bathroom and turned on the light.

I leaned on the doorframe and folded my arms across my bare chest. "So, pussy is preferable?"

She picked up my toothbrush from the cup and opened the medicine cabinet. "I'd prefer you not call it anything. Just ravage it."

I laughed. "I can do that. You have no idea how I can do that."

She smirked and loaded the toothbrush with paste. "Oh, I think I have an idea."

I pushed off the door and stepped behind her, looking at the two of us in the mirror. "No, you don't."

That blush. That blush was the best thing to ever happen to me.

She slipped the toothbrush into her mouth, and a new objective manifested: distract Annika by any means necessary.

I leaned back as she started scrubbing, looking down her back as she watched me in the mirror. First, her hair, my big hands making quick work of the hair tie holding it together. I shook it out — the bun had left it in soft waves that fell over her shoulders. My head tilted, hands running from her waist to her hips, then around to the back, to her zipper. I unzipped it and slipped my hands inside, down her hips, the band catching on my wrists, and I pushed until the material was a pile around her long, white legs.

She braced herself with her free hand on the counter, her chest rising and falling with shallow breaths.

The white silk shell had tiny straps, and I slipped one off her shoulder, bowing my head to kiss and lick in the wake of my fingers. The strap fell to her elbow, exposing one breast, sheathed in a nude, strapless bra that I wanted out of my way, but there was plenty of time for that.

I noticed her hand had stopped scrubbing.

"Keep brushing," I said into her skin and kissed down her back.

She did as she was told, though the motion was slow. It had maybe been twenty seconds. I had a full minute and a half left, according to the American Dental Association, and I'd take advantage of that time. I smirked at her over her shoulder as I ran my hands down her hips and around the front of her thighs, sliding them up until I found what I was looking for and slipped a finger inside.

Her lids fluttered, and her hand faltered.

"Keep brushing, egg breath."

She let out a small, muffled laugh, and spit into the sink before she got going again. With my free hand, I pressed my hand to her back and leaned in to whisper in her ear.

"Spread your legs."

She hinged at the waist and widened her legs as I dropped to my knees and grabbed her hips, pulling her toward me until I connected. She was so soft, so warm against my tongue, and I moaned, the sound rumbling through me.

"Oh, fuck," she breathed and dropped my toothbrush in the sink, opting to hang on for leverage. My lips were too busy to protest.

I buried my face in her, squeezing her hips, guiding her to move just how I wanted her to until she moved on her own, telegraphing to me what she liked, what she wanted, rocking against my tongue. Her back arched, and I reached up to grab a fistful of her shirt.

"God," she whispered into the basin, but I couldn't see her and didn't care what she looked like, not with all of my attention focused on making her come. She pulsed against my tongue and I knew she was close. I used my fisted hand to guide her, moving the hand on her hip between her legs, finding the sensitive spot with my thumb, circling it as she gasped. Then arched. Then shuddered against me, her body releasing. I slowed my lips, my tongue, easing her down as I hoped she wasn't tired. Because I was nowhere near done with her yet.

I kissed her long and slow as she panted, her legs trembling as I kissed the soft skin of her back, my hands skating up her ribs under her shirt, wanting it gone. She took the cue and pulled it off, and I spent a long moment kissing the skin between her shoulder blades as I flicked the snap of her bra open with my thumb and forefinger.

And just like that, Annika was naked, looking over her shoulder at me with wild hair and burning eyes, spread eagle in my bathroom.

"Go get in my bed," I said gruffly and kissed her back again.

She stood and turned to me, looking down my body as she reached for my hand, meeting my eyes for a split second before pulling me toward the bedroom. I followed her, admiring every curve of her long body — her shoulder, the dip in her spine, the slow wave of her waist to her hip — as she pulled me into my room and stopped in front of the bed.

She turned and looked up at me, her face young again, her lips wide and full, parted just enough to see a sliver of teeth. She brought her hands to my naked chest. Her fingers trailed fire as they slipped down my hips, under the band of my pants and back to my ass, pushing the elastic down and over until they dropped. I stepped out of them — her eyes hadn't left mine.

I cupped her small face in my hands, my fingers like tattooed wings against the flawless porcelain of her skin. She was so beautiful, so strong, so capable, but in that moment she was vulnerable, and that made her strength that much sweeter. She could move heaven and earth. She could move my heart, which I thought was immovable.

I closed my eyes and pressed my lips to hers to stop me from thinking anymore. I didn't want to think. I only wanted to feel her.

Her lips were sweet and supple, moving with mine, her tongue slipping past my lips and into my mouth. And as the kiss deepened, she wound herself around me, and I wound around her, pulling her flush against me.

She broke away after a moment and whispered into my mouth, "Lie down."

I smirked, my heart banging as I followed orders, stretching out on the bed, slipping my hands behind my head. Her bottom lip was between her teeth, one corner of her mouth pulled up too, eyes combing me over. I wondered if she'd ever seen anyone as tattooed as me — I was covered from neck to heel — but it was only a passing thought. I couldn't take my eyes off of her, the shadows across her body in the low light of the room — the curve of her breast, the peak of her nipple, the bridge of her small nose.

She was art, made of shadows and light.

I was almost startled when she moved — my brain had been calculating the strokes it would take to recreate her on paper, but it would be impossible. She was too real.

She crawled onto the bed and between my thighs, her hands skating up the outside to my hips as she dipped her head and trailed her tongue down the V of muscle that led down. She followed the path, tilting her head so the tip of her nose grazed my shaft, and I hissed, slipping a hand into her hair. She tilted her head again, replacing the tip of her nose with the tip of her hot tongue — my fingers clenched, twisting her hair in my fist. And then she looked up at me and smiled, licking up my shaft until she reached the crown, her lids closing softly as she opened her mouth, and I disappeared inside of her.

I held onto her hair as she rose and dropped, my eyes on her lips, my brain trying to match what I saw with what I felt — the wet heat as it surrounded and disappeared, her tongue as it rolled, her fingers as they dug into my hips, her breasts between my thighs.

She hummed, and my eyes closed, chin tipped. She took me deeper with every wave of her body, her hand leaving my thigh to touch me low, cup me, rolling her fingers in time with her mouth, dropping again and again until I couldn't let her go on.

I hissed her name, and she backed off me slowly, her eyes on mine, my cock leaving her lips so hot, it took all my reserve willpower not to slam back into her.

"Come here," I growled, the words barely audible as I rose to meet her, our mouths connecting, breath heaving, all hands and skin, the two of us pressed against each other and touching each other until I couldn't tell where one of us ended and the other began. I lay on my side with Annika in the crook of my elbow, her hair in my fingers, our legs scissored together as we kissed and kissed, rolled and tumbled. Until I needed her so badly that the only thing I could do was to take her.

I backed away, and she rolled onto her back, chest heaving, lips swollen and red, lids heavy. My hand slipped between her legs, cupping her, squeezing her as I leaned toward my nightstand for a condom. She whimpered, clutching my wrist, riding my hand, begging for me to touch her without saying a word, and I slipped a finger into her, then another as she gasped and whispered my name.

I groaned, lips together, letting her go to rip open the package, trying to focus enough to roll the condom on as she writhed on the bed, her thighs squeezing, looking for pressure. Pressure that was mine to give.

I opened her knees, one hand gripping my base as I hovered over her, pressing myself against her until she parted for me, let me in.

We both moaned as I slid into her, and I paused for a breath, then another, bending to kiss her, my lips feverish, hips still, feeling her all around me. I pulled her thigh into my ribs, and she raised it higher, resting her knee against my tricep, her hips rolling against me to give her the weight she wanted to ease the aching I knew she had to feel. I felt it too.

I pulled out and flexed, slamming back into her, and she kicked her head back into the bed. Then again, and a cry passed her lips. I pulled her other thigh up, and she squeezed my ribs before bringing her knees as close to her shoulders as she could. I leaned into her, hovered over her, her shins hooked under my arms. Our open lips were inches apart as I pumped my hips and she gasped for air, and when she came, when she pulled me into her with her breath and her body, I followed her, pulsing and shaking with the release. And as I slowed, I looked into her eyes, finding myself reflected in them, hoping she saw herself in mine.

HONEY PIE

Annika

I COULDN'T KEEP MY EYES open, not just because Joel saw more of me than I wanted him to, but because I was exhausted. My body was heavy — my arms slung around his neck, my legs caught under his arms, every breath labored. He was heavy too, his body on mine a comfortable weight. I liked being surrounded by him. It was comforting. Safe.

But I couldn't look into his eyes when he looked at me like that.

He released my legs, and I stretched them out, winding them around his waist as he buried his face in my neck, his breath huffing, lips closing occasionally to kiss my skin. I leaned into his ear, nestling into the bend of his neck.

We lay like that for a long time, long enough that I think I fell asleep for a few seconds, woken with his movement as he rolled over.

I twisted my hips to ease our bodies' separation, then put them back where they were, leaving me lying flat on the bed, feeling like a fat, lazy cat after a feast of milk and honey. Sweat had beaded all over my skin, and now that we weren't pressed against each other, the cool air prickled the moisture. It felt glorious.

The bed bounced as he got up — my eyes were still closed, my body reveling in its current state — and dipped again a moment later when he returned from the bathroom, if the flushing toilet was any indication. I sighed when I felt him next to me, turning my head, prying my lids open as I smiled at him where lay, head propped on his palm, smile on his lips, eyes on my face.

I convinced my body to roll onto my side so I could face him more comfortably, tucking my hands under my head and curling toward him.

"I'm so tired," I muttered.

His smile pulled up on one side before he started singing "I'm So Tired," by The Beatles in his off-key, gruffy timbre.

I chimed in on the chorus, and his tone shifted, trying to match mine without luck, but I didn't care. The look of surprise on his face as we sang all the lyrics together was absolutely perfect.

He laughed when we were finished, and I found myself smiling like a fool, lying next to Hairy, singing The Beatles.

"I never would have pegged you for a big enough fan of The Beatles that you'd know that entire song."

"It's on one of my favorite albums."

"*The White Album*? Really?" he asked, his face colored with disbelief.

"Yes, really. I know every note of that album just as well as I know my own name."

He shook his head, still chuckling.

"Is it really that unbelievable?"

"Yes, actually."

"More unbelievable than me reading romance novels?"

He laughed. "That's different, but close. Classic, stuffy, Regency era fiction seems like just your kind of story."

I pushed him in the shoulder. "Hey, you're reading it too, last I checked."

He laid a hand on my hip, slipping his thigh between mine. "I am. And it's not even that bad — I kinda love it. Well, once I figured out what the hell they were saying, at least."

I chuckled and shifted to move closer to him. "I'm glad you're reading it. It shows a particular level of persistence that you'd brave Jane Austen just to impress me."

That smirk of his made my insides feel all fluttery. "Psh. I don't even have to try when it comes to impressing you."

I full on laughed at that.

"So," he said, "explain to me how you became a mega-fan of the Beatles, because I can't figure out a theory that makes any sense."

"My parents have the original vinyl albums."

His mouth dropped open at that. "You're kidding. Do you know what number it is?"

My brow quirked. "What do you mean?"

His eyes lit up. "So the album covers all have numbers printed on the back," he said, speeding up a little as he spoke, "and if the number is under a hundred, it could be worth near ten grand."

I blinked. "Oh, my God."

"Yeah. I mean, I don't even know if I could sell something like that, if it were mine."

"No, they would never."

"Even to help their retirement?"

I shook my head. "It's too important to them. Mama loves to tell the story about when they lived in Israel and couldn't find a record store that carried it, so Roxy's dad sent them a copy from America. It was so rare to them, so valuable — did you know their music was banned in Russia? Well, anything Western was banned in Russia."

He shook his head.

"I think to them it was a tangible representation of their freedom, you know? No one would stop them from listening to it. There was no one to tell them no. So it's invaluable to them, along with most of their record collection." I smiled. "Papa still has his old record player, in mint condition. I remember being a little girl, dancing with him in the living room to 'Honey Pie.'"

Joel smiled and brushed my hair back from my face. "Who would have thought."

I laughed. "Not you." The last word stretched into a yawn. "But I really am so tired. I wish I could stay."

He leaned in for a kiss. "Then stay." His soft lips brushed mine, and I sighed.

"I can't. I have no clothes, and your apartment is in the same building where I currently work." I'd all but stopped smiling. "I don't even know how I'll get home other than a cab — if I call my driver, Laney will have a trail to follow."

"You can't just say you were working late?"

I chuffed. "Maybe if the show wasn't an around-the-clock operation. Someone's always here, and they'd tell her I wasn't if she asked. Which she would."

He was frowning, and I realized I was too.

"I dunno. Maybe I can walk to a bar and have him pick me up there. Pretend I had a drink."

"I don't like the idea of you running around alone."

I laughed. "You act like I didn't grow up in Brooklyn. I'll be fine, Joel. Really. I'll sneak out, take a little walk, and call my driver to get me home. Or call a cab and pay a small fortune to get over the bridge."

"Maybe you should just bring clothes over. You know, just to make things easier," he offered.

"Maybe I will," I said, leaning in for a kiss, wishing I had anything to wear tomorrow because going home felt like the equivalent of asking me to climb Everest. But I peeled myself out of Joel's bed and shuffled around the room, picking up my clothes and putting them on my exhausted body — he only had to reach off the side of the bed for his pants, swinging his legs over the side to pull them on.

When I was dressed, yawning hard enough for my eyes to water every thirty seconds, he walked me to the door and cupped my face, a gesture that made me feel small and precious.

"Next time, stay the night. Make it easy on both of us."

My heart lurched, something about his words giving me a sense of foreboding. "All right," I said anyway, and tipped my chin up, reaching for a kiss that he gave me, a gentle connection of our lips that swept away the feeling, replacing it with a wisp of a flutter in my chest.

He opened the door quietly and checked the hallway, even going so far as to trot down the stairs, barefoot and blissfully shirtless, to make sure the sidewalk was clear before finally letting me leave. Though he wouldn't let me go until I granted him another kiss, one a little deeper and hotter, like he wanted to leave his mark in parting, giving me something that would stay with me.

As if the night hadn't been enough.

I hurried out of the building, feeling less anxious about being spotted once I hit the sidewalk. And once I was near the corner, reality began to seep in.

I had no idea what I was doing. My first reaction was shame — not of being with him or doing what I wanted with him, but for not remembering the consequences. For not letting those consequences stop me. Because now? Now I'd had a taste, and there was no walking away. Not easily, at least.

I sighed as I walked toward a bar that, according to my phone, was down Broadway, barely recognizing myself. As different as Joel and I were, we fit together like clasping hands. Never in my life had I been with a man who knew exactly what to do to my body, a man so sure of every move he made, a man so … *equal* to me. It seemed to me, I realized suddenly, that every man I'd been with up to that point had been safe, unaffected. Ambitious, sure, but without true passion. Not like the lust for life that emanated from Joel like some crazy pheromone.

What are you doing, Annika?

It wasn't even a question I could answer, so instead I texted my driver before ducking into a bar called Habits, ordering a shot of Stoli to calm myself down as I waited. The bar was nearly empty, besides a middle-aged man slumped over a table in the back, and the bartender — a woman who I guessed was in her thirties and not used to working a bar, given the *Help Wanted* sign in the window and her open laptop displaying Quickbooks the far end of the bar. I was also glad she was too busy with her work to bother with me.

I heard Laney in the back of my mind, calling Joel a meat puppet and telling me not to get involved. I heard Joel telling me it didn't have to be complicated, that we would both walk away at the end and it would be over. *Like it never happened*, he'd said. I didn't know if I could ever pretend that Joel Anderson never happened.

I sat up a little straighter and turned the shot glass with my thumb and forefinger. We were hot for each other, that was obvious, and I told myself I'd imagined that there was anything more to it. It was just chemicals, that was all, and Joel said himself that he was a loner. He didn't do relationships, and he wouldn't want to start with me. And all of that was for the absolute best.

As I picked up the shot glass and tossed the liquor back, I did my best to convince myself that I was right.

JUNE GLOOM

Annika

EARLY THE NEXT MORNING — MUCH too early given the long night before — I found myself hauling the heavy box of ledgers up the stairs and into my office. Laney was already at her desk and on the phone, and I set the box down with a thump, shaking out my fingers from the strain. She glanced over at the box, then at me quizzically as I took a seat and opened up my laptop to go over the schedule for the day.

The big segment was a piece Joel would do for a woman we'd cast weeks before. She wanted a graphic piece in black linework, the concept simple enough that it could be done in a day, though it would take all day to film. We wanted to show the process of getting a tattoo, start to finish, including the sketching. Though we were sort of cheating — Joel already had an idea of what she wanted and had sketched a draft that she'd approved in advance so we could expedite things. I smiled to myself, looking forward to spending the day with him, wondering how it would feel to work that closely with him for an entire day after last night.

"Thanks, Paul," Laney said into the receiver. "Yeah, no problem." She set her phone down on the desk and leaned back in her chair. "What's all that?" She nodded to the box.

"Paperwork for my parents' retirement. Joel offered to help me with it."

"Look at you, making friends," she said snidely.

I frowned. "God, what's with you? I mean, you were practically pushing me into his lap when we started this."

Her face softened. "I know. It was funny, seeing you all worked up, but I'm now convinced it's a terrible idea."

"I wasn't worked up."

"Whatever you say, Annika. You know how I feel about it. What's on deck today?"

I let out a breath in an attempt to let her judgments go. "Joel's big tattoo segment. Tomorrow I have interviews. And Shep relinquished a key to Ramona's place for a scene we're planning to do with him setting up a romantic dinner at her apartment, but I sent a PA to copy the key and go over there to wreak havoc."

Laney laughed. "I like it. What's the plan?"

"Take a pair of Penny's shoes and hide them here in the office in the hopes that she blames one of the other girls for stealing them. Throwing out food in the fridge marked for Veronica. Taking Ramona's toothbrush. That sort of thing."

"Great. Where are you at with Veronica and Patrick?"

This was one of the topics I wasn't crazy about. "There's not much there. Patrick's living with his girlfriend now, and they're rock-solid. Veronica doesn't seem too hung up on it, either. I've pressed her in her interviews, but I really don't think anything's there."

"Maybe you should make something, then."

"This wasn't supposed to be that kind of show."

She sighed. "I know, but it's like a disease. I can't help but see the weak spots and try to exploit them. It's been years of conditioning, and you have to admit, it would make good TV."

"It would, but let's just focus on conflict outside of the store instead of creating conflict in it."

"That works for me," she conceded without a fight.

I relaxed a hair. "Thank you."

"For now."

I gave her a look.

"Don't give me that. We need a hit, you know that."

"I do, and I think we have one. You're right, they're going to love Joel and the shop. They'll get to learn, see a little drama. It's going to be great."

"They're going to want a lot of drama. But that's what Hal is for."

I took a breath and let it out. "Right." The word was far less emotional than it felt. It sounded apathetic, which was a massive crock of shit. And I was tired of feeling like I didn't have control over my own show.

I snapped my computer closed as if I could leave my discomfort there, in a spreadsheet or an email or somewhere harmless where it couldn't do damage.

"I'd better get down there to make sure everything's set up. I'll see you later."

"Let's do dinner tonight. How does cold pizza on our desks sound?"

I chuckled. "Sounds like heaven. Let's see if we can make it work. Have your people get in touch with my people."

"I'll pencil you in."

I waved at her over my shoulder as I walked out and headed downstairs, feeling a little raw. Mostly because Laney was right after all. Joel was already clouding my judgment, and I didn't think the problem was going to get any easier.

Downstairs in the shop, everyone was already bustling. Crew hurried around testing lighting and cameras. The shop had been cleared for the day so we could focus on Joel alone without any other noise, since we couldn't edit any background chatter out. I answered a few questions from various crew when I came in about positioning, timing, running any ideas they had by me. But I got away as quickly as possible, heading to the back room where I was hoping to find Joel.

I wasn't disappointed. He sat in a makeup chair, looking a little sullen as a girl dabbed his face with foundation. I tried not to laugh. I also tried not to let the sight of him rattle me. His hair was neatly combed, the line of his hard part bright against his dark hair, and he sat straight up in the chair, filling it to the brim, making it look tiny in comparison to his broad shoulders and muscular arms. He wore a

Henley, the top buttons undone, the sleeves pushed up his forearms, the taper of his waist apparent even sitting down.

Gorgeous, hairy bastard.

His eyes found me in his periphery, though he didn't move his head.

"Morning," I said, stepping around the makeup artist, clipboard in hand. I didn't realize that his client was already there, and I paused, surprised. In part because she was much prettier than I remembered.

Her hair was platinum blond and tied in a knot on top of her head, though her roots were dark, which somehow looked purposeful and cavalier rather than unkempt. Her features were all big, except her nose, which was pierced in several places, including a large septum ring. Sitting next to Joel, she looked like she belonged in his world — an alternative girl with gauges and surface piercings, tattoos, combat boots. And there I stood across from him in black and white, tailored and pristine, heels and hair tight and impeccable, about as cavalier as a judge.

I smiled at her, and I knew it looked genuine, though it was a lie of massive proportions.

"June, right?"

"Yeah," she answered with a wide smile.

"Are you two ready for today? It'll be a long one, but I think it'll be worth it."

Joel had a strange look on his face, though he was smiling. "Oh, yeah. I'm ready. Are you?"

I just kept on smiling. "I was born ready. Can I get either of you anything before we start?"

June shook her head, and Joel said, "I'm good," unable to move with the dabbing still happening.

"All right, just let me know if that changes. So the first thing we'll do is film June walking into the shop a few times, greeting you, Joel, behind the counter. Shake hands, and then June, I want you to tell Joel what you're looking for. We'll stop there and I'll go over the next steps again, but that's really the most talking you'll have to do. After that it'll just be getting the work done. I'll be asking you questions as we go." I looked them both over, unnerved again at how different she and I were, even though we could have been related, we looked so much alike. "Any questions?"

June looked to Joel, shaking her head. The dabbing had stopped, so he shook his head too.

"Great. Then let's get going, if you're all set, Kyla?" I asked the makeup artist.

"They're ready for you, Annika."

"Perfect. Come on, you two." And with that, we walked into the front of the shop, and I took my seat next to the director of photography, who was geared up with his camera and ready to roll.

Everyone milled around for a moment, getting last minute instructions, including June, who had a PA instructing her on where to go and what to do one more time.

I felt Joel all around me as he laid one hand on the arm of my chair and the other on the back, his fingers brushing my shoulder as he leaned into my ear.

"I hope your night was better than mine, because mine was terribly lonely."

I tried not to grin down at my clipboard, biting my bottom lip to stop myself. "Can't say that mine was any better."

He laughed, a single simple sound through his nose, but he was smiling, I could feel it. "Good. I'd hate to think I was the only one. Come back tonight."

I leaned away and turned to look at him, speaking loudly enough to not look secretive. "Oh, I brought the ledgers for you to take a look at. Maybe we could start tonight?" One of my brows rose, hoping he got that I was leading him.

He straightened up and smiled down at me. "Sure. Bring it by my apartment whenever you're finished with work for the day and I'll take a look."

"Mr. Anderson?" one of the PAs called, and Joel turned to him. "Can I get you behind the counter here? We just want to test the lighting one more time."

"Sure," he said, and I tried not to stare at him as he walked away, smiling to myself that I knew what was etched on every inch of his skin. But I looked toward June so I wouldn't give myself away about Joel and found her watching him too with her bottom lip between her teeth.

Jealously flared in my chest, and I felt my blood simmer. I took a breath to stave off the blush climbing up my neck and turned my eyes to the clipboard in my lap, flipping through the pages without actually looking at anything. In the back, I found my dick drawing of him that I'd done what felt like ages before, which made me feel somehow a hundred times better.

"Places," I called after a second, and everyone scattered, quieting down. "And, action."

The cameras rolled, and June entered the shop, smiling. I watched her long legs span the entry, extending her hand to take his. They were both smiling. Smiling and touching hands. She tucked her hair behind her ear, and the action made me want to get up and push her.

Four times we recorded it, though it was perfect the first. Then we moved on to June sitting across from him in the waiting area, looking at his sketches, still nodding and smiling. It was ridiculous — she wasn't coming on to him, but her body language told me she was into him. His was neutral, which somehow upset me. I don't know why, but I thought he'd shut her down hard, make sure she knew there was absolutely nothing between them. It would make terrible television, and I imagined me having to pull him aside and tell him he had to at least pretend to be somewhat interested in her, but he did exactly what I needed him to. And for some reason, that pissed me off.

We turned around to our secondary setup around Joel's booth and filmed him walking up with the transfers, with tight shots of him putting on his black latex gloves with multiple cameras, setting up his station. Then shots of June taking off her shirt and lying on her stomach on the table. Makeup had given her a sticky bra to wear, but it did little to hide the fact that she was pretty much naked from the waist up.

She laughed, her nose wrinkling up as he laid the long transfer — a single black line that ran from her tailbone to her hairline — on her spine and wet it down. We recorded it all. Him smiling, asking if it was too cold, her laughing and saying it tickled, me grinding my teeth to dust next to the camera. Then the second transfer, a fractal design, was applied, spurring off the line of her spine and up her shoulder. Then a third, spurring down in the opposite direction and around her hip. It was a huge piece, but it was composed only of lines, all the same width, in a pattern that was somehow fluid and linear, delicate and masculine. It was beautiful, hugging the curves of her body, turning her into a canvas.

She stood and looked using two mirrors to make sure it was placed where she wanted, though she told Joel she trusted him, to which I replied, *Cut!*

Joel smirked and gave me a look that said he knew exactly what I was thinking. I tried not to stare at his bottom lip when he swept it into his mouth with his tongue.

I was unsuccessful.

June stretched out on the table again, her face turned toward the cameras, worry creeping in as Joel took his seat and rolled up to the chair.

"All right," he said, his voice deep and comforting. "Just tell me if it gets to be too much and we'll take a break. Wrap your arms around the underside of the chair and hang on."

Seriously, everything he said sounded sexual, and I couldn't even deal with it.

She nodded, her smile gone, lips pinned between her teeth.

"You ready?"

She nodded again as he picked up his gun and turned it on. She flinched at the sound.

"Okay, June. Take a deep breath and let it out."

She did, her back rising and falling.

"Good girl."

He dipped the needles in a black ink cup and started at the bottom of the line on her spine. The second the needles made contact, her eyes widened, face ashen, her arms tensing around the bench.

"You okay?" he asked.

"Mmhmm," was all she could muster, the sound muffled, her lips a tight line between her teeth, where they'd stay for hours.

He worked his way up the line, the only sound in the room the buzzing of the gun. We'd cut the segment down to probably thirty seconds, but we'd record the whole thing and time lapse it, cutting in the questions I had prepped and anything else I came up with on the fly.

"So," I started once he was midway up her back and moving quickly, "what are the challenges of this kind of tattoo?"

Joel dipped the needles in the cup and picked up where he left off, wiping the ink and blood away with a paper towel as he went. "Line art is some of the hardest tattooing to do, especially things like this, geometric designs." Buzz. Press. Wipe. Repeat. "Straight lines, essentially freehand?" His eyes were on his hands, though his speech didn't seem overly focused on what his hands were doing. "Getting straight lines is one of the most difficult things any artist will do. It takes a lot of practice, a lot of patience. One tremble of your hand and you blow out a line, and there's no undoing that."

"How do you get good at it without messing up?"

He chuckled. "All of us mess up, it's just a fact of life. Doesn't matter your profession."

I offered a small laugh at that. "True enough."

Press and wipe. Dip the gun. Poor June looked a little green.

"Most of us learned by practicing on bananas."

"Bananas?"

"Yeah, or oranges. But bananas work best. The skin is tough and porous, smooth, too. If you can make a straight line on a banana, skin should be pretty simple. You can buy pig skins to practice on too, which is almost identical to human skin in terms of how it takes ink and moves under your fingers." He dipped the gun in ink again. "Still doing okay, June?"

"I think so." Her voice was thin.

"Okay. Let me know. Don't be a hero — no need to puke in the middle of the shop with Annika's cameras rolling."

Everyone would have chuckled if they hadn't been trained into silence. Instead, they glanced around and pursed their lips to stop themselves.

"June," I said, "are you able to answer questions?"

She paused for a second as he pressed the buzzing needles into her back. "I don't know." Her voice was thin, touched with trepidation.

Joel paused, his brow dropping. "June, look at me."

Laboriously, she turned her head, and he tilted his so it was angled the same as hers, looking into her eyes like he was diagnosing her. When he looked up, he didn't look happy.

"Somebody go grab me a cool washcloth from the back, a glass of water, and some crackers."

The PAs glanced at each other before springing into action as Joel turned his machine off and set it on his tray.

"Come here," he said softly, helping her to sit. "Did you eat today?"

She shook her head, chin tipping down like she was swallowing down a burp. "I was too nervous."

He chuckled. "This is one of the most painful places to get a tattoo, especially for a skinny little thing like you." His hand was on her arm, and he peered into her eyes in a way that made me want to stab him in his.

He was just being a good guy. Taking care of a client. I thought about when the light knocked me out and realized he probably would have done that for anyone. And that realization made me feel insignificant.

The PAs came scurrying back in, one with a bottle of water, another with crackers, and the third with the washcloth and a bag of ice. The foresight gained a solid nod from Joel, and he helped get a little food in her belly, holding the washcloth and ice on her neck while she nibbled the crackers.

After a few minutes, the color was back in her cheeks, and she was ready to go again. I tried to think about it in terms of ratings. Half-naked girl almost passes out on the table, Joel takes care of her like the hero he is. It would be an adorable, swoony blip in an episode. Laney would love it.

It was a win on all counts except the one in my achy chest. He'd barely even looked at me since he'd gotten started. *He's working,* I told myself. *You're being ridiculous,* I chided. *Get a fucking grip, Belousov,* I said in my head, honest to God wondering what was the matter with me. I'd never been jealous before, and it made me feel terribly petty and disgusting.

The only thought that set me back on course was that I'd screw his brains out later and show him exactly why girls like me were exactly what he needed.

My heart skipped a beat.

Joel had turned me into an animal. A jealous, feral animal. And I didn't completely hate it.

FIRE AND ICE

Annika

THE TATTOO SESSION LASTED JUST over three hours, and I kept my cool, reminding myself every time I got weird that I would, in fact, have his naked body in front of me within a matter of hours.

My eyes lasered in on where he touched her skin, thinking about his hands on *my* skin, cranking up my body heat through the course of the day. What I'd do to him when I got my hands on him played in loops, changing every time. There was so much I wanted from his body, and I didn't know just how much time I had left. I mean, if the show was picked up for another season, we could repeat the process again, but the thought of walking away from him before I was satisfied narrowed my eyes and sped up my heart.

Somehow, the genial smile stayed on my face, and I asked them both questions, her about her piece, him about his process, the tools he used, all the classics. We recorded the reveal of her tattoo in the mirror a handful of times, though I know we'd use the first, her tear-filled eyes, fingers pressed to her lips and nose as she whispered its perfection.

Joel smiled, lips together, arms folded, looking relaxed, like this was just something he did every day, nothing new. But I could feel the pride radiating off of him. It was the same feeling we'd talked about with my tattoo — her happiness was tangible. I definitely didn't feel that way when I'd gotten mine, and I considered asking him to draw something up for me after all, wanting to see that pride on his face, happiness on my own, something we could share. His mark, on me.

I was overwhelmed by the thought and cleared my throat. "June, let's get you two saying goodbye and then I think we'll wrap for the day." I was glad we were still rolling, because she smiled and nodded before bounding into Joel's arms, her brows together and eyes pinched closed.

He looked a little surprised, eyes widening just a touch as he wrapped tentative arms around her. I couldn't even be jealous — the embrace was so pure and genuine that I found myself smiling and warmth blooming in my chest.

They walked to the door where we went through a few rounds of her thanking him, walking out, waving, smiling. And then, we cut. The crew milled around for a while, moving back to the makeup room where the table of food stood, everyone wiped from the long day of filming, though I knew the editing crew was just gearing up to run all night upstairs.

I could barely breathe the same air as Joel, circling around him like a magnet, keeping that invisible barrier between us so I wouldn't give myself away. Instead, I made myself busy with directing everyone on what to do next, even though they mostly knew. June left. The crew began to disperse, the cameramen taking their gear upstairs to pass off, the engineers storing equipment, the PAs cleaning up. Joel walked up with a sandwich in each hand, offering one when he reached me.

I waved it off, my heart thumping. Zero chill. He's stripped me of my ability to be professional. "I'm good, thanks."

He shrugged and took a bite of his. "Did you bring the ledgers?"

"I did," I said, thankful for the light topic.

He smiled at me, a small, salacious turn of his lips. "Bring your box to me, Annika." The words were low and hot, tinged with amusement, and I felt myself blushing.

I mirrored his smile. "I will when I'm ready."

He turned to walk away, but his eyes were on my lips. "See you in a few then."

I let out a breath, annoyed and turned on: the familiar cocktail of Joel I found myself craving. And then I spent a little too much time watching him walk away.

I gave some final instruction to the lead PA and walked toward the door, past a smirking Hairy, who watched me like he was thinking about all those dirty things he'd do to me just as I had been all day. And I tried to keep my body in check as I hurried up the stairs and into my office for the box with every neuron in my brain firing Joel's name.

But Laney was there, sitting at her desk with an open box of pizza in front of her.

"Oh, good. Right on time," she said, reaching for a slice. "It just hit room temperature."

I reached for the box of ledgers and smiled at her, turning for the door. "Can't, sorry. I ate downstairs — long day."

I heard her pizza hit the box as she tossed it back in. "Hold up, really? Just like that?"

When I looked back, she was dusting off her hands, frowning. "Sorry, Laney. Joel needs to get started on these tonight if we have any hope of getting with a financial advisor next week."

"So come back up here after you drop them off."

My face gave nothing away, my mask firmly in place. "I've got to show him what's up and down. I mean, he can't even read them — they're in my mother's handwriting. In Cyrillic."

She ran her tongue over her teeth behind her lips. "Convenient. Have you slept with him yet?"

"That's not the plan, like I mentioned," I answered, avoiding a direct answer.

"Sure would be easy to convince him to meet with Hal."

"Oh, so now you want me to sleep with him? Make up your mind, already. You're giving me whiplash."

"What I want is to see that you have a plan that makes sense."

I shifted the heavy box in my arms. "My plan is to run the show. And running the show has very little to do with Joel. Past that, does it matter?"

155

She didn't answer.

"Don't you trust me at all?"

She considered the question for a second. "I do trust you, but —"

"Then maybe you could act like it. Because whatever this is, it's getting old." And with that, I turned and walked out of the office, through the busy control room, and out the door, more ready for the escape of Joel's body than I had been all day.

Down the stairs I flew, finding myself in the empty stairwell with my heart clanging, suddenly unsure that he'd be home. I wondered what I'd do with myself if he wasn't. My fingers ached from the heavy box as I shifted, propping it against the wall with my hip so I could knock on the door.

The sound of his boots from the other side of the door could have been a chorus of angels, it was so sweet.

When the door opened, I all but shoved him out of the way, dropping the box on the table with a thunk before whirling around to face him as he closed the door, my fingers already unbuttoning my blouse.

"Take off your pants."

His eyes twinkled, and he smirked but obeyed. My eyes were on his hands as he unfastened his belt. I pulled off my blouse and dropped it, moving on to my pants as he kicked off his boots and dropped his own pants to the ground. I stepped into him, slipping my hands under his shirt, my mouth angled up to his.

"Naked. I want you naked."

His breath was hot on my face as he reached behind him, momentarily disappearing through the neck, reappearing again as he tossed it away. And then I took a breath as I closed the small distance between us, my mouth clashing against his, his warm skin under my palms. His hands wound around my bare hips and lower back, pulling me into him. And it felt so good. I wanted him even closer.

One hand snaked up my back, flicking the snap of my bra, and I didn't let our lips disconnect as I took it off and let it fall, not considering the scrap of lace and underwire again, not once my naked breasts pressed against his chest. I found myself panting and writhing against him, so I turned and moved us toward his bedroom, my hands against his chest, pushing him toward his bed, his hands on my face and in my hair as he let me guide.

We stopped when he hit the foot of the bed, and I pushed him, half playing, half as serious as a heart attack. He fell back on the bed with a bounce, his long, tattooed body stretched out, propped on his elbows, waiting to see what I'd do. He didn't have to wait long — I hooked my thumbs in the band of my panties and pushed them down my legs, climbing onto the bed as I stepped out of them, pulling Joel's underwear down as I brought my lips to his crown as soon as it was visible, making no pomp about it, just wanting him in my mouth. I took him deep, my eyes closed and body rocking, reveling in the feeling of his hands in my hair, squeezing until it almost hurt. But it didn't hurt. It felt like everything I needed.

I let him go and crawled up his body, laying the line of me against the length of him, my hands on his rock solid chest, bracing myself as I rolled my hips. My lip was between my teeth, heart pounding, and I moaned, already close without even having him inside of me.

I climbed off of him before I did something stupid, reaching for his nightstand, where I knew he kept condoms. I came back until I hovered over him, knees pressed into the bed next to his waist, thighs parted, my shaking hands ripping open the condom and rolling it onto him as quickly as I could. And then I lifted him by his base and lowered my hips until he pressed against me, then into me. Neither of us breathed as I sank and sank, deeper and deeper until our bodies were connected completely, and we both drew a breath, letting it out with a sigh from the sheer relief of the sensation.

I leaned forward, my hands finding his hard chest again, elbows locked, my breasts squeezed between my biceps as I lifted my hips. He slipped out of me slowly, though I didn't let him go, just let gravity bring me back down.

His hands found my hips and squeezed.

My thighs trembled as I did it again, lifting my ass, dropping back down faster, rolling my hips when they were against his once more.

The feeling was so divine, I didn't want it to end. Ever. His strong body lay beneath me, the hard length of him inside me, his big hands on my hips, letting me do what I wanted. And my body rocked, humming with satisfaction at the sensation, the want and the need for him keeping my pulse thumping in my ears. I opened my eyes, wanting to see his face — his eyes were hot, lids heavy, full lips parted and hair mussed.

My gaze locked on his lips, so plump and wet, and I hinged over, bringing myself flush against himt, forearms against his chest and shoulders, hands splayed on the side of his face, and I kissed him. I took his lips like I took the rest of him, controlled and demanding as much as it was free and compliant. But the longer we kissed, the less control I had. His hands were on my ass, guiding me, and I wondered if I'd ever had control in the first place.

One hand found my hip again, the other slipping between my cheeks. His fingertips touched where we met, touched us, feeling both as he slammed into me, pulled out of me, again and again. He slipped two fingers around himself at the seam of our bodies in a V, flexing them gently against me. I moaned, my body speeding toward the edge.

I whispered his name, a plea.

His fingers slipped away, and he dragged his hand up, back between my cheeks, the tips of his fingers slick and hot, and before I knew what was happening, he slipped one into the tight hole and flexed gently.

I gasped, the sensation unfamiliar and satisfying, sending adrenaline through me in a shot like lightning. And within a second, I came unraveled, my body exploding and contracting, my breath frozen, heart stopped. The orgasm pulsed through my entire body, my toes curling, hamstrings tightening, bringing my calves up to the backs of my thighs. I gasped for air, my body still squeezing him inside of me, his hands still rocking me against him, knowing I wasn't finished, though my body had abandoned all function other than the one, only the one.

He moved to sit, taking me with him, cupping my face, taking

Tonic

my lips, and I was helpless, caught in a haze. He rolled us over, our bodies never separating, though he pulled my thigh into his ribs, holding it there as he pumped his hips. My head lolled to the side, eyes closed, my body still shuddering and heavy, nose brushing the edge of his wrist bracing him. I lifted my chin, parting my lips, closing them over his skin, dragging my tongue, closing my teeth to nip him.

His hand on my thigh tightened, his pace speeding, his breath heaving, and he came, slamming into me hard, head dropping down, his hair tickling my exposed neck. He buried his face in my neck, and I wrapped my arms around him, skating fingers around his back as it rose and fell with his breath. We lay there for a long while, long enough for him to turn his head so he could breathe easily with his cheek pressed against my chest, and my fingers danced across his back in wide loops and gentle turns.

When he spoke, the words rumbled through me. "You smell good."

I laughed. "After the long day and … *that*? I doubt it."

He turned his sleepy face to run his nose against my skin, inhaling. "You do. Like some flower, but I haven't been able to figure it out. Magnolia?"

I smiled up at the ceiling. "Gardenia."

"Yes," he said, the single syllable full of relief at knowing. "It's been driving me crazy, trying to figure it out." He nestled into my neck, and I found myself smiling.

My fingers spread flat against the smooth, hard curves of his back, hands sliding in opposite directions as I squeezed him.

He hummed. "Remind me to make you jealous more often."

My hands stilled. "I don't know what you're talking about."

Joel laughed, lips closed, and kissed my neck. "Sure, princess. Whatever you say."

I frowned. "Who would I be jealous of?"

He lifted his head, propping it on his hand so he could look down on me. He was smirking. Stupid, hairy smirker. "You're really going to deny it?"

"Deny *what* exactly, Joel?"

"You are. You're going to pretend like you didn't want to grab poor unsuspecting June by the hair and throw her out of my shop."

I smoothed my face. "Did I think she was attracted to you? Absolutely. Don't tell me you didn't see it."

He was still smirking as his hand trailed down my ribs, to my hip. "Nice try. Don't try to turn it around on me. It drove you crazy, didn't it?"

I felt the flush, this time angry. Because he could see right through me — there was no hiding from Joel. "If the tables had been turned, would it have driven you crazy?" I asked, still evading.

His eyes were green, with flecks of blue and gold shooting out from his pupils like starbursts, but they darkened at the question. "Without a doubt. And if he'd had his hands on you all day like I did June, I would have considered breaking every one of his fingers that touched your body. If I even gave him the chance to touch you in the first place."

I swear to God, my body physically responded, his words hitting me low in my body, in my lungs that drew a shallow breath. "You're a brute," I whispered, wishing that fact didn't turn me on so very much.

He leaned in. "I am. Unapologetically. And you hate that you love that about me."

Transparent, translucent, like the ice that I was. Freezing him out would never work, not when he could see the fire in my heart.

His lips were against mine, sweeping all other thought away, and for a long time, we just lay there, tangled up in each other, kissing like we had no other purpose. When he broke away, I sighed, wishing the rest of the world would just go away. But it wouldn't.

Joel moved my hair from my face, peering down at me. "We should get started on those ledgers."

I drew I another breath, trying not to sigh, but I just didn't want to. I wanted to lay there, wrapped up in Joel. "I suppose we should."

He rolled over and climbed out of bed, and I watched him with unabashed appreciation. Tattoos. Everywhere. Well, not *everywhere*, and thank goodness for that. A tattooed dick would be terrifying. But his sculpted back, ass, thighs ... all of him covered in ink that told stories, gave glimpses into his heart and soul. It was the most intriguing thing I'd maybe ever seen. I wondered if I'd have enough time to memorize the patterns on his skin, and my heart squeezed in my chest.

"Need something to wear?" he asked as he pulled on a pair of slate gray sweats, and I mourned the loss of the view.

I stretched and yawned, rolling onto my back. "I brought stuff."

He looked over his shoulder at me with one brow up and the other side of his lip raised. "You're staying?"

I sat and swung my legs over the side of the bed. "I mean, we have so much *work* to do."

He snorted as he left the room, heading toward the bathroom. "You have no idea how much."

I chuckled and walked through the apartment and to the kitchen where I'd tossed my bag, which was heavy with a smaller bag inside full of rolled up clothes. I set it on the table and unzipped it, revealing neat little rows of fabric — pajamas, panties, and a skirt and top for tomorrow.

Joel chuckled from behind me. "I bet your sock drawer looks like an advertisement for Ikea."

I grabbed my pajamas, another sheer, muslin tank and short set, though this one was black. "I don't really have a designated sock drawer, but if I did, yes, it would."

"You can't stand a mess, can you?"

I stepped into my shorts, seeing no point in being modest. "No. I can't."

"Then don't look in my sock drawer."

I chuckled as I pulled on my top and turned for the bathroom. "Deal."

He caught me around the waist as I passed and pulled me into his chest, kissing me once, sweetly, before letting me go again with a burning look and a smirk, saying nothing. And I did my best to calm the flurry of butterflies in my chest, trying to ignore the little voice in the back of my mind that whispered that I'd crossed an uncrossable line, and I couldn't go back.

GIRL

Joel

WHEN SHE CAME BACK A few minutes later, I was already at the table with the ledgers stacked in front of me, working on sorting them. But there was nothing I could do — all of the markings on the ledger covers were in Cyrillic.

She twisted her hair into a bun as she took a seat next to me.

"I can't read any of these, Annika," I said with a frown, wondering how I was going to be of any use.

She smiled and reached into her bag for a little notepad and pen. "Don't worry. It's not too hard."

My brow dropped, very much doubting that. But she jotted out a series of lines and squiggles, noting each one with the Western numbers they represented before ripping off the page and lying it between us.

"Here's your decoder."

I found myself frowning. "This is going to take forever if I have to translate the numbers."

"Only at first. You'll get the hang of it, I promise. Plus, that's why I'm here."

I sighed. "Okay. Let's start by getting these in order by year."

She reached for the first stack, and I tried not to look down her loose tank as it hung down, exposing her through the draping. I was unsuccessful and unremorseful, suddenly wishing we were finished here and back in my bed.

Annika flipped through the first stack. "I'll tell you the years and you can keep them in order. Do you have Post-Its?"

My brow quirked as I thought about if there were any in my apartment. "Uh …"

"Don't worry," she said as she reached into her bag. "I've got some." When her hand reappeared, it held hot pink sticky notes, and she passed them to me.

"What else do you have in there? A lamp, maybe?"

She smirked. "And a carpet. I also have ruler tape that will tell me exactly how you measure up."

I smirked back. "I'm curious to see what that would say. I'm betting *Practically Perfect in Every Way.*"

She chuffed. "More like *Rather Inclined to Giggle, Doesn't Put Things Away.*"

"I don't giggle, I chortle."

Annika laughed, that glorious sound, and I continued on.

"And I like to think I'm pretty tidy."

"For a hairy brute, I suppose I'd agree."

"Yours would definitely say *Extremely Stubborn and Suspicious.*"

She shook her head, though her eyes were on the ledgers as she sorted them in front of her. "Why am I surprised that you can quote *Mary Poppins*? You'd think I was immune to surprise, when it comes to you." She handed me the first ledger. "1994."

I jotted the date on the note and stuck it to the cover of the book, setting it aside. "It was Shep's favorite movie when we were kids. Don't tell anyone."

She laughed and passed me another book. "2002. You just told the producer for your show, *Don't tell anyone*," she said, chuckling again.

I wanted to laugh, seeing the humor, but something about it hit me funny. "So, we're not off the record?" I labeled it and set it next to the other one.

Something flickered across her face. "1990. We are and we aren't. Do you really object to me bringing up Mary Poppins to Shep? I'd really like to try to convince him to do the chimney sweep dance on camera."

"No." I labeled it and slipped it under the '94 ledger. "But I'd like to think most of this is private."

"2010. It is." She reached for another as I wrote the number. "Just not *all* of it."

"'96. Joel, I wouldn't ever exploit you like that."

I took the ledger and wrote the number, not offering a response.

"Hey," she said as she rested her long fingers on my forearm. I met her eyes, which were honest and open. "I mean it. I'll even swear not to say anything unless I've passed it by you. No matter how trivial."

"I believe you."

Her hand flexed, and she smiled. "Thank you for that. And thank you again for your help with this." She let me go and gestured to the stacks.

"You're welcome. I'm just glad I have something to offer in the way of help."

"That you do. 2012."

I smiled and labeled it.

We dug into the work, spending several hours getting everything sorted and organized, working through the ledgers together, absorbed in the work until Annika was yawning with every sentence she spoke.

I stacked up the book we were pouring over — 2015 — and pushed back from the table.

"Come on. Let's go to bed."

She sighed, looking over the books with an air of defeat, something I was unaccustomed to from her. "It's just so much. I wonder if I've bitten off more than I can chew."

I knelt down next to her chair and cupped her face, turning it to mine. Her hand hung on my forearm as she looked down at me.

"You haven't. We'll get it done."

Her face softened at that, and she leaned into my hand.

"Now, come to bed," I said softly, and she turned her face to press a kiss into my palm.

Snow was cold, fire was hot, and I couldn't walk away from

Annika like I'd promised her I would. The facts were as black and white as math, with no room for debate.

I wondered fleetingly if we would ruin each other. If my fire would melt her ice until it evaporated. If her ice would snuff my fire out of existence.

I pushed all of that down, deep down into my chest, and I kissed her. Because I had that moment. Later would figure itself out.

When I broke away, I took her hand, and she followed me wordlessly through the apartment. I flicked off the lights on the way through the apartment and guided her to my bed. I reached for the lamp, throwing us into darkness, and we slipped silently under the covers, into each other's arms. The weight of her, the warmth of her, familiar and foreign. I found comfort in her after a thousand nights alone. Because I'd been alone, even though I hadn't, not really, only finding momentary reprieve in women who I would never hold through the night. Women who I never considered keeping for more than the moment. It was easier that way.

With Annika in my arms, I realized just how easy it had been, how smart it had been to close my heart. Because when you opened your heart, you put it on the line. And my heart was most definitely on the line, exposed, raw against the touch of unfamiliar air.

It was stupid and reckless, and I didn't care. One day, I probably would. But until then, I'd revel in the feeling, the exhilaration of her.

This was my last cognizant thought, and I sealed it with a kiss in the dark. It was ownership without expectation, submission without consequence. It was her skin against mine, her heart and my own, our bodies together. It was a moment that stretched to an hour and into a night. And I knew I was lost, and she could never know just how lost I was.

Morning came too soon.

It was still dark when her phone chimed to wake her. I'd been awake, still and quiet, holding her in the dark, thinking. Thinking too much. But as soon as she opened her sleepy eyes, I smiled like I didn't have a thought in my brain past that very second.

We dressed for the day, chatting and smiling, eating bagels and drinking coffee around the stacks of books on my kitchen table. I leaned on the doorframe of my bathroom while she put on her makeup, watching fascinated under the guise of conversation as she leaned toward the mirror and darkened her long lashes. My eyes followed the angle of her body, the comical 'o' of her lips, even more enthralled as she twisted a tube of red lipstick and pressed the creamy pigment to her lips.

She was art. I wanted to draw her. My fingers itched to.

I had a flash of clarity — I realized just how deep the shit I found myself in went. And it went really, really deep.

I left first, scoping out the scene. The stairwell was empty, as was the shop, and even upstairs seemed more quiet than it did once things got going. So we parted before she left with a simple kiss before she walked down the stairs and onto the sidewalk, toward the coffee shop and away from me.

The distance felt like a chasm, and I was afraid of heights.

I closed the door with a snick and looked around my apartment. Ledgers on the table. Two coffee cups in the sink. Her makeup bag on my bathroom counter and clothes in my room. My bed rumpled, sheets still smelling of her.

"Fuck," I said to myself, raking a hand through my hair. And then I picked up my phone.

Tell me you're awake, I texted my brother.

Little dots bounced as he typed, and a breath, heavy with relief, slipped past my lips. *I am now.*

Good. I need to talk to you.

What did I do?

Nothing. It's what I did.

A pause. *What did you do?*

I ran a hand over my mouth. *Annika.*

That's not news, dude.

Just get up and come home.

No response.

I huffed as my fingers banged out a single word. *Please?*

Bouncing dots and a hallelujah chorus. *All right, all right. Be there in a bit.*

So I paced for a minute. Then I made my bed, erasing any visible remains of the night before. I did the dishes, putting our cups across from each other on the rack, like I could keep her out of my heart just as easily. But it was too late. I already knew that.

I'd never wanted anyone so viscerally before. That was the perfect word. Visceral. Animal. Deep and instinctive, beyond my ability to control. It wasn't love. Not yet, anyway. But if I didn't stop it right now, that's exactly where it would go. I could feel the allure of it pulling at my insides, twisting and squeezing to get my attention. As if I could ignore it.

God, how I wanted her. All day, every day, insatiably, selfishly — I wanted her. And more than anything, that scared me.

Years of convincing myself that I was fine. Years of loneliness. Fourteen long years of believing that love was too complicated, too rare to be real. Too rare to be mine. And then Annika walked through the doors of my shop and took a sledgehammer to everything I thought I knew.

Shep walked in looking sleepy and disheveled, closing the door behind him. He took a seat at the table and made to move a stack of ledgers.

"Whoa, don't touch those," I snapped, and he glared at me, lips frowning behind his beard.

"You really *are* wound up. Tell me there's coffee," he said as he folded his arms across his chest.

"There's coffee." I turned to pour him a cup and collect my thoughts. He let me have the silence, probably too tired to pry the truth out of me. I handed the mug over, and he grunted his thanks.

He watched me for a second, and I leaned against the counter, my turn to cross my arms.

"I'm not gonna beg for it, Joel." He took a sip and cursed when he burned his lip.

I chuckled. "That's what you get for being a smartass."

His glare sharpened.

I sighed. "Thanks for coming home. I just needed to talk."

"Then talk already." He took another, more tentative, sip.

"I'm in deep shit."

"How deep?"

"Bottomless."

He frowned. "Explain."

"I'm not really sure how to. That's part of the problem."

He kicked the chair across from him out a foot. "Sit and give it a shot."

I took the seat and propped my elbows on the table, slipping my hands into my hair. "I don't know how to explain it. She's under my skin, in my head, and I don't know what's happening or how to shake it. I don't know if I want to shake it."

Shep watched me, his mug in one hand, assessing me. "She's enough that you're willing to entertain the idea of actually being in a relationship?"

"Yes." The word stung coming out, like it held the power to set me on fire.

"And on the Liz scale?"

"Doesn't even register. Annika is a scale of her own, and it's stratospheric."

He thought about that for a second, though his face gave nothing away. "And what does she think of all this?"

"Haven't told her."

"So, what are you two doing?"

"Nothing, so far as we've said out loud. We're keeping it a secret — her boss thinks it's a bad idea. Laney's worried about me clouding Annika's judgment."

"I don't see how it couldn't."

"That's part of the problem."

"And what's the rest?"

I chewed my bottom lip for a second. "I told her not to think about me. To just do her job, do what she had to. That I wouldn't hold it against her. And that when it was over, we'd part ways like it never happened."

He sighed. "So, you lied."

I sighed in echo. "I lied."

"You're right. You are in deep shit."

"Deeper now that I'm realizing how much I care about her."

Shep rested his boots on the seat of the chair next to him. "What are you gonna do?"

"I don't know, man. That's why I needed to talk to you about it."

His jaw was set as he leaned back in his seat, propping his elbows on the arms of the chair, cupping his mug over his stomach with both hands. "Well, the way I see it, you have two options. Be with her or don't."

I rolled my eyes. "Deep, Shep."

He shrugged a shoulder. "Do you see a third option?"

"No, but it's not that simple. I don't want to put her job at risk, but I don't want her to lie to me. I want to trust her, but I don't know if I can or should. I don't know whether or not my blessing to treat me like a puppet was setting myself up to get hurt or a test to see if she'd hurt me."

"Probably both."

I let out a breath. "Probably both." I looked down at the surface of the table, and my eyes slipped out of focus. "What do I do?"

"Be with her or don't."

"It's not so black and white."

He shifted, setting his feet back on the ground as he leaned on the table toward me. "Sure it is. Do you want to be with her or don't you?"

I met his eyes, which were hard on mine. "You know I do."

"Then there's your answer."

"And what about the risk?"

"You've never been cautious before when you want something."

"But this is different. The fate of the shop is tied up in this. My heart is tied up in this, and so is hers. And what about the logistics? What if I can't deal with her or she hates me after it's all said and done? How do we keep working?"

"Man, fuck logistics. You like her. Like *really* like her, after years of being emotionally crippled." He shrugged again. "No pain, no gain. Right? No risk, no reward."

Pain surged in my chest. "And if she ruins me?"

Shep's eyes were sad. "Then that's the price you pay for knowing. And if she doesn't, then maybe you have a chance to find happiness. A chance to not be alone."

I nodded, swallowing the lump in my throat. "Well, then I don't really have a choice. Because now that I've had her, I want to keep her. I need to."

He smirked at me from across the table like he'd already known what I'd say and answered, "Well, then go get her."

GOOP

Annika

I FOUND MYSELF SMILING ALL damn day.

A cameraman screwed up a shot, and I didn't care. Laney was up my ass about Joel and Liz and Hal, and I just smiled. Joel watched me all day like I was a Michelangelo, and someone could have tarred and feathered me without being able to touch my mood.

Joel.

Joel, Joel, Joel.

Everything about him felt good. The way he looked at me. The way he touched me. The words that passed his lips and hit me in all the right places. I briefly thought back to the time when I thought he and I were nothing alike, had nothing in common. When I thought he was *wrong* for me.

I'd chuckled to myself at the idea, garnering a look from a PA. I didn't care about that either. Because Joel existed and wanted me, and it felt *good*. I felt good. Better than ever. Like a million bucks laid out on a mattress for me to roll around on.

Once the day was done, I met him in his apartment for 'work' on the ledgers, which we did. Eventually. But first, there was naked Joel and naked me and lots of smiling. My cheeks hurt, out of practice. A whole day of smiling. It was wrecking my Resting Bitch Face.

Didn't care about that either.

I laughed to myself again, and Joel smirked at me from across his kitchen table. I closed the ledger in front of me with a thump and sighed, sitting back in my chair with a yawn.

"It's late."

He closed his ledger too. "It is. Let's go to bed."

I smiled again. "Not tonight, Joel."

He honest to God pouted, that lush bottom lip of his sticking out comically.

"Oh, don't look at me like that. I've got to go home and shower."

He stood and walked around to sit on the table just in front of me. "I have a shower. A perfectly great shower with a massaging head."

"I'm sure it's divine, and I'd love to give it a shot, but I really do have to go home," I said lightly and stood. He pulled me into him, sliding his hands around my waist and down, coming to a stop on my ass.

"Why?" He nipped at my still-smiling lips, and I sighed, laying my hands on his chest.

"Because I need a change of clothes at least. I can't wear the same thing I wore yesterday to work or Laney will know."

He sighed.

"Plus, my *little lady* needs a rest."

"I thought you said not to call it that?"

I shrugged. "Well, it's mine, so I can call it whatever I want."

He smirked. "Kiss it and make it better?"

I giggled — I actually giggled like a teenager, and in the back of my mind, the ice queen slugged the teenager in the face. I gave Joel a peck on the smirk. "Tomorrow."

"There's no changing your mind?"

"Nope. But I'll stay tomorrow, if you'll have me."

He flexed his hands, effectively squeezing my ass with enough gusto to make my thighs clench. "Oh, I'll have you all right."

I rolled my eyes, not at all annoyed, kissing him on the cheek before attempting to pull away. But he pulled me back just as I stepped back, tugging me back into his chest for a kiss, a real one. A really real one, one that wavered my determination. But when I broke away, I found it again.

"Tomorrow."

He sighed again. "Tomorrow."

I made my way around the apartment, gathering my things, packing them away and more than a little disappointed about it. I didn't want to leave any more than he wanted me to, and I chased the fleeting thought that it should feel weirder than it did, the attachment to him. But it didn't feel weird at all. In fact, it felt perfectly natural.

It's like my mental alarm system was offline, leaving my heart ripe for burglary.

He'd followed me around, looking morose, leaning on door frames like James Dean, talking to me about nothing and everything, keeping me laughing as I packed, and when I finished up, I turned to where he stood, blocking me from leaving his room with a smirk on his face.

"Troll toll. Pay up," he said and leaned in for a kiss.

I happily obliged, leaning right back.

He broke away and took my hand, walking me to the door. "Let me know you made it home okay."

"I will."

"Tomorrow," he said, stopping us at the door before he opened it. And then he laid a kiss on my lips that seared through my body.

I broke away after a long, hot minute. "How do you do that?" I mumbled.

"Do what?"

"That. Turn me into goop."

He shrugged. "It's not hard. You're goopier than you think you are."

I rolled my eyes, but I was smiling still. Maybe permanently. "Goodnight, Joel."

"Goodnight, Annika."

He opened the door and leaned on the doorframe again as I walked away, and I didn't hear the door close until I'd hit the bottom landing.

Part of me wanted to run back up the stairs, but that would end up with me staying for hours, and I was dead on my feet. So I climbed into the car waiting for me and trained my eyes out the window, smiling silently at the city as we drove the distance between the Upper West and Park Slope.

When I unlocked my door and stepped inside, I was surprised to find Roxy still awake, sitting on the couch sketching. She glanced up, looking tired, but she smiled when she saw me.

"Hey. Didn't expect to see you tonight," she said.

I closed the door behind me and set my bag next to the stairs. "I didn't think I'd see you either."

"How's Hairy?"

"He's great. Just great." I sat next to her sideways and leaned on the back of the couch, kicking off my shoes before tucking my legs under me.

"Looks like it." She smiled as she assessed me. "How's it going with the ledgers?"

"It's going well. We've got half of the books translated by totals per month and should have the rest finished tomorrow, I hope. Then he'll start working on charting those while I dig deeper into the months themselves."

"That sounds terribly boring."

I chuckled. "Joel makes it more fun than it would be otherwise. What are you working on?" I asked, nodding toward her notepad.

She sighed and looked over her drawing. "Just gearing up for our next show. I'm not happy with some of the pieces in the collection and have been racking my brain to fix them. But I'm tired of that subject. That subject has consumed my brain for weeks. I'd much rather hear about Hairy." She leaned to lay her sketchbook on the coffee table and tucked in her legs, mirroring me.

I found myself grinning again. "God, Roxy. Look at me. He's turned me into a fool."

"I think he's just turned you *on*."

I laughed. "That too."

"So you slept over there last night?"

I propped my head on my hand, elbow on the back of the

couch. "I did, and woke up with him this morning. We worked together all day and then tonight on the ledgers."

"A solid thirty-six hours with the beast? Sounds dreamy."

"It was. I feel like a kid in a candy store, Rox."

"You look like one too. I don't think I've ever seen you like this. Not even with Paul DeMarco in the seventh grade."

"Well, Paul didn't have muscles, tattoos, a beard, *or* a sense of humor."

"Funny that 'hairy' is now in the *pros* column."

I smirked. "Funny, isn't it?"

She laughed. "Man, you really *do* have it bad."

I sighed, still smiling. "I really do."

"Does Laney suspect what's really going on?"

"Oh, without a doubt. But now I have the ledgers as an excuse to be seen with him outside of filming."

"Smart."

"I thought so."

Her smile fell a hair. "What are you going to do, though? About the show?"

My heart flexed, folding in on itself for a beat. "My job. But I'm the EP. I don't have to do anything I don't want to. And I don't want to hurt him. I don't want to betray him. So I'll find another way to do what I need to do, to get the drama that's demanded of me. But I'm not going to use Joel."

"What if you have to?"

"Then I'll tell him, and we'll get through it together."

She looked impressed. "Well, you seem to have it all figured out, then."

I smiled. "He's too good, too ... I don't know, Rox. I have no idea what it is about him that makes me so crazy, but I'm drunk off it. He's larger than life, full of lust for it, for me. It's like bingeing on ice cream, except you can't get fat."

Roxy laughed.

"I can't remember the last time I spent that much time with one person and didn't want to kill them. But I could have stayed tonight and been perfectly content."

"Why didn't you?"

"Because I know it's wise to take a break. Plus, I was out of clean panties."

She snickered. "I don't think he would have cared."

"No, he would have been just as happy if I weren't wearing any at all. But it's smart. I don't want Laney to know — she'll get in my head, pressure me to do something I don't want to."

"You really don't think she'll figure it out?"

"I'll tell her when the season is over, after I prove to her I can do what I need to without compromising my relationship."

"Well, I hope it works."

"Me too." The heart clench again, warning me that it wasn't as sure of a thing as I had convinced myself. "I need a shower so bad," I said as I hauled my tired body off the couch.

"Will I see you tomorrow?"

"In the morning, but I think I'm staying at Joel's again tomorrow night."

She waggled her brows, and I laughed.

"Night, Rox."

"Night, Anni," she sang from behind me as I scooped up my bag and headed up the stairs.

My room felt almost unfamiliar, as if I'd changed on a level so minuscule that I hadn't noticed until it effected my perception. Kaz mewed at me sleepily from my mattress, and I scratched his head, murmuring to him in Russian as I set my bag down next to him. The urge to sit was strong, but I knew once I did, I wouldn't get up again. So I sighed and headed to the bathroom where I closed the door and turned on the shower, truly alone for the first time in days.

I peeled off my clothes with my mind on Joel and the whirl of thoughts and feelings that accompanied him. He was like a hurricane, a force of nature, and I found myself swept up in him. It was strange, I thought as I tested the water streaming from the shower head, that I would be caught up in someone else. I'd always considered myself the strongest in every relationship I'd been in, requiring some level of submission strictly because of my ability to convince the other that it was necessary. It wasn't conscious, that drive, but I'd never met a man so wholly like me in that regard. And now that I had, I reveled in riding in the currents of him without having to dominate, in closing my eyes and just letting go.

THE BEAR AND THE FOX

Joel

I SAT AT MY DESK the next afternoon, working on the ledgers as I waited for my next client. The music was on, the shop running as it normally did, before the show at least, before Annika. It was strange, having Stone Temple Pilots playing after days of silence in the shop when we filmed. It was stranger still not having seen Annika all day.

She'd been working on interviews upstairs in the green room across from her office, and my artists had taken turns heading upstairs to talk to her. And I'd worked down here, tattooing and sketching, working on the ledgers when I could. My decoder lay next to the open ledger, a little crinkled and dirty after being handled so much over the last few days. But she had been right — I was starting to recognize the numbers that looked so much like letters, and what I found was strange.

I checked my numbers again, comparing them to the key to make sure I had them right. But I did, and I wasn't sure what to make of it.

I slipped the paper into the ledger I'd been working on and closed it when my next client arrived, going through the motions of greeting and transferring and needles and ink, though my mind was on Annika all the while.

The night before had been strangely lonely without her. It took me a long time to fall asleep, and I woke up earlier than usual, anxious to get downstairs to see her, even though I knew we wouldn't really see each other today. I held onto the thought that I'd see her tonight, that she'd stay the night, that I'd wake up with her in the morning. But it wasn't enough to make the clock move faster, and the minutes seemed to tick by, mocking me with every jump of the second hand.

I was the last to be interviewed, and I climbed the stairs to the control room, trying not to feel giddy. But I was. I felt fifteen years younger than I was, before I knew how hard life could be, when I still had hope in the idea that I'd be happy forever. I felt like nothing could hurt me, nothing could touch me, because I had her. Nothing bad could happen if I had her.

We shared a smile when I walked in, the relief at breathing her air almost tangible between us. She seemed lighter too, smiling more, happier. The ice had melted, and I'd found spring underneath, sprouting green and smelling of gardenia.

She kept it all business, asking questions that I answered readily, never pressing or pushing for more as I suspected she might. I'd been prepared for it — I'd told her to do her job, and I wanted her to. Within reason. But I was willing to bend, to give her something she could use as long as it wouldn't hurt me, and I'd redefined the perimeters of what I'd take offense to.

Once we were finished, the filming crew broke up and dispersed, and I approached her chair as she flipped through the pages of her clipboard.

I caught a glimpse of a drawing of a dick with a smirk and a beard, and I laughed.

"Is that supposed to be me?"

"If the shoe fits."

I took the clipboard from her and turned to the paper so I could inspect it, holding it out in front of me as I stroked my chin with my free hand. I shook my head as I handed it back.

"My beard's thicker than that."

She laughed freely, and I thought back to the time when I couldn't even make her smile, never mind kick her head back and actually *laugh*.

"So, I was working on the books today and found something … well, something I want to talk to you about. When are you finished here?"

She glanced at her phone to check the time. "In just a bit. It's an early night tonight — all we really had on the schedule were the interviews, and you were my last one."

"Good. I'm finished too. Meet me at my place."

Her smile held a spark of mischief. "I'll be down in a few."

I smiled right back, hoping she knew I was thinking about how far *down* she'd go. Judging by the blush that spread across her cheeks, I figured she did.

I left the green room, unwillingly catching the eye of Laney in her office. She nodded at me like she knew all my secrets as I passed, and I nodded right back, telegraphing that I didn't think she knew shit. Then down the stairs I went and into my apartment, heading to the ledgers to look over my notes again.

Shep had been staying at Ramona's by my request, and he didn't seem overly upset about staying gone. In fact, he didn't seem at all unhappy, but excited at the prospect, taking a suitcase with him like he was moving out. It hit me a little sideways, seeing him leave so willingly, but with Annika filling his place so fully, I wasn't at all sorry to watch him go.

I was double checking the numbers on my hand-drawn line graph when she knocked on the door.

"Come on in," I called through the door, and she walked in, sucking all the air from the room with her.

She was smiling, her cheeks rosy and eyes urgent as she closed the door behind her. I didn't know when I stood, but I found myself moving across the room toward her. She met me half way.

My hands were in her hair, my lips against hers without needing to command them, and she melted into me. I felt like I hadn't seen her in a week, like I hadn't kissed her in a year, like I hadn't breathed in a lifetime. So I breathed, sipping the sweet smell of her into my nose, tasting her lips, touching her petal-soft skin.

She hummed and broke away, looking up at me with smoldering eyes, smiling with her lips together and hands on my chest as she leaned into me.

"I missed you too," she said, her voice raspy and rough, and I laughed, brushing her cheek with my knuckles.

"As much as I can't wait to get you out of these clothes, I want to show you this first. Then I want to undress you slowly and get reacquainted."

She laughed. "You act like I didn't see you yesterday."

"Yeah, but I didn't *see* you."

"But you *saw* me three times the day before that."

I brushed my lips against hers. "I want to *see* all of you, all the time."

Another laugh, and I smiled, pulling away before I *saw* her right then.

"Come here," I said, taking her hand to pull her toward the table. I picked up the graph and handed it to her, looking at it with her over her shoulder.

"What am I looking at?"

"So, this shows the cash sales of the dry cleaners by month, over the course of the last five years. Look at this." I pointed to the peaks of the curve, happening every three months before dropping off like a heartbeat. "Every three months like clockwork, the cash flow skyrockets, then tapers off. I've never seen anything like it."

Annika didn't respond — her eyes were locked on the paper, and she was still and quiet as stone. So I kept talking.

"I was thinking that maybe they had a company they worked with, like uniform cleaning or something like that. Something that had them cleaning every three months. But it doesn't make sense. Places like that already exist just for laundering, and those kinds of companies wouldn't use cash, they'd use credit. There would be receipts or a trail, but this ... this has nothing. It doesn't make any sense to me."

She still didn't respond, so I just kept talking to fill the silence, figuring she just didn't understand quite what I meant.

"Do you have any ideas? Because this goes back all the way to when they opened the store. At some point in the late nineties, the cash would have dropped way off when people started using debit cards, but it doesn't. It's almost the exact same amount of money, every three months on the nose, like someone is dumping dirty money into the dry cleaners." I chuckled at the thought.

Her eyes were still on the paper as she stepped toward the table and pulled out a chair, sinking into it slowly.

My brows dropped. "Annika? What's the matter?"

She swallowed. "I think I know what's going on." She set the page on the table and looked up at me, and the worry and anger in her eyes alarmed me. My jaw clenched.

"Tell me." I sat next to her, resting my elbows on my thighs as I leaned toward her.

She nodded and took a breath. "They're laundering money."

I blinked. "Are you serious? I was just kidding. Why the hell would that be your first guess?"

"Because my uncle is in the Bratva."

More blinking as my mind raced to keep up. "As in the Russian mafia, Bratva?"

Another nod. I ran a hand over my mouth, whispering a swear.

"They can't sell their business, Annika. When they have the business and books appraised, it's going to be obvious that something's going on. These numbers aren't real."

She mumbled something angry in Russian, something that sounded like a curse.

I rubbed my face again, trying to figure out what I could do to help, but before I could come up with anything, she stood and turned for the door, grabbing her bag.

"I've got to go talk to them."

I stood and made to follow her. "I'll go with you."

She shook her head and turned, laying her hand on my chest when I reached her. "No. I don't want to drag you into this."

I gave her a look. "Nice try, princess. I'm coming with you."

"Why would they want to talk about money laundering with a stranger? There's nothing you can do, Joel." Her angry eyes bounced around my face, though I knew she wasn't angry with me, just angry in general. Her hopes had been dashed, and she'd been duped.

Tonic

The absolute last thing I wanted was for her to leave me like that, to face it all alone. She could have handled it, I had no doubt. But I didn't want her to be alone. I wanted to be there for her. So, I tossed the strongest excuses I could at her.

I rested my hand over hers against my chest and clasped her fingers. "Sure, I can. First of all, I already know what's going on — I'm the one who figured it out. And secondly, maybe someone was cooking the books for them and they didn't know, in which case I can help explain it to them. I can answer their questions and help you come up with a plan for them."

She didn't seem convinced.

"Then I can take you home and fuck your brains out."

She laughed at that, the tension unraveling just enough to let me in.

"Let me come with you. Let me be there with you." The words were soft with my real reason for wanting to go, and I touched her face.

She leaned in and looked up at me as her smile fell and the weight of the situation rested on her again. "All right."

I kissed her forehead. "Thanks."

"No, thank you. I'm sorry to have wasted your time with all this."

"It wasn't a waste of time. Think of all that *work* we got done."

She chuckled, and we headed out as she texted her driver to pick us up from Habits down the street, opting to duck into the bar for a shot of fortitude.

Within an hour, we pulled up to a row of red brick houses, each entry framed with a porch, with cheery yards and flower boxes on the rails. We thanked the driver and climbed out, and Annika fumed as we walked up the path to the door, walking in without knocking.

I hung back on the porch for a second, not as comfortable barging into her parents' house as she had been. She stopped a few steps in and turned when she realized I didn't follow, motioning me in.

I took a reluctant step across the threshold as she stormed toward the back of the house.

"Papa? Mama?"

Her father's voice boomed from the kitchen, whatever he said beyond my comprehension as it was in Russian, a cheery sound, even when tinged with confusion.

Annika responded as I caught up, her words biting and angry, faster than I could keep up with, not that I had any idea what she was saying.

Her parents looked mildly confused, their confusion deepening when they saw me step into the room behind her. Her father asked a question, and Annika glanced over her shoulder at me, her anger softening by a degree.

"Papa, this is Joel, a friend of mine," she said in English.

I extended a hand. "It's a pleasure to meet you, sir," I offered, not sure what else I could say, given the circumstance.

He smiled, the big, jovial man with a slate gray beard and a newsboy cap on his head. The point of the visit seemed to be forgotten, though her mother wrung her apron between her fists, her lip between her teeth.

"Ah, hello, my friend. I am Maxim, but my friends call me Max. And this is my wife, Dina."

She nodded, stepping forward to offer her hand. "Hello, Joel."

I took her hand and shook it. "Nice to meet you, ma'am."

Max took a deep breath before opening his hands to us. "Now, come. Sit."

He shepherded us into their dining room where we sat at the long table, though Annika was ramrod straight as she took her seat, her lips a thin line. Max assessed her coolly from the head of the table and touched his wife's hand where it rested on the surface.

"Dina, I think maybe *vodachka* may be in order."

I must have looked confused because he smiled at me and winked.

"Vodka." The word was heavily accented, the sound of it so right for the drink, and I felt like a fraud for pronouncing it so crassly for the entirety of my life. "Vodka helps us solve all our most pressing problems. Yes, Annika?"

"Yes, Papa," she answered, but the word was perfunctory — she slung it at him as Dina entered the dining room with four small glasses and a bottle of Stolichnyaya.

Annika didn't offer more, seeming to wait for her father to lead. But he didn't say anything, not until we all had a glass in front of us.

Max picked his up. "This is about our books, yes?" He took a sip.

"You know very well this is about the books, Papa."

"And why did you bring your friend? I am happy to meet him, *zvezda moya*, but this is not something I wish to discuss with strangers."

"He's not a stranger — he was helping me dig through your books, and I wouldn't have accepted his help if we couldn't trust him. And he's the one who figured out you've been putting Andei's cash through the store."

Dina and Max were very still.

Her face hardened at their reaction. "So you did know. Did you think I wasn't going to find out?" The flush climbed her neck, her cheeks, her eyes icy. "You can't sell the business because it's been involved in illegal activity since you started it. So, why? Why did you waste my time? And Joel's? Why did you let me run a fool's errand when you knew it was pointless to even consider selling?"

Max didn't answer right away, just drained his glass. No one else had touched theirs. When he set the glass down, he pressed his palms on the table, his eyes on his hands as he spoke.

"I did not consider that we could not sell. Andrei had given us instructions, and I believed that we had done right to sift the money in."

"Done right? Papa, this is *illegal*. Don't you understand? You could go to jail. They could have taken everything from us, and for what? Tell me, what did he give you to convince you to do this for him? To take such a risk?"

His eyes were sad when he looked up at her, the same cold blue as hers, though his were tinged with wisdom and pain that hers couldn't know. The depths of his were unfathomable, giving me a glimpse of his past that left me humbled.

"Annika," he said her name as a plea, soft and accented in the way it was meant to be spoken, "you must understand. Andrei saved me. He saved your mother and her sister. If not for him, we may never have had you. We may not have lived, trapped in Russia. You would not have the life we wanted for you, the life you have had. So, yes. When my brother came to my shop, the shop he helped me to build, with a bag of crisp money and instructions on how to help him, I did it without question. Because he gave me everything, and he is my brother. He loves us, and you, and I owe him all of our lives."

Annika didn't respond as I sat there next to her, feeling like I didn't belong, like I should have listened to her and stayed home. But I knew I'd made the right choice when I looked over and realized she didn't speak because she couldn't, not with the tears in her eyes and jaw clenched tighter than a steel trap. Whether they were angry or sentimental, I couldn't know, but she picked up her glass and lifted it, tilting her chin as she poured the clear liquid down the hatch until it was gone.

She took a breath. She let it out. And then, she spoke.

"I don't know how to help you, Papa. I don't know if you can stop working, maybe not for years. There's not enough in your retirement. There's just not enough …" she trailed off, her voice smaller as she shook her head at her empty glass.

"Then we will work," Max said, and Dina picked up her glass with a sigh, tilting it to me almost imperceptibly, inviting me to do the same. I did, gratefully, feeling like an intrusion.

"I don't think you have a choice, Papa."

"I did not ask for a choice. That choice was your doing, *zvezda moya.*"

She nodded, and I reached for the bottle of Stoli to refill her glass. A grateful smile was my thanks, and she took a sip, leaning back in her seat, looking defeated when she spoke.

"I just wanted you to enjoy this time in your life. You've been through so much, worked so hard."

Max smiled at her, elbows on the arms of the chair, hands clasped on his belly. "You say that as if I am an old man."

She almost smiled. "Papa, you're seventy."

He made a guttural noise in dissent. "I am no old man, frail and unable to work. And your mother is no old woman. We are strong. We can work, and so we will."

"But you don't have to. Most people are retired at your age."

Another noise, this one a little more mocking. "Perhaps in America, but not where we come from. There is no *retired*, or playing of the golf in silly hats." He wiggled his fingers over his head as if to conjure one.

Dina chuckled at that.

"Well, Papa, you're not in Mother Russia. You're in America."

He nodded. "Yes, yes. And you, my daughter, are so very American. It was our wish that you be. Our greatest wish. But I am not afraid to work, and you should not be afraid for us to work."

Annika sighed and took another sip of her vodka. "We'll come up with a plan to fill up your savings so you can leave the shop, and Andrei will have to figure out what to do with the store. Because you *can't* sell it, Papa. If you try, you may go to jail yet still."

He nodded. "*Da*. I will speak with him. He will know what to do." Max turned to me with mirth at the corner of his lips, effectively changing the subject. "It is not often that Annika brings someone to our home — you must be very special. Thank you for helping her, though I am sorry to have wasted your time."

"It was my pleasure to help, sir. As I told Annika, it wasn't a waste of time, not by a long shot."

Annika smiled at me, and Max watched the two of us, eyes knowing. "I can see that it was quite productive."

"Papa," she started, changing the subject, "Joel owns the tattoo parlor where we're filming. He's one of the cast for the show."

"Ah," he said as if he'd discovered a clue. "I suppose I could have guessed your profession. And how is the show?"

"Good," I answered. "Surprisingly more entertaining than I thought it would be."

Max laughed at that. "Yes, Annika has that gift. And I would think she maybe did not think much of you at first, hmm?"

I smirked. "You'd be right."

"Too … *glupyy*," he said, motioning to Annika for the right word.

"Silly," she said, and I laughed.

"Too silly for Annika, yes. She is not at all silly, my snow bird. No, she is a winter fox, white and clever. Quick to hide, but when she strikes, you listen."

I smiled over at her.

"But you are like a great bear, the lumbering beast who has no need to hide, just makes himself known and invites what may come." He nodded and put a fist to his chest. "I am a great bear, too."

Dina laughed. "Maxim, you are an old dog."

He frowned comically, feigning hurt. "*Nyet*, I am the great bear, and you are my sweet, summer fawn, and I will eat you for supper."

Her cheeks were rosy and high, and I saw Annika in her. "If you can catch me, old man." She kissed his cheek, and he leaned into her, laying his big hand on hers where it rested on his shoulder.

And the moment struck me, the two of them, the two of us. The bear and the fox. I saw myself in Maxim and Annika in her mother, and when I glanced over at her, I knew she saw it too. But I couldn't read her expression, didn't know what it meant to her.

Only what it meant to me.

INK AND MILK

Joel

AN HOUR AND THREE VODKAS later, I found myself standing next to Max in the living room, admiring his old record player and receiver, which was in mint condition, just as Annika had said. He handed me his original *White Album*, and I took it reverently, pulling up a footstool to sit on so I could inspect it properly.

The first thing I did was to check the album number printed on the cover. My hands went numb.

"Sir, I don't know if you realize this, but this album is worth quite a bit of money."

Max smiled and sat in the chair I'd stolen the footstool from. "Yes, I know. But do not tell Dina, eh? Or Annika. If she tried to convince me to sell something so precious to me, I might not be able to choose between the two."

I chuckled and pulled out the first album, inspecting it. "For as much as Annika says that this was played, it's in excellent condition."

"*Da.* It is one of the few possessions that I would risk much to protect." He sighed, but I could feel him watching me. "I am sure that sounds … silly," he said after searching for the word again, "but when you have very little, sometimes it is the silly things that mean the most."

"I can appreciate that. May I?" I asked, gesturing to the record player.

He extended a hand toward it. "Please."

I knew how to work the old Panasonic receiver — my parents had one just like it when I was a kid — and I lifted the glass lid of the record player, setting the vinyl on the deck gently. I pressed the button to start the spin, the familiar click bringing back memories of my childhood, and lifted the arm, bringing it down as softly as I could to the edge of the record.

Max smiled as the beginning chords of "Back in the USSR" played through the speakers.

"I was Annika's age when this album came out," he started with nostalgia in his voice. "It was all so exciting, the forbidden music, the Western culture. The promise of freedom. More than anything, that album and a few like it were symbols of that freedom. They were *hope*. I did not understand what it meant though, not until we came to America and I saw that freedom myself."

I nodded, and he reached for a picture frame on the side table next to him. He held it away from him before passing it over to me. It was black and white, from the 40s or 50s, two women with rifles over their shoulders, looking sober.

"This picture is of my and Dina's mamas. They were snipers in Hungary, during the revolution. I was just a boy, thirteen, but I also had a rifle in my hand, and so did Dina. We fought for freedom even then, but that freedom does not compare to what we have here, in America."

I looked down at the photograph, running my thumb across their faces, considering just how little I knew about the world, about suffering. Considering how much I missed having a family of my own.

But Max waved a hand, smiling. "Maybe Dina is right. I am just an old dog, telling old stories."

"I'm not quite the pup myself," I said with a chuckle.

"No, I can see that. But Annika is not either. She was always much older than she appeared. Roksana was the pup and Annika the wise one, with eyes that knew more than they should." His smile fell. "I should have told her of Andrei's money before. Long before."

"You didn't want to trouble her. You knew she would be disappointed."

He nodded. "You know her well, it would seem."

"I'd like to know her better," I added.

"I think you may have that chance. Or at least, I hope that you do. Us old dogs and silly bears must stay together. Keep them safe from harm." He nodded toward the kitchen where Annika and Dina were. "She likes you. Not many men have come here."

I smirked. "Well, I wouldn't have either, if I'd taken no for an answer."

He chucked. "One cannot, not with *zvezda moya.*"

"Pardon my asking, but what does that mean?"

Max smiled, his cheeks rosy. "My star. She is moonlight, starlight, the light in the dark. She is my hope. She is what I leave behind."

I found myself unable to speak.

"But she burns hot. It is not always easy. I know this. But her light is good and true. Her light is worth getting burned to hold. *Da?*" His eyes searched mine for understanding.

I nodded, swallowing my heart, knowing just what he meant. Knowing all too well.

Annika rounded the corner into the room, smiling. "You ready?" she asked.

I smiled back and stood, still moved, and Max knew it. He stood too, clasping my hand as we said our goodbyes. Dina kissed my cheeks and told me to come back again for dinner. And then we left, heading toward Ocean to catch a cab.

She hooked her arm in mine, and we walked silently for a moment. "You'll stay with me tonight?"

"If you'll have me," I said, repeating her words from yesterday.

"Oh, I'll have you all right," she said with a smile, taking the bait.

I chuckled, and we fell back into silence.

"Are you okay?" I asked after a bit.

She sighed. "No. I don't know. I'm working on a plan for Andrei, but I've got to talk to Roxy first. See what she thinks."

I nodded, feeling a little worried about Annika dealing with the mafia, uncle or not. "Is it safe?"

She laughed. "It's safe. He's my uncle, and Papa was right. He loves me, and he loves Mama and Papa. I think there's something to be done, but my hopes of doing it by the books are shot. He could have saved us so much time just by telling me from the start."

"I didn't mind. And I don't think you should tell Laney that the plan is off. I think we should be working on ledgers for a *very* long time."

Annika leaned into me. "Deal."

I moved my arm to wrap it around her, and she slipped hers around my waist, and we walked that way for some time, neither of us speaking. Catching a cab once we reached Ocean was no problem, and we rode the quarter-mile up the road to her brownstone. It wasn't terribly late, but I was ready for the quiet of her room, of her company, and she seemed to feel the same. We climbed her steps and ducked inside, thinking everyone would be asleep.

We were wrong.

Kira squealed and ran down the stairs, naked as day and dripping water everywhere, her long, blond hair plastered to her back as she streaked past where we stood in the entry.

"Bunny, get *back* here!" Roxy called, trying to hurry down the stairs, towel over her shoulder. Her foot slipped, and she grabbed both handrails to stop herself from toppling over. "Ugh, my groin!" she whined and continued her descent a little slower than before.

Kira giggled from the kitchen, and Roxy tossed me the towel. "Head's up," she said as she went in one entry, so I took the other, scooping the slippery, giggling girl up like a burrito, depositing her into her mother's arms.

She sighed, relieved and annoyed. "Thanks, Hairy," she added gratefully as she carried the little girl back up the stairs, chiding her all the way.

Annika was nearly finished wiping up the wet footprints from the floor and the stairs, and I followed, smiling to myself at her efficiency. When she reached the top of the stairs, she stood, brushing a fallen piece of hair from her face, and when she turned to me, I didn't breathe, and I don't think she did either. I climbed the steps to meet her, stopping at the step below hers, our faces level, her eyes hot as I closed the space between us.

Just before our lips connected, Kira's door burst open, and she giggled, feet thumping as she ran down the hall. Annika smiled, her cheeks flushed, and Kira — now in a nightgown — stopped in the threshold of the bathroom.

"Ew, kissing!" Bubbling laughter rolled out of her like tinkling bells. "*Anni loves Hairy, Anni loves Hairy,*" she sang, wiggling her hips back and forth to the words, and Roxy appeared, smiling at us conspiratorially.

"Come on, Bunny. Leave Anni and Hairy alone or you might have to see more kissing."

Ew! they both said as Roxy ushered Kira into the bathroom, winking at me as she closed the door.

Annika cupped my jaw and kissed me sweetly. "Come on, Hairy. Let's get you to bed."

I found myself smirking, my hand slipping down her arm to twine my fingers with hers as I followed her to her bedroom.

"Hairy, huh?"

She shrugged. "Short for *That Hairy Fucking Guy.* You used to bug me, remember?"

I chuckled. "Seems like a million years ago," I said as I stepped in behind her.

And then the door was closed, and the quiet enveloped us in the dim light of her room. The rest of the world disappeared right then, right there. She walked across the room to her bed and turned to face me. Her fingers slipped into her hair and untied her bun, the loose locks tumbling down around her face, her eyes locked on me.

I didn't move — she'd pinned me with her eyes, and I stayed just where I was, watching her. Long fingers worked the buttons open one at a time, neck down, leaving the white, tailored shirt open, exposing a sliver of her skin and bra. Her black pants were high-waisted, circling the smallest part of her, just below her ribs, and I held my breath as she unfastened them, bending to slide them down her legs.

Everything about her was beautiful, the light shining through the back of her shirt, casting a glow around the shadow of her body, and when she rose, her eyes were open, her soul open, and I could see her. All of her. And she was mine.

I stepped into her, slipping my hand under her shirt to the soft curve of her waist, pressing my forehead to hers as she wrapped an arm around my neck, fingers in my hair. And she closed her eyes behind a curtain of lashes as my heart pumped in my chest like it was reaching for her.

Her eyes didn't open as she lifted her chin, finding my lips without the necessity of sight, the softness, the sweet demand of them against mine all I wanted, all I needed.

There was no urgency, not now, not yet, and I reveled in her as she touched every one of my senses. The sight of her alabaster skin in the soft light as I slid the shirt off her shoulders. The sweet scent of flowers as I ran my nose up the line of her neck. The sound of her sigh, a hot breath in my ear. The feeling of her body under mine as I lay her down and she wrapped herself around my waist. The taste of her lips — lips that would be the end of me.

She was everywhere, and I was lost.

I broke away and ran a hand across her throat and down, fingers dipping in the hollow, skating down between her breasts. Ink and milk. Black and white. Her and me.

She lay stretched out underneath me, hair lying around her face like a halo, legs parted and hooked around my thighs, arms bracketing her head, hands clasped above it, eyes full of heat and want and something else, something more. Maybe she saw all of me, too. I wanted her to. I wanted to give her all of me and take all of her, so I did, the way I knew how.

Her skin between my lips was the sweetest pleasure, and I moved down her body, my hands on her thighs, opening them wider as I trailed my nose toward her hip. Her panties were silky, slick and hot in the center, and I pressed my thumb to the sensitive tip of her, dragging my middle finger up to the crease, my eyes on her face as her chin tilted, lids fluttering closed. She moaned, and heat burned through me. I wanted to be the only one to hear that sound. I wanted my name to be the only one to leave her lips. I wanted her. Indefinitely.

I closed my eyes and opened my mouth, closed my lips over her and sucked, slipping my thumb in the leg of her panties and into her heat.

Her fingers were in my hair and mine on her thighs, pushing them against her ribs, wanting her open, wanting inside of her, first with my hands, then with my tongue. The rest of me would find its way later, but for that moment, I would own her with my mouth alone. I licked up the line of her, sucked and teased, rolled and moaned with her in my mouth until her legs shook under my palms. I rested them on my shoulders, freeing my hands to rid us both of the satin in my way with a fist full of fabric and a flex, shredding it.

My eyes were closed, hands and lips busy, my heart pounding in my ears as her thighs clenched. When I finally looked up, looked at her — hands on her breast, bra pulled down, fingers clenched around her nipple — she was looking down at me, her eyes full of exquisite pain and pleasure. And the second our eyes met, she gasped, then shuddered, then squeezed me with her legs, her hands, the rest of her pulsing against my hand and mouth as she gave me what I wanted.

The moment her body relaxed, she whispered my name, and I knew I'd do whatever she asked of me.

But I'd take my time, moving up her body with my lips to her skin, in the circle of her arms, and when I reached her mouth, she took mine with the possession I felt for her. So I gave it right back, telling her with my fingers in her hair, with my lips pressed to hers, with my body pressing her into the bed, that she was mine.

Her hands moved across my body, under my shirt, across my abs, to my chest. Everywhere she touched was on fire, branding me.

I broke away only long enough to pull my shirt off before my lips were against hers again, her hands fumbling at my belt, unfastening my pants, pushing them over my ass, freeing the rest of me. She halted the kiss to look down at her hands, pressing her forehead to my lips as she watched her fingers close around the length of me, and I sucked in a breath at the contact, flexing into her palms.

She squeezed gently, and I dropped my head, whispering her name with my lips to her ear, and hers to mine as she answered with a single word: *Please.*

I throbbed in her hand and pulled away, kicking off my boots, then my pants as she muttered something, reaching for my cock, back arched as she ran her fingers up the length of me, guiding me toward her, pressing me against her core.

I drew in a breath at the contact of my bare tip against her hot, wet center and pulled back.

"Hang on," I begged her or myself, reaching over the bed for my pants, praying my wallet was within reach.

"No," she begged, fingers digging into my ass, pulling me down as she lifted her hips, angling for me. "It's safe. I'm safe."

Safe. I knew what she meant, but my heart clenched, and I slipped a hand in her hair. "You sure?"

"Yes. Fuck, Joel, yes. Please."

It was all the permission I needed. I lowered my face as I lowered my hips, pressing my crown against her, flexing, sliding into her as I watched her face smoothing with every inch I filled her, stopping at the end, staying there for a long moment as I brushed her face with my thumbs, felt her all around me, our bodies connected. It had been years since I'd been bared this way, my heart, my body.

I'd forgotten. I'd forgotten how to trust, how to feel, how much I needed to be felt.

I took her lips, slipping my tongue into her mouth as I pulled out and flexed, pumping into her. Then again as her legs curled around me. Again and I was already close, but so was she, my body clenching, muscles contracting in waves as I rolled against her. There was no pride, just the honesty of that connection, just her body around mine, mine inside of her.

My name again, as if from a distance, and I wondered if she'd said it aloud or if her body had whispered it as she held me, as I rocked into her until the build was too much, my heartbeat too much, Annika too much. And I came with a soft cry, filling her, pumping my hips to get as deep as I could. She was right behind me, her hips swinging, sliding me in and out to the rhythm she needed as her body let go again.

I buried my face in her neck, eyes pinned shut, fingers clenched in her hair, clinging to her as she clung to me. I couldn't let her go.

CATCH A FALLING STAR

Annika

WHEN I WOKE THE NEXT morning, I was surrounded by Joel.

His big arms held me into his chest like a velvet cage, his legs scissored in mine and beard tickling my forehead. I'd never been so comfortable in my whole life. He was just like Papa had said — a big, hairy bear, silly and sweet and ferocious, all at the same time.

I probably should have been hot, but I wasn't at all, even though he radiated heat like a furnace. It was helped by the fact that we had a sheet draped over only the bottom half of us, but it was as if our bodies just regulated to each other rather than contributing heat. I could sleep wrapped up in him like this every night, and the feeling was so strong. I pushed away an errant thought of sleeping without him like a plate of lima beans. I didn't want to be without him. And as strange as I should have felt about that, I didn't. Not at all. In fact, it seemed like the most natural thing in the world.

He pulled in a noisy breath through his nose, signaling consciousness, but I didn't pull away or give him room, squeezing him instead, nestling under his chin. His answer was the tightening of his arms around me.

"Time is it?" he mumbled.

"Dunno," I answered against his collarbone. "Before six — my alarm didn't go off."

"Mmm," he hummed. "Then there's time."

Tonic

I laughed as he pressed exactly what there was time for against my stomach. And then I nipped his neck, and he growled, rolling me over to make a more distinct impression on me.

His lips were hungry — the rest of him hungry too as he slipped inside of me like he'd never left. It was my arms around his neck and his hand on my thigh, the sheet slipping as he rocked into me, harder and faster, hovering over me so I could see him, so I could look down the line of our bodies to the seam where they connected, and we both fell again and again, fell into each other.

It almost felt like a dream. We lay there for a little while, wrapped up in each other. He'd tuck my hair behind my ear, and I'd blush. He'd say something funny, and I'd laugh. In fact, I hadn't laughed so much in I didn't know how long, hadn't smiled, hadn't been *me*. I wondered just how long I'd been hiding, but shied away when I realized the vastness of time.

I kissed him to erase the thought, to live wholly in that moment in his arms.

But the daylight called. I climbed out of bed, my body aching in all the right places as I pulled on a black satin robe and opened my bedroom door, listening for Kira and Roxy, but they were still asleep, the house quiet. I waved Joel out behind me like we were cat burglars, and we snuck into the bathroom, stifling laughter while Kaz judged us from the hallway. Well, I was laughing — Joel just smirked, holding his clothes over his privates, which was the funniest part of all of it.

I turned on the shower, and we whispered and laughed some more before stepping in together. We hadn't planned on having sex again — or at least I hadn't. I wasn't even sure my body could have another orgasm until I was accosted happily by soaking wet Joel, slick with soap I'd made the mistake of rubbing all over him. He was so hard, all silky skin over hard muscles. He'd been rubbing soap all over me too, which was mistake number two. Before we could even stop ourselves, I was wrapped around his waist, hot water streaming down us as he lifted me by the ass and let gravity do its work, over and over until it happened again, my body giving him anything he wanted, anything he asked for.

I told you — Joel turned me into an animal, and I wasn't even sorry about it.

We snuck back out of the bathroom to the sounds of breakfast downstairs, and were safely in my room before anyone was the wiser. Joel stood in the middle of my room with a towel wrapped around his waist, running a hand through his hair, and I thought I heard my ovaries pop.

So we got dressed while I did my best not to climb all over him again, just to see if I had more hidden orgasms in my body that he might be able to coax out. But I kept my cool, and we headed downstairs to eat, effectively ending naked time with Joel for at least a few hours. I smiled to myself, thinking about working with him all day. Maybe we could sneak off. I'd definitely see him that night, but that seemed an age away.

I sighed, smiling at him from across the table as he talked to Kira about a show she was watching on her iPad, something about fingers. She sang a little song I'd heard a million times about Daddy fingers and Mommy fingers that repeated on and on, ad infinitum while Joel made her stuffed bunny dance on the table. Roxy had taken on the task of breakfast — bacon, eggs, and toast — and we ate, sipping coffee as we talked and laughed. And after I helped Roxy clean up, I found him and Kira on the floor in the living room, playing with Kaz, the two of them giggling and whispering. I swear to God, Joel Anderson giggling quietly was one of the most precious and ridiculous things I'd ever witnessed.

The whole thing felt so … *right*. I imagined him talking to a little girl of his own, one with blond hair and a button nose, with green eyes flecked with gold and blue, like his, and I was overcome by the vision.

How I'd gone from loathing him to this, I wasn't sure. But I didn't want to go back. Only forward. With him.

We shared a cab back to the West Side, stopping at the coffee shop down the street from Tonic to grab a cup and walk to work together, under the story that we'd met that morning over the ledgers, nothing more. Not that I'd spent my night and morning wrapped up in him. No, no, it was all business. It seemed laughable that anyone would believe it — I could feel his body calling to me like a blinking neon sign — but I prayed that they would buy it, because we weren't ready for the ramifications of being outed.

I hated to leave him at the door of the shop, but we said goodbye cordially, and I turned for the door to the apartments, climbing three flights to get to the control room.

It was busy as ever, and I greeted everyone as I made my way through, finding Laney in the office at her computer.

She glanced up at me with an unreadable expression on her face as she sat back in her chair, watching me as I set my bag down on my desk and sat across from her.

"Morning," I said, ignoring whatever she was doing.

"Morning. Sleep well?"

"Like a baby," I answered, not skipping a beat as I opened my laptop.

"Good. Because I have news that may keep you up tonight."

I cut my eyes to her, then back to my computer as I pulled up my mail and pretended to read it. "Oh?"

She reached across our desks and pushed my laptop closed. "It's about Hal and Liz."

I sat back in her chair, trying not to fume, my face smooth. "What about them? Last time Hal left here he didn't seem interested in coming back."

Her lips were thin, and she looked older for that moment, worry creasing her face. "They got their own show."

"What?" I shot louder than I meant to.

She nodded. "Another network. Apparently Hal pitched the idea to a producer, and it's happening. And? It's supposed to happen before we air."

"Fuck," I breathed, only thinking of Joel, of what he'd say. Of what he'd do.

"So, a couple of things need to happen. First, we need to ramp up production. So you and I need to sit down today and work out the schedule, figure out how we can speed things up."

I nodded, feeling numb.

"Second, we need to stage telling Joel."

I kept myself still, though my pulse ticked up a notch, and the traitorous flush climbed a hot path up my neck. "What do you mean?" I asked, knowing very well what she meant, hoping it wasn't true all the while.

"What I mean is that you can't tell him. Not until we have the cameras rolling and on him. Today is packed with filming we've had scheduled for weeks, and we can't rearrange it for this."

"We can do whatever the fuck we want. *I* can do whatever the fuck I want — I'm the show runner, for God's sake."

Her eyes narrowed. "So you're going to reschedule three different tattoos with three different artists today? You've got a grand plan?"

"There's a way. There's always a way."

"Not this time. I've already tried. This is it — we don't have time to fuck around with the schedule when we're trying to speed everything up. The simplest, most efficient and cost-effective thing we can do is not tell Joel until tomorrow."

My jaw clenched.

"What's the big deal? I mean, telling him about Hal isn't going to make him go ballistic, but he's going to be pissed, and I want real emotion. He can't fake that. So why is that a problem?" she asked, baiting me.

"I just think it's really shitty not to tell him."

She made a face. "Who cares? It's what we have to do to keep everything on track."

"You're saying we don't have twenty minutes to film telling him between all of this?"

"No," she volleyed, "because it's not twenty minutes. It's going to be a full day of not only following Joel around, but of interviewing the rest of the cast about it. So do your job."

She was right. I knew she was right. But the thought of keeping this from Joel made my stomach turn, sending my breakfast up my esophagus. I swallowed hard. Maybe I could tell him, tell him to act surprised. But Laney would know. Joel was no actor. That was part of what made him so appealing. He was real, as real as they come.

"Annika," she warned. "You cannot tell him until tomorrow."

I pursed my lips and narrowed my eyes.

"I'm going to ask you again, and you're going to answer yes or no. Is this a problem?"

She kept talking when I didn't answer.

"Because this is your job. This is exactly what I was afraid of and exactly why I told you not to get attached. But you did. You fucked him and instead of using him, you got attached."

My nostrils flared. "Says who?"

She rolled her eyes. "Oh, my God. Says your body language. Reading people is my job, remember? So you made your choice, and now it's time for you to face it. I'm sorry that you're here, but this is *exactly* what I was trying to avoid. This is why I've been pushing you about him, because here you are, and it was all your choice. So, it's time to face the music. Sack up, Belousov. Your job, or the guy? What's it going to be?"

My job that I'd worked so hard to get or the guy who I found myself falling for? It was impossible. My plans had been dashed, and there were no exits, no paths out of the mess when I thought I had it on lock. And now … now I had to choose.

Laney wouldn't forgive me for betraying the show, but Joel had given me permission to betray him from the beginning. He told me to do my job, and this was my job — to lie to him. He'd made the rules. And with that, the choice was made for me.

There was only one answer, and it settled in my chest like a block of ice, too cold to melt. "My job."

Two words. I spoke those two words, and I knew he'd never forgive me for them. I didn't know if I'd forgive myself. But I had no choice, just like I told him from the beginning. I'd worked too hard for too long to throw it away. I only hoped he'd understand, which was as likely as catching a falling star.

LIAR'S REMORSE

Annika

LANEY AND I SPENT THE morning going over the new, expedited calendar and the following day's filming, which would start with telling Joel through a horrible game of telephone. I'd tell Shep, and Shep could tell him, and like a coward, I was glad I wouldn't have to be the one to expose the truth I kept from him. I tried to work it out so I wasn't even in the room when they filmed, hoping she would take my place, but she pulled rank. I had no choice. No options. I'd been backed into a corner.

I'd been a fool to think I could have walked away from this unscathed. A blind, proud fool.

I floated through the day in a haze, without a single moment to myself. Joel went about work as usual, though I felt his presence, felt him watching me. The air had changed between us, crackling with questions and fear, but there was nothing to be done. There was nothing I could do but sit and wait for the train wreck, knowing it would come without the ability to save anyone, not even myself.

There was no time to contemplate, every minute of the day a whirl, moving from one segment to the next without even enough time to wolf down the catered food. We were packing up at the end of the day, everyone exhausted, when Joel finally approached for the first time since we'd parted ways in front of Tonic that morning. It seemed like a million years and a million miles had passed.

No one was close by — I sat in my set chair, working on paperwork to finish logging the day, and he stood near me, his body language tentative.

"Busy today, huh?" he said, his voice low and rumbling, comforting. But I didn't deserve his comfort.

"It was. How'd you do?"

He shrugged. "Fine. The usual." He moved closer, laying a hand on the back of my chair to look over my shoulder at the clipboard, as if we were talking about work. "Come see me tonight."

My heart burned in my chest. "I'm so tired, Joel. I was thinking about going home."

He smiled. "We can sleep."

I would have laughed if it didn't hurt so bad. I managed a small smile. "I doubt that." *Please, let it go. Please, leave it be. Please, take no for an answer.*

He pointed at an arbitrary spot on the paper and leaned in, his lips near my ear. "We don't have to talk. Just come to me tonight."

It was too much. "I can't. Not tonight."

"Tell me why." It was a demand, a quiet demand that scratched at my resolve.

"Joel, please," I begged with a shaky breath.

He paused — I listened to him breathe for a moment before he finally spoke, his voice tight with understanding he couldn't possibly possess. "Don't do this, Annika. Whatever it is, don't do it."

Emotion rolled through me, taking me over, needing out of the immediate situation. I stood, leaving the clipboard in the chair as I reached for his hand, not caring who saw, swallowing tears as I dragged him out of the shop and up the stairs, through his door.

I slipped into his arms when the door was closed, his shirt fisted in my hands, my head tucked under his chin, and he held me, rocking me silently in the dark. I was thankful for the cloak of night, hiding my face that broke with my heart.

I could tell him right then. It would be so simple — I could tell him everything, throw it all away. Because after the argument with Laney, after everything, I would throw my career away if I told him. Laney would fire me, and she'd be right to do it. Maybe Joel didn't really know what he signed up for, but I did.

The woman I'd been a few weeks ago was gone. He'd done what he set out to do — melted that façade I'd so carefully crafted when I was at work, the one that kept me separate, unaffected by the demands of my job. It was gone, and now ... now I had to rebuild it, brick by brick.

The one thing I didn't deserve — Joel's comfort — was the only thing holding me together. I would betray him because that was what I had to do. I'd talk to him afterward, beg him to understand. But if he didn't, if he couldn't forgive me, then this was it. And of what I knew of Joel, he would never forgive me for lying to him, about anything. And as hard as I'd tried to fight it, I'd have to manipulate him after all.

This was the last time I'd be in his arms. This was the only chance I would have to say goodbye. And I wanted to say goodbye. I needed to.

"I need you," I whispered. "I don't want to talk. I just want you."

His lips never spoke, but his hands told me everything. He would give me anything I wanted, if I were true, if I were real. But I wasn't. I was a liar. Cruel. And I'd fallen in love with a man I couldn't protect from myself.

He kissed me with all the fire in him, as if he could burn away my pain. He undressed me with care, with strong, tender hands, laying me down in the dark as tears slipped out of my eyes and into my ears. He didn't know, he didn't see, only did what I had asked. I needed him, and he gave himself to me.

I memorized every moment, every touch. His body against mine. The caress of his hand on the curve of my breast. His lips as they tried to kiss away the bad. The heat of him as he slipped into me, filling my body, my heart, splitting it in two. And I said goodbye. I kissed him knowing it was the end, and when he felt it, when he knew, he grew frantic.

His lips crushed mine, telling me not to go. He slammed into me, claiming me for his. And I opened myself to him, giving him all of me. Because I'd walk away from all of this his. I had no choice in the matter.

When our bodies were spent, he held my face, fingers finding the tears, and I looked into his eyes, the one thing I could see as they reflected the only light in the room.

"I'm sorry," I whispered, my voice heavy with tears.

"Don't," he begged.

I turned my face, pressing a trembling kiss into his palm. *I'm sorry. I'm sorry. I'm sorry.* The words spun through my mind like starlings. I shifted to try to leave, but I was pinned by his body, and he didn't budge.

"Annika," the word broke in his throat, broke in my heart, and when I moved again, he let me go.

I gathered my clothes, trying not to sniffle as I dressed. And when I turned to where he lay on the bed, I took a heavy, shuddering breath and said the only thing I could.

"No matter what happens, this was real."

And then I turned and hurried out of his apartment, leaving my heart with him where it belonged.

PULL THE TRIGGER

Joel

I DIDN'T SLEEP.

THE SECOND she walked away, I pulled on pants and followed, but she was gone, climbing into her car as I bolted through the building door. I'd called. I'd texted. And I'd gotten nothing but silence in return.

By the time I walked into the shop the next morning, I was crawling out of my skin. Dark shadows ringed bloodshot eyes, my jaw aching from the pressure of squeezing it as I stared at my ceiling all night, wondering what was happening.

Whatever happens, this was real.

The words haunted me, followed me through the night and into the day. I knew from the way she said goodbye to me with every kiss that it was over. I just didn't know why, and I hoped to God it didn't have to do with the show, with the lie I'd given her. But it felt inevitable, like an approaching storm, and I stood out in the wind, waiting for it, exposed.

Shep showed up just after me, his face falling when he saw me sitting behind the counter.

"What's the matter?" he asked when he was close enough not to be overheard. Because everyone was there, milling around their stations, crew all over the place.

"Have you heard any gossip about the show? Annika?

Anything?"

His brow dropped. "No. Why?"

I scrubbed a hand across my face, feeling old, used. "Nothing. Don't worry about it."

Shep opened his mouth to ask a question just as the door chimed and she walked in.

She didn't seem to have fared much better than me, though the half-moons of shadow under her eyes were lighter than mine, covered up with makeup, her dark lashes making her eyes shine like the cobalt in the center of a flame, where the fire burned the hottest. Just seeing her sucked all the air out of my lungs.

Annika kept moving, her eyes on mine before she broke the contact with the cut of her eyes toward my brother.

"Shep, can I have a word?" she asked as if I wasn't there.

His eyes were narrowed as he looked from her, back to me, back to her. "Yeah. Sure."

"Thank you," she said, all business as she walked toward the office, and he followed, tense and unsure.

My heart hammered against my ribs until they ached, and I sat behind the counter with my numb hands on the surface and eyes on the door. Cameramen had set up, red lights on. They were already filming.

Something was happening.

I felt like a pawn, like a piece in a game, without will, without a choice. A puppet. A tool.

When the door opened, Shep walked out first, his eyes connecting with mine like he was trying to tell me what had transpired. Annika didn't look at me, just took a seat in her chair and picked up her clipboard, crossing her long legs. And just as my brother approached, she met my eyes with a flash of pain.

Shep's jaw was set, his eyes darting to the cameras. He didn't want them there when he detonated whatever bomb Annika had set for us, the trap she'd laid.

He pulled in a breath through his nose and let it out as he leaned on the counter across from me, and a cameraman took his place to our side, catching the profile of two brothers. My pulse raced.

"Tell me," I said simply.

His Adam's apple bobbed. "Hal got his own show."

My nostrils flared at the shock of his words. "He what?"

"He pitched his idea for a show to another network, and they signed him."

My breath froze in my lungs, and the burn spread across my ribs as I realized what that meant.

It was all for nothing.

The show. The sacrifice of my privacy, my shop, my family. The sacrifice of my heart. All for nothing.

I barely noticed the cameras around me, filming every breath as I tried to keep still, but anger pitched and rolled through me.

Shep's jaw was set, lips flat. "Not just that, but Hal and Liz are the frontrunners for the show, which means—"

"They're going to talk about me." There I was, trying to protect Liz, protect our past, but she wouldn't hold back, and neither would Hal. My life, laid bare for the world, and I had even less control on that fact than I had before.

"Fuck," I breathed as my mind raced. I tried to keep my composure as I sorted through it all. Shep knew, and Annika told him.

Annika. She knew. And she kept it from me.

"Did you just find out?"

He nodded. "Just now."

I pushed back from the counter and stood, my eyes locked on Annika. "And when did *you* find out?"

She froze, eyes widening a fraction. She looked like a statue, a beautiful doll, made of ice and stone. Unbreakable. She didn't speak.

I stepped closer, the cameras following me. "Answer me," I growled.

"Yesterday morning." Her voice was quiet, calm. I snatched her clipboard out of her hands and threw it.

Everyone jumped at the noise of it clanging to the ground.

"You kept it from me."

Her cheeks were pink, her eyes hard. "This is my job. I had to."

"The hell you did, Annika. *The hell you did*," I roared. "You lied to me. You *lied*."

She stood tall, her chin up defiantly. "What was I supposed to do, Joel? You knew walking into this what I'd have to do, didn't you? *You* told me to do what I had to do, so I did."

"What, so this was all just to push my buttons?" Fury boiled through me. "You waited to tell me so you could film it? You fucking *knew* I would flip my shit, so you waited. You waited and you ignored me all day, then came over and fucked me to make yourself feel better. Well, do you? Do you fucking feel better, Annika?"

She sucked in a breath like I'd hit her, and my lip curled.

"You want me to wreck shit?" I screamed and reached for anything I could. My hands closed around a camera — I ripped it from its owner and threw it as hard as I could to a chorus of gasps as it slid across the floor. "Is this what you want?" I grabbed her chair and flung it, sending people scattering. "You wanted a show? Well, here you fucking go." I threw my hands up, face steaming.

I stepped closer, invading her space, arching over her. "You didn't even care, did you? Were you using me this whole time? Did you just fuck me to get what you wanted out of me? To get me to do what you wanted? Or is this how you've always gotten your way?"

Her eyes shone with angry tears, her jaw set and lips pinched as she pulled back and slapped me as hard as she could. I saw it coming a mile away and let her, felt the sting of it, the sharp pain fortifying me to withstand the damage she'd done.

"Fuck you, Joel. Fuck you, and fuck off. Get out."

"You can't kick me out of my own fucking shop, you lying bitch." I hated every word as it left my mouth. I hated every heartbeat as it burned in my chest. I hated her for what she'd done. I hated myself for believing her.

"I can, and I will. Shep, get him out of here. Now." Her voice shook only once, betraying her, as Shep stepped between us and tried to move me toward the door. "These were your rules, Joel. You told me it could be easy. You told me to do my job. *Your* rules. Not mine."

I shook Shep off and pushed him out of my way so there was nothing between her and I but air. "Yeah, well I was fucking lying, and you knew it. *You knew it*," I yelled, pointing at her. "You knew it, and you let it happen anyway. I don't even give a fuck about Hal or the show or any of this," I said with a wave of my hand. "It was *you*, Annika. All I wanted was you." The words broke in my throat, and I turned for the door, anger and emotion burning through my chest, pricking the backs of my eyes as I tried not to think about the sight of her standing there, looking just as betrayed as I felt.

PINK MIST

Joel

I DIDN'T KNOW WHERE TO go.

I stood on the sidewalk for a split second of indecision. Part of me wanted to run, find something to break, to punish. Part of me wanted to hide.

All of me saw red.

I turned for the door to the building just as Shep burst through the door of the shop behind me. I think he called my name, but I couldn't be sure, the blood rushing in my ears so loud, it was all I could hear.

Upstairs I went with my brother in my wake, stairs falling behind me two at a time, throwing my door open. My apartment, my home, tainted by her. Stacks of ledgers stood on the table still, and I roared, sweeping them from the surface with a single motion. She was everywhere, the smell of her assaulting me as I entered my room, and I grabbed my blankets, flinging them behind me, fisting the sheets in my hands, ripping them off the bed with enough force to set the mattress askew. I didn't care. She'd ruined them. She'd ruined everything.

My name again, a hand on my shoulder, and I swung blindly, knowing it was Shep, blaming him for all of it. For the cursed show. For trying to stop me from expending my rage. For letting me fall for her.

My fist connected with his jaw, his spittle slinging across my face with an *oof*, but he rebounded with a swing of his own, his meaty fist connecting in almost exactly the same place where I'd hit him. I spun around, catching myself on the bare mattress, chest heaving.

"Calm the fuck down, Joel," he growled, and my shoulders sagged, face throbbing, eyes pinched shut as stars danced in my vision. *Zvezda moya*. My star. But she'd never been mine. It was all a lie.

Another roar climbed up my throat, past my lips as I flipped my mattress, sending a lamp crashing to the ground and porcelain and glass skittering across the hardwood.

"*That's enough,*" Shep screamed, shoving me into the box spring. "Get a fucking grip! *Now.*"

I looked through my fury over my shoulder at my brother looming over me, ready to put me down if I got up again, I knew. So I didn't. I turned and sank to the ground, elbows on my knees, head cradled in my hands, breath sandpaper in my lungs, scratching and burning me raw from the inside.

He paced the length of my room, then back, not speaking. Then again as I sat on the floor, broken and used up. Shep was trying to solve the problem, the massive, looming problem we'd created. The problem *I'd* created. But I'd lost all ability to consider that. All I could think about was her.

Lies. Betrayal. Destruction. I'd given her my trust, the one thing I held above anything, and she'd broken it. And that break had turned me into a monster I hadn't seen in a long time.

Annika and I weren't so different than Liz and I had been. Fighting. Fucking. Burning each other down. Turning ourselves into ash. And I'd been stupid enough to think she was different.

This was why I was alone. And I couldn't just blame Annika — I was hell-bent on destroying myself, with or without her help. It wasn't a phase or a fluke. It was a pattern, one I was destined to repeat.

"I can't go back down there," I croaked, my throat raw.

"No, you can't. You're not going anywhere unless it's out of this building and miles away."

"I'm not leaving. She can fucking leave."

"You know she's not going anywhere."

I didn't respond.

More pacing. I opened my eyes, staring at the wooden floor between my knees, my eyes hanging on a knot in the wood, the grain sweeping around it like water past an immovable stone.

A sigh from Shep. "I've got to go back down there at some point."

"Go."

He huffed like a bull, and I reached for a shoe next to my bed, finally lifting my head to pitch it at him as hard as I could.

"Get the fuck out."

He dodged it, fuming. "I don't want to leave you here like this."

"There's nothing you can do. There's nothing she can do. It's already done, so leave me the fuck alone. I'm not a fucking child."

Shep's jaw flexed, and he motioned to my tossed room. "Sure, real grown up, Joel." He jabbed a finger at me. "Don't you fucking leave this apartment, or I'll beat the shit out of you."

He would. I knew it. "Fine, I already fucking told you I'm not leaving, so *get the fuck out already*," I yelled.

He squared his shoulders, pinning me with a hard look before he turned and walked away, slamming the door behind him. And I dropped my head into my hands once more as I counted my mistakes, every single one.

BOTTOMS UP

Annika

I COULDN'T BREATHE. I COULDN'T run. And I couldn't follow him.

I couldn't leave. I couldn't stay.

But I had no choice.

A sob fought its way up my throat, but I coughed instead, then swallowed hard, turning to the cast and crew. Every pair of eyes seared me, accusing and disgusted. So I did all I could do.

I turned to my director of photography. "Did you get that?"

He nodded and looked away.

"Good. Take it upstairs. Thirty-minute break and we're picking it back up in the green room. Mark, you have the schedule for one-on-ones, right?"

A perfunctory nod.

"Let everyone know when they're needed upstairs."

The room was silent. Patrick stepped forward, fuming. "You can't actually expect us to do this. Not after *that*." He motioned to the door of the shop. Toward Joel.

My heart ached, but my voice was cold and sharp. "I can and I do. This is exactly when I need to speak to each and every one of you privately. And the contracts you signed bind you to being there."

I couldn't say anything else or I'd break. So I turned on my heel and walked out, feeling all of their eyes on me, hearing the murmur of questions and speculation as the door closed, shutting them out. Up the stairs I flew, swallowing, swallowing, swallowing again, but I couldn't keep my emotion down as it climbed up my throat. When I reached his landing, a roar and a crash came from behind his door, and I jumped, pausing, heart frozen. But I couldn't stop. There was nothing I could do. I'd already done enough.

The final flight was the longest, my legs shaking, brain scrambling for a place where I could be alone. The control room was full of editors who glanced up at me when I entered, with questions in their eyes, not knowing what had happened. Laney sat at her desk, her face full of awareness when she looked up, but I couldn't deal with her. Not yet. So I ducked into the green room, finding it empty. I closed the door behind me, bracing my body against it as I closed my eyes, forcing the tears down my cheeks.

Laney had been right all along. I knew she was from the beginning, but I thought I was smarter. That I knew better. That I could sidestep the destruction. But we'd been doomed from the start. I wanted to blame Laney for pushing me. I wanted to blame Joel for pursuing me. But in the end, it was my own choices that had brought me to where I was.

I had no one to blame but myself.

And that was where I stayed for a long time, my back against the door, tears slipping down my cheeks, trying to press the pieces of my heart back together. The tears eventually slowed, then stopped. My heart burned down and hardened, frost climbing over the surface of it. And then, my thirty minutes of mourning were up, punctuated by a knock on the door.

I swiped at my cheeks and stood, smoothing my clothes and my face, opening the door to find Penny waiting in the hallway, arms folded, looking absolutely furious — her cheeks were nearly the same shade of pink as her hair was.

She brushed past me and stormed across the room, taking a seat in the interview chair. A cameraman, sound guy, and PA followed her in, quietly, though their judgment may as well have been screaming at me. I sat across from her as the cameraman took his place next to me, and the sound engineer mic'd her.

Staci Hart

Penny sat in the seat at an angle, scowling, defiant. "What, you don't have fifty million questions planned for this?" she asked, nodding to my empty hands.

"No, I don't," I answered simply, coldly, looking to the cameraman to make sure he was ready. He nodded. I nodded back and turned to her. "Tell me about what happened downstairs."

Her eyes narrowed. "You made a fucking spectacle of the most honorable guy in the world. On camera."

I swallowed hard and did my job, the job I'd coveted so much that I sold Joel out for it. "Why do you say he's the most honorable guy in the world?"

Penny's lips were flat. "Because he'd do anything for anyone. He's honest and good. He takes care of us. He loves us, and what he loves, he loves fiercely. With everything he is. But you don't really give a fuck about him or me or any of us, do you? We're all just a bunch of fucking toys for you and your fucking boss to throw around and make a joke out of. Does that answer your question?"

"I get that you're angry—"

She barked a joyless laugh. "Bitch, you have *no idea* how angry I am. He was right. This whole fucking thing is a joke, a horrible mistake. We should have listened to him from the beginning." She stood and tugged off her microphone, tossing it into her chair. "Fuck this shit. I'm not doing this right now," she said as she blew past.

"Penny, you're under contract."

She whirled around, jaw set. "Fuck your contract, you lying skank. Call my lawyer about it, would you?" Then she flipped me off and stormed out of the room.

My hands shook, and I threaded my fingers in my lap, squeezing to keep them still, turning to the PA. "Go get me whoever's next."

The next hour was one of the longest of my life. One by one, the cast came in to see me, each of them offering me nothing but their hurt and anger. There was no footage, no headway, just an audience with me, a place with a closed door where they didn't want

218

to be, spitting insults at me like nails.

I couldn't even be mad. I deserved every one.

It became painfully clear that we were getting nowhere, and I sent everyone away, finally exiting the room to face the bigger issue. The biggest issue.

Laney sat at her desk, typing away at her computer, eyes darting to me coolly before finishing whatever she was working on. I closed the door and sat down across from her like the seat was on fire, back straight and eyes on her.

She closed her laptop and leaned back in her seat.

"They won't work with me."

She didn't speak. Her face said she'd told me so.

"This is your fault."

She had the nerve to laugh. "*My* fault? Annika, be serious."

"If you'd let me tell him—"

"I'm not the one who sent you up there to sleep with him last night after you knew."

Knife in my heart. "Why did you even tell me yesterday? Why not wait until today?"

"Because it shouldn't matter when I tell you anything. Because my job isn't to protect your feelings. It's to get you to do your job. I'm not the one who got my wires crossed here."

She was right, and I didn't care, nor would I admit it to her. "So, what do we do?"

Laney gave me a look that was full of disappointment, resentment, sadness. "There's really not much more you can do. You should probably take the rest of the day. Take your laptop and work from home on the things you don't need to be here for. Or don't. Either way, I've got to take over."

"Until when?"

"Until maybe forever. I don't know."

Ice cold. My hands, my toes, my heart, my breath as adrenaline surged for the hundredth time that day.

We sat in silence for a moment before she sat straight, opening her laptop again, the beginning of my dismissal.

"Let's just get through today. Tomorrow, we'll see where we're at. For now, you should go."

I couldn't even speak, just nodded once and packed up my things after texting my driver. And then I stood and walked out, through the control room, down the stairs, to the sidewalk with everyone's eyes on me and mine trained ahead. The car pulled up just as I approached the curb, and I slipped into its cool, dark confines like a stone through black water.

Not a single tear fell as we drove out of Manhattan, across the bridge, into Brooklyn. I don't know that I moved, other than the even rise and fall of my chest as I breathed through the gaping hole in my ribs. When the car pulled to a stop in front of my house, I climbed out, walked up the stairs, slid my key in the door, and found myself standing in my entryway, feeling lost and utterly alone.

"Annika?" Roxy called from the living room, and I carried myself toward the sound of her voice, surprised and grateful to find her sitting on the couch. "What are you doing home?" she asked, her voice full of concern as she took me in.

"I …" My voice was thick, foreign. I couldn't even speak.

She set down her sketchbook and stood, brow low, clasping my shoulders with her palms when she reached me, looking me over. "What happened?"

I took a shuddering breath. "He'll never forgive me."

Her face softened, and she pulled me into her arms, sinking down to the couch with me. And my tears fell, the ice shattering as the heat of my emotion burned through me. I mourned every decision, every word, every touch that I stole from him. I didn't even care about my job in that moment. I'd lost the only real man I'd ever known, the only one I'd ever had for myself. The only one who'd wanted me like he did. I'd lost it all, and lost myself.

It was a long time that I sat with Roxy, first in her arms, then with my head on a pillow in her lap as she stroked my hair. She offered whispers of comfort and soft shushing like she gave to her baby, until my sadness had all burned away, leaving me empty, hollow. A shell.

When I had finally calmed, I sat, sinking back into the couch, wishing it would swallow me up so I could disappear. Roxy handed me another tissue and hauled herself off the couch, clanged around in the kitchen for a moment, and came back with two small glasses of vodka and a bottle of Stoli.

"*Peyhdodnah*," she said. *Bottoms up*. And we did just that, tipping our glasses to pour the liquor down our throats.

The burn felt good as it snaked through my body, and I reached for the bottle to pour myself another. Roxy extended her glass.

"What are you doing home?" I asked, not sure I could talk about myself yet. Kaz hopped up onto the couch, tail flicking as he looked up at me.

Roxy pulled her feet back, eyeing him. "Kira's sick — I picked her up from Max and Dina's shop earlier. The last thing we need is them getting sick too."

"True. I'm glad you were able to take off." I ran my hand down Kaz's back, and he stepped gingerly into my lap.

"Yeah, well, everything's on hold until I get this mess figured out anyway." She flicked her hand at her sketchbook.

I nodded, not having anything else to add. So I took a drink.

"What happened?" she asked tentatively.

I looked into my glass like I could find answers there. "I had to lie to him, keep something from him, and then tell him the truth on camera."

"Oh, Anni." There was no disappointment in her words, only empathy, and a pained smile touched the very corners of my lips.

"He didn't take it well." I drained my drink and reached for the bottle again.

"No, I imagine he didn't."

"And the entire crew is on revolt. Laney sent me home because none of them will work with me."

She drew in a breath.

"Yeah."

"So what happens now?"

I drained my glass and reached for the bottle, pouring until it was near the top. "Now, I drink until it doesn't hurt anymore."

She raised her glass, and we did just that.

ENOUGH

Joel

MY ALARM WENT OFF, A blaring assault ringing in my aching head. The sound was foreign to me — I couldn't remember the last time I hadn't woken before it.

I reached for my phone, tapping at the screen until it stopped without opening my eyes, and I was wrapped in blissful silence again. A sigh left me, and I rested a hand on my chest, my brain creaking into motion.

I felt like week-old garbage.

My entire body ached, including my head, and I worked my way backward through my memory, trying to figure out how I'd gotten where I was.

I remembered being at Wasted Words with Patrick, the bar his girlfriend owned, which meant lots of free drinks. That explained the headache. I remembered him coming over before that and dragging me to the gym, where I ran until my legs were glue.

Because of Annika.

Pain bloomed in my chest at the thought of her name alone, deepening when I replayed what she'd said, what she'd done. What I'd said and done.

Shep had sent Patrick to babysit me, and as angry as I was, as much as I'd wanted to wallow or break something or both, I'd been thankful for him forcing me out of the apartment, into the city, to the gym where I ran a dozen miles. I just wanted to burn away all of her with every drop of sweat, every aching muscle. I couldn't stop until I'd expended every ounce of energy I had and all the adrenaline in my body had burned out. And when it was all said and done, I could barely walk on my numb legs to the locker room, which explained my aching body.

We didn't go back to my place. I'd showered at the gym, and then we went to the bar, never speaking once about anything that had happened. He knew what I needed and helped me get there, with the assistance of a handle of whiskey.

I'd blacked out, and hoped I didn't get into a fight or have a breakdown in the time my memory failed me. I checked my knuckles — they were only scuffed up from hitting Shep, and I felt a little comfort at that. When I looked over at my nightstand for water, I found some right next to a bottle of ibuprofen and took both, grateful for whoever'd had the foresight to leave it for me.

I sat up in bed and pressed the heel of my hand to my eye socket to stop the throbbing before glancing around my room. Someone — must have been Shep — had put it back together, cleaned up the lamp, even put fresh sheets on my bed. I doubted that the rest of the mess I'd made would be so easily set to rights.

Yesterday, I'd hidden from my problems the way I knew how. Today I'd deal with it, whether I wanted to or not.

I had no idea what to expect. Not even a single clue as to what I'd be walking into, leaving me nothing to prepare for.

I swung my legs over the side of the bed, testing out my body. Seemed that the effects of the whiskey were limited to my thumping head, and I counted my blessings before climbing out of bed and pulling on clothes.

I found Shep in the kitchen, sitting at the table with a cup of coffee. He'd cleaned all that mess up too, packing the ledgers in a box that he'd pushed next to the couch. I tried to pretend they weren't there, moving to pour coffee in silence as my brother watched me, sitting with my back to them.

I rested my forearms on the table with my mug between my hands and met Shep's eyes.

"So," I said.

"So."

I swallowed. "I'd say this was all your fault, but I feel like you already figure I feel that way."

"Do you? Feel that way?"

I breathed through a couple heartbeats. "I wish it were that easy, that I could pin the blame on somebody else. But I can't really, can I?" I didn't wait for an answer. "Bring me up to speed."

He watched me for a moment, seeming to collect his thoughts before starting. "The show's a mess. Production is pretty much on hold, or at least it was yesterday, since the entire crew is on strike."

My brow was low. "The production crew?"

"I mean, they're still doing their jobs, but they don't look real happy with how things went down. But I meant *our* crew." He shook his head. "Annika tried to run interviews after you left and ... well, let's just say it didn't go well."

The pain was back, pressing against my ribs. "Good."

His eyes narrowed a millimeter, but he didn't acknowledge my response. "So, I don't know what's going to happen today. I didn't see Annika again, and no one seems to really know what's going on."

"What about Laney? Didn't anyone talk to her?"

"I did for a second. I spent all day yesterday trying to calm everybody down. Penny was ready to fight, so it's good Annika disappeared. I sent Tricky with you because I thought he might be ready to fight too. Everyone else is just ... well, they're pissed. They feel betrayed. They're angry."

My eyes were on the steam rising from the bottomless black coffee.

"Anyway, Laney basically said to let everyone breathe and that we'd pick it up again today, but I don't know what that means. No one wants to film right now, and there's talk of quitting, lawsuits ... all kinds of noise. I was really hoping she'd call it off for today, but I haven't gotten word yet."

I still didn't speak.

Shep scratched at his nose, waiting for me to offer him

something, anything, but I had nothing to give.

"Do you want to talk about it?"

"No." The word was final.

"All right, man. You know where to find me if you do."

I ventured to take a sip of my coffee, the sting of it against my lips and down my throat somehow a comfort. I was surprised I could feel anything at all.

"What do you want to do?"

I sighed through my nose and sat back in my chair. "Not much we can do except keep going. Right?"

He nodded, though he didn't look happy. "Far as I know."

"Then that's what we'll do." I took another sip. "Thanks for dealing with everything yesterday while I was … out."

He shrugged a shoulder. "You're not the only one who's capable of dealing with the shop, Joel. I know sometimes you feel like you are, but you put that on yourself. It was nothing. I'm just glad you're okay."

"I'm so far away from okay, I'm not even on the same continent."

His jaw flexed, his eyes full of concern. "Fair enough. But you don't have to go in there yet, if you don't want to. I can figure out what's going on and let you know. You can take time. You've earned that."

I took another sip, considering all I'd *earned*. "No. I'm done. Face the music and all that shit. Right?"

"If you want to. It's your call."

"I don't *want* any of this, but it's mine to deal with all the same."

"It's not just yours, man," he said, frustrated, and I fumed.

"Fuck you, Shep. It's my mess, my problem. She's my problem. She and I put us in this boat, so I'm the only one who can handle it. I appreciate the offer to help, but you can't fix this."

He sighed and raked a hand through his hair. "I don't think you can fix it either, but I guess we'll see."

I stood and picked up my mug, walking toward the bathroom. "Guess so," was all I offered.

Every motion was automatic — close the door, turn on the

shower, set down the coffee, take off the clothes, step into the stream, scrub the bullshit off. But there was no getting rid of it. The grime stuck to my soul, staining it.

Dry and dress. Walk down the stairs with my boots full of bricks. Push the door of my shop open. Brace self for the shitstorm.

My crew was all there, bright and early, faces full of anger, and all of them stood and rushed me, everyone talking at once.

"Are you okay?" Veronica.

"Fuck that fucking bitch." Penny.

"Tell me we don't still have to do this, Joel." Ramona.

Eli and Max huffed and puffed and rattled off insults, and Patrick just stood behind them, arms folded, watching me with the weight his eyes always had. They all kept talking, talking, talking, getting louder as my pulse thumped in my ears, ringing in my head like a bell.

My eyes slammed shut. "*Enough!*"

Silence.

I opened my eyes to find them all still, brows drawn, incensed. My voice was low when I spoke. "I told you, all of you that this was a mistake, but you wanted it. You wanted this. You signed up for it, every one of you, and so did I."

Penny's face was on fire. "You can't fucking expect us to work with her, Joel. I won't do it. If she threw you away, lied to you, then why would she give a fuck about any of the rest of us? This is bullshit, man."

"I know it's bullshit, but what do you want me to do about it? We've all signed contracts."

Her jaw clenched, arms folded, but she didn't have an answer. Neither did I.

"Trust me, I'm the last person who wants to be here," I said, scanning their faces. "But we're in this, and we're in it together."

Ramona shifted, popping her hip defiantly. "If we're all in it together, then we can all get out of it together."

I shook my head and ran a hand over my beard. "It doesn't work that way."

"Why the fuck not?" Eli that time, looking betrayed. They all looked betrayed, and my anger simmered, steamed, boiled.

Penny saw it and pressed the button. "Joel, we don't have to work with *her*. She fucked you up and fucked you over, and now we're supposed to act like she didn't? Fuck that shit. It's her or us."

Nods and noises of approval. My anger bubbled over, hitting the bottom of my heart with a hiss. "You act like this isn't hard enough without having every one of you fighting me." My voice grew lower, louder with every speeding heartbeat. "But I come down here and you're slinging insults when I need you to have my back."

Veronica frowned, her red lips dipping, jaw flexing. "But that's what all this is about. We've got your back so hard, we'll fight for you when you won't."

I shook my head, frustrated. They didn't get it, and I didn't have the patience to explain it to them. "Then do what I ask. All of you."

They waited for instruction, and I pointed at the chairs.

"Go to fucking work," I bellowed, startling all of them. "Do your fucking jobs. This isn't about *you*. It's not your fight." I turned for the door. "It's mine."

No one followed me. I walked out of the shop to complete silence, aside from the bell on the door, and I turned straight for the door to the building, heading up the stairs to the control room, praying Annika wouldn't be there.

I didn't see her in the control room, just the faces of some editors who looked as tired and over it as I felt. Laney was at her desk on the phone, and her eyes cut to me when I walked in.

"Let me call you back. Yeah. Okay, bye." She set her phone down and had the nerve to look at me with pity. "Good morning, Joel."

"The hell it is." I moved into the room, stopping about halfway in. "We've got a problem."

"We've got several problems."

I nodded, crossing my arms. "They won't work with her. They're talking about staging a coup."

She sighed.

"This can't go on. I don't know how you expect any of us to keep going after everything that's happened."

"You'd be surprised. It'll blow over sooner than you think."

My eyes narrowed. "Do you know something I don't?"

She shrugged and spun her chair to face me, looking unfazed. "Just that people are predictable. Everyone needs time, sure. But nothing is irreparable."

A laugh shot out of me, dry and painful. I shook my head. "You don't know us very well."

"You'd like to think that, sure. But you don't do this for as long as I have without it becoming second nature. We read people. It's how we produce. It may as well be in the job description."

I seethed. She stood.

"You knew what you signed up for."

I scoffed.

"Okay, maybe not exactly what you signed up for, but you knew this wasn't going to be a picnic. You knew there would be drama, so I'm still trying to figure out why you're surprised. Annika too, for that matter."

My jaw clenched, teeth pressing together until it hurt.

"She did exactly what she was supposed to do. The rub was that she got attached, and so did you. And here we are. So, what? Do you need a few more days? I can push it back a little to give you some space, but we can't just stop filming or we'll fall behind. And if we fall behind, Hal's show will air first. And if Hal's show airs first, we're all fucked."

I couldn't stand it, the loss of control, the loss of my choices, my options. There was no escape, and fury churned in my chest. I dropped my hands, squeezing them into fists by my side. We were at an impasse. I had no way to convince my people to work, and this was all *her* fault. But if I were gone, maybe I'd take the drama with me and the show could still go on. It was my only other option, and as furious as I was, I took it.

"Fine. Then I quit. I never wanted to do this fucking show anyway, and now that you're going to make a circus out of my life, then it's over. I'm done." I spit the words at her, waiting for her to react. To beg me to stay so I could say no again.

But she didn't. In fact, the pity was back. "You can't quit. I'm sorry, I really am, but you're under contract, and so is the shop and everyone in it. The network has sunk millions into this show. They're airing trailers and ads. And they're not going to shy away for a second from taking you down if you try to fight it."

"Tell them to come at me," I hissed through my teeth, an empty promise from a caged bear.

She shook her head. "You'll lose it all, the shop, everything. They'll take you down for compensation. I'm sorry, Joel. But this is it."

Rage. It took every ounce of willpower I had not to scream, to wreck something, to get the adrenaline, the frustration out of my body and into something else. But I didn't. I felt my blood pressure rise to the point of dimming my vision, the heat of my pulse in my tense neck climbing up my face. I had to get out of there.

So I turned to leave, and there she was, standing in the doorway, pale and beautiful. And I hated her more in that moment than I've ever hated anything in my life.

Annika

He was so angry, he seemed to suck all the air from the room into himself. His eyes locked onto mine, full of hate, burning into me. The shock of it sent physical pain through my chest, and he stormed past, nearly pulling me into him with his gravity. His eyes never left mine, and I couldn't look away, turning my head to follow him until he broke the connection, leaving me powerless. Empty.

Laney stood in the middle of the room, looking at me like she'd told me so, and I filled up the emptiness with rage. My lips twisted.

"What did you say to him?"

Her jaw flexed, eyes narrowing as she crossed her arms. "Don't act like I've betrayed you, Annika. You're the one who's put us all here."

I ignored the jab. "What's the matter with him?"

"You."

I pulled in a long breath and let it out slow, chin down, wishing

I could explode her with my mind. "Laney," I warned.

"He tried to quit. The cast won't work with you. He wants out, and he can't get out. So, he's pissed."

I was unsurprised at anything she said. "I can't do my job." It was a statement, a fact.

"Yeah, conflict of interest, like I said from the beginning."

"What do you want me to say? That you were right? That this is all my fault? What do you want from me?" My voice broke.

Laney looked tired, resigned. "I don't want anything from you, unless you've got a time machine somewhere you've been hiding."

I looked around the office, feeling out of place, alien. "What am I supposed to do?"

She sighed. "Sit in here and work on next week's art and history segments. Keep that door shut. Don't talk to anyone. Don't leave this room."

"And tomorrow?"

"I don't know, Annika. I honestly don't." The words were heavy, laden with her frustration. "But today, I've got to try to figure out how to calm everybody down, earn their trust back. And I can't do that with you around."

I held my chin high, even though I wanted to crumple to the ground and cry, and took my seat as she walked toward the door.

She paused just before walking out, though I didn't give her the satisfaction of meeting her eyes, focusing instead on my laptop screen.

"I'm sorry, Annika."

I didn't answer, not even giving her a nod, though she stood there for a long moment waiting. And then she closed the door, leaving me in the quiet room alone. It was *too* quiet. I scrambled for my earbuds in my bag and plugged them into my phone, putting them into my ears with shaking hands, as anger and sadness, pride and pain pumped through me to the aching beat of my heart.

MOLOTOV

Annika

MORNING CAME IN THE CLAWS of my alarm, and once it was shut down, I stretched in bed, wishing I could just sleep through the next week to wake up with everything behind me.

The day before had been bullshit. I'd hidden in the office. Laney sent the entire cast out drinking on a company card in the hopes they'd burn off steam and come back feeling better, and we spent the day working on the schedule, the segments we had, a trailer for the network. Busy work. We were otherwise shut down, and if Joel's reaction to me had been any indicator, we were a long way off from getting moving.

If I was in the picture, at least.

Honestly, Laney should have fired me on the spot, given the fact that I could no longer do my job, but she kept me working and busy while she tried to fix the mess. But she was treading water. If I were gone, everything could get back on track.

I sighed to vent the pressure in my chest, but it didn't help.

Kaz was cuddled up on the bed next to me, a new development for him. But he'd been so affectionate ever since things fell apart, and I just figured he knew I needed him. It'd been nice — the old bastard hadn't been so lovey-dovey since he was a kitten and I was eight.

I rolled over to face him, curling around him as I laid a hand on his furry back to pet him. But my hand froze — he felt ... *wrong.* Cold. Still.

Dead.

I jerked away from him in shock, scooting back in a flurry, but I didn't realize how close I was to the edge and whooped as I tumbled off the bed and hit the floor with a thump. But I didn't stop trying to get away, my eyes bugging and heart thumping as I crab walked across the room like a bug.

"Fuck, fuck, shit, fuck," I muttered in a loop as I blinked at the bundle of fur on the bed.

I stood and scrambled out of the room, down the hall, panic rushing through me as I threw open Roxy's door. She sat up in bed and moved her head like she was looking around, but her eyes seemed like they were closed.

"Huhwha?" she mumbled.

"Roxy," I hissed. "Fuck. Fuck! I think ..." I couldn't even say it out loud.

"Wassamatter?" Blinking happened and she peered at me through slitted eyes.

I tried to swallow, though my mouth was dry as bone, as I tried to catch my breath. "It's Kaz."

Her eyes flew open. "Oh, my God."

"Yeah," I breathed. "Yeah. Come with me."

"Okay," she said as she crawled off her bed, and we hooked arms, walking down the hall together with our eyes on my doorway. I could see him in my bed still, and my heart sped up.

We stopped at the edge of the bed, staring at him. He hadn't moved. We didn't speak for minute, both of us just watching him, wondering what the hell we were supposed to do.

"Touch him," I finally whispered.

"He's your cat, Annika," she hissed back.

"Roxy, you have to do it. I can't do it, you have to, please, you have to do it," I rambled, and my freakout must have been fully evident, because she let me go and stood up a little straighter, steeling herself.

She took a deep breath and braced her hand on the bed,

reaching into the middle to touch him. She flinched when she made contact, squinting as she ran a hand down him and felt his ribs.

After a second, she jerked her hand back and shuddered, hopping as she shook her hand out like she could get rid of the memory of it. "God, Annika, nope. Nope. Not sleeping. Definitely dead."

My hands flew to my face, covering my mouth and nose as I stared at my cat, my friend since I was a little girl. The fear dissipated, and I sat down on the bed as tears pricked my eyes, falling when I ran a hand over his silky fur. He looked peaceful, like he'd just come to comfort me, fell asleep, and drifted away.

Roxy broke the silence, her voice soft. "What should we do with him?"

I sniffled, swiping at my tears. "Maybe we could bury him at Mama and Papa's. Or find one of those … I don't know … cremation places?"

"And in the meantime?"

I stood and walked over to my corner to picking up his blanket before moving back to my bed to lay it flat. I picked up Kaz and laid him on top, then wrapped him up in it like a death shroud. We stood there and looked at him for a long time, both of us lost in thought, in memories.

My tears fell, my already broken heart fracturing again and again, just when I thought things couldn't get worse. Joel crossed my mind as all the hurt piled on, then I thought about work and the mess I'd left there.

Work.

There was no way I was going in today. I reached for my phone and texted Laney.

I'm sorry to do this, but I won't be in. My cat died this morning.

She texted back almost immediately. *Oh, God. Don't worry about things here. I've got it under lock. Probably best to give everyone here some air anyway. Take care of yourself, and let me know if you need a few days. K?*

K

I set down my phone, turning my eyes back to the bundle on my bed.

"Mama?"

We turned to find Kira in the doorway, hair mussed, rubbing her eye with her little fist, her bunny hooked in her elbow.

"Hey, Bunny," Roxy said, the words full of sadness and comfort. She glanced at me before turning for Kira, scooping her up.

"What's the matter, Mama?"

"Oh, honey," she clutched Kira into her shoulder and looked to me again. We shared a look full of wariness and weariness, and I got the sense that Roxy was trying to figure out how to break the news to her. "So, baby, I have to talk to you about something. Do you remember Lady Pearl?"

Kira leaned back to look at Roxy, her arms loose around Roxy's neck, bottom lip poking out just a hair. "Our fishy?"

Lady Pearl was our betta, a pink and purple explosion of color, and a male. But Kira insisted he was a lady and named him Pearl. And thus, our transgender fish was born.

"Yeah, our fishy," Roxy said. "Remember when we found her upside down in her bowl?"

She nodded. "Because she was an old lady?"

"Right. Because she was an old lady, and nothing lives forever."

"I remember."

"Well," Roxy started, pausing for a second. "Do you remember how old Kaz is?"

"Old-old. Almost as old as you, right, Mama?"

"Right," she said softly. "Well, baby, last night, Kaz went to sleep, but he didn't wake up."

Kira's chin quivered. "What?" she whispered, and a sob rose in my throat. I pressed my fingers to my lips.

"He's gone."

"No," she wailed, her little face bent. "No! Where is he? Where is Kaz?" She looked around and looked at the bed. And she cried, reaching for him as Roxy tried to soothe her, finally taking her out of the room.

I picked up the cat and walked down the stairs, not sure what to do with him, working through the biological part of what his death would mean. So I slipped him into a trash bag and put him into a box that I set on our back deck.

When I closed the door, I felt better by only a tiny degree. I could still hear Kira upstairs crying while I called my mother and told her what happened. More tears, hers and mine, and Papa got on the phone, his voice raw as he told me how sorry he was. They agreed to let us bury him in their back yard, said they would take off the next day so we could come over.

So, I'd be off for at least one more day, not that anyone needed — or wanted — me around.

I made my way back upstairs to Kira's bedroom to find Roxy holding Kira on her bed, sobs hiccuping through her little chest.

Roxy's eyes were wet, her hand skating up and down Kira's back. "Kira wants to have a funeral for Kaz."

I sat next to them, my heart broken. "Sure, Bunny. We'll have a funeral at Babushka and Dedushky's house tomorrow."

Kira nodded. "And Dedu Andrei has to come, and Hairy."

My breath hitched.

Roxy shook her head. "Hairy doesn't need to come, Kira."

Her little face wrenched again, and the tears slipped down her cheeks in rivulets. "He has to come! Kaz loved Hairy, they were friends, and Hairy has to come! He has to!" Her voice was shrill, edging on hysterical. I couldn't stand it.

"I'll ask him, Bunny, but he may not be able to come."

"He has to!" she squealed. "He has to, you have to tell him! Please, Anni, make him come!"

Roxy and I shared a look. "Okay, I promise, I'll tell him."

"Tell him now!" Her eyes were wide and wild, wet and sad. "Please?"

"Kira—"

She cried again, her words all running together, and I reached for my phone.

"Okay. Okay. Look, I'm gonna call him right now, okay? Don't cry, Bunny, please don't cry," I said as my own tears fell, and I pulled up his name, hoping he wouldn't answer. Because the last thing I needed was to hurt anymore. And hearing his voice couldn't do anything but tear me apart.

Joel

The phone rang on the kitchen table between me and Shep, flashing her name, bringing our argument to a halt.

"Speak of the devil," Shep said.

I pushed the button on the side of my phone to stop its buzzing, and hopefully my nerves.

"You're not going to answer it?"

I gave him a flat look.

"Just answer it. She wouldn't call if it wasn't important."

My jaw flexed. "Don't really care."

"You're not curious?"

I sniffed. "Not even a little."

My phone was still showing her number, the button begging me to answer. But there wasn't enough tea in China to convince me to do it.

He scowled, watching me until it went to voicemail. I picked up the conversation again.

"We can't get out of the show, Shep. So now it's our job to convince the shop to get back on board, and I need you to have my back."

He rubbed the back of his neck and sighed. "That's a tall order, man. Ramona and the girls are pissed, especially Penny. She's ready to Molotov Cocktail the control room."

"We don't have a choice."

"All right, then let's look at this objectively. All emotion out of it. Can you do that?"

My jaw clenched. "Yeah."

"So, the way I see it, we have two options. The easiest option is this — tell Laney to choose. Us or her. We might have a shot at convincing them to get back on board if she's gone. But otherwise, it might be hopeless. Laney paying for a night at the bar was great and all, but it wasn't enough. No one would go in today, which means the shop is closed too. We can't keep this up. So maybe if *she's* gone, it can get us back on track sooner."

As much as I didn't want to see her, the thought of getting her fired sent dread twisting through my guts. I wished, not for the first time, that she would just disappear without any consequence for any of us.

"Last resort," I said after a moment, and my phone buzzed again, alerting me that a voice message had been left.

Shep and I looked at each other for a split second, and his hand darted out toward my phone. I was a millisecond too late to stop him from grabbing it.

I stood, and so did he as he held up my phone.

"Give it back," I barked.

He had the nerve to smirk. "Why? What are you afraid of?"

I moved around the table, and he kept pace, keeping it between us so I couldn't reach him as he opened up my voicemail like a fucking traitor and played the message, putting it on speaker.

"You son of a bitch." I darted, and he sidestepped to stay right across from me.

The message began, and my chest ached at the sound of her smoky voice, muffled by a stuffy nose.

"I … I'm sorry to bother you." Kira wailed in the background, and the ache squeezed tighter. "My … my cat died last night." A pause, more crying in the background. A deep breath. "We're having his funeral tomorrow at my parents' house, and Kira wanted you to be there." Kira wailed *Hairyyyyyy*, and Shep's brow dropped. "I understand if you can't make it, really. But it would mean a lot if you were there." She rattled off the time for the funeral and her parents' address with a shaky voice before disconnecting.

Shep eyed me. "Dude, you have to go."

"No, I don't."

He slid my phone across the table toward me. "Yeah, you do."

I picked it up and put it in my pocket.

"Listen, Joel. I get it. I really fucking do, but you can't keep pretending that you didn't play a part in all of this."

"Trust me, I don't. You said we had two options, so what's the other one?"

He shook his head. "You're not gonna like it. But you need to consider it."

"Tell me, already."

Shep watched me for a beat. "Make up with her."

"What?" I shot the word at him like a cannonball.

"I don't mean you have to be with her, but if you can figure out a way to let it go, everyone else would fall in line. You're their fearless leader. They'd follow you anywhere, even down the path of redemption. But so long as you're wounded, they will be too. The longer they see you hurting, the more they dig in their heels."

My nostrils flared as a hot breath left them. It was impossible. But he was right. I deflected.

"I'm not going to her fucking cat's funeral, Shep."

He shrugged. "Even if you don't go for her, you should go for that little girl."

I glared at him. "It's a cat funeral. A funeral. For a cat."

"Yeah, I get what it is, I've got ears, asshole. But if you go, it's an olive branch to her. You're there for the little girl who I'm assuming must really want you there, since it convinced Annika to call you."

I blinked at the sound of her name. "I'm not going, dude."

He frowned. "Stop acting like you're the only one who got hurt. She's not wrong, you know. You gave her permission to do her job, and she did. You lied to her. She lied to you. You hurt each other."

"It's not the same," I growled.

"I'm not saying it is. I'm saying you led her on just as much as she did you."

"Yeah, well, I didn't lie to her and then fuck her."

He gave me a look. "That's exactly what you did."

"You know what I mean, Shep."

"I do know what you mean, but I'm saying that what you did *to each other* was shitty. You're both assholes. I'm not saying you have to be best friends with her. I'm not even saying you have to forgive her. But either you find a way to work with her or she's got to go. You can't have it both ways."

I turned for my room, not knowing where else to go. But I had to get away. "I'm not fucking going, Shep."

And he sighed as I closed my door to shut the world out.

BLACKBIRD

Annika

THE NEXT AFTERNOON, I FOUND myself in my childhood kitchen, milling around with my family, all dressed in black, somber clothes. It felt more like an actual human wake than I cared to really acknowledge, and with more people than I'd anticipated, including several family friends who I'd known all my life. Mama had cooked enough food to feed half of Russia, including all of Kira's favorites, and desserts galore.

All I'd had to eat was half a dozen chocolate pirogi, and I didn't even feel bad about it.

Papa had pulled me aside and asked me about Joel, after Kira wouldn't stop talking about him, wondering if he would come, and I'd told him everything, the two of us in the quiet bedroom hallway. And I cried again, loss piled on loss, and I couldn't find the edges of the two anymore to separate them.

After a little while, when we'd said the little service would start, we moved into the living room where a table covered in black cloth stood with Kaz's tiny cat-sized coffin on top. Papa had built it the day before out of simple pine and dug his small grave in our sliver of back yard, and Mama had covered the mirrors in mourning. I took my place next to the table as everyone sat in folding chairs lined up in the living room. Kira sat in front, her eyes big and shining, her stuffed bunny in her lap and hair braided in a crown around her head. Her small mouth was pinched, her rosy lips tight.

I took a heavy breath as they all got settled, blinking back tears, telling myself the show was for Kira. But it was more for me than I was really willing to admit. I fought the urge to lay my hand on his little coffin, winding my fingers together in front of me instead, squeezing them tight.

"I'd like to thank you all for joining us today to say goodbye to Kazimir, destroyer of peace, shoes, and sometimes, hearts."

A chuckle rolled through them, and I gave a small smile, feeling a little better. Until the door opened, spilling slanted daylight into the room.

Joel stood in the doorframe, massive, imposing, his brows low and lips drawn, his eyes connecting with mine immediately.

I couldn't breathe, the room suddenly hot, stifling.

Everyone had turned to the motion, and Kira cried, "Hairy!" before bolting around the chairs and into his arms.

He scooped her up, clutching her into his chest as her little arms wound around his neck.

"Hey, kid. You doing okay?" he asked softly.

She leaned back, arms still circling his neck, sniffling. "He's gone."

His face softened and bent, his eyes brimming with sadness. "I know. I know he is. I'm sorry."

She nodded, fresh tears slipping down her round cheeks. When he set her down, she slipped her tiny hand into his gigantic one and pulled him to the front. And he did her bidding, sitting right next to her.

Right in front of me.

I swallowed down a dozen emotions, his eyes heavy on me as I looked away. I felt cheated by his presence, no longer free to feel however I felt, everything complicated simply because he was there. So I looked at everyone but him, determined to keep it together.

"Mama found Kaz behind the shop, tied up in a trash bag with his brothers and sisters, the lot of them mewling and crying to get out. When she freed them, they took off, all of them but Kaz, who climbed into her lap and purred his thanks. She gave him milk and brought him here, brought him home."

Kira leaned into Joel, Roxy nearly forgotten altogether. She looked a little miffed at the fact too, shooting him looks, though it may have also been on my account.

"I was beside myself — Mama had refused me a pet since I'd been able to talk." Another chuckle. "But Kaz wiggled his way into our lives easily, mine easiest. You might remember me pushing him up and down the street in a buggy with a bonnet on."

Mama laughed, which turned into a sob. She dabbed the corner of her eye with her handkerchief and leaned into Papa.

"He slept in my bed and let me walk him with a collar. And even though Mama threatened to turn him out for scratching at the sofa and marking her closet when he was mad, she never did. I don't think she could have, because even though he was impossible, he was family. He was ours." Another swallow, another breath, another heartbeat. "He didn't have many friends, which made his affection that much more enviable. And they say that only the good die young, which is probably why he lived for eighteen years, and we all thought of him as immortal. But everything has its end in life, and nothing lasts forever."

Joel's eyes screamed at me, begging me to look, but I wouldn't. I couldn't. Instead, I forged on.

"And so, to Kazimir, we say goodbye. I hope that your heaven that awaits is full of bright yellow canaries and big windows where you can watch the cars all day. I hope there are warm squares of sun for you to nap in and couches to scratch without anyone to stop you. I hope your belly is always full of milk and fresh fish and that there's someone to hold your face and tell you how lovely and horrible and crazy you are. We'll miss you, old friend."

I bent down, extending an arm to Kira, and she slipped out from under Joel's arm and next to the table. I took her seat, twisting my hands in my lap, unprepared to be next to Joel. The heat of him, his body so close to mine — I could feel him through the space between us like he was calling me.

Kira clasped her hands in front of her, bobbing her head as she sang, in Russian, a children's song with a shaky voice, her eyes trained on the ceiling and around to the walls, avoiding looking at any of us. Even that young, she tried not to cry and knew that if she did meet our eyes, she wouldn't be able to stop her tears.

In a far, far away Kingdom,
Where there is a castle, a river and a garden,
Maybe a hundred, maybe two hundred years ago
Only lived cats,
And more cats,
Kingdom of the cats,
Kingdom of the cats was there.

Cats, cats,
Cats and cats
Cats, cats, cats,
Furry tails.

In be Kingdom of the cats, they happily lived-
Made fairytales, made songs, danced and sang.
Cat king, Princess kitten,
Ruled happily over their land.
Danced, had fun every day.
Milliner and washer woman cats,
Cooks, artists,
Kingdom of the cats,
Kingdom of the cats was there

Cats, cats, cats,
Cats and cats
Cats, cats, cats,
Furry tails.
In the kingdom of the cats,
Lived happily,
Made fairytales, made songs, danced and sang.

Throughout her song, I wanted to reach for his hand, which

rested in his lap. But I was no longer welcome to touch him, particularly for comfort. I'd done that and paid the price.

When she was finished, her cheeks were pink and she looked to me.

"And now," she announced, "Anni will sing 'Let It Go' for Kaz. It was his favorite."

I stood and we switched places again. In part, I hated the idea of singing a Disney song in front of anyone, not only for the fact that it was maybe the most played out song in the history of Disney songs, but because I never sang in front of people. But there was my whole family and the guy whose heart I wrecked, and Kira, my sweet Bunny, waiting for me to sing it to give her reprieve. And I couldn't deny her that.

So I took a breath and began to sing. I sang like she was the only one in the room, though it took me a second to find my footing. But when I did, I sang. I sang it loud and proud, my eyes on her the whole time, if they weren't closed. I told her to let it go, to be strong, to leave her hurt behind her and keep going.

When I was finished, she bounded out of her seat and rushed me, and I knelt to meet her, closing my eyes.

"I love you, Kira. I'm sorry," I whispered.

"I love you too, Anni," she whispered back shakily. "I miss him."

"Me too." She was so small in my arms, my hand splayed against her back as we hugged until I had to let her go.

She took her seat again, and I made the mistake of looking at Joel. His eyes told me a thousand things I couldn't decipher, and my heart said a thousand things he couldn't hear. But it said them all the same.

Joel

Annika looked away, and for that I was thankful. Because when she looked at me like that, I forgot why I hated her so much. When I witnessed her sadness firsthand, heard the catch in her voice as she sang a song I was sure she didn't like to a little girl who she loved so much, it was hard to remember.

But I had to remember. Because what she'd done couldn't be undone, not by something so simple as a song at a cat funeral.

When Kira took her seat again, Annika stood and spoke, avoiding my eyes. "I have one more song to sing for Kaz, and for Mama for saving him, and for Papa for taking care of all of us. And I wanted to thank you all again. It means so much to us that you're here." She looked to Kira, then briefly to me before threading her hands in front of her and taking a deep breath.

Somewhere in the first line of the song — "Blackbird" by The Beatles — my heart stopped, then started again with a painful thump in my ribs. She didn't cry, but her eyes were wide and shining, as she sang of his broken wings learning to fly, her cheeks flushed and knuckles white where they twined together as she sang of his freedom. And she said goodbye to her old friend as a little girl leaned into my side, her breath hiccuping as she cried with the openness that only a child could have.

When the song ended, we all stood, and Max walked from the second row to pick up the pine box. We followed him through the kitchen and to the backyard, under a hemlock tree where he'd dug a small grave. Some words were spoken in Russian and maybe Hebrew, and everyone reached down and grabbed a handful of earth, tossing it into the grave. Kira, whose hand was in mine, nodded to me, urging me to do the same, so I did.

It was somber, final, and the sadness of death seeped into me. I chided myself — it was a cat funeral, and not even for a cat I knew particularly well. But I couldn't shake the heaviness of it as we headed back inside single file. He was an old cat, a part of their family. And he only liked three people in the world, it would seem — Annika, Kira, and me.

Everyone gathered in the kitchen, moving toward the food, but I edged for the door, bending down to get level with Kira.

"Thank you for inviting me, Kira."

"I didn't, Anni did."

I kept my eyes on her when they wanted to look for Annika.

"Yeah, but she just invited me because of you."

She shook her head. "Nu-uh. She wanted you to come too. Kaz would have been sad if you didn't come, Hairy."

I chuckled. "Maybe so. I'm glad to see you, but I've got to get going."

She pouted. "You haven't even had Babushky's pirogis yet. They're my favorite."

"I bet they're delicious, but I really do have to go. I'm sorry about Kaz."

She nodded down at her shoes. "He was super old. Babushky says he's in heaven now." She didn't sound like she believed it.

"Is that what you think?"

She rolled one shoulder in a shrug. "I dunno. It makes me happier to think he is."

"Then you should think about him there with a big bowl of cream and a can of tuna fish."

She smiled at that and grabbed me around the neck, surprising me. "Thanks, Hairy."

I hugged her to me and smiled. "Anytime, Bunny."

When she let me go, Annika was there, and I stood as ice ran through my veins. Kira hugged Annika's leg with her bunny hanging in her arms, and Annika rested a hand on the back of the little girl's head. We watched each other for a heartbeat.

"Thank you for coming, Joel. I know this wasn't—"

"I didn't come for you," I said, the words harsh, harsher than I'd intended. I swallowed and turned for the door, leaving her there with splotchy cheeks and brimming eyes. I couldn't. I couldn't talk to her. I couldn't deal with her. Not then. Maybe not ever.

I'd almost reached the door when Max materialized on the stairwell in the entry.

"Ah," he said, smiling jovially, "the bear has come to bid the cat farewell?"

I kept my back to the rest of the house, anxious to be done with the whole affair. "Only because the bunny asked me to."

He nodded, slipping his hands into his pockets as he descended the last few steps. "I see. Do you remember *zvezda moya*?"

"I remember," I answered quietly.

"It hurts, I know, but to hold the star in your hand is worth the pain." His eyes were so much like hers, crystalline, somehow cold and warm all at once, bottomless, and they looked into mine, telling me things I didn't want to hear.

"Not if it burns me to the ground, Max."

His smile fell, making him look older, and he nodded, clasping my shoulder and squeezing once. And we turned away from each other like conspirators after their last deal was settled and done.

Annika

Papa's eyes were heavy with sadness as he walked toward me and Joel walked away, never once looking back. I stood there with Kira clinging to me, feeling like I'd lost the whole world, like I'd never be happy again. And when Papa reached me, I leaned into him with a burning throat, comforted by his big, strong arms as he whispered consolations in Russian. But I kept it together, transferring Kira to her mother before making a plate under my mother's watchful eye.

So much of Russian happiness is tied up in food and the care of others, and they're not afraid to tell you exactly what to do if they're worried about your well-being. Like eat.

I picked at my food, opting mostly for pirogi. Because if ever there was a food that would solve problems, it would be chocolate-stuffed dumplings.

Our family friends left after a little while, and then it was just the Belousov clan, including Andrei. Once Mama, Roxy, and I had moved the food from the table and into the kitchen, we all sat down, with the exception of Kira, who had fallen asleep on the couch.

I scanned their faces, landing on Andrei. He sat next to Papa, the thinner, harder, less hairy version of his older brother. They had the same icy cold eyes, the same color hair, all salt and pepper, but that was where the similarities ended. His smile was thin and frosty where Papa's was big and warm, Andrei's jaw clean and sharp where Papa's was hidden under his heavy beard.

"I want Mama and Papa to retire," I said in Russian, without the energy to beat around the bush. "They can't sell the business because you've been laundering money through the store. So, I have a proposition."

His smile pulled up on one side. "Of course you do, Annika. You have my ingenuity. What do you propose?"

I sat straight enough it almost hurt, but he didn't intimidate — I was angry and determined, but not intimidated. It was hard to be intimidated by a man who had given me piggyback rides and bought me ice cream.

"Pay Mama and Papa to manage the shop and hire some of your goons to run the day to day. They can't sell, and they can't quit the shop, so this way everyone wins. They can stay home, you can keep your front, and no one is the wiser."

He shrugged lightly, still smirking. "This is fine. Better, even — we can do more without putting Maxim and Dina in harm's way. I agree to your terms," he said with a single nod in my direction.

I blinked, surprised it had been so easy. At least until I thought about it. He cared less about what my parents did and more about their happiness, which I knew. But for some reason I'd expected a fight. I relaxed, smiling back. "Thank you."

"You are welcome. Anything else?" Still with the smirk.

"No, uncle."

"Then it is my turn to thank you. You did all of this for Kira, and you helped your papa — you want the best for all of us. And Max, Dina, you have run that shop, never asking questions of me. For that, I am grateful."

Papa nodded solemnly. "I would do anything you asked, brother."

"And that is why I will happily agree to let you stay home without strings, without anything but my gratitude."

Mama poured us all drinks, and we raised our glasses.

"Brotherhood is the best wealth," Andrei said, and we poured the vodka down our throats in unison.

Exhaustion slipped over me as soon as I set my glass down, all my responsibilities now checked off, and I sagged a little. Roxy bumped me with her elbow.

"You ready? We should get Bunny home."

I nodded. Mama loaded us up with leftovers, and we said our goodbyes before loading into the cab I called for the short ride back to our place. Kira didn't wake at all that I saw, not as Roxy carried her inside or hauled her upstairs to put her in bed. I kicked off my shoes and walked into the living room, sinking into the couch with a sigh. Tears pricked my eyes when Kaz didn't appear to jump in my lap, and everything felt lost, changed, foreign.

Roxy joined me a few minutes later, sitting silently next to me.

My eyes were on my feet propped on the coffee table. "That was a lot."

She nodded, propping her feet next to mine. "It was." She paused. "He came."

I rested my head against the cushion behind me. "He did."

"How do you feel?"

"Gutted."

She didn't speak for a second. "But he came."

"Not for me. He made sure I knew."

"Yeah." More silence. "I'm sorry."

My eyes were locked on a chip in my big toe's polish. "It's okay. Or it will be. I hope. Eventually."

"You're working tomorrow?"

I nodded.

"Is there any way to make it right with him?"

A lump climbed up my throat, and I swallowed, forcing it down. "I don't know," I answered quietly. "I don't think so."

"But you miss him."

I bit my lip and nodded again.

Another sigh. "There's got to be a way to fix this."

"He's done. I betrayed him, and that's the unforgivable transgression in his world. I don't even know how I still have a job, honestly. In fact, I'm pretty sure I'm going in tomorrow just for the firing squad. I can't do my job. Joel is done with me. The whole shop is. I thought I was so smart, thought I had a big plan to protect us both." I laughed, the sound dry and tired. "I should have listened to

Laney from the start."

"But … I don't know, Annika. I've never seen you like that with a guy. You were with him like you are with us, with your family. You were *you*, not work *you*, but the real *you*. I know he did that."

"It doesn't matter." The ache in my chest twisted and burned. "I humiliated both of us. I've been insulted and rejected, and I can't blame anyone but myself. I can't even be mad because I earned this." I took a breath. I let it out. "I don't want to talk about this anymore."

"All right," she conceded.

But the white flag wasn't enough, so I hauled myself off the couch. "I'm heading to bed."

"Okay. Thanks for everything today. I'm glad it's over."

"Me too," I said as I turned for the stairs, wishing the whole thing was over, even as I knew it had barely begun.

WORST CASE

Annika

I WOKE UP STILL EXHAUSTED from a fitful sleep, and as I got ready for work, I tried to prepare myself for the day. But I had no idea what I was preparing myself for. I had the suspicion that this was it — I couldn't see a way to keep working on the show. Never mind Joel, that cause was lost. So lost. And I was still picking shrapnel out of my heart, piece by bloody piece.

I imagined talking to him, imagined him freezing me out again. Imagined him yelling, screaming like he did that day, the day when everything went nuclear. Imagined him forgiving me, holding me, telling me he understood, but only for a moment. A moment was all I could stand before I closed that hope behind an iron door.

The ride to work was quiet, and I steeled myself, ready as I could ever be for the unknown.

No one noticed my exit from the car or my entrance to the control room, everyone going about their business as if I were a ghost. The thought gave me no comfort as I walked into the office, finding Laney just where I knew she'd be. But when she looked up and smiled, I found a dangerous glimmer of hope again.

"Hey," she started, closing her laptop. "How are you holding up?"

I assumed she was talking about my cat and said, "I'm okay, thanks. Kira wanted to have a funeral for Kaz, so we did that

251

yesterday." I took my seat, feeling stiff and uncertain. "How's it going here?"

She sighed. "Better. It definitely helped having you out for a few days. I've got everyone starting to get back into a little bit of a rhythm, and they're talking to me in one-on-ones, but it's still tense." She watched me for a beat. "You saw him yesterday?"

I nodded. "We didn't really speak though."

"I gathered that. He hasn't said much, when he's been here." She folded her hands in her lap, sitting back in her chair. "I owe you an apology, Annika."

I blinked once, stunned. "I'm sorry?"

She chuckled. "No, that's my line." She let out a slow breath, assessing me. "I'm sorry about this. About Joel. The show. My behavior. It's just ... this is exactly what I was trying to avoid. I saw this — you and Joel — coming a mile away, and it didn't take me long to figure out that there was no way out of it for you without someone getting hurt. I know I didn't go about it the right way, and I'm sorry for that too. I only wanted to stop you from this. Exactly this. You being unable to produce the show. Me being put in a position to have to figure out what to do with you. The shop being in the middle of a coup. I wanted to protect you, and I handled it all wrong, and for that, I'm sorry."

I sat there with numb hands, surprised and full of shock. "I'm sorry for not listening. I thought I could handle it. Produce my way out of it."

"And you might have been able to do it. But it just didn't work out that way. I'm sorry we couldn't film right away, but it just wasn't possible, and I'm sorry you couldn't tell him."

"It's all right. You were right — I know there was nothing we could have done." I took a breath, steeling myself for the question I didn't want to hear the answer to. "So, what are you going to do about me?"

"Well, I have a plan. But I don't know if you're going to like it."

"Are you firing me?"

Her brow quirked. "What? No. Why would I do that?"

"Because you should have done it already."

"I probably should have, but no. I'm not firing you. But you might find that preferable to what I have to offer."

I recrossed my legs in an effort to relieve the squirmy feeling racing through me. "All right. Let's hear it."

"Well, as we well know, Tonic doesn't want to talk to you. The footage from Joel's table flip all included you. The interviews, you. You're everywhere."

A tingle worked its way up my neck, across my cheeks. "Oh, God. Laney, no."

She nodded. "You're a part of the show, and the only way out I can see is to stop fighting it and put you in front of the camera."

I dropped my face into my palms, trying to keep my breath steady. "Fuck," I said into my hands.

"You'll still produce, just nothing inter-personal, and they're going to fight you, but it'll be on camera. You'll work on the big segments and with scheduling and all, but I'll do the rest. Basically, we'll split the production up, both of us EP, but you'll be in front of the camera too."

I couldn't even look at her. "You're right. This might be worse than getting fired."

She chuckled, and I sat up, feeling a little faint.

"He's never going to go for this."

She let out a long, slow breath through her nose. "It's the only way I can see to keep you on the show in any context, so I hope you're wrong."

"When are you going to tell him?"

"Well, that all depends on you. First, do you accept?"

I thought it over for a second, but in the end, I knew she was right. "If it's the only chance at keeping my job, then it's worth a shot."

"Good. So the next question is, do you want to tell him or should I?"

That one wasn't answered so easily, and I sat back, considering it.

Sure, Laney could tell him, but I found myself not wanting to let her. Because the truth was, I missed him. Over everything, through all of it, he wouldn't talk to me, *really* talk to me, and this was a chance, an opportunity to get him face to face. Maybe now he'd listen to me after the long days of silence, the two of us hurting in our own corners, alone. Maybe he'd talk to me. Maybe I could convince him to at least begin to forgive me.

"I'll tell him," I said and only hoped I wouldn't regret it. I nibbled my bottom lip, already rolling over the speech I'd give him. "When?"

"Whenever you want. He's downstairs now in the shop."

"Now?" The word squeaked a little on the end.

"Yes, but you don't have to go down there now. I was only saying he's there."

The thought of going down there made me feel sick. The thought of waiting, sitting here for any length of time just thinking about it, made me feel even sicker. So I stood and smoothed my skirt.

"Now's good."

She nodded. "You sure?"

But I was already heading for the door. "I'm sure."

So down the stairs I went, adrenaline rushing through me until my hands were icy and shaking. Out the door of the building and into Tonic I walked, chin up, looking far more confident than I felt.

Joel sat at his desk sketching, his shoulders broad in a Henley. He turned and looked over his shoulder with a jovial expression that hardened the second he saw it was me. But I didn't waver, just walked up to his booth with everyone watching me.

"May I have a word with you in your office?"

He didn't answer, just burned a hole through me with his eyes as I stood there, waiting.

"It's about the show."

It was one of the few things he couldn't refuse, just like I'd hoped. He stood, and I turned, walking back toward the office with my heart thumping like a drum.

He followed me in, and I nodded to the door. "Privately, please."

Another hard look before he closed the door and stood almost against it, folding his arms across his wide chest, closing himself off to me.

I took a breath, my eyes on his. "Laney has a new plan for the show, and I need to discuss it with you before we can move forward."

"Why couldn't Laney talk to me about it?"

"Because it involves me, and I wanted to be the one to tell you." His eyes narrowed. "Tell me what?"

All of a sudden, I didn't want to say it. I fought the urge to leave, to tell Laney she could tell him herself, or better yet, that I could just leave the show. But really, it was the last thing I wanted to do, to give up, to walk away from Tonic. From Joel.

"We can't edit me out of the show. I'm already a part of it, and that's what she wants me to do. Join the cast and produce the segments unrelated to the relationships in the shop."

He said nothing. I waited. He didn't speak.

"Joel, I know …" *you're angry, this isn't easy, this sucks.* It all felt wrong, shitty, trite. "I know I fucked up. I'm sorry for what I've done. I thought … I hoped you would understand. You told me you did, before, in the beginning. Because there was no way out for me. You have to know that. And now, the only way for me to keep my job is to join the cast. This is it."

He swallowed, watching me like a wolf. "What do you want from me?"

Forgive me. Kiss me. Take me back. I took a breath. "I want to know if you're okay with it. If you agree to work under those conditions."

A flush crept into his cheeks as he drew in a breath. "You want to know if I'll work with you in front of a camera when I don't want to work with you behind the camera?" Incredulous, that was the only word to describe it.

"At least if I'm in front of the camera, it's honest."

A mirthless laugh shot out of him. "Honest. That's fucking rich."

My heart flinched at the insult.

Joel shook his head. "So, what? You want my blessing? Well, I'm not here to make you feel better about any of this, not when you've

255

made the entire shop miserable. Not after what you've done."

He couldn't say it, what I'd done to *him*. I opened my mouth to speak, but he kept going, cutting me off.

"I can't with you. I can't hear your voice. I can't see your face. I just … I can't. But I don't really have a choice, either. Do I? Because you and Laney will do whatever you want, and who gives a shit who you ruin along the way. It's about your job. It's always been about your job. There's no room in you for anything else. Not me, at least."

"Joel, that's not fair." My nose burned, and I blinked to keep the tears back.

He fumed. "Don't tell me what's fair and what isn't, Annika." My name was a curse on his lips. "I don't want to do this. I don't want to see you, not in any context, in front of the camera, behind it, in the shop or out. I don't want to even think about the fact that you exist in the universe because it's just easier that way. So no. I won't give you my permission to fuck with me any more than you already have." He unfolded his arms, clenching his fists at his sides. "Anything else?"

I shook my head, my lips pursed, and he turned and pulled open the door with a whoosh before disappearing from the threshold. He'd taken everything I had left to give, except for one thing. Just one. And I'd give it gladly.

BULL IN A CHINA SHOP

Joel

THE REST OF THE DAY was a blur, a wash of emotions that I couldn't sort through. I hated her. I wanted her. She hurt me. She healed me. And now, everything between us would be exposed and exploited on national television.

It was the absolute worst case scenario. And I knew she didn't feel any better about it than I did. That, at least, gave me some comfort.

That night, I found myself sitting in my living room with Shep, sipping my beer to the sound of The Dandy Warhols. We hadn't spoken in probably an hour, both of us lost in our thoughts. I was drained, sapped of all energy.

Until someone knocked on the door. Then I buzzed with anxiety that it was her.

Shep and I exchanged glances, and he got up to answer it as I stared straight ahead of me.

"What are *you* doing here?" he said in a tone that made me turn to see who it was.

It had been a couple of years since I'd seen Liz, but she looked much the same — chin-length black hair with straight bangs, big, blue eyes that went from sweet to crazy in a heartbeat, red lips that would curse you and kiss you in a breath.

"Good to see you too, Shep." She met my eyes. "Can I come

in?"

I stood, nodding my assent to Shep, who moved out of the way with a huff. "Guess so." He watched her for a second as we stood across the room from each other. "Well, I'm gonna make myself scarce. Try not to break anything, okay?"

Neither of us laughed as he walked to his room and shut the door, leaving me alone with her for the first time in nearly fifteen years.

"You look good, Joel."

"You too, Liz. Wanna sit?"

"Sure, thanks." She took a seat at the table, and I stepped to the fridge for a beer.

"Beer?" I asked, looking over my shoulder.

She shook her head. "I'm in recovery. Weekly meetings. Twelve steps. That old chestnut." She dug around in her bag as I closed the fridge door, shocked. "Mind if I smoke?"

I shook my head, grabbing an ashtray off the counter. I slid it in front of her and sat down as she lit her smoke and took a long drag.

"Thanks," she said.

"What are you doing here, Liz?"

She sat back in her chair and crossed one arm, propping her elbow on it with her cigarette in the air. "I came to call a truce."

My brow rose. "So Hal sent you?"

"He doesn't know I'm here." She took a drag and blew the smoke toward the ceiling. "I get the bad blood between all of us, because it's never been good or easy. We don't really do easy, you and me."

I took a pull of my beer in lieu of a response.

"But we both have shows, and they're going to be pushing us to fight. If we can truce, we can control how it all goes down. Otherwise, we'll all be at each other's throats. I don't want that, and you don't either. Our shops already hate each other. Throw the show into the mix, and it could really get bad. I don't want my guys actually fighting with yours. I don't want to deal with any actual damage. Do you?"

"Of course I don't."

"Then we should work together." Another puff of her cigarette. "He's not a bad guy, Joel."

"Ha."

Her brow dropped. "He's not, and you know he's not. You know he's always idolized you. And you also know that when he and I got together, he couldn't stay at Tonic. He didn't leave to spite you. He left for me."

I ran a hand over my mouth, elbows on the table. "Hadn't thought about it like that."

She smiled, lips together. "No, you wouldn't have. Hal's a good man. He's taken care of me and I've taken care of him. You've gotta understand that me and Hal is nothing like me and you. You made me crazy."

"I made you crazy?" I smirked.

"I'm an alcoholic, Joel. I hurt you and you hurt me back for five years straight, over and over again. It wasn't until I started this whole sobriety thing that I really understood what I'd done. Hal's doing it with me. Makes it easier."

"But you never fought with him?"

She shrugged. "I mean, sure. We fought, but not like *we* fought. But part of why I'm here too is to make amends."

I chuckled softly. "Twelve steps?"

She smiled and took a drag. "Twelve steps. I'm sorry for hurting you. I'm sorry for fucking you up more than you'd probably admit to me. You don't have to forgive me for any of it, but you needed to hear it, to know it's true."

I swallowed and nodded. "Thanks for telling me."

"You're welcome. So, back to the shop and the shows — can we work out a truce?"

I blew out a breath. "I suppose it wouldn't hurt to try. But I've got to think on all of it."

She nodded. "That's fair," she said as she snuffed the butt of her cigarette into the ashtray and watched me for a second. "Listen, it's none of my business to say anything, but I've heard some gossip about you and one of your producers. That you were seeing each other. Big fight?"

I frowned. "How could you know that?"

"One PA tells another PA. It was on our set before lunch."

"I fucking hate this show." It was almost a groan.

She chuckled. "Yeah, I mean, I was pretty shocked you ended up agreeing to it, even if it was just to stop Hal."

I frowned. "Seriously, how do you know everything?"

"I'm not kidding about the gossip. Our makeup artist has a big fucking mouth. But anyway, shut up for a second so I can make my point." She waited to make sure I was going to keep quiet before continuing. "She's not me. If you care about her, you need to remember that or you'll never survive."

"There's nothing to survive. She made sure of that."

"Nothing's unfixable."

I gave her a look.

"Okay, other than you and me, nothing's unfixable. She's not me. Hal's not you. That's why he and I work — he's the polar opposite of you. When I show my crazy, he keeps his cool where you just pushed me right back."

"So, you're saying that I'm to blame for you and me?"

She huffed and rolled her eyes. "Joel. Seriously. Stop talking." She leaned in. "You've got to remember something important about us."

"What's that?"

"It wasn't your fault." She sighed, the sound full of regret. "I'm not going to make excuses for either of us, but it wasn't because of you alone that we were bad together. I don't know how much power I have over how you feel about that, but I wanted to say it anyway. Because I want you to be happy."

I looked at my beer bottle as I twisted it slowly in a circle. "I don't really know what to say to all of this, Liz."

"You don't have to say anything. I've had plenty of time to get up the nerve to come talk to you, and you've been blindsided. So, just think about it." She stood and grabbed her bag. I did the same, walking her to the door. "See ya around, Joel."

I nodded, and she walked away, leaving me more exhausted than ever.

When I walked into work the next morning, I didn't know how to feel. Mostly, I was resigned to the fact that I had to be there, on the show, unwilling to risk everything I'd worked so hard for. In that, I could see where Annika was coming from in trying to protect her job, but that was where the similarities ended. I wasn't willing to put the people I loved at risk. I wasn't willing to lie.

Or maybe I was, I thought as I took a seat at my desk, surrounded by cameras.

I hadn't seen her since I walked out of the office the day before. She'd disappeared, up into the control room I figured. Probably plotting with Laney all the ways they could use their new angle to their advantage. I imagined them laughing deviously with little horns on their heads, throwing darts at all of our faces. But I knew it was more honest than that, which almost hurt more.

Laney walked in and gave us instruction, put everyone in their places to film for the day. Annika never showed — I expected her to walk in the door and pick a fight with me on camera, or for Laney to sit the two of us down and force us to talk with the whole world listening. I'd braced myself for it all day, but the shoe never dropped.

I worked that afternoon on a large hip piece that required the girl be in her underwear, so I spent the time in the back room, the same one where I'd touched Annika for the first time. And though I'd scrubbed and sanitized the room myself, there was no getting rid of the memory. She'd been everything I thought I wanted and everything I needed, but didn't know it. She fed my soul, and I felt that loss completely.

But she'd scared me too. I'd slipped back into the old dynamic I had with Liz without even realizing it, into the push and pull that had almost ruined me once before. I heard Liz in my mind — *She's not me.* And I knew she was right. Annika was different, but even a hint of that relationship dynamic, full of anger and manipulation, still terrified me.

I couldn't go down that road again. Even though for a moment, I'd seen Annika let go. The fighting had been gone and behind us for that moment when she was mine and I was hers. I'd caught a glimpse of her, the real her, and I'd thought we'd turned a corner and stepped into something happy, equal.

But she'd lied. And that lie wrecked everything we'd built. But in the end, it was a maze of mirrors, and the only way out was to smash them, to step through the shards of the wreckage and walk away. Only I was still trapped. Just not by her.

When the tattoo was finished, Laney had already left the shop, and once I was free, I made my way upstairs to her office. I told myself I just wanted to know how they were going to use me, my only condition to the whole farce. In a dark, dusty corner in the back of my mind, I wanted to know where she was, if she was all right, when she'd be back. As much as I reminded myself it was for my protection — knowing would help me brace myself — I ached to know just for my own peace of mind, and I hated myself for it.

Laney stood in the control room behind an editor, directing them on a trailer they were cutting, but she stood when she saw me, her face drawn.

"Joel," she said in way of a greeting.

I nodded. "Do you have a second?"

"Sure." She turned for her office, and I followed, though she held the door open for me, closing it behind me when I'd passed. "What can I do for you?"

My jaw clenched, fighting the words, wishing she could just offer me all the information I wanted without stooping to ask. "So." I cleared my throat. "Annika told me about your scheme to integrate her into the show, and I wanted to know just how you planned on doing that. I've been in the dark long enough. If you want me to play, you're going to have to tell me what's coming before it happens. I won't be manipulated anymore. That's my only condition."

Laney leaned against her desk. "That's fair. But it's no longer necessary."

My brow dropped. "What do you mean?"

Her face was sad, and she looked like she hadn't slept any more than I had. "Joel, Annika quit."

"What?" I breathed, uncomprehending.

"Yesterday, after she spoke to you. She didn't give me much, and I didn't ask because her reasoning is crystal clear to me."

"Well, enlighten me. I can't imagine a single reason why she'd leave this show, not after ... everything."

She smiled sadly, narrowing her eyes, amused. "You really can't think of *any* reason?"

I made a face.

Laney sighed, shaking her head at me. "She left because of you."

I didn't speak, just stood there stupidly, trying to sort through what I'd heard.

"She told me that the show couldn't function with her here, which is only partly true. What she didn't say, but what I know to be true, is that she left because you couldn't bear for her to be here."

I dropped into Annika's chair — her old chair, she was gone, gone — and stared at a spot on her desk.

Laney watched me, hands folded on her lap, sitting side-saddle on the edge of the desk. "I've known Annika for a long time, and as long as I've known her, as well as I know her ... she would only risk everything she'd worked for, including the protection of her heart, for one reason."

She waited until I looked up at her before telling me something I knew but couldn't truly fathom.

"She loves you, Joel. I don't know if she knows it, if she realizes it, but that doesn't make it any less true. She walked out of here sad and dejected, sure. But she left here completely certain she was doing the right thing. Your happiness is more important than hers. Your dreams are more important than hers. She put your needs above her own. And the only people who she's ever done that for are her family."

I still couldn't speak, the words all piled up in my throat like a train wreck. But Laney didn't need me to speak, she was still going.

"I know she hurt you. I know she lied to you, but she did that for me, for her job, and she hoped you would understand. That when you told her to do what she had to do, that it meant you would forgive her. Annika wanted to tell you the truth. Joel, she fought for you. She did everything she could not to hurt you. And deep down, I know you know that."

I touched my lips, rubbing them gently before I spoke. "You're right," I said, my voice raw and quiet.

"And I'm sorry to be the one to tell you all this. But you won't listen to her or your brother or anyone. Frankly, I didn't think you'd listen to me, either. But I'm the only one who knows her, *really* knows her, and I owe this to her, to you."

My thoughts crashed through my brain like a bull in a china shop, smashing and snorting, with clumsy hooves that tried to piece it all together. But I'd only made it worse. Made it harder. And now, I had to make it right.

I nodded at Laney.

Her eyes narrowed a tick. "You haven't really said anything. What are you going to do?"

I stood, feeling the fire of decision licking at my ribs, flickering with every beat of my heart. "I'm going to get her back."

HAIRY 2.0

Annika

A KNOCK RAPPED AT MY bedroom door, and Roxy cracked it open.

"You awake?" she asked, her head floating bodiless in the gap.

"Yeah," I muttered, my voice gruff from disuse.

She slipped into the dim room and crawled in bed, settling in so we were face to face, curled toward each other.

"It's been two days, and I've only seen you leave this room for food, vodka, and to pee."

I shrugged my free shoulder. "It's not like I have anything else to do."

"I mean, I've been trying to get you to take a vacation for years, but this is excessive." She smiled, joking, and I tried to smile back.

Apparently, it was weak. Roxy kept on me.

"You're kind of stinky, too. I don't think I've ever seen your hair greasy in all my twenty-six years of knowing you."

"To be fair, you can't remember the first five or so."

She made a face. "I'm sure Dina never let you get this bad. Seriously, you look borderline homeless."

I sniffed, not having anything else to say.

Her face softened. "Come on. Come get out of bed. Get cleaned up. Maybe we can walk down to DUMBO, take Kira to play at the park under the bridge."

I sighed. "I don't really feel like it, Rox."

"What have you even been doing in here?"

"Reading. Sleeping. Pretty much just that."

"Have you talked to Laney?"

"No, but I don't even know where my phone is."

Her face twisted up, lip curling. "Who are you?"

"Don't be dramatic."

She snorted. "Tell me not to breathe, why don't you."

"What do you want, Roxy? Should I go over it all again? Because I just don't want to talk about it anymore. There's nothing anyone can say to fix this. I had to leave so Joel can get on with his life. So the shop and the show can keep going. I was the problem, the gum in the gears. So I let it go, and that's that. All better."

"Except for you."

"Doesn't matter."

She sighed. "Of course it matters. You matter. How you feel matters."

"Not this time."

Her eyes were so sad, full of pity.

"It's fine, really. It'll be fine. I just needed to wallow, that's all. When I'm finished laying here, hating myself, I'll work on my resume and start looking for a job. I'm sure Laney will give me a good reference, and I have loads of experience. I'll be fine." *Eventually. Hopefully.*

"If you say so," she said quietly. "I love you."

"I love you, too."

She slipped out of the bed, looking cowed, but she spun around once her feet were on the ground and grabbed my comforter, ripping it off me with a cruelly amused look on her face.

"Hey!" I yelled.

"And it's *because* I love you that I won't let you keep on rolling around in your stinky pity party. So get up, smelly. I bet your nooks and crannies smell atrocious."

I curled up in a ball, feeling around for my top sheet. "Ugh, fuck off, Roxy." My fingers closed around it only to have it ripped away too.

"Ah, ah, ah. You're getting up and getting some vitamin D before you turn into a vampire."

I pulled a pillow over my face and groaned, but that disappeared too.

"Come on, mopey. Party's over. Time to go wash your undercarriage before you develop a fungus."

I lay there, staring at the ceiling. "I hate you."

She scooped up my bedding and headed for my door. "Tell me that after you're clean." She disappeared, but popped her head back into the room. "Oh, and if you don't get up in the next two minutes, I'm sending Kira in."

Kira was even more relentless than her mother. I groaned, and she smiled before disappearing again.

I sighed once I was alone, feeling that loneliness, that emptiness. Loss of purpose, that was part of it. Loss of Joel. That was a bigger part. But he couldn't be any more clear. It was over. And the only silver lining was the comfort of having done the right thing, even if the right thing for everyone else was the complete and utter sacrifice of what I wanted.

I hauled my body off the bed and shuffled into the bathroom, turning on the shower once the door was closed. I stripped down automatically, sticking my hand in the stream until it was hot enough to burn, climbing in to let the water beat down on me. Roxy was right — the shower was cleansing, the soap crisp and fresh in my nose, bringing me back into humanity by a degree. I even shaved my legs, feeling inspired by the thought of walking down to the ocean with the sun shining, the wind blowing with the little bit of crispness the water gave to the air.

I even brushed my teeth, mostly because they didn't really feel scummy until the rest of me was clean. Roxy was waiting in my room when I walked back in, wearing nothing but a towel. She sat on my bed — which she'd made neatly — with her legs folded in lotus, looking terribly pleased with herself. The curtains were thrown open, making the room look almost cheery. A little part of me hated her for it.

"Still hate me?" she asked.

Staci Hart

"Yes," I said as I opened my closet door.

"Liar."

I chuckled, reaching for a sundress I hadn't worn in a couple of years. It was white and gauzy, like a slip, probably the least tailored article of clothing I owned that wasn't pajamas.

"Kira's already ready to go," she said as I dressed and toweled off my hair. "Are you hungry? We could pick something up on the way."

"Food sounds terrible."

"Well, let me at least make you a smoothie." She unfolded her legs and stood just as the doorbell rang.

We shared a look.

"I'll get it," she said as she left the room and trotted down the stairs. The door opened. A rumbling voice echoed words I couldn't quite hear downstairs, and my heart stopped.

"Annika?" she called, and I stepped into the hall, my eyes down as I descended the stairs with numb hands.

First I only saw his shadow, then his shoes. Then his legs, his arms, his chest. His face, so changed from the last time I'd seen him, but just as familiar as it ever was. Our eyes locked, and I moved to him like I was caught in a tractor beam. Roxy disappeared. Everything disappeared, and for one, long moment, it was just the two of us in the whole universe.

Something squirmed in Joel's arms, and he looked down, shifting his arms and hands to hang onto it.

A kitten.

Joel Anderson was at my doorstep, holding a kitten, smirking at me like a beautiful, hairy bastard.

My mouth was open, I realized distantly, and my eyes found his, so bright, so green, the blue in them more vibrant than I'd remembered. It seemed like a lifetime since he'd looked at me like that.

"So, are you gonna invite me in?" he asked, still smirking.

I blinked at him and tried to smile, moving out of the way so he could step in. I closed the door, so utterly shocked that I didn't even know where to begin.

"What are you doing here?" I asked his back as he walked into my living room and sat down like he lived there.

"Come here and I'll tell you."

I walked in silently and sat next to him on the couch, hoping this all meant what I thought it did, telling myself I was wrong.

He turned on the couch and handed me the kitten, a snow white ball of fur with crystal-blue eyes. It mewed and nestled into me, trying to crawl up my arms, small and warm and the most precious thing I'd ever seen in my whole life.

I watched it wiggle around, petting it as my heart threatened to explode with happiness.

"I'd like you to meet Hairy."

I laughed for the first time in a week as my nose burned. Ice Queen, my ass — I was a gooey mess, stripped and bare, with no armor to hide behind.

"Joel ... I don't know what to say." My eyes were on the little cat. I couldn't look at Joel.

"You don't have to say anything, Annika. I have plenty to say for the both of us."

I swallowed, my attention still on Hairy 2.0.

"You quit. Because of me, because of the shop. I know ... I know what I said hurt you. That was why I said it. I wanted to hurt you like you hurt me, but I didn't expect you to quit. I don't want you to sacrifice everything, not when it was just as much my fault as it was yours."

I nodded down at Hairy, not trusting my voice.

"So, I want you to come back. I won't fight you, and neither will the shop. Come back to the show."

Elation and pain — those were the acute emotions I felt at his words. This — him being here, the kitten as a peace offering — wasn't about him and me. It was about the show. But that wasn't all I wanted. I looked up at him, finally meeting his eyes. It wasn't what I wanted, but it was all I would get. And maybe we could be friends. Maybe there was hope.

I smiled past the pain of knowing he wouldn't be mine. "If you're sure."

"I'm sure, and so is everyone." He chuckled. "Well, almost everyone. I'm still working on Penny."

I laughed softly with him, clutching the furry bundle to my chest.

He reached over to scratch Hairy's head. "I thought this little guy might make you feel better. Not that Kaz could ever be replaced."

I smiled. "Please, I don't think a cat exists that could ever be so ornery as Kaz."

He smiled back, his hand still on the cat. "But you can only keep him under one condition."

My brow dropped, my chest tightening. "A condition?"

Joel nodded, his eyes on mine, open and honest and earnest. "You have to come back to me, too."

My breath hitched. "What?" I whispered.

His eyes fell to the cat as he resumed his scratching, and Hairy leaned into his hand. "I ... I understand if it's too much to ask, after everything I've said, after the way I've treated you. I was wrong, Annika. I was wrong to treat you the way that I did. You lied to me, but I lied to you, too. I told you what you needed to hear to convince you to stay with me, told you there would be no consequences. But the truth is, I've been falling for you since the second you walked into my shop."

"Joel ..."

He looked up. "Not yet. Don't answer me yet. Let me finish."

I nodded, and he took a breath. "Your lie split me open when I was already raw, exposed from trusting you, and I just couldn't handle it. It hurt too much."

Emotion climbed up my throat, my vision blurring as I reached for his face. "I'm so sorry," I whispered.

He closed his eyes and turned his head to press a kiss into my palm. "Shh. It's okay. It's all right, Annika. I betrayed your trust too. I was scared because I haven't loved anyone in so long. And then, I found you." His eyes searched mine. "Forgive me. Come back to me."

I closed my eyes and answered him with a kiss. It was sweet

relief, washing over me in waves as I breathed him in after believing I never would again. After thinking I'd lost him forever. And then he showed up at my door with a kitten and a smirk, asking me to forgive him when I hadn't been able to forgive myself. But the weight of it fell from me like shackles, and I kissed him, telling him without words that I needed him.

He broke away and pressed his forehead to mine, holding me there for a moment while we just breathed and listened to our heartbeats as they pumped heavily in our chests.

"I can't believe you came," I finally said. "I can't believe you're here."

"I'm here, and I'm not going anywhere."

I smiled and pulled back to get a good look at him. "And you brought me a cat."

He smiled back, the color rising in his cheeks, just a touch. "I found out yesterday that you quit, and I decided to come here, but it was too late to find one, so I had to wait to come see you. You have no idea how hard that was, not coming straight here. I kind of still wish I had."

"Me too. But this is maybe the best surprise I've ever gotten. A hot, bearded, tattooed, apologetic man with a kitten. How could I say no?"

He laughed. "Oh, I'm sure you could have found a way." His fingers skated across the line of my jaw. "But I'm sure glad you didn't." He laid a sweet kiss on my lips.

The kitten wiggled again, and I broke away to keep a hold of him. "God, Joel. This cat is adorable." I held him up, inspecting him, and he mewed at me.

"I knew the second I saw him that he was the one. He reminded me of you, the snow fox with icy eyes. But he's just a little pile of fluff," he said as he petted Hairy. "Just like you."

I couldn't help but laugh, and a second later I heard Kira running down the stairs.

"Hairy!" she squealed, sprinting through the living room and into Joel's arms.

"Hey, Bunny."

She squeezed him. "I'm glad you came back."

"Me too, kid. Did you meet my friend Hairy?" he asked as he pulled away, and she turned to me, her face stretching open when she saw the kitten.

"Oh my gosh," she breathed and reached for him, picking him up under his arms. She clutched him to her chest and gasped. "A kitty! Oh my gosh, *a kitty*!"

I laughed and smoothed her hair as Roxy came in shaking her head, but she was smiling.

"You've outdone yourself, Joel."

"Psh, please. This is nothing. I'm reserving the big guns for the serious fights."

I glanced at him to make sure he was kidding.

He was. I think.

Roxy knelt down to pet Hairy. "Well, Kira and I are going to get out of your hair for the day, aren't we?" she asked Kira.

She pouted. "I wanna play with the kitty."

"I know, and you can. Later." Roxy smiled at us. "Much later."

Kira handed the cat over, and they left after a few minutes. And then it was just us. I stood and reached for Joel's hand, and he took it, the humor leaving him, replaced by quietude as he followed me up the stairs and into my room.

We lay down facing each other, heads propped on our hands, the kitten between us, pawing at an old toy of Kaz's.

"I'm sorry, Annika."

I smiled at him. "You already said that."

But he didn't smile back. "I mean it. At least you didn't mean to hurt me. I wanted to hurt you. I ... I don't know if I'll forgive myself for that."

"Please, don't do that. I felt the same way — I didn't know if I could forgive myself for what I'd done to you. I never meant to hurt you. I had this big plan to navigate the show around you, to refuse what I could, tell you what I couldn't. Show Laney at the end just how clever I was to be able to have my cake and eat it. I fought her — I wanted to tell you."

"I know," he said softly.

"When you said you wouldn't work with me, that you didn't want to see me ... I knew there was really only one way to make it right. So I left. I didn't want to hurt you anymore."

His eyes were sad as he leaned forward, cupping the back of my head to kiss my forehead.

I scooted closer to him, moving the cat out of the way, twining my legs with his as Hairy jumped off the bed and went exploring. "For so long, I've been split in two. There was the me I had to be for my job, the job where I spent eighty hours a week, and then there was the real me. Those two parts of myself have been at war for so long, and I didn't even realize it. But you saw *me*. You made me realize that everything that other part of me thought was right was bullshit. You're real, and everything else is a cardboard cutout. I just couldn't tell until I found the real thing."

He smiled, but his eyes brimmed with emotion. "You think I'm the real thing?"

I laughed. "I do." My fingers fiddled with the buttons on his shirt, and my gaze was pinned there, away from his eyes. "Did you mean what you said about falling for me?"

He rested his hand on my hip and nodded. "From the minute I first saw you."

"Me too, you know. Even though I fought it."

He smirked. "Well, I *am* hard to resist."

I laughed, and he pulled me closer until our bodies were flush. "You really are. Maybe it's all that hair."

"Or the tattoos." He leaned over me, angling for my lips.

My hand smoothed over his bicep. "Or the muscles."

He smiled and kissed me deep, pressing me back into the bed as my arms wound around his neck. He felt so good against me, his lips, the weight of his body.

When he broke away, he stroked my cheek, looking down at me. "I'm sorry," he said again, a whisper.

"It's all right," I whispered back.

He closed his eyes and bowed his head, trailing the tip of his nose up the bridge of mine. "It's not, but I'll make it up to you. I'll make it right." And he kissed me again, telling me with the action alone that he meant it, that it didn't matter how long it took.

But he'd already fixed it, and I told him so with my own lips, forgiving him with every heartbeat. It was a long time that we lay there wrapped around each other until kissing turned to roaming hands. His fingers skated up my thigh, under the hem of my dress, cupping my ass, pulling me into his hips.

I moaned — I couldn't help it. I felt like I was starving, like the week I'd spent without him sent my body into sleep, and his kiss, his touch woke it again, and it was hungry for him. His fingers trailed fire, slipping between my legs, teasing me with his fingertips as I rolled my hips, wanting him to touch me, wanting to touch him. So I teased him back, slipping my fingers into the top of his pants to graze anything I could get to. His shaft. His crown. He hissed against my lips when my nails slipped over his skin, his hand flexing, forcing a finger into me.

My mouth hung open, and he dipped his head, kissing down my neck, to my breasts. I couldn't reach him anymore, so I settled unhappily for my arms around his neck, clutching him to me, grinding my hips against him to relieve the pressure. His hand left the warmth of me to pull the low neck of my dress down, to stroke the curve of my breast and squeeze it in his palm, thumb brushing my nipple before I felt the wet heat of his mouth, his tongue rolling, teeth against the peak, gentle and demanding all at once.

He took his time, and I let him, watching him with my pulse rushing in my ears, dress hitched up around my waist and tugged down at the neck, his fingers, covered in ink, holding my breast like it was precious, kissing it like it was delicious, his lips opening, closing. My back arched in offering.

I'd give him anything. My body. My heart. It was all his.

He pressed against me, the denim of his jeans rough, and I longed for the softness of his skin. My hands skated down his chest, to his belt. He sucked hard and let me go, the cool air tightening my nipple at the loss of him, but he gave me more than that, backing away to take off his clothes. I watched him, trying to catch my breath, my eyes on his hands as they gripped his belt and unfastened it, then his button and zipper. Then his shirt, leaving his pants gaping, the ridges of his abs leading down to the shadow as he reached behind him and grabbed a handful of jersey and yanked it off. Then his pants, pushing them to the ground, leaving him gloriously naked, a beautiful man who was a work of art in so many ways, in all the ways.

I opened my arms, and he climbed into them, wrapping himself around me as I wrapped around him, the warmth and comfort of him filling my heart and my soul. And I knew I didn't want to be without him again. The loss of him had been so complete, it had left me in shock. But now he was mine, and I wouldn't let him go so easy.

All I'd put on was the dress itself, and he didn't take it off of me, but dropped the straps from my shoulders until they draped in my elbows, baring my breasts. He kissed down my body again, his hand lingering on my breast as the rest of him went lower, spreading my legs. I watched as he trailed his fingers up the inside of my thigh, as he stroked me gently, his eyes on his hand. He spread me open and brought his lips down, kissing me deep, sucking and pulling, stroking me as I twisted my fingers in his hair, and his eyes closed, his dark lashes brushing his cheeks.

I wanted the weight of him against me. I wanted him in my arms. I wanted him inside of me, and I told him so. So he climbed up my body, dragging up the hem of my dress to meet the neck, then ran his fingertips down my ribs, over my hip, down my thigh as he settled in between my legs. First the length of him lying against me, sending my hips rolling. Then his lips against mine, promising me his heart. And he guided himself until he pressed against my core and flexed, slipping into me, giving me what I wanted with a sigh and a whisper.

I was caged in his arms, his fingers in my hair, his body against mine, and I was safe. I was whole. I was his.

He slipped out of me and flexed, slamming in with a satisfying jolt. Again — rolling his body, and I opened my thighs, wanting him as deep as he could get. And he took my permission, pushing harder until he hit the end of me. My eyes had closed — I hadn't realized it — and when I opened them, he was watching me, his lids heavy and full of emotion. And I saw him, and I knew he saw me, and there was nothing between us.

Faster he moved, faster went my heart, faster my shallow breath slipped past my lips, and he said my name, a whisper, full of pain and adoration and love, and my body let go. I came with a crash and a gasp, my hands on the backs of his thighs, squeezing, pulling him into me with my entire body. He kissed me hard, slipping his tongue into my mouth, his breath heavy and sharp, and he came right behind me, his body pumping and shuddering, head hanging down to press his forehead against mine.

He collapsed and rolled, wrapping his arms around me, taking me with him. One arm was around my waist, the other around my back, his hand cupping the back of my head, holding me against him like he'd never let go. And I never wanted him to.

SCIENTIFIC FACT

Joel

SHE LEFT ME SHAKEN. SHAKEN from pleasure, from emotion, from breathing her breath and touching her skin, she shook me to the core. She was an earthquake, and I was changed forever because of her.

I held her for a very long time, until we had to part, cleaning up and coming back together so I could hold her some more. We talked about the time we'd spent apart, and we talked about the future. We talked about our fears, and then there was no more talking, only the comfort of her body, only the sweetness of her against me for a long afternoon and a long evening. I fell asleep with her in my arms and woke with her body wound around me.

It was like the universe had been knocked off kilter without her, and now, everything had been set straight. The rightness of her, the peace I found, it was more than I'd ever known before, through everything I'd been through. I'd been missing her my whole life. And even after I'd found her, I'd lost her. But not again. Never again.

She stirred against my chest, squeezing me.

"Hey," I said softly and brushed her hair from her face.

"Mmm," she answered with a smile, though she didn't open her eyes.

So I wrapped her up again, resting my cheek on the top of her head.

That is, until she shot out of my arms with wide eyes that were locked on mine.

"Hairy."

"Shit," I said as I flipped off the covers and climbed out of bed. I found him asleep in the bottom of her closet and picked him up, carrying him back to bed.

She looked at me like I was a slab of naked, tattooed, kitten-holding meat. "My God. That might be the sexiest thing I've ever seen."

I chuckled as I set the cat down and slipped back under the covers. He pranced over to her and wound up in a fluffy ball against her chest.

"I can't believe you got me a cat," she said, smiling.

I propped my head on my hand. "Believe it."

"You can't just get me a cat every time we fight, you know?"

I shrugged. "Says you."

She laughed. "I'll be the crazy cat lady, shaking out cat food on the fire escape."

"You're only crazy if you live alone and have lots of cats. That's a scientific fact."

"Well, I can't live with Kira and Roxy forever, so eventually it'll become a truth."

"Well, maybe you won't ever be alone. Maybe you'll find forever with someone else."

She smiled at me, the soft, rosy flush of her cheeks filling my heart with a warmth I couldn't put into words. "Oh, you think?"

And I smiled back, leaning in to steal a kiss. "Princess, I don't think. I know."

EPILOGUE

Joel

ANNIKA LAY STRETCHED OUT IN front of me, her naked
back under my fingers. Her skin was unmarred, smooth and pale,
not a freckle on her entire body. I'd know — I'd spent the last nine
months getting to know every inch of her.

The machine in my hand buzzed, the needles bouncing faster
than the naked eye could follow. She'd been in my chair for hours
and endured the pain like it didn't faze her. And of course she
would. She was stronger than anyone I'd ever known.

"Almost done, babe," I said gently, and she nodded as I finished
shading the ice around her heart.

I'd come up with the idea just after we'd gotten back together,
and when I drew it up, I was sure she'd never go for it. For someone
who had no visible tattoos, letting me tattoo her back down to her
tailbone seemed a stretch. But when I showed her, she pressed her
fingers to her lips and said yes. I hoped it wasn't the only yes I'd ever
get from her when it came to the impossible.

I'd planned on painting it, if she'd refused — her naked back,
skin split open to reveal her heart of ice. But inside, it glowed with
fire that burned the ice away, sending it down her back in rivulets.
I'd covered her old ice tattoo with silhouetted wildflowers that
sprang up into watercolor in the same blues, reds, and oranges of
her fiery heart.

I turned off my machine, though my hand still tingled, making it feel like it was vibrating as I wiped the extra ink and blood from the art. I stretched and pulled at her skin, turning my head to inspect it for mistakes. But it was perfect, and so was she.

The cameras around us kept rolling as she sat, and I showed her the piece in the mirror. Part of me wanted to step between her and the camera to hide her body, the body only I had the pleasure of seeing so bare, even with the sticky bra on, but the look on her face when she saw her back made everyone else in the room disappear. Her eyes were wide and wet, her breath short as she looked it over, telling me I'd done well. I'd done right by her.

"Joel ..." she breathed.

I smiled, my heart expanding in my chest with pride and emotion. I couldn't speak.

She was still looking in the mirror, her eyes scanning the piece. "It's ... God. It's beautiful. It's perfect."

I stood and hugged her, pulling her into my chest, my fingers in her hair. There were no cameras, not other people, just us in that moment, and I kissed her temple as she wrapped her arms around my waist.

"You okay?" I asked, and she nestled into my chest.

"Yeah. I can't believe it's over. I can't believe how it looks."

I chuckled. "You doubted me?"

She pulled away to look up at me, smiling. "Never for a second. It was just more than I imagined."

I pressed a smiling kiss to her lips and let her go to finish up. I rubbed the salve all over her raw skin, then taped a plastic covering over it to protect it for a few hours. She pulled on a loose tank afterward, and Laney smiled at us.

"Cut." The cameras lowered — all except one — and everyone chatted. The whole Tonic crew was there to watch us film the second season's finale and the wrap party.

Season one had ended with a bang. We worked Annika into the show, and Laney softballed the editing for all of our sake. When they approached us for season two, we'd almost refused. But we'd gone all in with Hal and Liz — which was bizarre in its own right — and with that control over our fate and Laney on our side, we decided to go for it.

The ridiculous amount of money they offered us didn't hurt either. Because the show took off. We were a household name, and it wasn't the absolute worst thing in the world.

Annika had moved in months before — we filmed an entire moving-in episode. Surreal. — and we'd merged our lives. Merged our hearts. And I didn't ever want to be without her again.

Laney caught my eye and gave me a slight nod.

I reached for Annika's hand and pulled her back to the chair, adjusting it so she could sit. Her eyes were full of questions, though her lips still smiled sweetly at me. She'd changed so much and somehow not at all. But that hardness was gone, letting what was inside of her go free. And that made her all that much more beautiful.

I held her hands in mine as everyone hushed. And I looked into her eyes and took a breath, ready for what would come, hell or high water.

"I never thought I'd fall in love. Didn't think it was for me, figured it was me who was broken. But then you walked into my shop and proved me wrong. You proved me wrong about everything, about who I thought I was, about what I thought I wanted. Because in the end, I only wanted you. The girl who pushed me, who wanted me, who loved me despite my many shortcomings. And it didn't take me very long at all to realize I didn't want to be without you. Not ever. I love you, Annika."

She smiled, her cheeks flushed and eyes shining with tears. "I love you too, Joel."

And then I reached into my pocket as I dropped to one knee, and her eyes flew wide, her fingers pressed to her lips, and the whole room gasped, even though almost all of them knew what had been coming. I opened the velvet box where a simple ring lay, two bands criss-crossing back and forth on each other, covered in small diamonds that made it shine and shimmer when the light hit it like sunshine on snow.

"Marry me," I said quietly, simply, and her eyes jumped from the ring to my face, her hand falling away to reveal her smile, and she reached for me, cupping my face, as she said the word I'd longed to hear.

"Yes."

It was shaky and sweet, and she pressed her lips to mine, wrapping her arms around my neck to the whoops and cheers of the crew. And I stood, cupping her face, kissing her to seal the promise.

I held her for a long moment, though not long enough, kissing her, whispering to her. And then I pulled away and slipped the ring on her finger with shaking hands before kissing her again. As much as I'd hated the idea of doing this with everyone around, in the end, it had felt completely right. The show brought us together, and they should all be part of our forever.

We walked around, hugging and receiving congratulations from everyone. PAs came back from the break room with flutes of champagne, and we toasted and laughed. And she was tucked into my side for all of it. But I could feel all the things she wanted to say, and I wanted to hear them, anxious for the moment when we could be alone.

But before that, we made our way up to the control room and to the green room where we filmed the engagement interview with Laney, answering questions and laughing and holding hands. And the second we were finished, we flew out the door and down a flight of stairs, into our apartment.

I'd hoped she'd say yes, and had planned for all of this, from wine next to the bed to rose petals everywhere. And she walked into our room, shaking her head.

"You did all this?"

I nodded, smirking.

She turned to me, laying a hand on my chest as she popped up on her tiptoes. "You're just an old romantic, aren't you?"

I wrapped a hand around her waist, mindful of her tattoo. "We're both gooier than we let on, aren't we?"

She kissed me. "That we are. I think we bring out the goo in each other."

I chuckled, touching her face. "You said yes."

"Of course I said yes. How could I ever be with anyone else? You've ruined me for all other men, Joel Anderson."

"Good. Because you're mine, and I'm yours. I'll give you my name, my heart, my soul. Anything you want, so long as you return the favor."

"I will. I already have. You're it for me." She paused for a second, watching me with her big, blue eyes. "Are you scared?"

I shook my head and thumbed her bottom lip. "Not even a little. I never thought … I didn't know it could be like this. I didn't know love until you, and now that I have you, I want you forever."

And her smile could have moved mountains. "I'm yours."

Acknowledgements

As always, I need to think my husband Jeff first. Thank you for always supporting me, for always stepping up, for being the one part of life that's always easy and fun. You're my hero, my ultimate, the reason why I write romance.

To Kandi Steiner — And here we thought it would be harder to write a book on the same schedule. You've pushed me, motivated me, loved me, supported me through writing this story, even when it was hard and things were ugly. I only hope I was able to do the same. I love you forever. #SteinHarts

To Becca Mysoor — Even though you weren't a part of this book every day (THANKS A LOT, TRIP TO ASIA), your love and support has always been food for my soul, and this was no exception. Thank you for always having my back, and for making sure I've got panties on and that my lipstick is on point. I love you, boo.

To Brittainy Cherry — For always being there when I needed a friend. For always knowing just what to say, just what I needed to hear, even when I didn't know it. Thank you for your heart. Thank you for your soul. Thank you for your friendship.

To Karla Sorensen — For being my ramble partner, my voice message queen, my cheerleader and cloned brain. I couldn't have done this without your daily support.

To Tina Lynne — Thank you for kicking my story in the teeth when it needed it. Thank you for your honesty and for your organization and for your spreadsheets and reminders and Googling fingers.

To Amy Daws — For holding my hand and always telling me straight. Thank you, Dawsome.

To my betas:
Lex Martin — thanks for letting me blow up your vagina with my words.
Monique Boone — with the most thoughtful feedback, and for all the time you spent talking through this story with me.
Melissa Lynn — for always being my non-romance voice of reason.
Miranda Arnold — for always making me laugh

in your comments, and for giving me such useful feedback.

Brandy Mello — please tell me you're in for life, because your notes were brilliant.

Jenni Moen — please finish your book so I can beta read for you. PLEASE! *Cracks whip*

Ilsa Madden-Mills — for sending me the most helpful, adorable, blush-worthy voice messages. Praise from you is equivalent to it raining diamonds.

Zoe Lee and Matt Maenpaa — thank you for reading under duress and sending me your notes (also under duress)

To Sahar Bagheri and Meghan Quinn — thank you for reading the final version to make sure I didn't walk out into the world with my dress tucked into my undies.

Special thanks to Jenn Watson of Social Butterfly for petting my hair and feeding me chocolates, and to Lauren Perry of Perrywinkle Photography for once again SLAYING my photoshoot.

And to Rebecca Slemons and Ellie McLove — thanks for making my words all shiny and pretty.

And YOU, readers. Thank YOU. You're the

reason for all of this, and I'm forever grateful for each and every one of you.

A Love Letter To Whiskey

MY BEST FRIEND KANDI STEINER just released her book, A Love Letter To Whiskey, and if you loved this book, I know you'll love hers too. Her's her first chapter, just to prove it.

Amazon US: http://amzn.to/2dD4EkX

Chapter One
First Taste

The first time I tasted Whiskey, I fell flat on my face.
Literally.

I was drunk from the very first sip, and I guess that should have been my sign to stay away.

Jenna and I were running the trail around the lake near her house, sweat dripping into our eyes from the intense South Florida heat. It was early September, but in South Florida, it might as well have been July. There was no "boots and scarves" season, unless you counted the approximately six weeks in January and February where the temperature dropped below eighty degrees.

As it was, we were battling ninety-plus degrees, me trying to be a show off and prove I could keep up with Jenna's cheerleading training program. She had finally made the varsity squad, and with that privilege came ridiculous standards she had to uphold. I hated running — absolutely loathed it. I would much rather have been on my surfboard that day. But fortunately for Jenna, she had a competitive best friend who never turned down a challenge. So when she asked me to train with her, I'd agreed eagerly, even knowing I'd have screaming ribs and calves by the end of the day.

I saw him first.

I was just a few steps ahead of Jenna, and I'd been staring down at my hot pink sneakers as they hit the concrete. When I looked up, he was about fifty feet away, and even from that distance I could tell I was in trouble. He seemed sort of average at first — brown hair, lean build, soaked white running shirt — but the closer he got, the more I realized just how edible he was. I noticed the shift in the muscles of his legs as he ran, the way his hair bounced slightly, how he pressed his lips together in concentration as he neared us.

I looked over my shoulder, attempting to waggle my eyebrows at Jenna and give her the secret best friend code for "hot guy up ahead," but she had stopped to tie her shoes. And when I turned back around, it was too late.

I smacked into him — hard — and fell to the pavement, rolling a bit to soften the fall. He cursed and I groaned, more from embarrassment than pain. I wish I could say I gracefully picked myself up, smiled radiantly, and asked him for his number, but the truth is I lost the ability to do anything the minute I looked up at him.

It was an unfamiliar, warm ache that spread through my chest as I used my hand to shield the sun streaming in behind his silhouette, just how you'd expect the first sip of whiskey to feel. He was bent over, hand outstretched, saying something that wasn't registering because I had somehow managed to slip my hand into his and just that one touch had set my skin on fire.

Handsome wasn't the right word to describe him, but it was all I kept thinking as I traced his features. His hair was a sort of mocha color, damp at the roots, falling onto his forehead just slightly. His eyes were wide — almost too round — and a mixture of gold, green, and the deepest brown. I didn't coin the nickname Whiskey until much later, but it was that moment that I saw it for the first time — those were whiskey eyes. The kind of eyes you get lost in. The kind that drink you in. He had the longest lashes and a firm, square jaw. It was so hard, the edges so clean that I would have sworn he was angry with me if it weren't for the smile on his face. He was still talking as my eyes fell over his broad chest before snapping back up to his sideways grin.

"Oh my God, are you fucking blind?!" Jenna's voice snapped me from my haze as she shoved Whiskey out of the way and latched onto my hand, ripping me back to standing position. I'd barely caught my balance before she whipped around to continue her scolding. "How about you brush that long ass hair out of your eyes and watch where you're going, huh champ?"

Oh no.

I didn't even have time to call dibs, I couldn't even think the word, let alone say it, before it was too late. I watched it, in slow motion, as Whiskey fell for my best friend before I even had the chance to say a single word to him.

Jenna was standing tall, arms crossed, one hip popped in her usual fashion as she waited for him to defend himself. This was her standard operating procedure — it was one of the reasons we got along. We were both what you'd call "spitfires", but Jenna had the distinct advantage of being cripplingly gorgeous on top of having an attitude. She flipped her long, wavy blonde ponytail behind her and cocked a brow.

And then he did, too.

His smile grew wider as he met her eyes, and it was the same look I'd watched fall over guy after countless guy. Jenna was a unicorn, and men were enamored by her. As they should have been — she had platinum blonde hair, crystal blue eyes, legs for days, and a personality to boot. Now, before you go thinking that I was the insecure best friend — I had it going on, too. I worked hard, I was talented — just not at the things traditional high school boys valued.

But we'll get to that.

"Hi," Whiskey finally said, extending his hand to Jenna this time. His eyes were warm, smile inviting — if I had to pick the right word for him, just one, I'd say charming. He just oozed charm. "I'm Jamie."

"Well, Jamie, maybe you should make an appointment with the eye doctor before you run over another innocent jogger. And you owe Brecks an apology." She nodded to me then and I cringed at my name, wondering why she felt the need to spill it at all. She always called me B — everyone did — so why did she choose the moment I was face to face with the first boy to ever make my heart accelerate to use my full name?

Jamie was still grinning, eying Jenna, trying to figure her out, but he turned to me after a moment with that same crooked smile. "I'm sorry, I should have been watching where I was going." He said the words with conviction, but lifted his brows on that last line because he and I both knew who wasn't paying attention to the trail, and he wasn't the guilty party.

"It's fine," I murmured, because for some reason I was still having a difficult time finding my voice. Jamie tilted his head just a fraction, his eyes hard on me this time, and I felt naked beneath his gaze. I'd never had anyone look at me that way — completely zeroed in. It was unnerving and exhilarating, too.

But before I could latch onto the feeling, he turned back to Jenna, their eyes meeting as slow smiles spread on both of their faces. I'd seen it a million times, but this was the first time I felt sick watching it happen.

I saw him first, but it didn't matter.

Because he saw her.

* * *

It was just over a week later that Jenna and Jamie put a title on the flirting relationship they'd been having for a solid eight days. That's how it was when we were in high school — there were no games, no "let's just hook up and see where this goes." You were either with someone or you weren't, and they were very together.

I had the privilege of watching them make out between classes, and as much as I wanted to hate them together, I just didn't. In fact, I'd pretty much forgotten that I'd seen Jamie first because they were disgustingly cute together. Jenna was taller than me, but she was just short enough to fit perfectly under Jamie's arm. She was a cheerleader, he was a basketball player — different seasons, but popular and respected nonetheless. His dark features complimented her light ones, and they had a similar sense of humor. They even sounded good together — Jenna and Jamie. I mean honestly, how could I be mad at that?

So I dropped it, dropped the idea of him, moved easily into the third wheel position I was used to with Jenna and her long list of boyfriends. Jamie was the first of them who seemed to enjoy me there. He was always talking to me, making jokes, bridging the gap between awkward and easy friendship. It was nice, and I was sincerely happy for them.

Still, I had opted out of tricycling that particular afternoon after school. Instead, I swung my Jansport onto my bed and immediately started ruffling through the clothes in my top drawer for my bathing suit, desperate to get some time on the water before the sun set. Daylight Savings hadn't set in yet, but the days were slowly getting shorter, reminding me that summer was far away.

"Hey sweetie," my mom said, knuckles rapping softly on the panel of my door frame. "You hungry? I was thinking we could go out for dinner tonight, maybe to that sushi bar you love so much?"

"I'm not really hungry yet. Going to go check out the surf," I replied, my smile tight. I didn't even look up from my drawer, just pulled out my favorite white, strappy top and avoided her eyes. It wasn't that I was a dramatic teen who hated her mom, I wasn't — I loved her, but things were different between us than they had been just two short years before.

Okay, this is the part where I warn you — I had daddy issues. I guess in a way, mommy issues, too.

But let me explain.

Everything in my life was perfect, at least in my eyes, until the summer before my sophomore year of high school. That was the summer I opened my pretty gray eyes and looked around at my life, realizing it wasn't at all what it seemed.

I thought I had it all. My parents weren't married or even together, but then again they never had been. I was used to that. It was our normal. Mom never dated anyone, Dad dated but never remarried, and somehow we still always ended up together — just the three of us — every Christmas. I'd always lived in my mom's house, but I'd spent equal time at my dad's. My parents never fought, but they never really laughed, either. I assumed they made it work for me, and I was thankful for that.

We were unconventional, me bouncing between houses and them tolerating each other for my sake, but we worked. Dad's skin was white, pale as they come, freckled and tinged pink while Mom's was the smoothest, most delicate shade of black. Ebony and ivory, with me the perfectly imperfect mixture of the two.

They may not have made enough at their respective jobs to shower me with birthday gifts or buy me a shiny new car on my sixteenth birthday, but they worked hard, they paid the bills, and they instilled that mindset in me, too. The Kennedy's may not have been rich in dollars, but we were rich in character.

Still, not everything is as it seems.

I never understood that saying — not really — not until that summer before tenth grade when everything I thought I knew about my life got erased in a violent come-to-Jesus talk. My mom had drank too much one night, as she often did, and I'd humored her by holding her hair back as she told me how proud she was of me between emptying her stomach into our off-white toilet.

"You are so much more than I ever could have wished for," she kept repeating, over and over. But then the literal vomit turned to word vomit, and she revealed a truth I wasn't prepared for.

You see, the story I'd been told my entire life was that mom and dad were best friends growing up. They were inseparable, and after years of everyone around them making jokes about them dating, they finally conceded, and it turned out they were perfect together. They had a happy relationship for several years, a bouncing baby girl who they both loved very much, but it just didn't work out, so they went back to being friends. The end. Sounds sweet, right?

Except it was a lie.

The truth was much uglier, as it so often is, and so they hid it from me. But mom was tequila drunk that night and apparently had forgotten why she cared so much about lying to me. So, she spilled the truth.

They had been best friends, that much was true, but they had never dated. Instead, my dad had turned jealous, chasing every guy who dared to talk to my mom out of her life. But he didn't stop there. One night, when she was crying over the most recent guy who'd dumped her, my dad had come on to her. And he didn't take no for an answer.

Not the first time she said it.

Not the eleventh.

She counted, by the way.

Mom was seventeen at the time, and I was the product of that night — a baby not meant to be born from a horror not meant to be lived.

I guess this is the part where I tell you I immediately hated my dad, and in a way I did, but in another way I still loved him. He was still my dad, the guy who'd called me baby girl and fixed me root beer floats when I'd had a bad day. I wondered how the soft-spoken, caring man I'd grown up around could have committed such an act.

For a while, I lived in a broken sort of limbo between those two feelings — love and hate — but when I finally had the nerve to ask him about it, to tell him that I knew what happened, he had nothing to say. He didn't apologize, he didn't try to defend himself, and he didn't seem to hold any emotion other than anger that my mother had told me at all. After that, I slipped farther toward hate, and I stopped talking to him a short five months after the night my mom told me the truth.

And though I shouldn't have resented my mom for not telling me sooner, I did. She didn't deserve me to blame her for letting me think my father was a good person, but I did. And so, my life was never the same.

Like I said, it wasn't that I hated my mom, because I didn't. But there was a raw wedge between us after that night, an unmovable force, and I felt the jagged splinters of it scrape my chest every time I looked at her.

So, more often than not, I chose not to.

"Okay," she replied, defeated. "Well, I hope you have fun." I was still rummaging, searching for my bottoms, and she turned to leave but paused long enough to call back over her shoulder. "I love you."

I froze, closed my eyes, and let out one long breath. "I love you too, Mom."

I would never not say those words. I loved her fiercely, even if our relationship had changed.

By the time I found my suit, dressed, strapped my board to the top of my beat-up SUV and made it to the beach, the weight of the day was threatening to suffocate me. But as soon as I set my board in the water and slid on, my arms finding their rhythm in the familiar burn that came with paddling out, I began to breathe easier.

The surf in South Florida was far from glorious, but it worked for my purposes. It was one of my favorite ways to waste a day, connected with the water, with myself. It was my alone time, time to think, time to process. I used surfing like most people used fitness or food — to cope, to heal, to work through my issues or ignore them, depending on my mood. It was my solace.

Which is why I nearly fell off my board when Jamie paddled out beside me.

"Fancy meeting you here," he mused, voice low and throaty. He chuckled at my lost balance and I narrowed my eyes, but smiled nonetheless. Everything I thought I knew about his body was erased in that moment and I swallowed, following the cut lines along his arms that led me straight to his abdomen. There was a scar there, just above his right hip, and I stared at it just a second too long before clearing my throat and turning back toward the water.

"Thought you had plans with Jenna."

He shrugged. "I did. But there was a cheerleading crisis, apparently."

We met eyes then, both stifling laughs before letting them tumble out.

"I'll never understand organized sports," I said, shaking my head.

Jamie squinted against the sun as we rode over a small wave, our legs dangling on either side of our boards. "What? You'll never understand having a team who works toward the same goal?"

I scoffed. "Don't be annoying. You know what I meant."

"Oh, so you hate fun?"

"No, but I hate organized fun." I glanced sideways at him then, offering a small smirk, and I grinned a little wider when the right side of his mouth quirked up in return. "I didn't know you surfed."

"Yeah," he answered easily. "Believe it or not, us organized-fun people enjoy solo sports, too."

"You're really not going to let this go, are you?"

He laughed, and I relaxed a bit. So what Jamie was impossibly gorgeous and had the abs of the young Brad Pitt? I could do this, be friends, ignore the little zing in my stomach when he smiled at me. It was nice to have a friend other than Jenna. Where she made friends easily, I tended to push people away — whether by choice or accident. Maybe the Jamie-B-Jenna tricycle wouldn't be so bad, after all.

But when I truly thought about that possibility, of having a guy as a friend, my stomach dropped for a completely different reason. A flash of Mom bent over our toilet hit me quickly, her eyes blood-shot and her truthful words like ice picks in my throat. I swallowed, closing my eyes just a moment before checking the waterproof watch on my wrist.

"We should try to catch this next wave."

I didn't wait for him to answer before I paddled out.

We surfed what we could, but the waves were sad that day, barely offering enough to push our boards back to shore. So eventually, we ended up right back where we started, legs swinging in the salt water beneath us as we stared out at the water. The sun was slowly sinking behind us, setting on the West coast and casting the beach in a hazy yellow glow.

"Where do you go when you do that?"

"Do what?" I asked.

"You have this look, this faraway stare sometimes. It's like you're here, but not really."

He was watching me then, the same way he had the first day we met. I smoothed my thumb over one of the black designs on my board and shrugged.

"Just thinking, I guess."

"Sounds dangerous."

He grinned, and I felt my cheeks heat, though no one would know but me. My skin didn't reveal a blush the way Jenna's did. "Probably is. You should steer clear."

Jamie chewed the inside of his lip, still staring at me, and opened his mouth to say something else, but didn't. He turned, staring in the same direction as me for a few moments before speaking again.

"So what are you thinking right now?"

I let out a long, slow breath. "Thinking I can't wait to get out of here, move to California, and finally surf a real wave."

"You're moving?"

"Not yet. But hopefully for college."

"Ah," he mused. "I take it you have no interest in going to Palm South University, then?"

I shook my head. "Nah, too much drama. I want a laid-back west coast school. Somewhere with waves that don't suck."

Jamie dipped his hand into the water and lifted it again, letting the water drip from his fingertips to the hot skin on his shoulders. "Me too, Brecks. Me too."

I cringed at the use of my name. "It's just B."

"Just B, huh?"

I nodded. "You want to go to school in California, too?"

"That's the plan. I have an uncle out there who has some connections at a few schools. You have a specific one in mind yet?"

"Not yet. Just somewhere far from here."

He nodded once, thankfully not pushing me to expand on that little dramatic statement. We sat in silence a while longer before paddling back in and hiking our boards up under our arms as we made the trek back to the cars. The sand was a bit course under our feet, but I loved the way it felt. I loved everything about the beach, especially surfing, and I glanced over at Jamie, more thankful than I thought I would have been running into him.

He helped me load up after we rinsed off, strapping my old lime green board to the top of Old Not-So Faithful. And just like the reliable Betty that she was, the 1998 Kia Sportage failed to turn over when I tried to start her up.

"Great," I murmured, my head hitting the top of the steering wheel. Jamie had just finished loading his own board a few cars away, and he made his way back over.

"Not starting?"

"Seems to be my luck today."

He smiled, tugging the handle on my door to pull it open. "Come on, I'll drive you home."

I didn't know it then, but that one small gesture, those six small words, they would be what changed everything between me and Jamie Shaw.

Grab A Love Letter To Whiskey on Amazon, FREE on Kindle unlimited!

More Books by Staci Hart

Hearts and Arrows

Deer in Headlights (Hearts and Arrows 1)
Snake in the Grass (Hearts and Arrows 2)
What the Heart Wants (Hearts and Arrows 2.5 Novella)
Doe Eyes (Hearts and Arrows 3)
Fool's Gold (Hearts and Arrows 3.5 Novella)

Hearts and Arrows Box Set

Hardcore (Erotic Suspense Serials)

Volume 1
Volume 2
Volume 3
Box Set

Bad Habits (Romantic Comedy)

With a Twist
Chaser
Last Call

Wasted Words

Once
Short story on Amazon

Sign up for the newsletter to receive a FREE copy of Deer in Headlights

About the Author

Staci has been a lot of things up to this point in her life: a graphic designer, an entrepreneur, a seamstress, a clothing and handbag designer, a waitress. Can't forget that. She's also been a mom to three little girls who are sure to grow up to break a number of hearts. She's been a wife, even though she's certainly not the cleanest, or the best cook. She's also super, duper fun at a party, especially if she's been drinking whiskey, and her favorite word starts with f, ends with k.

From roots in Houston, to a seven year stint in Southern California, Staci and her family ended up settling somewhere in between and equally north, in Denver. They are new enough that snow is still magical. When she's not writing, she's gaming, cleaning, or designing graphics.

Follow Staci Hart:

Tonic

Website: Stacihartnovels.com
Facebook: Facebook.com/stacihartnovels
Twitter: Twitter.com/imaquirkybird
Pinterest: pinterest.com/imaquirkybird

Made in the USA
Charleston, SC
24 November 2016